THE MURK

ROBERT LETTRICK

DISNEY • HYPERION

LOS ANGELES   NEW YORK

Printed in the United States of America
First Edition, April 2015
1 3 5 7 9 10 8 6 4 2
G475-5664-5-15032

Library of Congress Cataloging-in-Publication Data
Lettrick, Robert.
The murk/Robert Lettrick.
pages cm
Summary: Seeking a rare flower that might cure her baby sister's illness, fourteen-year-old Piper Canfield, her brother Creeper, friend Tad, and two guides go to the heart of the Okefenokee Swamp, where great danger awaits.
ISBN 978-1-4231-8695-3 (hardback)
[1. Adventure and adventurers—Fiction. 2. Okefenokee Swamp (Ga. and Fla.)—Fiction. 3. Sick—Fiction. 4. Plants—Fiction. 5. Monsters—Fiction. 6. Friendship—Fiction. 7. Brothers and sisters—Fiction. 8. Horror stories.]
I. Title.
PZ7.L56895Mur 2015
[Fic]—dc23   2014031438

Visit www.DisneyBooks.com

SUSTAINABLE FORESTRY INITIATIVE   Certified Sourcing
www.sfiprogram.org
SFI-00993

THIS LABEL APPLIES TO TEXT STOCK

*For my sister Suzanne, the intrepid explorer,
and my brother Ron, the determined healer*

"All nature awakes to life and activity."

—Naturalist William Bartram (*Travels*, 1791)

PROLOGUE

Piper Canfield took a full breath and began.

    While prepping for delicate surgery, she stared out the small latrine window of the rented American Eagle RV. Off in the distance, the majestic Cascade Mountains rose up like barnacles on the back of the world. Or at least that's how she saw them after talking to a station attendant in town. The old man, a native Inuk, told her that the Cascades were once great whales that had grown too large to swim, beached themselves, and died. Looking at the mountains framed within the porthole, she could almost believe they had been living, breathing things at one point. They were quite magnificent. The Cascades' highest peaks, marbled with snow, whispered to her spirit of adventure, and she was listening intently. Piper's snowboard was practically vibrating in the RV's equipment closet.

    Nothing could spoil her mood, not even the horrible stink coming from the loaded Huggies she was carefully peeling off her baby sister's bottom.

    "Ugh, this is the worst one yet!" Piper declared, recoiling in horror. She dropped the sinister diaper into a plastic bag, closed the ziplock seal, and envisioned herself hurling the whole mess into outer space. She eyeballed the offender, six-month-old baby Grace. The great love of Piper's life. Grace was flailing her arms in little circles on the changing table and blubbering her lips, oblivious to her big sister's ordeal.

"How you manage to convert strained peas and mashed pears into *this* biohazard, I'll never know. Maybe I should call an exorcist, because there is definitely something evil going on inside you. No wonder you got a rash this week. But no worries—big sis is here to save the day."

Grace blinked and flashed a heart-melting, four-toothed grin. Piper tickled her belly, and the grin turned into a burst of happy giggles.

"Oh, you find this funny, do you? You're lucky I love you so much, Grace Lynn Canfield, or I'd let Mom change you, and we both know she's chintzy with the diaper cream."

As if on cue, the RV's entrance opened with a *whoosh* and folded into the stairwell. Piper's mother came aboard. Jane Canfield leaned into the bathroom and smiled at the sight of her daughters. "Almost done changing the little poopzooka?"

"Almost," Piper answered, slathering her sister's bare bottom with rash cream. She cleaned her hands then plucked a fresh diaper from the box. "Wrapping things up. Literally."

It was pretty clear which parent Piper favored in the looks department: slightly hooded brown eyes so light they bordered on gold; long auburn hair; a faint smattering of freckles. She had her mom's everything. As for the rest of her genetic inheritance, she shared her dad's heart-shaped face and athletic build, but that was all. This imbalanced combination made Piper a true Southern beauty with more than a few admirers at school. Not that she cared about romance. Her heart belonged to Grace.

Piper pressed the fresh diaper's Velcro tabs together at Grace's waist and tugged on the hem to test the seal. It passed inspection.

"Clean as a whistle and sharp as a thistle," she proclaimed, then hoisted her sister to her chest and gave the baby a kiss on her pudgy cheek. "She's ready for the paparazzi."

"Great. Bring Grace outside, would you, sweetie?" said Jane. "Once we flush your little brother out of his tree, we're setting off on our hike to Lake Heather."

Piper snorted. "Good luck with that. Want me to fetch Dad's rifle from the storage bay?"

"I appreciate the offer, but let's leave shooting him down as a last resort." Jane winked, then went back outside.

Piper hollered after her, "Lead with what gets results!"

Despite her brother's annoying antics, it had been the best summer of Piper's life. At the start of the school break, her family rented a forty-foot motor coach in their hometown of Jesup, Georgia, sixty miles southwest of Savannah, and set out on the open road. They'd spent the next three months exploring the country, driving in a jagged diagonal line across the United States, making several stops along the way. They'd visited Graceland in Memphis; spent a week with Jane's parents in Topeka, Kansas; white-water rafted the Snake River through the Grand Canyon; and, just two days ago, they'd fly-fished in Butte, Montana. The plan was to end their journey in Washington (although if Piper had her way, they would have continued on to Alaska; she'd always wanted to see the northern lights). They were running behind because of a flat tire in Spokane, and now there was only one day left to explore the Cascades' scenic trails before the deadline to return the RV in Seattle. They would spend the night in the city and fly home the following day.

Piper, like the rest of her family, was most happy in the great outdoors. She'd inherited more than just her parents' good looks. She possessed their love of nature too. Piper wasn't afraid to get her hands dirty, which was why she ended up on diaper duty more than half the time. No, that wasn't honest. She took care of Grace because of a promise she'd made even before her sister was born. A promise between Piper, Grace, and the universe, and that was nobody's business but theirs.

With the baby cooing in her arms, Piper dropped the dirty business into the disposable diaper sack, then stepped outside the RV and into the shade-dappled campsite. Surrounded by forest, the fragrance of pine was so intense it made her a touch woozy. The tree-shaped air fresheners hanging strategically throughout the RV (several of them clustered above her brother's smelly bunk) didn't come close to the real thing.

The ground was springy, a little muddy in spots. The air was cool and bug-free. They'd crossed into Washington on the tail end of a powerful rainstorm, but it had passed on to the Pacific Ocean, leaving behind a world as crisp as before the dawn of man. There was little at the site to suggest human activity, just an old, weathered picnic table and a rust-crusted barrel for refuse. There were no electrical or water hookups like those you'd find in a modern RV park. Not that the Canfields needed them. The RV was fitted with solar panels, and there was an enormous tank in the underbelly bay that could provide them with showers and drinking water for days. It was the perfect vehicle for dry camping, or boondocking, as her dad called it. This style of bare-bones living suited the Canfields just fine.

Piper's parents were standing at the base of a tall pine tree, their heads craned upward toward the highest boughs. Her ten-year-old brother, she knew, was somewhere high above. She caught a glimpse of him, then tracked him by following the bouncing branches and the traveling rain of pine needles.

"Hit the ground, Creeper!" Brad Canfield hollered up at his son. "We've got a five-mile round-trip hike ahead of us. We'd best get a move on!"

A creature more lemur than boy came sliding down the tree trunk, bits of bark shredding away like sparks under the soles of his tennis shoes. "I made it to the top!" Creeper announced proudly. "I could see everything from up there, even the lake. That has to be the tallest tree in Washington."

"Not quite, buddy," Brad said. "Your tree is maybe sixty feet tall. There are a few three-hundred-footers in Olympic National Park."

Creeper's eyes lit up. "Really? I'm gonna climb them all someday!"

Brad ruffled his son's hair. "I believe it, champ."

Piper's brother's real name was Monty, but his dad nicknamed him Creeper for the way he was always climbing trees like a creeper vine. The boy's life goal was to sit atop the tallest trees in every part of the world, especially there, the Pacific Northwest, home of cloud-tickling sequoias. He hoped to one day make a living competing in lumberjack contests, but Piper predicted he'd grow up to be one of those telephone-pole repair guys.

"We'll be back in two hours," Brad told Piper. "If you hear anything suspicious, take Grace into Rolling Thunder"—his nickname for the RV—"and lock the door behind you. You keep one walkie-talkie, I'll take the other. Keep yours close. Just say the word, and at a full sprint, I can be back from the lake in ten minutes. If Godzilla attacks and you need to call in the marines, the satellite phone is charging in its cradle. That one's for emergencies only."

"We'll be fine," Piper laughed. "It's totally safe here. Go. Have a great time."

Creeper said, "There's nobody around for miles. I saw everything from the top of the tree. Heather Lake is all ours."

Brad seemed puzzled by Creeper's scouting report. "All to ourselves? On such a beautiful day? That's a little odd, but I suppose that's fortunate for us."

"I don't know. . . ." Jane was still on the fence about leaving her girls alone. "I could carry Grace."

Brad took Jane's hand. "Sweetie, it's not the most difficult hike, but the guidebook says the trail gets steep and rocky at points. It'll be safer to leave Grace here with Piper. They'll be fine. You heard Creeper—there's no one around for miles."

"Are you sure you're okay with this, Piper?" Jane triple-checked. "I can stay with the baby if you'd rather go to the lake with the boys."

"Go, Mom," Piper insisted. "You deserve to have fun too. Besides, I like hanging out with Grace. She's my sidekick."

"Okay, just promise me you won't leave her side."

"I won't," Piper assured her mother.

Brad said, "Everyone knows that steel is more breakable than a promise from Piper Canfield. You got that from your uncle Jake."

Uncle Jake was Brad's brother, and like all the Canfield men, he'd served in the military. Uncle Jake was Piper's hero. He died in a desert three years earlier, keeping a promise he'd made to the men in his charge—a promise to get them all home safely. They survived because Jake was an honorable man who did an honorable thing. Piper missed him, but she was also deeply proud to be his niece.

Jane relaxed at once. "That's good enough for me. You're such a thoughtful sister."

"Says you!" Creeper scoffed. "Nobody asked my opinion."

Brad gave his son a withering glare. "You're right about that."

"I don't get it!" Creeper argued the injustice of it all. "How come you guys believe whatever Piper tells you, but I'm always guilty until proven innocent?"

"Maybe because I never lie, and you've lied six times already today. And it's still early."

"That's not true!" Creeper flared. "Name one lie!" Suddenly realizing the ease of his challenge, he quickly revised it. "Name *three* lies!"

Piper ticked them off on her fingers. "You said you'd make breakfast this morning, but you slept in, so Dad had to make it. You promised to straighten my tackle box after I let you borrow it, but when I checked it an hour ago, I found a tangled ball of line, lures, and Almond Joy wrappers. And third, you told Mom you brushed your teeth, but instead you just closed the bathroom door and ran the water so she'd *think* you were brushing them."

"How would you know if I brushed my teeth or not?"

"I washed up after you," she replied. "Your toothbrush was as dry as a cracker. Plus I can smell your stinky breath from here. It's the worst thing I've smelled all week, and remember, I just changed Grace's diaper."

"Shut up!" Creeper snapped. "You think you're so perfect!"

"Creeper!" Jane said, appalled.

Brad handled the situation. "Listen, if there's one thing I've tried to drill into your heads, it's the importance of keeping your word. Your word is the foundation of your character. It's the measuring stick by which people judge you and by which you should judge yourself. Your uncle Jake understood that, Creeper. Your sister understands it. Hopefully, you will too someday."

Creeper groaned, overcome by itchy impatience. "Fine. She's Perfect Piper, and I'm a big fat liar. Can we just go already?"

"Yes, let's." Brad kissed each of his daughters on the top of the head, then he and Jane set off down the trail toward Heather Lake. Creeper hung back so he could stick his tongue out at Piper without getting caught, and then he ran to catch up. He was lucky she had her arms full with Grace, as she had an overwhelming urge to peg him in the back of the head with a pinecone.

Piper decided to get comfy. She brought Grace's portable bassinet (Brad called it "the Moses basket") outside the RV, set it on the picnic table, and placed her sister inside. Feeling clean, adored, and drunk on fresh air, Grace quickly fell asleep. Piper fished a Coke from the cooler and sat down on the bench. She took a sip, then opened up her ragged copy of Jack London's *White Fang*. London's tale of a three-quarters wolf seemed a fitting read. It was exciting to think that she was likely within a mile or two of real, live gray wolves—there were several in the Cascade valley. How amazing would it be to see one in the wild? Maybe she'd get lucky before the day was through.

A noise disturbed her daydreaming. Something was buzzing nearby. It took a moment for her to register that the sound was coming from inside the RV. It was the intrusive hum of technology. The satellite phone. She'd never heard it ring before. It was for emergencies only, like her dad said, so she figured the call was important. She checked the bassinet. Grace was still fast asleep and Piper didn't want to wake her.

She went inside the RV and answered the phone. "Hello?"

"Hey, stranger!" said a familiar voice on the other end.

"Tad!" It was her classmate and best friend from back home. She hadn't spoken to him since she'd left her grandparents' house in Kansas two weeks earlier, a record. "I'm so glad to hear your voice! We can't talk long, though. My dad'll have a fit when he returns the RV and the rental guy hands him a phone bill."

"C'mon, it can't be that expensive," Tad said.

"Um, yuh-huh, four dollars a minute!"

"I stand corrected."

"How'd you get this number, anyway? It's for emergencies only."

"A little detective work," said Tad. "You know me. Besides, this *is* an emergency. I haven't talked to you in literally forever!"

"I don't think you know what 'literally' means, and no, that's not an emergency," she said, laughing. But she knew what he meant. They'd met outside the local Food Lion when they were five. Tad put his quarter in the coin-operated horsey, but he let Piper have the ride. They'd been inseparable ever since. It was weird being apart for the whole summer. "I'm glad you called, though."

"I'm glad I called too," he replied. "Having fun?"

"Of course," said Piper. She plopped down on the plastic cushioned L-shaped bench that made up the seating in the RV's dining nook. Through the window she had a great view of the mountains. "It's been an amazing trip. You should see this place."

"You're in Montana, right?"

"No, we left there yesterday," she told him. "We're in Washington now."

There was a pause on the line. A subdued static hiss. Then, in a deadly serious tone, Tad said, "Washington? Where in Washington?"

"A camping spot near Mount Pilchuck in the Cascade Mountain valley. I remember Dad saying we exited off the Mountain Loop Highway to get here. You sound worried. Is Bigfoot back in the news?"

Another pause accompanied by a distinct rustle of paper. On his end, Tad was fidgeting with a map.

"Tad? You still there?"

He didn't answer. Piper thought she'd lost the connection and was about to end the call, when Tad blurted out, "Piper, haven't you been listening to the news?"

"No. Dad doesn't like to drive with the radio on. It gives him a headache. Plus this trip was about getting away from it all, remember?"

His next words came out in a frantic jumble. "Turn on the radio, any channel. It's national news. You may be in danger—"

Tad's warning was tamped down by growing static. Piper listened for a few seconds, then realized she'd lost the signal. She checked the phone's screen. It showed she had only one signal bar, indicating a very weak connection to the satellite floating somewhere far above in space.

The urgency in Tad's voice had frightened her. She wondered if the mountains were somehow interfering with the signal. She decided to move to higher ground before calling him back. Piper didn't possess Creeper's agility to climb trees or his innate comfort with heights. The top of the RV would have to do. She went outside and walked around to the backside of the American Coach Eagle, where a curved ladder was bolted to the vehicle's frame. She climbed up to the roof, stepped around an array of solar panels, and sat down on top of the hamburger-box-shaped air conditioner, carefully so she wouldn't dent it with her butt. She checked the phone. This time she had two bars. She dialed Tad's number. He answered in half a ring.

"Piper? Piper, can you hear me?"

"Yeah, the connection is better. What were you saying when—?"

"Listen to me! Yesterday a very bad dude released some crazy airborne version of the rabies virus into the air. It happened in the Cascade Mountains area. A summer camp was attacked by infected animals, not far from the Mountain Loop Highway. The animals went crazy, biting everyone they came across. I don't know how you even got into that area; the military set up roadblocks, and—"

"My dad took a dirt road off the Mountain Loop Highway," she told him. "It wasn't marked. He almost missed it. Are we going to get in trouble? Will they lock us up for trespassing?"

"That's not important!" Tad was almost yelling now. "If you see an animal acting weird, whatever you do, don't let it near you!"

Piper scanned her surroundings for signs of wildlife and saw none. "Tad, you're freaking me out. What's going on?"

"You should get out of there right now. It only takes one little bite . . ." Tad trailed off, holding something back.

"What happens when the animals bite, Tad?"

"Piper, more than a hundred kids were killed at that camp. The animals are sick. One bite and you'll be dead before you hit the ground."

Piper went numb. It dawned on her that she hadn't seen a single mammal since they'd arrived. Not even a squirrel or chipmunk. Nothing. She'd felt like something was amiss, but couldn't put her finger on it. Then she remembered they'd spied an unusual amount of roadkill the last few miles before the turnoff: a couple of deer, a raccoon, and a dog. The smell of skunk—clearly more than one—had brought tears to their eyes, and they'd been forced to roll up the windows. None of the carcasses looked particularly mangled or bloody or had tire marks on them. Now that she thought about it, none of the animals had looked injured at all. Just dead. She thought of her parents and Creeper, so far from the safety of the RV.

"Tad . . ." she said, lowering her voice to a whisper. "I think we may have driven right into the middle of it."

"Piper, you have to get your family inside the RV. Then get out of there. Head to Seattle and don't stop until you get there. If any animals survived the"—*crackle crackle*—"you might not be able to"—*crackle crackle* . . .

The signal failed and Tad was gone again. Piper started to redial his number, but something—a faint breeze, a smell in the air, or maybe her secret bargain with the universe—told her to check on Grace. She looked down at the bassinet. Her blood ran cold.

Piper dropped the phone. It clattered against a vent pipe, tumbled over the side of the RV, and shattered against the portable barbecue grill with a loud clacking sound. The noise drew the attention of the furry creature peering hungrily into Grace's bassinet. It aimed its beady black eyes at the phone dangling by its wire guts from the grill's lid handle. Nostrils flaring, it raised its muzzle to the roof of the RV. Piper saw the foam dripping from its mouth. She recognized the animal. A wolverine, the largest member of the weasel family, and a vicious predator. Although wolverines weighed less than forty pounds, one could still take down a weak caribou. She'd never seen one in person before, but it fit the description. It had a head shaped like a bear's. Its elongated body was covered in fur. The fur was black and white, a reverse in the stripe pattern of a skunk. This one was clearly sick, just like Tad said. *One bite. One bite and then death.* The creature's foamy jaws were inches away from her sleeping sister.

Piper leaped to the ladder and slid down the side rails, ignoring the rungs entirely. She landed hard, twisting her ankle, but she couldn't let that slow her down. She needed a plan. Her dad's hunting rifle was the first thing that came to mind, but it was locked in a case in the cargo bay. She'd never get it out in time. What else?

Piper looked on the ground for anything she could use as a weapon and saw the water hose attached to the RV. Her dad had spent the morning washing Rolling Thunder from bumper to bumper. If the water pressure was strong enough, maybe she could blast the wolverine away from her sister.

Piper turned the spigot on, and water flowed from a holding tank in the RV's belly, through the hose, and out the nozzle, pooling on the ground. She picked up the sprayer. The wolverine threatened Piper with a noise that sounded like a cross between a lion's roar and the grunting of a pig.

"That's right!" she yelled at it. Piper spotted the long grill fork and grabbed that too. "Stay focused on me!"

But the animal would not be distracted. It turned its attention back to the baby. Globs of saliva dripped from its mouth into the bassinet.

Screaming and brandishing her two makeshift weapons, Piper charged at the wolverine. The hose uncoiled like a striking snake behind her.

1

A full year had passed since the horrific rabies outbreak in Washington. For the most part, the world had moved on. It was early August, two months deep into summer, a time when the kids of Jesup, Georgia, were running around outside with their tongues hanging out, like crazy dogs that had slipped their leashes. They spent their days sugar-powered by Kool-Aid and ice cream, and they wore bathing suits as uniforms. Fun in the Southern sun was all anyone could think about. Except for Tad. He couldn't get his mind off Piper. It didn't help that he was now lost in a sea of boys clamoring for her attention. She'd always been pretty, but seemingly overnight she'd blossomed into the kind of girl who turned guys into silent-film comedians, tripping over their own feet, slap fighting one another over who would get to retrieve the book she'd dropped in the school hallway. She'd turned into what his dad would have called "a stunner."

It wasn't just her looks that had changed. Her personality had changed too. She wasn't a tomboy anymore, and she'd stopped hanging out with "geeks" like Tad. She was part of the pageant crowd now, a group of girls who entered—and usually won—every pageant in eastern Georgia. The Beauty Queens. Piper was the most beautiful of them all. In fact, she seemed even more radiant since he'd last seen her, before the start of summer. That was two months ago. Two months, one day, seventeen hours, and some change. When Tad found out she'd been invited to cut the ribbon at the opening of the new Jesup Nature Center, he started a countdown, using a red marker to X out days on the calendar over his desk. Today was Red Circle Day.

Tad watched from the crowd as Piper, dressed in a lovely pink sundress and a white sash printed with glittery gold letters that read JUNIOR MISS JESUP, used a pair of oversize novelty scissors to cut the ceremonial red ribbon hanging across the entrance door of the shiny nature center. He lost sight of Piper as Mayor Stodge escorted her into the building and the throng funneled in behind them. Tad loitered outside a bit for no particular reason he could think of before heading up the steps.

Tad knew the layout of the building because the curator, Mrs. Ham, had given him a preview tour when he accompanied his mother in July to deliver some family heirlooms for a special exhibit. Tad headed there now to consult with a dead man.

He entered a room labeled THE FLORA OF GEORGIA and nosed around. Mrs. Ham had done a bang-up job of displaying his family's donated items. Most of them—including a botanist's satchel, a microscope, and a rusty pair of pruning shears—were resting on satin pillows. Placards framed on metal stands told visitors what each item was and how it might have been used in the field. An oil painting of their original owner hung on the wall behind them, bathed in the apricot glow of the track lighting above.

Tad stepped in front of the portrait, glanced around to make sure he was alone, and then, in a familiar tone, he spoke to the man in the painting. "Hey . . . um . . . how's it hanging, sir? Hope you're comfy here. It's a lot roomier than our basement. Definitely an upgrade. So . . . I need to ask for some advice, if that's okay. It's about a girl. . . ."

Tad nearly jumped out of his sneakers when a ghostly vibrato voice replied, "Speeeeaaaak, my son." He whirled to find his friend

Grafton Connor standing behind him, grinning and fully satisfied with the outcome of his prank.

"I'm sorry, buddy." Grafton chuckled. "I didn't mean to interrupt your heart-to-heart chat with Lord Boringdude. But if you need some advice on your love life, you should talk to the photo of Dian Fossey over in the primate exhibit. She was an expert on monkey mating rituals."

"Har, har," Tad replied. "What are you doing here, anyway? Didn't you just get your driver's license? I figured you'd be out making the roads unsafe for humankind."

"I was. And then I drove here to check out the Birds of the Southern States exhibit. It's kinda lame, though—too many song-birds, not enough raptors. But observing a dodo bird talking to a wall made the trip worthwhile."

At six foot two, Grafton was big enough to be a varsity attraction at Jesup Middle School, and there were certainly unfair expectations of him to play sports, but Grafton was a science geek, like Tad, and had zero interest in athletics. He was a birder, the type of guy who'd rather spend his time in a tall field than on a ball field. "You want to tell me why you were soliciting dating advice from a painting? Who is that guy, anyway?"

"Dr. Brisbane Cole. He was a famous botanist back when America was fairly new. He was only fifteen when he joined the Lewis and Clark Expedition as a page. He was even pals with Thomas Jefferson. He's kinda my hero."

"Cole . . . Cole . . ." Grafton stroked his chin. "That name sounds familiar."

"Picked up on that, Sherlock?" Tad snorted. "Brisbane Cole is my great-great-great-great-great-great-great-great-great-great-grand-father."

"That's . . . um . . . great. But I'm a little offended. I thought *I* was your hero. Oh well. I guess that explains your weird fascination

15

with plants. Genetics. I can sorta see the resemblance between you two. Same goofy grin. He's a much better dresser, though. Maybe if you worked on your wardrobe a little, you wouldn't need help in the dating department."

The man in the painting was in his early thirties, attired to fit a bygone era and portrayed as possessing a noble mien. He was wearing a double-breasted tailcoat with a high collar made of velvet, and under the coat a white waistcoat, and under that a white shirt. His neck was hiddden by a cravat—a scarf-like precursor to the necktie. Cole's waist looked pinched (girdles weren't just for women back in his day). This gave him a waspy, cartoonish torso. His hairline had receded, but tufts of golden locks jutted forward from his temples to frame his bare forehead like a laurel wreath. Cole had a gaunt but handsome face, made even more pleasant by his crooked, toothy smile, the kind you rarely see in nineteenth-century portraits of self-important muckety-mucks. Cole was cradling a golden cylindrical canister in his hands.

Grafton peered into a glass case to inspect a two-hundred-year-old flower press. "How'd the museum get all this junk?"

"It's not junk, goober. It's here on loan. When I was a baby, my mom inherited Cole's estate. There wasn't much left to it by then. His brownstone in Manhattan was foreclosed on by the bank when my great-grandfather couldn't afford to pay the city's high property taxes. You ask me, we got all the good stuff: His botany equipment, the painting, some of his field journals. I've read them all. My ancestor was like the Indiana Jones of plant hunters, traveling all over the world to collect specimens. My mom thought it would be a nice gesture to donate his stuff to the museum so other people could appreciate it. I'm not thrilled about parting with his stuff, but at least she let me keep his final journal."

"So what's the deal?" Grafton asked. "He your romance coach or something?"

Tad shifted in his shoes, embarrassed. "I was just talking out loud.

It's not like I expected him to answer or anything." The fact was, Tad wished he could go back in time and ask his ancestor how to fix things with Piper. If there was one thing he and his long-dead relative had in common—besides a deep interest in botany, of course—it was their unwavering devotion to one woman. Grafton was his buddy, but Tad didn't feel as though Dr. Cole's tragic love life was any of his business.

"So . . . I'm assuming you're still hung up on you-know-who?" said Grafton. "Because if so, it's like I've told you a hundred times, you need to let her go. For your own sanity."

"Let who go?" Tad asked innocently.

"You know who I'm talking about, dude. Miss Peanut Festival 2014. Piper Canfield. Is that why you came here? Are you hoping to take her aside and have a little chat? Seriously, dude. I have to watch you like a sharp-shinned hawk. Someone has to keep you from making the biggest mistake of your life."

"Look, not that it's your business," Tad said, "but Piper and I have history."

"So? I have History with her too. And Math and Chemistry. Jesup Middle is a small school. What's your point?"

"I didn't mean it like that," said Tad. "I meant we *share* a past."

Grafton raised one eyebrow. "But not a *present*, right?"

Tad didn't offer a reply.

"Thought not. Look, I get that you have a thing for the girl. She's hot. Heck, you can't throw a paper plane in Jesup without hitting some dude who has a crush on Piper Canfield. But there's a reason why guys steer clear of her and the rest of the Snooty Queens. They're heartbreakers, every one."

Piper's clique referred to themselves as the Beauty Queens, on account of their combined twenty-six pageant wins, but most of Tad's guy friends called them the Snooty Queens behind their backs. It wasn't a particularly clever play on words, but it was accurate. In Tad's opinion, the Snooty Queens were as shallow as a plate of water. He'd never given them much thought until Piper joined their ranks, ending their lifelong friendship in the process. It's not wise to approach someone who's surrounded by angry pit bulls.

"Look, you need to be careful," Grafton warned. "Even if Piper doesn't drag your heart through the mud—and she probably will—those other harpies won't be so gentle with your reputation. Before you get within ten feet of their pack, they'll brand you as the creepy stalker guy and your social life will be a wrap. Did you know they've actually started handing out restraining orders? Check this out." Grafton reached into his book bag and retrieved a six-by-two-inch piece of pink laminated cardboard. Printed on one side were the words YOU ARE NOT ALLOWED TO COME WITHIN 100 FEET OF THIS PERSON EVER AGAIN. Tad turned it over and saw that the back was covered in glitter and shiny star stickers.

He was amused. "What did you do to earn that?"

"I was behind Patty Myers and Olivia Price in line at Dairy Queen last week, and I asked them if they were having a good summer," Grafton said. "Patty handed me this. It's laminated, bro. Laminated! That's serious business."

"Why'd you bother keeping it?" Tad asked.

"I don't know how it works. Maybe if I collect five, I'll win a free soda or something."

"They're ridiculous," said Tad. "Look, I appreciate your concern, but I still have to talk to Piper. It's important."

Grafton gave Tad a pitying look. "I figured. But what kind of buddy would I be if I didn't at least *try* to talk you out of committing social suicide?"

"Your concern has been entered into the record."

Grafton shrugged, then picked up a twined bundle of corncob husks from one of the exhibit tables. "What's this? Some kind of camping pillow?"

"That's what Cole used to . . . uh . . . wipe. Toilet paper wasn't produced in America until the eighteen fifties."

Grafton dropped it like a hot potato. "Ew! Gross, dude!"

"It's not used, dummy! That would be unsanitary. How did you think Native Americans cleaned themselves back then?"

"I don't know! I just figured they grabbed a passing squirrel, something soft and fluffy! You could have warned me!"

"Nobody told you to pick it up," Tad reminded him. "This is a museum. Look, don't touch."

Piper Canfield and the rest of the mayor's entourage entered the room with much commotion. Piper's eyes met Tad's, then she quickly looked away. The exchange felt like frostbite. Grafton put a comforting arm around Tad's shoulders and said, "That's good advice, dude. Look, but don't touch. You should leave her alone."

After Grafton left, Tad waited for more than an hour for Piper to break away from Mayor Stodge and the others. He paced back and forth between the Spiders of the Carolina Coast exhibit and the restrooms. If there was one thing he knew about girls, it was that they went to the restroom a zillion times a day. Needing a distraction from his anxious thoughts, Tad picked up a pair of headphones and listened to an audio commentary about the black widow spider. Apparently, the females bite the heads off the males when they get sick of having them around. He tried not to forge implications.

When Piper finally made her way to the restroom, she was so focused on adjusting her sash that she didn't see Tad until she was right next to him.

"Hey, Piper!" he said, mustering a chipper voice. "Can we talk for a sec?"

"Oh . . . hey, Tad. Um . . ." She looked extremely uncomfortable. Not good.

"It'll only take a second."

Piper fished into the little purse that hung by a thin gold chain crisscrossed over her sash. Tad feared she'd spring a homemade restraining order on him, but instead she took out her cell phone and checked the time.

"Okay," she said, "I have a couple minutes. What do you want?"

Tad got straight to the point. "I have something for you. Can you come by the house later to pick it up?"

"Oh. I don't know, Tad. . . . I'm supposed to meet my friends. We're working on pageant stuff—the talent portion. We have to practice."

Piper's cagey response wasn't the reaction Tad was hoping for. He knew that if he gave up now, this would become the site of his final defeat. His Alamo. His Waterloo. His Death Star. He had to be persistent. "It won't take long, I promise. You don't even have to come inside the house. Your gift is in the backyard. In the greenhouse."

"You have a greenhouse?"

"Yes, built it myself this spring. Wait until you see it."

Piper frowned and started tugging on her sash again, even though it was perfectly aligned and all the glittered lettering was readable. Tad was sure she'd turn him down, but then she nodded and said, "All right."

"All right?"

"Yes, I'll stop by, but it'll be around six, if that's okay. Like I said, I already promised the girls I'd meet up with them this afternoon."

Tad lit up. He could barely mask his joy. "Six is perfect!"

"Okay."

"Six it is!" he called to her as he watched her walk away.

But six it wasn't. Six o'clock came, but Piper didn't. As the minutes ticked on, Tad descended gradually through the stages of grief:

denial, anger, depression, and finally totally bummed. He gave up on her, went inside the house, and ransacked the freezer for bad-mood-food. He was about to kick off a world-class pity party featuring a sandwich made out of cookie dough ice cream smashed between two Pop-Tarts when Piper's text came through.

Running behind. Be there in 15 min.

Never before had seven words so quickly reversed the tide of despair. Tad checked himself in the mirror by the coatrack, combed his hair with his fingers, and searched his pants pockets for gum but found none. He headed back outside. The sun was setting. The interior of the greenhouse would be dark soon, and since his mother forbade Tad from doing the electrical wiring himself, the greenhouse didn't have lights yet. Piper wouldn't be able to stay long. Maybe that was her plan. Tad lifted the door latch, opened the door wide, and propped it with a brick. He went inside.

The greenhouse was Tad's crowning achievement. Thirty-five feet long by eighteen feet wide, with an A-frame ceiling. Both roof and walls were made of clear, shatterproof polycarbonate panels he'd cut to size with a chop saw. He'd spent many evenings and weekends assembling the building with the help of Mr. Patel, Tad's cantankerous next-door neighbor. Mr. Patel had bartered labor in exchange for some space to store his outdoor plants during the winter months. Jesup wasn't exactly Alaska, but at times the temperatures did drop below freezing.

Tad set to work watering flowers to keep from going crazy while he waited, but mostly he just went over in his head the lines he would say to Piper. Good lines. The kind of lines that won the girl over in the chick flicks he'd sometimes watch with his mother because when she watched them alone she cried. Tad was so lost in thought that he jumped when Piper rapped her knuckles on the inside of the door frame.

"Sorry I'm late," she said.

Tad waved her inside. He tried to act nonchalant, hoping she wouldn't notice that his hands were shaking. "No problem. I was just finishing up some work."

"Wow . . ." She panned around the greenhouse. "This is impressive. I was expecting something a little more . . . amateur."

"You know what they say: go big or go home." He shouldn't have said "go home." He had to choose his words more carefully. His future hinged on careful words.

Piper peeked down at the time on her phone. "I can't stay long— I've already missed dinner. You said you had something for me?"

"I do. Can you spare ten minutes? Please? I'll give you a tour."

Before Piper could object, Tad started down the center aisle, pointing out his various projects. Piper lagged behind, keeping a fair distance between them. He could tell by her body language—arms folded close to her chest, hands knifed deep into her armpits, eyes darting everywhere except for his face—that she was uncomfortable being alone with him.

"We've got your standard salad fixings here. . . ." He moved the tour along at a brisk pace. "Some perennial flowers over here . . . Potatoes . . . Did you know potatoes are in the poisonous nightshade family? Here's my mom's herb garden—mostly stuff you'd find in Indian food. She loves Indian food."

"What about these plants?" Piper asked. Her curiosity was piqued by a lone potter's bench set against the back wall. It looked like a table in a mad scientist's lab. The plants on its shelves were experiments in various stages. "Are you going all Frankenstein in here, Tad?"

"Not exactly." He laughed. "I've been reading up on Charles

Darwin, the guy who came up with the theory of evolution. In the years before he died, his interest shifted his focus from animals to plants. He conducted a bunch of experiments on them."

"What kind of experiments?"

"This may sound crazy. . . ." Tad said. "Darwin wondered if plants had souls. Or at least some sort of higher awareness than we give them credit for. In order to make a determination, he first had to find out what plants know, which meant finding out which senses plants possessed, if any."

"Senses?"

"The five senses: sight, touch, smell, taste, and hearing."

Piper chuckled. "So you're saying Darwin went a little bonkers toward the end?"

"Not at all! In fact, his experiments proved that plants possess many of the same senses we do. They just receive and process the information a little differently. For example, we know now that plants can see certain colors, like white, red, and blue. The sensory cells that detect and process colored light are located in the tips of a plant. If you shine a red light in the dark, a plant will grow toward it. But if you cover the tip of the plant with an opaque cap, then the plant stays dormant. It doesn't grow or flower. Different colors of light have different effects on plants. Blue light is good for leaf growth, while red light encourages the plant to bloom."

"Cool. What about the other four senses?"

"Well, there's touch. . . ." Tad's fingertips accidentally brushed against Piper's arm and his heart fluttered. "Plants know when something brushes up against them."

"Nuh-uh," she said.

"It's true. I'll show you." He lifted a leafy plant from the potter's bench and held it out to Piper. "This species is called *Mimosa pudica*. Go ahead. Pet it."

"Excuse me?"

"Stroke the plant," he insisted.

Piper ran her fingertips over the leaves. Immediately, they folded in half like tiny books and moved away from her touch. She yanked her hand back. "Oh no! Did I hurt it?"

Tad smiled. He thought her concern was adorable. "No, it'll forget about you in a few seconds, and then it'll open back up." *Forget about you? Who could forget about you?*

Sure enough, the plant sprang back to form.

"I didn't know plants could move so fast," said Piper. "Or *at all.*"

"It's called rapid plant movement," Tad explained. "Most plants aren't capable of it—just a few, like my mimosa and the shrinking violet. It happens when electrical signals acting on motor cells make the leaves move. Now, the plant's *awareness* of your touch is called something different: tropism. Most plants experience tropism, but unlike the *Mimosa pudica*, they can't react to it quickly. When they get scared, they can't just uproot and run away." *Like you did.*

Piper pondered this. "If plants can feel touch, can they also feel pain?"

Tad shook his head. "No. Plants don't have brains like animals do. Without a brain, they can't process pain." *Lucky them.*

"That's good," said Piper. "I'd hate to think the broccoli au gratin I had for lunch suffered horribly. Can they hear too?"

"Some scientists believe so," Tad said. "But if I had to guess, I'd say plants are as deaf as a doornail."

Piper giggled.

"What's so funny?"

"My mom. She sings to her house ferns every day. She thinks it helps them grow. She has a terrible singing voice, so I was worried she was doing more harm than good."

"Ha! I know what you mean. Mr. Patel, the neighbor who helped me build this greenhouse, curses up a storm. If plants could hear, all of his would have shriveled up and died a long time ago."

They were having fun. Tad decided this was the moment he'd waited for. It was time to tell her exactly how he felt about her.

A tiny flicker of green light outside caught Piper's attention through the glass wall. Then another. Her smile disappeared. "Fireflies are out. It's dark. I really need to go."

"Oh. Okay. I'll get that thing you came for."

Tad led Piper to the greenhouse sink. Above the shelf was a solitary shelf. It held a single plant, an orchid in a clay pot. He'd written the words FOR PIPER! MR. PATEL, PLEASE DO NOT USE THIS POT! in permanent marker on the side. The orchid rose from the soil and hooked at the point on the stem where its gorgeous pink-and-white flowers began. "It's a hybrid. A new species. I named it *Denbrobium* Piper Anne."

Piper was confused. Piper Anne was *her* name.

"I made it for you," Tad said, holding the pot out to her. "This orchid is a brand-new hybrid species. Took me a year to grow. Take it. It's yours."

"Oh." Piper blushed. "Thanks." Other than the sudden color change, her face was stony. Unreadable.

"No problem."

She accepted the orchid from his hands. "It's pretty."

"I'm glad you think so."

"I should go." Piper turned and headed for the door. Tad followed.

They walked across the lawn toward the street. The porch light from Tad's house illuminated the way. Neither of them spoke. Tad scoured his mind for the right words. Words that would reopen the door that had closed between them a year ago when the sick wolverine changed everything. He wanted things to be the way they used to be. He wanted *Piper* to be the way she used to be. But as desperate as he was for those magic words, they never came.

They reached Piper's bike, and she unchained it from pole of the basketball hoop in Tad's driveway. It was the first time anyone had used the hoop all year. Shooting baskets after school used to be their thing.

Piper set the orchid in her book bag. The flowers poked out of the unzipped top.

"Well . . . I'll see you at school," she said coolly, then straddled her bike seat.

In a moment of panic, Tad said the stupidest thing (which was, ironically, the most honest thing). "I've missed you, Piper."

Piper didn't reply. She just froze, staring at the handlebars, with one foot up on a pedal and the other on the pavement.

Tad forgot to breathe. *Say something, Piper! Say anything!*

A fat firefly floated in front of Piper's face and blinked on. Green light means go.

"Good night, Tad."

She rode off into the night.

June 31, 1823

In my travel-worn Bible, the apostle Paul warns that money is the root of all evil. Today, in this humble botanist's view, the common gingerroot is the source of all that is good.

I, Dr. Brisbane Cole, am a passenger aboard the tea clipper *Eastern Sun*, a trade ship packed to the gunwales with teas and silk, sailing from Kwangchow, China, to New York. For five days I endured the most wicked bout of seasickness. At times the vomiting was so severe I considered flinging myself overboard for relief. The ship's crew members, an unsavory lot who resent sharing our limited supply of freshwater with the three hundred exotic plant specimens I gathered along the Biejiang River, have taken no pity on my condition.

It was the chief cook who resolved my tender stomach! The cure? A teaspoon of infused gingerroot added to a cup of water every day has soothed my flopping innards. I shall be in the man's eternal debt. It has not escaped this botanist's sense of irony that my deliverance "stems" from a type of plant. The curative properties of plants have been recorded in modern science and in ancient legends, in the epic tales of Gilgamesh and Achilles, for example. . . . I believe that the most enduring myths spring from seeds of truth. And perhaps I believe in these stories of miracle plants because it gives me hope to do so.

We find ourselves in a golden age of medicine. The Silk Road trade between China's Qing dynasty and the Americas has opened a whole new world of discovery. The Orient is a great source of plant species previously unknown to Westerners. The people there have used these plants as medicine for thousands of years and have guarded their healing secrets from foreigners with ferocity, but I was able to earn their trust. In the span of three months, I gathered a trove of unique plant specimens and learned of their medicinal uses: *dang gui* for the health of the

heart, *chai hu* for the stomach and liver, *gan cao* to harmonize
the body, to name but a few. While I was forced to end my visit
abruptly, it brings me great satisfaction to return to the States
with a wealth of wellness as my reward. Now that the gingerroot
has lifted my spirits, I am able to gather my thoughts, which are
as roiling and dark as the tumultuous sea below. I think of my
wife, Edwina. My beloved. Two weeks ago I received an urgent
missive from our estate's caretaker, Mrs. Muldoon, and learned
that Edwina is eight months pregnant with our firstborn, and
while this should be cause for much jubilation, it seems that
my wife's condition is complicated. She has taken sick with a
mysterious ailment. Her body grows weaker by the day, and the
doctors hold little hope that she will survive childbirth. I cannot
accept this prognosis, and yet I feel helpless to change the
outcome. For despite their curative potential, there is not a sprig
or seed or sapling among our cargo that can save her life. And
so my thoughts and sights return to America. It is with steely
determination that I will venture into a dark, foreboding realm
to seek the flower of Edwina's salvation in the black heart of
Georgia's Okefenokee Swamp.

2

When Piper got home, her mother had nearly finished clearing the table. Her dad was dunking dishes into the sudsy sink. Neither of them scolded her for missing dinner. She'd called ahead to let them know she was stopping by Tad's, and this seemed to make them happy and surprised. Happy because they'd always liked Tad, and surprised because the last time he'd been a visitor in their home (the day the Canfields had flown back from Washington), Piper had screamed at him and shoved him out the door, slamming it in his baffled face. He'd teetered on her welcome mat, stunned. The last words she'd said to him were "I never want to talk to you again!" and despite her parents' repeated efforts to convince her that Tad had done nothing wrong, she'd stubbornly stuck to her guns.

"There's some leftover chicken in the fridge," Jane told her. "Help yourself."

"I'm not hungry, thanks."

Jane noticed the orchid sticking up like plumage from the top of Piper's backpack and gushed over it. "Wow, that's gorgeous! Did Tad give it to you?"

Piper slipped off the pack to give her mother a better peek. "Yes. That's why he asked me over."

"Well, it's positively lovely," said Jane.

With the last dinner plate set upright in the drying rack, Brad wiped his hands with a dish towel. "He's such a nice kid, that Tad. It's a shame . . ." He didn't finish his thought. He didn't have to. Piper knew how her parents felt about her ex–best friend.

"I'm going to put the plant in my room. I have homework to do, so I'll see you tomorrow."

She said good night to Creeper, who was playing with his Xbox in the living room, his eyes glued to the TV screen. He waved good night or he waved her away—she couldn't tell which.

On the way to her bedroom, Piper stopped by the open door of the nursery. The lights were off inside, but she could make out the silhouette shapes of the crib and the teddy bear mobile dangling above it. The room's occupant was awake, standing up on short sausage legs, smiling and reaching out to Piper with little clutching hands.

"Pippy!" the baby squealed.

Piper sighed and stepped into the nursery. She reached into the crib, but instead of picking Grace up, she fished the plastic baby monitor from the bedding and spoke into the microphone, knowing her voice would be received in the kitchen. "Mom, your youngest is awake. I told you I have to do homework—she's all yours."

Piper considered her sister's joy-filled face and chubby arms reaching eagerly for her Pippy.

"Go to sleep," Piper whispered, diverting her gaze to the mobile. She pressed its button, prodding the plush teddy bears into a slow circular waltz to the tune of "Rock-a-bye Baby" and the faint clicking of the mobile's motor. "I'll see you tomorrow." Piper turned her back on Grace and left the bedroom. She waited in the hallway until she heard her mother starting up the stairs, then she ducked into her own room and quickly shut the door. Inside her safe zone, she made a place of prominence for Tad's orchid by pushing some of her pageant trophies to the back of her dresser top. She kicked off her shoes, changed into her nightclothes, washed up (in the bathroom adjoining her room to Creeper's), and then sprawled out on her bed. She set her alarm clock to go off an hour earlier than usual; homework would wait until morning.

Piper's phone pinged with a text message. She checked the screen thinking it might be from Tad. He had her new number now because she'd texted him earlier to tell him she'd be late. But the text was from her friend, Olivia Price.

Hey, bestie! Don't forget we're going dress shopping for the pageant this Saturday. Let me know what time. P.S. I saw you at the new nature center, cornered by some geek. Do you need me to print more restraining orders? ROFL!

Piper didn't reply. She was friends with Olivia and the other girls in their clique, but she didn't agree with some of their crueler antics. The restraining orders were especially stupid. If she didn't feel like talking to someone, she just wouldn't. She didn't need to make a spectacle out of it.

Piper knew that people thought her friends were shallow. She knew that people thought *she* was shallow too. Even her guidance counselor had lowered his expectations of her. During their last visit, he'd suggested she consider a career as a showcase model. A showcase model! The kind that stands by expensive cars at auto shows and waves vapidly at people as they pass by. Her counselor said, "It's super easy. All you have to do is smile and occasionally ask people to sign up for raffles." She would have been offended if she'd actually cared. Nobody asked much of her anymore. That's exactly how she wanted it.

Piper stared at the orchid and recalled the look of disappointment on Tad's face when she'd met his kindness with indifference. She thought about him until she drifted off into a pine-scented nightmare in which squirrels the size of grizzly bears ate babies by the wheelbarrowful.

In the moments before the alarm went off, Piper was climbing into a giant squirrel nest as big as a swimming pool in a daring attempt to rescue Grace. It was nothing new; she'd been in the nest plenty of times and knew the plot of the nightmare well. Only this time when the giant squirrel attacked, Tad climbed up a colossal orchid stem, jumped into the nest, and fought off the creature, giving Piper a chance to escape with the baby for the first time ever. Tad. Her hero. She was jarred awake by the buzzing alarm before she could return to help. She considered hitting the snooze button to go back for him, but she had a debt of homework to address, so she slid out of bed and into her slippers.

Piper showered, dressed, and cranked out her assignments with little difficulty. She thought to water the orchid, and it dawned on her that she didn't know the first thing about taking care of one. She would have to do some research. Of course, she could just ask Tad, but that would be awkward after how she'd behaved in his driveway. She packed her book bag for the day and headed downstairs.

"Good morning, sweetheart." Jane mouthed the words so she wouldn't startle the baby. She was sitting at the table, cradling Grace in her arms. A cup of yogurt sat on the table with a little spoon sticking upright out of the top. Grace had some yogurt on her chin, but her eyes were closed. It looked as though she'd fallen asleep in Jane's arms right in the middle of breakfast. "I hate to do this to you, Piper," Jane whispered, "but I need you to stay home from school today."

"Me too?" Creeper asked. He was sitting across from their mother, hunkered over a mountain of bacon and a heap of scrambled eggs. His eyes were alight with hope.

"No, not you, mister," Jane said. "Finish eating and brush your teeth. No dragging your feet. The last thing I need is for you to miss the bus this morning."

"Aw." Creeper pouted. "No fair."

Piper wasn't thrilled about her arrangement either. "Why do I have to stay home? I've got a million things I need to—"

"And I need you, Piper," said Jane. "Grace isn't feeling well today. Your father left for work before the baby woke up, and I have a presentation this morning at the office. I want you to keep an eye on your sister until I can get home, which should be around noon. Can you please do that for me?"

Piper went into panic mode. The last time she'd been on solo babysitting duty was a year ago in Washington. She'd managed to wriggle her way out of it ever since. But this time it was an emergency. She'd have to wriggle harder.

"Mom, Mr. Traynor has been threatening a pop quiz in math class all week. If I miss it—"

"If you miss it, you'll live. I'll speak to your teachers this afternoon so they understand the situation."

Piper scowled. "I'll fall behind in class."

Disappointment was etched on Jane's face. "What happened to you, Piper? You used to dote on Grace, but lately you treat her as if she has the plague."

Piper fell quiet. She'd hoped she hadn't been that obvious.

Jane stood with the baby. "Please clean the table. I'll get Grace comfy in her crib, and then I have to get going. I expect you to watch over her."

"Fine," Piper muttered.

"That doesn't mean taking the baby monitor into your room and closing the door. I want you to sit with Grace. Bring your laptop into her room if you want; just keep the volume low. You're to call me if

33

your sister shows the slightest sign of feeling worse. Are we clear?"

"Yes, ma'am."

That was that. Creeper was on time for the bus and Jane was on time for her presentation. Piper, as she viewed the situation, was the only one inconvenienced by her mother's master plan.

Piper dragged a beanbag chair and her laptop into the nursery. She spent the first hour surfing the Web for pageant gowns. She planned to go to All Things That Glitter with Olivia on Saturday to buy a dress in person, but it wouldn't hurt to get an idea of what she wanted in advance. Her search yielded a blue strapless number she liked, and she e-mailed the link to Olivia for a second opinion. But despite her best effort, she couldn't purge Tad from her mind.

She searched for instructions on orchid care and found a website that told her everything she needed to know. There were pictures of different kinds, though none as pretty as hers. *Denbrobium* Piper Anne was one of a kind. Tad had created something extraordinary just for her. Perusing the website, she realized how much work he'd put into raising hers. A ton. She felt even worse for the way she'd treated him. Piper started typing him a text, but when she finished, she deleted it and set the phone down.

It was almost ten o'clock when Piper thought to check the crib. Grace was awake but barely moving. Usually, whenever the baby saw her Pippy, she got all giddy and did a wormy dance on her back. This time she just stared up at her older sister without connecting, eyes wide and unblinking.

"You really *are* sick, aren't you?" Piper hoisted Grace up into her arms and held her close. The baby felt heavier than Piper remembered. She struggled to think back to the last time she'd done this. Feeling Grace's limp body pressed against her chest, she had the same pangs of guilt she'd felt over Tad, only a gazillion times worse.

Piper paced the floor speaking softly to her sister. Grace remained unresponsive. Her arms hung limp like a rag doll's. At eleven o'clock,

Piper decided she was in over her head and texted both her parents with an update. Jane responded first:

Heading home now. Hang tight.

A few minutes later, her dad replied with a similar message.

The next hour was a blur of frantic activity. Brad was the first through the door. He took the baby from Piper, and she brought him up to speed. With Grace cradled in one arm, he used the other to stuff a diaper bag. Jane showed up five minutes later and stole Grace from Brad. Since Jane's car was the last in the narrow driveway, they would take it to the hospital. While Jane fastened the baby into her car seat, Brad put the diaper bag in the trunk.

"I'm coming with you," Piper insisted.

"Someone has to be home when Creeper gets off the bus," Brad reminded her. "I promise we'll call you as soon as we know something."

Piper watched the car curl around the cul-de-sac and then speed off down their street in the direction of the highway.

For the rest of the afternoon Piper was a nervous wreck. She hadn't been this scared for Grace since that terrifying day in Washington when the rabid wolverine peered into her bassinet with murder in its glassy black eyes. Piper had been lucky then. She'd managed to spray the crazed animal with the hose before it could bite Grace. She blew it off the picnic table and onto the ground, then she speared it with the barbecue fork, killing it instantly. She'd snatched up Grace, sprinted into the RV, and locked the door behind her. She used the walkie-talkie to warn her family, and they hurried back immediately. An hour later they were on the road to Seattle, shaken but thankful to have made it out of the woods unscathed. The Canfields listened to the radio as they sped down the Mountain Loop Highway and learned all about the airborne rabies outbreak that had spread through the forest of the Cascade Mountains. The big rain killed off most of the infected animals—extreme hydrophobia was a symptom of the virus, and the ones that got wet literally died of fear—but there were reports of isolated attacks still coming in, most of them within a few miles of Heather Lake. Her friends and family called her a hero (although that was the farthest thing from the truth). Whatever was happening to Grace now wasn't something Piper could solve with courage and a water hose. This time she was utterly helpless.

Shortly after four, Creeper arrived home from school. Piper was sitting at the kitchen table listlessly poking at a piece of key lime pie, occasionally taking a bite. She didn't care about the calories. The last thing on her mind was squeezing into a pageant dress.

"Where is everybody?" Creeper dropped his book bag onto the table and started gutting it clean of homework. The rule was he wasn't allowed to play Minecraft until he'd finished his assignments, so as usual he jumped right into it.

"At the hospital," Piper mumbled. "Grace got worse."

Creeper looked up from organizing mini-stacks of textbooks and papers. "Really?" He sounded genuinely worried. "Is she going to be okay?"

"I don't know. I hope so. I'm waiting to hear from Mom and Dad. There's more pie in the fridge if you want some."

"Pie before dinner? You're gonna get in trouble," he said, as though nothing would please him more.

"Fine, then don't eat it," said Piper. "I don't care."

Creeper wavered for a moment, then he went to the fridge and carved out a huge wedge of pie, bigger than the piece he left in the tin. He sat down across from Piper and attacked it. Between goopy gulps he asked, "What do you think is wrong with her?"

"How should I know?" Piper snapped. "Do I look like a pediatrician?"

"Why are you barking at me?" he shot back. It was a fair question—he hadn't done anything wrong.

"Just leave me alone, okay?" Piper shoved her plate away, got up from the table, and stomped out of the kitchen and into the living room. Creeper followed her.

"You sat for Grace today," he reminded her. "You know more than I do! Tell me what happened."

Piper rounded on him. "Oh, so it's *my* fault she went to the hospital?"

"I didn't say that!" he hollered, stomping his foot.

Neither of them would be able to recall the fiery words that led up to their brawl—hot tempers fueled by fear can short-circuit a person's memory—but for the first time in years, Piper and Creeper were locked in a wrestling match, rolling around on the carpet in front of the TV, screaming like banshees. Piper, three years older, was bigger than Creeper, but he was wiry and had done nothing to deserve her anger. Sometimes right makes might; it was an even match at first.

"Get off me, you ugly troll!" he screamed.

"Stop kicking me, you little dweeb!" she yelled.

"Ouch! That hurts!"

"Let go of my—*ow!*"

Things got *really* ugly when Piper sunk her heels into Creeper's stomach and kicked out, launching him backward across the room. He landed with a sickening *crack*. At first Piper thought she'd busted his skull; fear gripped her like a vise. Her brother rolled over, and she saw that Creeper had landed on something he valued way more than his head: his video game console. This brought the fight to an immediate halt as Creeper inspected the damage.

"Please be okay, please be okay . . ." he muttered under his breath.

The console wasn't okay. There was a split down the center of the plastic case.

"No, no, no," Creeper whimpered as the circular green power light dimmed dark, like the eye of a dying robot. The boy turned beet red. His body began to tremble. His fists clenched. It just got real.

Piper tried to calm him. "Creeper . . . I'm sorry, it was an accident. . . ." It was no use.

"Why are you so mean to me?" he roared.

"I'll pay for it," she promised.

"You'll pay for it, all right!" Creeper snarled. He pounced on top of her.

The second round of the fight was much shorter than the first.

"Stop it! Both of you, right now!" Their father was standing in the doorway. Brad's posture was slack; he looked emotionally spent. His eyes were pink and watery. The kids had seen their father cry only once before, in their parents' wedding video during the recitation of their vows. But that had been a happy cry. They could tell right away this time was different. They stopped fighting immediately.

Piper rose to her feet and wiped a gloss of blood on her lip. "What happened, Dad?"

"Yeah, what's wrong?" Piper had pulled Creeper's shirt up over his head to blind him. He was peeking out at his father through a sleeve hole.

Brad shut the door behind him. "You two are ridiculous! I can't believe with everything that's going on . . . Dang it! You're not babies anymore! You're not babies. . . ." He trailed off.

"Where's Mom?" Creeper asked, pulling his shirt back into place. It was all stretched out now and looked two sizes too big.

"And Grace?" asked Piper. "Dad, where's Grace?"

"Both of you, sit on the couch. Opposite ends, please." Brad dropped his keys into a bowl by the door, then sat down between them, his head bowed, elbows on his knees. He sighed heavily, deflating at the chest and shoulders.

Piper was afraid. "Dad?"

"We need to have a talk," he said softly. "We need to talk about Grace."

3

It was a Friday afternoon; the weekend had arrived, but Tad wasn't exactly thrilled about it. Two weeks had passed since Piper was in his greenhouse. Whatever he'd hoped to accomplish with the orchid had been a colossal waste of effort. Fourteen months of effort to be exact, the total length of time it had taken for him to patiently coax the plant from seed to flower. He'd intended to give her the sprout as a welcome-home gift when she came back from the cross-country RV trip. Instead, he'd watched it grow in his bedroom, and then his greenhouse, until he could barely stand to look at it. Did she even like it? In the end nothing had changed. He was still the Ghost of Piper's Past.

He considered riding his bike by her house to see if her family was home or away on vacation. The last time he'd been at the Canfield residence was a year ago. It'd been a total train wreck. Remembering, he could almost feel the puff of air as Piper slammed the door in his face. Today he'd made it halfway to her house, then turned around and went to Dairy Queen for ice cream. Dark times called for dark chocolate.

Tad barely made it home ahead of a summer downpour. It was so gloomy outside that his mother had turned on both overhead lights in the kitchen—a rarity in August, when the sun stayed up late. Mrs. Cole was standing at the center island, mincing vegetables on a butcher block. Tad, deciding to fix a predinner snack, raided the fridge with the barbarity of a Viking.

"Get your big head out of there!" his mother scolded. "I'm serious, Tad. You see me making dinner here."

"I see you chopping celery," he replied. "When you start kneading pizza dough, then we'll talk."

"Don't test me, kid. I've got a big knife here." With a bemused expression on her face, she held it up to show him.

He snorted. "So I have two choices: starve to death or risk you gutting me like a fish? Would Dr. Phil approve of your parenting method?"

"Starve to—? Tad Bartholomew Cole, I can see the ice-cream stain on your shirt. So help me, if you ruined your appetite . . ."

Tad knew better than to tell her why he'd self-medicated with ice cream. His mother didn't like Piper very much. *Forget about that girl*, she'd say, as always. *If she doesn't want your friendship, then she's not worth your time.* But his mom only felt that way because she didn't understand. He and Piper hadn't drifted apart, like kids do sometimes when they grow up. They'd been *ripped apart* by a single unfortunate event. He didn't think Piper hated him. How could she? The rabies plague in Washington wasn't his fault. And wasn't he sort of the co-hero in the story? Or at least the hero's sidekick? After all, if he hadn't called when he did, she might never have known the wolverine was rabid until it was too late.

His mother passed him the fruit bowl. "A banana will do."

"Yes, ma'am." He tore the ripest banana from the bunch and peeled it.

Mrs. Cole went back to her prep work. "So what's new, kiddo? You seem a little crabby lately. Everything okay in your world?"

Tad shoved the banana into his mouth. Sometimes he had to guard his thoughts around his mother. Since his father died three years ago, the two surviving Coles had become so close that sometimes Tad felt she could read his mind, especially when he was troubled. He wasn't in the mood to talk about his feelings for—

"Piper Canfield?"

Tad looked up from a stack of mail to find his mother leaning over the sink, staring out the window at the greenhouse. "Huh? What about her?" he asked.

Mrs. Cole tapped on the windowpane. "A girl who looks *exactly* like Piper Canfield just ran across the yard and went into the greenhouse. Tad, were you expecting—?" But Tad was already sprinting for the back door.

"Stop!" his mother ordered. "Raincoat!"

Tad yanked his dad's yellow slicker off the coat hook across from the door; no time to go upstairs for his own. He threw the slicker on. To his surprise, it fit perfectly. He bent quickly to flip the hood over his head. Before his mother could say another word, he was out the door, hurdling puddles on a mad dash to the greenhouse.

Upon entering the glass building, Tad was hit by the scent of rich dirt and a sense of disappointment. The greenhouse was empty. Had his mother imagined seeing Piper? There were some plants that when fussed over too long could mess with your vision, but celery wasn't one of them.

He heard muffled sobbing.

"Piper?" There was no reply. He followed his ears through the aisles.

He rounded a corner at the eggplant and found Piper sitting on the ground, slumped over, drenched, and shivering despite the humid recirculated air. She was clutching her orchid pot snugly to her chest. Tad saw that the flower's stem was broken at the top of the spike, between two gnarled nodes. Its petaled face was dangling by a thin strip of splintered cellulose, the plant's version of skin. The victim's broken body shook in Piper's hands.

"What's wrong, Piper?" was all he could think to say.

Piper looked up at him, eyes bloodshot and watery, lip quivering, strands of wet hair slicked across her forehead. *Brittle*. This was the word that came to Tad's mind. Hard, but likely to shatter easily. Brittle was a divot of soil that crumbles away from the base of an uprooted flower. Brittle was the brown leaves of the ficus plant Mr. Patel had forgotten to water while Tad was away on vacation. As an amateur botanist, he knew brittle.

She didn't answer, so he asked again.

"Everything, Tad," she choked out. "Just everything."

Tad sat down across from her on the uncomfortable pea-gravel floor. "It'll be okay. Take your time. Tell me what 'everything' means."

Tad heard all the horrible facts: Piper's parents had taken baby Grace to the emergency room. The doctor ran a blood test and concluded she had an infection. Antibiotics cleared that right up, but a few days later Grace was lethargic again, and this time the doctor called for a more thorough examination. She ran a battery of tests and determined that Grace had something called Alpers syndrome, a degenerative disease that attacks the nervous systems of babies and toddlers. "It's horrible . . ." was Piper's only added commentary.

And it *was* horrible; of course it was. But Tad, as was his nature, focused on the fix.

"Okay, your dad is retired military, which means he has awesome health insurance, right? Grace will get the very best treatment, and she'll be back to crawling the walls in no time."

Piper blinked hard, and a new surge of tears escaped her eyes. "You don't get it." She screwed the base of the clay pot into the loose gravel, jumped awkwardly to her feet, and loomed angrily over Tad.

She yelled at him, just as she had a year ago as he tottered on her welcome mat. "This disease is always fatal! Grace is going to die, Tad! She's going to die, and it's all my fault! Because I broke my word! I broke the pact!"

Tad was confused. "What pact? What are you talking about?"

The cell phone in his pocket sounded. He knew from the ringtone—Darth Vader's theme song—that it was his mother, calling from thirty yards away. The timing of the menacing music was embarrassingly inappropriate.

He leaped to his feet to make fishing the phone from his wet jeans pocket easier. "Yes?"

His mom: "Dinner, bud. Invite her or send her home." *Click.*

Tad glanced back at the house. Through the slanting rain he saw his mother scowling at him from the kitchen window. What was it about mothers and bad timing? He snapped off a sarcastic soldier salute at her through the glass. *"Jawohl, mein Kommandant."*

He turned back to Piper. "Um . . . my mom wants me to come in for dinner. You're invited. Will you stay?" He figured she'd say no and fade from his life again, this time forever. He'd clearly failed to comfort her, and that was why she'd come, wasn't it? "I wouldn't blame you if you'd rather—"

"I don't want to go home yet." She sniffled. "Not right now."

"Okay, then," he said. "Let's get out of here." He took the broken orchid from Piper and set it on a table. He didn't ask her why it was broken. All things weighed, it didn't seem important.

The Field Notes of Botanist Dr. Brisbane Cole

July 12, 1823

The *Eastern Sun* docked in Manhattan's harbor early this rainy
morning. I am home. The afternoon was spent supervising the
transfer of my plant specimens from ship to shore, then on to
their final destination, my private nursery on Staten Island.
Although fewer than half of my samples survived the journey,
I was pleased to find that any had endured the damnable salt
air. During my absence, the plants will be cared for by a staff of
horticulturists in my employ. I arrived at my brownstone in the
early evening and was dismayed that my beloved Edwina was
not able to greet me at the door. I found her laid up in bed, her
illness far worse than Mrs. Muldoon's tone had suggested. Still,
our reunion was a joyous one. Edwina joined me in the parlor
after supper and reminded me that today is my birthday, a fact
that I, overwhelmed by my concern for her health, had plumb
forgotten. She presented me with a magnificent gift. I decided
right then to commission a portrait of myself holding it proudly.
Mrs. Muldoon suggested we might hang the painting on the wall
across from the fainting couch by the window, in the hope that it
will coax Edwina to sit for a spell in the sunlight while I'm away.
She looks so pale. . . .

My beloved has requested I extend my visit. While I worry
that delaying my quest will return to haunt me, I cannot say
no, for fear that denying her wish may hasten her decline. She
is certain that my trip to the Okefenokee Swamp will be a fool's
errand. She'd greatly prefer that I forgo the expedition so that
we might spend her remaining days in each other's cherished
company. I will stay on in New York for an additional three
weeks, but travel arrangements have been finalized. On the
first day of August, I set sail for Savannah, Georgia. I must go,
for the chance that I may yet save her. On the outskirts of the
swamp lives a great Seminole chieftain named Micanopy, who

claims to know of an extremely rare silver flower with the power to cure all ailments. Tension between the Creek Indians and the white settlers has been stoked by recent skirmishes in the Oke's hinterlands. Regardless of the danger, I will go to Micanopy and ask for his help in finding the silver flower. Beg for it, if I must. If he takes my life, so be it. It is worth but a pittance compared to that of my darling wife.

Just this moment, Mrs. Muldoon informed me that Edwina has awoken from a fitful sleep and is calling for me. I make haste to her side.

4

Tad loaned Piper his dad's rain slicker for the short walk to the house. "Don't want you catching a chill," he told her. "Even though it's August, the drop in temperature from the greenhouse into the rain can be harsh." He covered his own head with a plastic plant tray, but there were drainage holes in the bottom and the water pooled there and funneled through in thin streams, spattering on his ears and shirt. He barely noticed; his entire focus was on Piper.

"You don't have to tell my mom what's going on," he assured her. "She'll ask if you're okay, but she won't force you to talk if you don't want to." When it came to Tad's personal life, his mother could pry like a crowbar, but she was surprisingly respectful of the boundaries of people who weren't her son.

"Okay," Piper muttered.

Tad was right. His mother asked generic questions at dinner, but when Piper wasn't forthcoming, she didn't press. They ate quietly, the clinking of dishware and the patter of rain on the domed skylight over the table substituted for conversation. After dinner, Piper excused herself and went to the bathroom. As soon as they heard the door creak shut, Mrs. Cole's questions came in a hissing fury. "Why was Piper in the greenhouse? What's wrong with her? Was she crying because of you? Is she in some kind of trouble? Are *you* in some kind of trouble? Start talking, mister."

"Why were you spying on us, Mom? It was embarrassing."

"Because I'm your mother and spying is my job, that's why. And because I don't trust that girl. It's a small town—I've bumped into Piper and her gaggle enough times to tell that she's changed, and not for the better." She took a calming breath. "You're a good kid with a big heart. When you lose people, it affects you deeper than most. I saw it when your dad died, and I saw it when Piper pushed you away. I don't want you getting hurt again. Now spill."

Tad kept it simple. He explained that one of Piper's family members was very ill. He didn't offer details, but this information alone was enough to change his mother's attitude from suspicious to compassionate. *"That* girl" became *"Oh, that poor girl."*

When Piper returned to the table, she was ready to leave. Mrs. Cole offered her a ride home. Piper declined, so Tad's mom sent him to fetch a spare rain slicker from his bedroom closet. "I don't want you catching pneumonia," she said, and patted Piper's hand. She didn't even try to stop Piper from following Tad up the stairs. "Leave the door open, bud!" was her only condition, and that was a bona fide miracle. His mom was strict when it came to girls, but she knew Piper hadn't come over for that kind of monkey business.

Piper found a spot on the corner of Tad's bed that wasn't buried in an avalanche of laundry, and sat down. Tad rummaged through the back of his closet and retrieved a blue rain slicker he'd outgrown last year. It would fit Piper perfectly. He'd sprouted nearly a full foot since their friendship went into deep freeze. If they hugged, his chin would rest squarely on the top of her head—and, yes, he knew this because he'd worked it out in his wild imagination.

"It's weird. . . ." Tad hung the jacket over one of the bed knobs; he wasn't ready for her to leave just yet. "You haven't been in my room since we were, what, eleven?"

"Sounds about right," she said. "Where'd all the *Star Wars* posters go?"

"I trashed them. I still love the movies, but the posters weren't doing much for my street cred." Glancing around his room, seeing it through a guest's perspective for the first time, he realized that the shelves, groaning under the weight of science books, didn't exactly scream gangsta. Neither did the lithographs of exotic plants painted by Walter Hood Fitch that decorated the walls where his movie posters had hung last year.

"I like the changes. They suit you." Piper took a peek through the telescope on the tripod by the window, but the lens was capped, so she turned her attention to the metal globe on his nightstand. Tad had placed magnetic flags on the countries he'd visited personally—eighteen flags in total, not bad for a guy his age. He wasn't exactly Indiana Jones, but he wasn't sheltered either. Piper batted the globe, setting his world spinning.

"I didn't get rid of *everything*," Tad told her. "I still have this." He handed her an ugly ceramic mug with THADDEUS, his full name, written on the side in blue sparkly paint. If it wasn't for the writing, the mug could have been mistaken for something a caveman might have owned. It was little more than a sad, misshapen hunk of pottery with a handle.

"I can't believe you kept that ugly thing," said Piper.

"Why wouldn't I?" he asked. "You made it for me."

She turned the mug over in her hands. There was her signature on the bottom, glazed, fired in a kiln, preserved for all eternity. "But it sucks. If it were any more lopsided . . . Doesn't it tip over when you fill it?"

"Nope, it works fine." He didn't tell her that he'd used it every day since she gave it to him for Christmas four years before, despite the fact that he'd chipped a tooth on the too-thick rim. "It was a thoughtful gift."

"Not as thoughtful as yours. I'm really sorry I broke the flower."

"It's okay," he said. "I'm sure it was an accident."

She blushed. "I wish I could say it was. I was so angry when I got the news about Grace. I threw a blind tantrum. I broke my laptop and, worse, the orchid. That was days ago. I should have brought it to you sooner, but I was embarrassed. I didn't want you to see what I'd done to your beautiful flower."

His heart flickered. She valued his gift over an expensive laptop. She'd loved it after all. "It's okay," he told her. "I still consider it an accident. Or at least temporary insanity."

"Can it be fixed?"

Tad examined the patient by memory. "Maybe. If I use pruning shears to cut the broken stem off at the base of the plant, then it might survive. But there won't be any more flowers until the next blooming cycle. Plants are resilient, for the most part," Tad told her. "As long as their roots are healthy, they can usually make a comeback."

Piper stared down at her phone's screensaver, a photo of Grace. "It's strange, isn't it? People think flowers are so delicate, but humans are the fragile ones. Or maybe it's just me. Everything I care about seems to break."

Tad burrowed his butt into the pile of laundry, creating a seat for himself next to Piper. He sat there quietly for a while, arms folded across his knees. Then he took a deep breath and asked *the* question.

"There's nothing the doctors can do for Grace? Nothing at all?"

"No."

"I'm so sorry, Piper."

"It's not your fault," she said.

Of course it wasn't his fault. Neither was the incident in Washington, yet she'd still blamed him for that. Severed their friendship over it. He was surprised to find a heartworm of bitterness living inside him, still gnawing away, despite having missed her desperately. But this wasn't about him, and feeling sorry for himself at that moment would be shameful, so he pushed past it.

"There's no medication that can help?" he asked.

"I mean, sure, they'll stuff her with all kinds of drugs," Piper told him, "but only to keep her from suffering. They can't actually cure her."

"I can recommend some holistic herbals if you'd like," he offered. "Some of those hospital drugs can be harsh stuff with bad side effects. Herbals might balance them out a bit. I have some plants growing in the greenhouse that may help."

"Thanks," she said, "but what I really need is a plant that'll save her life. Nothing like *that* in your greenhouse, I suppose."

"A cure-all plant? No. I'm afraid not. Not inside my greenhouse, anyway."

Piper tilted her head and studied him curiously. "What do you mean?"

"What do you mean, what do I mean?"

"Is there such a plant *outside* your greenhouse?"

"Huh?" It took Tad a moment to see what she was driving at, but when he understood, he backpedaled in earnest. "Piper, I didn't mean to suggest that somewhere in the world is a magical plant that can fix everything, if that's what you're asking."

"Then what?" She leaned in close, locking on to his eyes. She'd found some kernel of hope in his words and had latched on to it like a starving bird. She was making him uncomfortable.

"There's nothing," he said. "Really."

She didn't believe him. "Tell me, Tad."

"I just think there are plants we haven't discovered . . . in the rain forest, on the mountaintops, in caves . . . that can cure specific diseases *if* we can find them before lumber companies tear them up or ranchers burn them to the ground to make grazing land for their cattle. There are examples—"

"Examples? What examples?"

"The yew tree, for one. The bark is used to make drugs that treat cancer. And the prickly burdock is great for poison ivy—can vouch for that remedy personally. Sage isn't a cure-all, but it has more than one purpose. It relieves cramps, fights colds, and is a great salve for burns. It can even bring color back to graying hair—ask my mom and she'll tell you I'm the cause and sage is the cure."

Piper didn't care about gray hair or poison ivy. She needed a plant that could eradicate the evil sickness that had settled into her sister's tiny body. "Tad, think. Please. Is there anything growing in the wild? Something Grace's doctors may have overlooked? If the yew tree can cure cancer—"

"I didn't say *cure*," he corrected her. "I said *treat*. The yew bark *treats* cancer. That's a huge difference."

"Still . . ." Piper got up off the bed and had a look at Tad's bookshelves. She scanned his stacks of old textbooks. Most of them were written by stuffy dead guys like Charles Darwin, the father of evolution, and David Douglas, a Scottish botanist. All the books were thick and heavy. In Piper's opinion, they'd make better nutcrackers than reading material. She ran her finger across a row of books. "Maybe there's something in one of these old bricks that might help."

Tad thought for a moment, then went to his cluttered desk. "None of those. But maybe this one."

He moved some papers around and found a small square book with a plain brown cover. A blue tongue of silk ribbon lolled out from the pages. He handed it to Piper. "This was written two hundred years ago by my great-great-great . . . by an ancestor of mine."

Piper read the title aloud: *"The Field Notes of Botanist Dr. Brisbane Cole."* She flipped the book over. "No author photo?"

"It's a personal journal. Besides, Dr. Cole went missing a year before chemical photography was invented." Tad hoped that bit of obscure knowledge would impress her.

Piper opened the journal to the title page and scanned the entry dates. "Eighteen twenty-three? That's like . . . ancient."

"Dr. Cole was a big-time plant hunter back in the early nineteenth century. He spent most of his time overseas looking for exotic species, but before he died he returned to the United States to search for a rare plant. One said to produce a single silver flower every year. The Creek Indians claimed it could cure anything. It grew in only one place, the Okefenokee Swamp."

"That's an hour's drive!"

"Yes."

"It's okay if you want to spoil the ending of the book, Tad. Did Dr. Cole ever find the silver flower?"

"Nobody knows," said Tad. "My ancestor went into the Okefenokee and never came out. Some people think he was killed by his swamp guides, two Seminole Indians. This all took place a year before the Seminole Wars broke out. Whites were moving into the swamp, cutting down trees and tearing up the land. Apparently, one of his guides disappeared with him. The other, a thirteen-year-old Seminole boy, fled. He was caught and interrogated by men from one of the timber companies. The kid claimed Dr. Cole had been dragged away by demons living in the swamp. Nobody believed him, of course. They made plans to hang him for my ancestor's murder, but they never got the chance. He escaped and disappeared. If anyone found the flower, we'll never know. This journal covers their expedition up until the point where Dr. Cole went missing. Some lumberjacks searching for clues found it at his abandoned campsite and delivered it to the authorities. They searched for him, of course, but his body was never found."

"Do you think the flower might be there still, waiting to be discovered?" Piper asked. "Do you think *we* could find it?"

Tad considered the possibility. "The Okefenokee is the biggest blackwater swamp in the country. Thousands of acres, and much of it still unexplored. Maybe the silver flower is more than a myth, but the odds of finding it are a billion to one. Dr. Cole was a legendary plant hunter, yet this was the quest that most likely killed him."

"But *we* have a plan!" she said.

"A plan?" Tad couldn't see it. "We do?"

"Yes!" She patted the book. "This journal will be our guide! We'll start at Dr. Cole's last location and see if we can pick up his trail from there."

"That's some plan, Piper. We'll just head over to the Okefenokee and try to find a trail that ran cold two hundred years ago?" He didn't mean to sound dismissive, but he couldn't help it. It was a crazy scheme.

"Look here. Dr. Cole drew a map in the book. See?"

"I've seen it a thousand times. So?"

"So the last place he visited before he disappeared was this island, here." She showed him. "Maybe he left clues behind that will tell us where he went next."

Tad humored her. "Let's say we do find a marker, and it points to another, and another. What if it takes us down the exact same path my ancestor went? One that ends in danger, or worse?"

"I think we can rule out demons, right? And I doubt there are any vengeful Native Americans hiding in the swamp, waiting to do us in."

"I suppose not," Tad said. "Okay, but we don't have a boat. That's a big problem."

"There are plenty of swamp tours there. I have money saved up for my next pageant dress. Entry fees too. We can use every cent of it to hire a boat and a personal guide. We don't have to tell him why we're there. We'll just . . . nudge him in the right direction. If we're paying, what will he care?"

Tad didn't know what to say. Piper's plan was insane, of course.

There was virtually no chance they'd find such a flower in a swamp covering 650 square miles. It was like looking for a needle in a . . . well, a needle in a freakin' big swamp.

"I don't know, Piper. . . ."

She placed her hand on his shoulder and leaned in so close that he could feel her breath on his lips. She locked on to him with her soft golden eyes. He could see himself, helpless, in their reflection. "Maybe this is the way it was supposed to happen," she said. "Maybe you were meant to find the flower your ancestor never could. You inherited his love of plants. What if you also inherited his quest?"

Tad knew Piper would say just about anything to persuade him to go. But there was no doubt that finding the flower was the best possible way to honor a man he'd clearly inherited so much from. It would put the Cole name in the botany books like no other discovery would.

"Please, Tad. I know this is a long shot, but at least we'll be doing *something*. I can't just sit on my hands and watch Grace fade away."

Tad caved, as if there was any doubt in his mind that he would. But he added a stipulation. "If I'm going to allow you to kidnap me, I have one condition."

"Name it!"

"There has to be a time limit to this quest. One day. Sunup to sundown. That's it. If we don't find the flower by dark, then you have to promise you won't pursue this any further. We go home and that's the end of it."

"Agreed! We have a deal!" She grabbed his hand and pumped it up and down. "I promise you'll be the best-treated hostage in history."

"I'm more worried about your comfort than mine. It won't be easy," he warned. "The Okefenokee Swamp is no place for a pageant princess."

"I swear I won't complain about bugs or the smell or anything. You know I'm an outdoorsy girl at heart."

Tad turned somber. "That was a long time ago. You've changed since then." There. He'd said it. And he wasn't just talking about her transformation from tomgirl to priss. He was referring to the fact that she'd turned her back on him in the process.

"I know, and I'm truly sorry," she said. "You've always been a good friend. I—"

"We should wait until next weekend," Tad said. "That'll give us time to prepare and study the journal. We'll need to get creative— come up with cover stories for our parents. We probably won't get home until late."

"I hate lying to my mom and dad. But if we find the flower, it'll all be worth it."

"We'll work out the details this week, then we'll leave Saturday morning, weather permitting." An entire week spent huddled over Cole's journal with Piper. Despite his conflicted feelings toward her, Tad couldn't be happier. "It'll be an adventure," he said.

"You bet, buddy!" She soft-punched his shoulder then reached for the rain slicker. "Just like old times."

"Ouch." Tad feigned a sniffle and rubbed his shoulder. But the pain was real. It wasn't the punch that had hurt him; he was made of tougher grit than that. It was the word *buddy* that had stabbed him through the heart.

"Sure, pal," he replied dully. "Just like old times."

August 1, 1823

Before my trip to Asia, I had the opportunity to visit my friend
William Bartram, the renowned naturalist, at his family's lavish
garden in Kingsessing, near Philadelphia. Always spry and of
good humor, he regaled me with stories of his travels through the
southeastern portion of our fledgling nation. Ever his own man,
William once turned down an invitation from Thomas Jefferson
to explore the Red River in the Louisiana Territory.

During his solo exploration of the south, William discovered
many unique plant species, including the bizarre Venus flytrap
(found growing nowhere else in the world except for the coastal
Carolinas) and a tree that he named the Franklin tree, after
another of his esteemed cohorts, the statesman Benjamin
Franklin. In Georgia, William came upon a Seminole Indian
who harbored deep hatred for white men and had intent to kill
any and all that crossed his path. William charmed the bitter
fellow with his good nature, and the Indian became his traveling
companion for a spell. During one of their daily discourses, the
man told William of a plant in the Okefenokee that bears but a
single silver flower, the source of miraculous healings. He even
went so far as to claim it could restore broken bones to their
original state of congruity, a boast I find dubious, at best.

I asked William if he thought his companion was playing him
for a fool, but he did not. On the contrary, William was so taken
in by the story that he journeyed to the Okefenokee in the spring
of 1774 to search for the flower, only to abandon his quest upon
realizing how ill-equipped he was to explore such a vast and
inhospitable terrain. I, however, shall not be deterred so easily.

Tonight is my last night with my darling Edwina. I set sail
for the port city of Savannah, Georgia, in the morning. From
there I will travel by train to Old Nine, a military post just north
of the swamp. A soldier stationed there has offered to arrange

a meeting with the Seminole chief Micanopy. I shall attempt to enlist his help in my search for the silver flower.

The portrait is finished. The artist has outdone himself, capturing not only my external likeness but also the anticipation I feel inside. For tomorrow, finally, I mobilize my effort to save my beloved's life. No longer must I sit idly by and watch her wither away. Her condition has worsened considerably since my arrival. For her sake, and for the sake of our child, I dare not tarry a day longer. I will say my good-byes tonight and then depart for the dock at first light. I relish the challenge of exploring this new and perilous place.

5

"I'm all packed to go. You ready to do this?"

It was still very early; the rays of the ascending sun were slicing sideways like laser beams through the blinds of Piper's open window. She was sitting on her bed, her backpack resting on the floor, cradled between her feet, being turkey-stuffed with supplies such as sunblock, antibacterial soap, and various odor-killing sprays Piper hoped would keep the scent of swamp from being absorbed into her clothes. Her cell phone was pressed between her shoulder and her ear.

"Just about," Tad answered on the other end of the line. "My mom left for work. Lucky for me she picked up a weekend shift at the last minute. I didn't have to lie to her after all. I'm still going over my checklist to make sure I'm not forgetting anything." His supplies were more practical. "I've got a disposable camera, binoculars, some snacks, a first-aid kit, and ziplock bags for everything I want to keep dry. Plus bug repellent . . . lots of bug repellent. The yellow flies will be out in droves."

"Don't forget Dr. Cole's journal," Piper reminded him.

"Of course not. That was the first thing I packed."

Tad and Piper had spent the entire week combing through every page of the plant hunter's journal. They'd filled the empty margins with notes that might be useful during their search for the silver flower. While much of Cole's writing was a bit stuffy—especially the minute details about every boring plant he came across in the Okefenokee—he'd been certain that the legendary cure-all flower was real, and that surety was infectious. Cole even had Tad semi-convinced that the flower existed, but he knew the odds of finding it were slim to none. The journal had a much greater impact on Piper. It gave her real hope for the first time since Grace was diagnosed. Today was the day. She was in an upbeat mood, raring to go.

"My dad went to Home Depot to pick up some fertilizer for the yard. Mom has to take Grace in for another treatment later this morning. She's busy running around getting ready. I'll meet you at the gas station on East Cherry Street, like we agreed. You sure the ride you arranged for us will be there?"

"Yep, he's reliable," Tad assured her. "All I had to say was *Okefenokee* and he was in."

"Weird, but whatever." Spending a sunny Saturday running around a giant swamp wasn't her idea of fun. Maybe in the past it would have been, but not anymore. She'd learned a lesson in Washington: nature was dangerous. She had to keep reminding herself she was doing this for Grace.

Piper picked up her backpack and slung it over her shoulder. "I'm heading out soon."

"You're sure nobody knows about this trip, right?" Tad asked, sounding worried. "You didn't tell any of the Snoot—uh . . . any of your girlfriends?"

"Of course I didn't. They can't keep a secret to save their lives."

Tad didn't doubt that. "If anyone found out what we're about to do—"

"Stop worrying. Nobody knows, I swear."

"Good enough," Tad said. "See you soon."

As Piper ended the call, she caught a glimpse of movement out of the corner of her eye. A flash of red in the tree branches just outside her window. The flutter of a launching bird, maybe. Whatever it was, it was gone.

In the kitchen, Piper made herself a bologna sandwich. Jane paused from her battle to get Grace to eat, and eyed her elder daughter suspiciously. "You're fixing your own lunch? But you *never* fix your own lunch." Jane leaned in close to Piper, one eye squinted in parental scrutiny. "Who are you, and what have you done with my daughter?"

In a thick accent, Piper said, "I am really Russian spy named Viper, sent to infiltrate and observe family, learn to bore enemies to death. Is ultimate torture."

"I see." Jane chuckled weakly. She hadn't produced a genuine laugh in weeks. "I won't blow your cover. I just wish things were a little *more* boring around here lately. We could use more boring."

"True," Piper agreed. She scooped a glob of mustard out of the jar and slathered it on her sandwich. "By the way, I'll be home late. I'm going to Olivia's. I'll grab dinner at her house."

There. She'd told the lie. Now she'd have to live with it. She just hoped Grace would live *because* of it.

"Okay, but don't stay out too late," her mother warned. "Don't make me come looking for you."

If that's her plan, thought Piper, she'll need a boat. "Yes, ma'am."

She finished making the sandwich, then made one more. Lunch and dinner. She sealed them in individual ziplock pouches, and placed them in a plastic grocery bag.

Creeper came downstairs and joined them in the kitchen. Piper was in such an upbeat mood that not even his sour face could spoil it. "What's up, Creepo?"

"'Morning," he grumbled. Normally, he would have shot back with a snarky nickname of his own (his preferred zinger of choice was

Pooper), but today he was unusually quiet. He fixed himself a bowl of cereal and proceeded to eat it over the sink. Creeper watched as Piper finished packing her lunch sack. She tossed a couple of granola bars and an apple. The apple wasn't her first choice of fruit, but she suspected pears and bananas might bruise more quickly in muggy swamp air.

"That's a lot of food," he said.

"Yeah, I'm a growing girl," Piper replied.

"Especially your nose, Pinocchio," he said under his breath.

Piper didn't get his meaning, nor did she care enough to ask. Creeper was being a creepo, as usual, just in a peculiarly creepy way.

While Jane's back was turned, Piper sneaked four bottles of water out of the fridge and dropped them into her backpack. With her supplies gathered, she did something she hadn't done in a long time. She bent over the sleeping baby and kissed her on her wispy-haired forehead. "When I come back," she whispered in Grace's ear, "I'll have a special gift for you."

She hoped.

Piper arrived at the Citgo gas station on Temple Street and chained her Schwinn to the freezer on the sidewalk, the one with the pillow-size bags of ice inside. The machine looked like it weighed a thousand pounds—two thousand when full, which it was. If anyone wanted her bike, they'd have to take bolt cutters to the chain. It would be safe until she returned. She sat on the curb and waited for Tad and their mystery driver to show.

The gas pumps were occupied by crews of men driving pickup trucks loaded with tools of all kinds. These men were construction workers and landscapers, hardworking people who spent their days outside and liked to get cracking early to beat the heat. The "worm getters," as her dad called them. None of them seemed to notice her. So when someone called out to her, she was startled.

"What's up, sis?" Creeper was sporting a rucksack and an impossibly obnoxious grin. "Going somewhere without me?" He skidded to a stop on his bike in front of Piper, set one foot on the ground for balance, and held the other up mere inches from her face. He was wearing his oldest, rattiest, *smelliest* sneakers. "Got my swamp shoes on."

Piper was livid. "Who told you? How do you know where I'm going?"

It made no sense. She'd been *so* careful. The only way Creeper could have found out was if Tad had—

"A little birdie told me," Creeper snickered. "A little birdie in a tree."

It hit Piper. That flash of red in the tree outside her window wasn't a bird. It was her stupid tree-climbing, pain-in-the-butt, eavesdropping eleven-year-old jerk-face brother. She jumped to her feet and roared, "You were spying on me?" She grabbed the handlebar of Creeper's bicycle and shook it so hard that he nearly fell off the seat.

"I wasn't spying!" He slammed his feet down to steady the bike. "I was practicing!"

"Practicing for what? A career as a Peeping Tom?"

"I was just climbing! It's the best climbing tree on our property. I can't help that it goes past your window. Trust me: you're not interesting enough to spy on. All you care about is tiaras and stupid dresses covered in fish scales."

"They're called sequins! But that's not the point! You invaded my privacy!" Piper realized that some of the men at the pumps were staring at them, and she simmered down to a low boil.

Creeper broke free of his sister's grip. "I wasn't trying to invade your stupid privacy, but I'm glad I did, Piper. I'm going with you to the Okeenokee, and you can't stop me."

"It's called the Okefenokee, and no you are not! Listen, Creepo, this isn't some school field trip. It could be dangerous. Besides, Mom is probably already wondering where you are."

"I have a Little League game today, remember? It's doubleheader day. She's expects me to be gone till dark."

"Look, I get it. You want to climb around in the swamp, but I'm not going there for fun and games. You're too young to understand. There's no way you're—"

"She's my sister too!" Creeper thundered. He looked like he was about to cry.

Piper's attitude softened instantly. She felt like a big jerk.

A horn honked. A beat-up red Mazda came rattling into the gas station parking lot and pulled into the space in front of them. All the windows were rolled down, which meant only one thing in Georgia in August: the car's air conditioner was busted. It was going to be an uncomfortable trip.

"Your chariot has arrived, milady," said the driver, a huge African-American kid with a cute smile. Piper recognized him from chemistry class. His baby face made him look fifteen, but she knew he was at least sixteen; you had to be sixteen to drive without an adult in the car in Georgia. "My name is Grafton," said the driver. "In case you're too stunned by the awesomeness of my car to remember, I sit behind you in Chemistry."

"Hey." Piper waved. "Thanks for the lift."

Tad jumped out the passenger side and slammed the car door. He looked upset. "What's your little brother doing here?"

Piper shook her head. "He's coming with us."

Creeper's eyes lit up with joy. "For real?"

"Yes," she answered.

"This trip is already risky enough," Tad reminded her. "Now we're endangering little kids too? Our parents are going to kill us."

"I know," she said. "I'll take full responsibility for him."

"Hey, do you mind wrapping this up?" Grafton was resting his arm on the door's window track—he lifted his wrist and glanced at his watch. "We need to get on the road, gang. I've got a Class D license, which means I can't drive after midnight. The more time we spend sitting in this parking lot, the less you'll have to play around in the swamp."

"Fine!" Tad huffed. "He can come."

Creeper threw his arms up like a referee calling a touchdown. "Yes!"

Piper took Creeper's bike and chained it to her own while Tad put their backpacks in the trunk. They all piled into Grafton's car, Piper in the front, the two boys in the back. It was Grafton's idea to separate the siblings.

When they were all buckled up, Grafton craned in his seat to face the group. "I'm happy to take you guys to the Oke," he told them. "As a birder, I've been dying to go there ever since people started reporting new evidence for the ivory-billed woodpecker. The bird was supposed to be extinct. It's kinda like the Bigfoot of the bird world, if you know what I mean. Lots of hearsay, but little proof."

"We'll keep our eyes peeled," Tad said.

"So look," said Grafton, "I hate getting tough, but there're two things I need to make clear. If you want a ride home, you'd better get your butts back to the car no later than ten thirty P.M. That'll give me enough time to get you back here and then get myself home before midnight. I just got my license, and I'm not about to lose it. Not for anyone. Miss our departure time and you'll find yourselves stranded."

"No problem," Tad assured him. "What's the other thing?"

"Yeah . . . the second thing. You're all related to me."

"Huh?" the group asked in chorus.

"You're all related to me," Grafton repeated. He looked as serious as a heart attack. "If we get pulled over by a cop, that's the story I expect you to stick to. In Georgia, the law for driving with a Class D license says that during the first six months, only immediate family members can ride in the car. So, Piper, you're my sister, and you two knuckleheads in the back are my bros. Got it?"

"There's one obvious flaw to that plan, don't you think?" asked Tad.

"Right. So as of now, you're all adopted. Welcome to the Connor family."

Grafton turned the ignition key, pulled out of the parking lot, and with a clunk from the motor and a loud bang from the muffler, they were on their way.

The fifty-mile drive from Jesup to Waycross, where the north entrance to the Okefenokee Swamp is located, was almost a straight shot on US Highway 84 west. They stopped just once, at a Subway in Blackshear; both Canfields needed to use the restroom.

While they waited, the two older boys sat on the scratched-up hood of Grafton's car, ate Subway cookies (Grafton bought a dozen), and talked.

"I told you not to pursue that girl," Grafton said. "Didn't I? Now look, she's dragging you down to a swamp. What's the next stop on your honeymoon tour? The sewers of New York? How romantic."

"Hilarious," Tad said, polishing off an oatmeal-raisin cookie. "You don't know what you're talking about. I'm excited about this trip."

"Yeah, alligators and snakes are way better than dinner and a movie. I hope this pans out for you, dude. My bet is you'll be getting a glittery pink restraining order by the end of the week. Maybe by the end of this trip."

Before Tad could reply, Piper and Creeper appeared. Grafton handed them each a white paper sleeve of cookies.

"Mmm, dessert for breakfast! I'm starving."

"Lucky for you, I packed two sandwiches," Piper said. "We'll eat lunch once we get on the water."

"Speaking of water," Grafton said, "you *do* have a boat waiting for us there, right? I mean, unless you've got an inflatable pool raft in your backpack."

"We're covered," said Tad. "I found a website and hired a tour guide over the phone. From a company called Oke Dokey Boat Tours. I talked to a man named Perch Gentner."

"Perch?" Grafton raised an eyebrow. "Like the fish?"

"I guess so. I didn't ask."

"What's he like?"

"I dunno. He had a deep voice. A bit of a Southern accent. He's probably in his thirties; really friendly type. He said he has a boat that can fit eight people. The *Mud Cat*, I think he called it."

"*Mud Cat*. Lovely," Piper snorted. "Sounds like a first-class operation."

"The man seemed pretty knowledgeable," Tad said. "I think we're in good hands."

"We'll find out soon enough, right, little man?" Grafton fist-bumped Creeper.

They finished their cookies to the last crumb, then got back on the road.

The Okefenokee Swamp Park's entrance was a one-story gray building with a cedar shake roof shaped like an oversize Pilgrim's hat. Carved on the welcome sign out front was a menacing alligator stalking prey among the reeds and lily pads. Grafton parked the car, and they gathered up their supplies.

Grafton pointed to the fat, blue pouch secured around Tad's waist. "Um, did you just put on a fanny pack?"

"This? No, it's not a fanny pack!" Tad said. "It's a utility belt. Like Batman wears."

Grafton snorted. "Dude, it's a fanny pack. You look ridiculous."

"Whatever. I like being able to reach down and grab whatever I need. It's efficient."

"It's a babe repellent."

"We're heading into a swamp. Who cares how I look? It'll be fine."

"If you say so." Grafton chuckled. "Mr. Fanny Pack."

They went inside.

The welcome center was part gift shop, part information center, part museum. The centerpiece of the room was a glass display case with the skeleton of an enormous alligator skeleton inside.

"Cool!" Creeper ran over to check it out.

"That's Oscar," a roaming greeter told him. "He was our star attraction while he was alive. Weighed a thousand pounds and was the park's dominant alligator for the last sixty years. We think he was roughly a hundred years old when he died."

Creeper noticed damage to the giant reptile's head. "What happened to him?"

"Before the park's alligators were granted the protection of the state, they were hunted regularly for their meat and hides. You can see here"—the greeter pointed out holes in the skull—"Oscar was shot three times and even survived a shotgun blast to the face."

Creeper was impressed. "Wow, he must have been one tough customer."

"The toughest in the swamp. He was the dominant predator for most of his life, and no creature has stepped up to replace him since he died peacefully of natural causes. We all miss him. But in a way he's still with us."

"What do you mean?" Creeper asked. "Like his ghost?"

"Ha! No, as far as I know, there aren't any ghosts in the Oke, despite what the swamp guides may tell you. Oscar had a lot of girlfriends and spawned hundreds of children. And many of those gators had children too. So, you see, his legacy is all around us."

While the greeter gave Creeper a personal tour of the other exhibits, Tad, Piper, and Grafton made a beeline for the information desk.

"Welcome to the park," said the cheerful desk worker. She handed them a map of the refuge. "Take one—they're free."

"We're looking for Perch Gentner," Tad told her. "Do you know where we can find him?"

"That scallywag? Sure!" The woman pointed toward double glass doors at the back of the center. "Head outside and you'll find the boat dock. If the *Mud Cat* and its crew are around, that's where they'll be."

"Any new ivory-billed woodpecker sightings?" Grafton asked.

"Ah, a fellow birder! Glad to have you here." The woman extended her hand and Grafton shook it. "A couple from Alabama claimed they heard the ivorybill's distinct double-knock sound a month ago, but it might have been a hunter shooting at ducks in the distance. They couldn't be sure. The last verified sighting of the bird was in 1944, a long time ago." She pointed to a painting of the bird hanging high on a wall. "Take a good look. Memorize its markings. There's a fifty-thousand-dollar reward for concrete proof that the ivory-billed woodpecker is still alive."

The bird was very pretty, with its red tufted head and black-and-white feathers. It would be a shame, thought Piper, if it was really gone from the Earth forever.

The desk worker added, "The refuge covers four hundred thousand acres. That's a lot of room for the woodpecker to hide in."

Piper's eyes met Tad's. They were thinking the same thing. A lot of room for a flower to hide in too.

"Listen," the woman said, "if you folks are here for the birds, I'm leading an ornithology tour into the swamp in ten minutes. You can sign up if you want. I'll take you to some of the most likely woodpecker nesting spots. We'll follow the clues and see what we find. Maybe we'll get lucky."

Grafton gave the others a sheepish look. "Would you guys mind if I . . . ?"

"Nah, it's okay," Tad said. "You go on your bird tour. We can meet up at the car."

The woman handed Grafton some paperwork, and he got busy

filling it out. Tad, Piper, and Creeper went out the back doors to look for Perch Gentner.

The welcome center was set along a canal connected to the swamp. They followed a walk path to a long covered dock. There they found a dozen or more boats moored in the water, parallel against the platform, waiting for tourists to board.

"Which one is ours?" Creeper asked.

"Not sure." Tad scanned the boats for a clue. He pointed out a johnboat toward the back of the flotilla. The name *Mud Cat* was stenciled in blue letters on the side. "There. That black one."

Two people were prepping the boat. A large man with a gray crew cut and dressed in overalls was leaning over the transom, fussing with the outboard motor. His back was turned to them. Flitting around the man was a kid who looked no more than a year or two older than Tad and Piper. Fifteen or sixteen at most. He was busy moving supplies from the dock to the boat. The kid saw them approaching and paused to give them a whole-arm wave.

He was wearing a pair of old jeans and a company T-shirt that read OKE DOKEY BOAT TOURS. It had a cartoon of a turtle in the water with tourists riding on its back. The smiling stranger was tanned, with a messy shag of sun-bleached hair kept in check by a pair of mirrored sunglasses on top of his head. He had an athletic build, the kind earned through hard physical work. Handsome in a not-so-subtle way.

"Wow, he's cute," said Piper, too preoccupied to notice the hurt look on Tad's face.

"You think so? I don't see it."

"Why would you?" Piper asked.

Tad turned red and fell quiet.

When they reached the boat, the kid held his hand across the water in greeting. Tad walked right past him and on down the dock to the back end of the boat. He tapped the burly boat man on the shoulder. "Mr. Gentner, sir? I'm Tad. We spoke on the phone."

The broad-shouldered person with the crew cut turned to face them. Tad's jaw dropped.

He wasn't a *he* at all. *She* was a woman in her sixties, with a flattened nose like a boxer's and a faded tattoo of a battleship on the right side of her neck. Her upper lip rose in a slight snarl. If a mama polar bear was ever reincarnated as a woman, here she was.

"Do I look like a sir to you?" she asked in a thick Southern drawl. "Call me that again and I'll cancel your birth certificate."

The woman shook her head and returned to her work.

"Don't mind Macey," said the handsome kid, leaping easily from the boat onto the dock. His Georgian accent was less pronounced than that of his crewmate. "She's former navy. Toughest woman I know. Not overly sociable, but she's the best boat mechanic you'll ever meet. Out on the water that's way more useful than politeness." He leaned in and whispered, "Don't call her 'sir,' though. For some inexplicable reason, she *hates* that."

He winked at Piper and she smiled. Tad didn't find the kid funny.

"You must be Mr. Cole," Perch said, offering his hand again. This time Tad gave it a halfhearted shake.

"Call me Tad. I didn't mean to offend anyone. I just didn't realize there'd be *three* guides taking us out today." He looked up and down the dock, searching for the man he'd spoken to on the phone.

"There won't be, friend," the kid said, his voice dropping to a deep baritone. "This is my phone voice. You'd be surprised how many people hang up when I use my real one. It's funny how folks equate youth with inexperience and will dismiss you for it. My bloodline reaches far back in Oke history, to when Waycross was called Old Nine. I know this swamp better than most. Believe me when I say you're in good hands."

"I don't understand," said Tad.

Piper did. "You're—"

"Perch Gentner!" he introduced himself. "Captain of the *Mud Cat* and professional rascal, at your service!" He grabbed Piper's wrist and lifted the back of her hand to his puckered lips. Despite the sweltering summer heat, goose bumps appeared on her arm.

Tad noticed. "You're a friendly one," he seethed. He was pretty sure their captain had kissed plenty of hands on the job. If he tried it again with Piper, Perch would be kissing Tad's fist instead.

"That's a sweet fanny pack," said their young captain.

Tad corrected him. "Utility belt."

Still holding Piper's hand, Perch said, "Are you three ready to embark on the greatest adventure of your lives?"

"We sure are!" Piper was keyed up and ready to go. "We're all yours!"

"All righty, then!" Perch took Piper's backpack. "All aboard!"

August 8, 1823

My voyage along the continental coast to Savannah was
uneventful; as was my passage by train to Old Nine. (The rather
unimaginatively named military outpost is the ninth westward
stop of the railroad beginning in Savannah.) There currently
exists a cease-fire between the United States government and
the Creek Indians, but the soldiers stationed at Old Nine say it's
unlikely to last. They recount skirmishes with the Creeks and
paint a picture of a perfidious, savage people. Raids on white
settlements occur on a weekly basis, and of course this behavior
must be quelled at all costs. It was only five years ago that
General Andrew Jackson descended upon the Okefenokee Swamp
with five thousand men and drove the Seminoles out. They have
since returned, and they have obviously *not* forgotten. Still,
it is my good fortune to have arrived at a moment of peace,
fragile though it may be. A soldier named James Cash, a rather
unsociable man made memorable only for his grim aura and
silver ponytail, accompanied me to Chief Micanopy's village on
the periphery of the swamp.

I was received there in an unexpectedly cordial manner,
which I appreciated all the more when compared to the rather
frosty companionship provided by my escort. I was impressed
immediately with Micanopy; my observation of the man reveals
a gracious host and a benevolent leader. He attends to his people
with thoughtful wisdom, ensuring their village is a safe haven
not just for his people, but for escaped slaves, as well. In contrast
to the horror stories I'd heard from the soldiers at Old Nine, I
found the Seminoles and their culture to be warm and welcoming.
Their dwellings, called chickees, are open hut-like structures
supported by posts, with palmetto thatched roofs and raised
floors. During the cold months they hang canvas walls, but come

spring, the canvases are dried and hung in the rafters. For most
of the year, the chickees are as open as the people who live in
them. The Seminoles are an industrious people. During the day,
the men hunt and gather while the women tend to the gardens
and the children. Micanopy's village consists of nine chickees
set in a circle, protecting a center courtyard where the children
learn and play in safe sight.

Micanopy's turban is adorned with lovely white crane
feathers and is really quite fetching. Had I brought my beaver
hat, I would have engaged him in trade for it. Bearing the loyalty
of a fallen acorn to its tree, Mr. Cash took his leave directly and
without fanfare. I joined Micanopy and the entire tribe in the
eating house for supper. The women set a lavish feast consisting
of all manner of foods, including a delicious stew the likes of
which I'd never tasted before. After I had wolfed down two
heaping bowlfuls, Micanopy revealed that the mystery ingredient
was alligator meat! It was a well-played joke, and I instantly felt
right at home. After supper I shared a smoke with Micanopy,
and I asked him about the silver flower. He was, to my surprise,
quite forthcoming. The chief confirmed the flower's existence
and touted its healing prowess. He claimed the village medicine
man used it to snatch back a person from the brink of death on
more than one occasion. Apparently, Mr. Cash was among those
fortunates. I asked the chief if he would be kind enough to point
me in the right direction and perhaps provide transportation for
my journey. His generosity is without limit. Tomorrow at dawn,
accompanied by two of Micanopy's men and traveling in canoes
equipped with a week's worth of provisions, I will venture into
the swamp. My new friend made only one request: that I not hurt
the plant itself in any way, so that it may continue to heal his
people in the future. I may pluck the flower, but that is all. This
seemed a most reasonable request. I gave Micanopy my word.

The crickets sing me to sleep.

6

The *Mud Cat* wasn't the most impressive vessel, but at sixteen feet it was large enough to be comfortable and its sturdy aluminum hull made Piper feel perfectly safe. "All the boats out here are flat-bottomed," Perch told them. "They're designed for stability on placid waters. The greatest danger we swampers face in the Oke isn't the wildlife. It's the occasional underwater eruption of swamp gas whooshing to the surface. Flatter hulls keep the bubbles from flipping us over. Oh, I should mention, if any of you folks would feel safer, there are life jackets in the benches."

"Do you have one with sequins for my sister?" Creeper joked.

"Shut it, Creepo," Piper ordered.

There were four cross benches dissecting the hull into five sections: bow, bow-middle, stern-middle, back, and the motor well. The motor well was where Macey set her tree-trunk legs while she steered the boat, swiveling the outboard motor by its tiller handle. In boating terms, Macey was called the sternman, which is sort of what she looked like too: a stern man. Perch sat on the bow, facing his guests and making charming patter as they headed out into the vast expanse of the Okefenokee Swamp. It was hard to ignore him, with his tussled hair, square jaw, and unreasonably green eyes.

"First-timers, right?" Perch asked, but he already knew the answer. "I can always tell by a passenger's reaction to the scenery. The Oke is never what people expect when they first see it. They think *swamp*, and split pea soup comes to mind. Then folks get here and the water is so reflective, like a mirror. It catches them by surprise. Don't get me wrong—the Oke has stagnant areas too; but for the most part, it's open water or flooded forest or prairie."

"Like *Little House on the Prairie*?" asked Creeper.

"Sort of, but not quite." Perch chuckled. "It'll be easier for me to just show you when we get there."

Piper, who was sitting on one of the middle benches next to Tad, nudged him in the ribs, spurring him to speak up. They were there for a reason. Minnie's Island was the last location Dr. Cole had visited before he disappeared. The last marker would be there, as would any evidence to explain what had happened to him next.

Tad said, "Actually, we were hoping we could start with a visit to Minnie's Island."

"Minnie's Island?" Perch sat up straight, as though a balloon had popped in his face. "Nobody ever asks to go there."

"We did a little research before coming," said Piper. "In fact, we have a few specific sights we'd like to check out today, if that'd be all right."

Macey looked at Perch and rolled her eyes as if to say, *Here we go—bossy tourists.* The crusty woman hadn't said another word since she'd put Tad in his place, nor did she have to. Macey spoke volumes with her lined, expressive face. It was clear she wasn't thrilled to be toting three kids around the swamp all day.

Perch studied Tad and Piper suspiciously. "You folks didn't come to the Oke to start trouble, did you? You're not alligator poachers?"

"Wha—? I . . . no!" Tad slipped all over the question. "Of course we're not—"

"Relax, I'm just joshing you." Perch laughed, his eyes atwinkle.

"You don't look like hunters to me. 'Cept for maybe that little one over there. I can tell he's bad news. Little fella's got a real tough-guy look about him. Right off the bat, I had him pegged for an alligator hunter, or maybe the leader of a motorcycle gang."

This tickled Creeper. "I'm not an alligator hunter! Besides, if they're all as tough as Oscar, I couldn't kill one if I wanted to."

"You're all right with me, then." Perch gave a sharp nod of approval. "Here in the Okefenokee, we're all about protecting the wildlife. This swamp is just a young one. So we have to look out for it."

"What do you mean, 'a young one'?" Piper asked.

Perch explained. "The Oke started life as a large lagoon before sandbars built up and cut it off from the Atlantic, turning it into an inland sea. Over time it curdled, and now it's a swamp, some thirty-eight miles by twenty-five miles in size. In the grand geological scheme of things, it's just a baby, seven thousand years young. But it's *our* baby, so we appreciate people who treat it right."

Our baby. The words hit Piper like a tack hammer. She needed to stay focused on Grace. Perch was a real charmer, and easy on the eyes, but she would have to lead him around by the collar if they were going to have any chance of finding the silver flower by the end of the day.

"I'd like to go to Minnie's Island straightaway," she insisted.

Perch shrugged one shoulder. "Sure, why not. You're paid in full. I'll take you in that direction. Can I ask what it is you're after?"

"What we're after?" Piper frowned. Had she been so obvious? Did Perch sense they had a hidden agenda?

He clarified. "I mean, are you folks birders? Adventure seekers? History buffs? Lots of great history in the Oke. You know, there have been swampers here for thousands of years . . . the Swift Creek, the Weeden Island tribes. The Seminoles were the last to inhabit the swamp before the whites drove them all out. Of course, then you've got the swampers like me, just regular folk making a living on the water."

"That's all very interesting," said Tad. "But we're here for the flowers."

Macey grumbled in the back. "No surprise there."

Perch, to his credit, didn't seem to think this was strange at all. He stroked his chin. "Flowers, eh? You came to the right guide, my friend. We've got over six hundred species of plants in the Oke, and I know all the pretty ones. And the rare ones too."

Piper perked up. "We'd like to see the *rarest*."

"You won't find them on Minnie's Island, that's for sure," said Perch. "You certain you want to go there first?"

"Yes, we want to go there first," Piper answered.

"You heard the lovely lady, Macey!" Perch smacked his knee. "Head us on over to pretty Minnie."

Macey leaned into the tiller and twisted it toward her body; the boat lurched forward and picked up speed. It skimmed southwest across the surface of the water, following in the two-hundred-year-old wake of Dr. Cole's canoe.

Perch told them it would take an hour to get to Minnie's Island by following the Red Trail. (He explained that the six public trails were named after colors, and the red would take them to Minnie.) As they wound through the waterway, which was no more than five to ten feet wide at most points, they had time to drink in the surrounding scenery. Piper was feeling as reflective as the surface of the water. While reading Cole's journal she'd learned a lot about the swamp. He'd written that the Oke was a world of duality, and she understood that now. It was simultaneously bright yet haunting, open yet confining. It was water, but it was land too. It was natural yet otherworldly. It was a cusp. A threshold. A brink. A place forever on the verge of transition. The one thing it was not was "swampy." In fact, there was a gentle southward current, a trait of meandering rivers, not bogs.

"The water is pretty fresh in most of the preserve," Perch said. "Cleaner than city water, that's for sure. Technically, the Okefenokee is one great big peat bog. There are definitely some slimy parts to it, but most of it is like what you see here. It's one of the most pristine blackwater swamps in the world."

Creeper peered over the side of the boat. "Blackwater? It looks brown to me." He was right; the water was not black at all. Instead, it had a bronze tint, the color of weak tea.

"Good eye . . . What did you say your name is?" asked Perch.

"Creeper. It's a nickname. My dad gave it to me because I can climb anything, like a creeper vine."

Perch gave him a thumbs-up. "As nicknames go, it's a good one." He addressed Creeper's point. "*Blackwater* is just a term for any darkly stained waters. The swamp here gets its color from tannin that dissolves in it when trees decay. Tannin is the same dye people used to tan leather with. It's mildly acidic, which is great, because bacteria and mosquitoes don't fare well in acidic water. Helps keep the pests away."

"Except for tourists," said Macey.

Perch chuckled. "Well, don't be shy, Mace! Tell us how you really feel!"

Macey glared at Tad and Piper. "I've never been a fan of insects. I'll be happy when summer's over and the shutterbugs go home."

"I have to apologize on behalf of my partner," said Perch, although he seemed more amused than embarrassed. "She usually waits at least an hour into a trip before insulting our passengers. This may be a new record. I think ol' Macey ate too much alligator meat as a kid, and it turned her cold-blooded. Sometimes she forgets we're in the hospitality business. While I personally get a kick out of her surly attitude, I am, at heart, a humble businessman. I love tourists, especially the ones who bring lots of cash and leave the chain saws and duck guns at home." His gaze drifted. "Speaking of waterfowl . . ."

Two large shorebirds flew across the bow. They were grayish, with white cheeks and a cap of glinting ruby-red feathers covering their foreheads. They glided low to the water, staying aloft with an occasional flap of their wings until they disappeared as chevron specks in the distance.

"Those are sandhill cranes," Perch said. "They're incredibly romantic birds. That pair we saw is bonded for life." He flashed a pearly grin at Piper.

It looked to Tad as if there were *some* tourists in particular that Perch Gentner "loved" more than others. The last thing Tad expected or wanted on this trip was competition for her attention. He hated the way their guide was staring at her like a hungry alligator.

Piper noticed it too and blushed. "Why are you looking at me that way?"

Perch leaned into the space between them to study her face. "I've seen you before, haven't I? Maybe on TV or in a magazine? Ain't you a model or an actress or something? Were you on the Disney Channel? You've got that wholesome look they like."

"No," she replied. "I've won some pageants, though. Mostly in my home county, not far from here. Maybe you saw me on the local news."

"So you're a princess!" Perch proclaimed. "I confess I haven't been to a heck of a lot of beauty contests, and I sure don't watch the news. Two much war, not enough love. But no, I don't think that's it. You just have one of those faces."

"And what kind of face would that be?" Piper bristled.

"The kind of pretty that'd give any flower in this swamp a run for its money."

Tad rolled his eyes. He hoped Piper was clever enough to see through Perch's cheesy act. He needn't have worried.

"You're making me uncomfortable," she told Perch.

"Am I? Then please accept my apology." Perch leaned back on the bench, tapped his shades down over his eyes, and smiled, unfazed.

At about ten A.M., the *Mud Cat* motored into a lake dotted with purple water flowers. The blossoms rose above the surface on stalks. Perch told Macey to cut the motor. They slowed to a drift.

"Why are we stopping?" Piper asked impatiently. She'd just peeled the wrapper off a granola bar. "We're not at Minnie's Island yet."

"This is our first destination on the Oke Dokey Flower Extravaganza Tour!" said Perch. "If you like unusual flowers, you're in for a treat. This here purple one is about as unusual as they come."

"How so?" asked Creeper.

"It's called the bladderwort," said Perch. "You came at the right time of the year. These flowers only bloom in July and August. For the rest of the year, the plant stays hidden underwater."

"They're pretty," Piper said, so as not to be rude. Inside she was indifferent. The purple flowers wouldn't help Grace. Stopping for them was a waste of precious time.

"Like several plants in the park, bladderworts are carnivorous," said Perch. "They eat meat."

"No way!" said Creeper. "Plants that eat meat? You mean if I fell overboard, they'd rip me to shreds like piranhas? That'd be so cool!"

"That's disgusting, Creepo," Piper said. "You *are* kidding, right? Plants can't eat meat."

"Some can," said Tad. "Haven't you ever seen a Venus flytrap kill a bug? It traps them inside its leaves and slowly digests them."

Piper groaned. "There goes my appetite." She started to rewrap the granola bar, but Creeper held his hand out hopefully and she gave it to him. "Fine. Eat it. It's spoiled for me, anyway."

"So these bladderworts eat meat? What's the deal?" Creeper asked. "Do their flowers have teeth or something?"

Perch gave a hearty laugh. "Now, *that* would be creepy! Here, I'll show you how they work."

He reached over the gunwale and plunged his hand into the water directly under a cluster of bladderwort flowers. He fished around for a bit, then lifted a whole specimen into the air. First he broke off the purple flower and presented it to Piper. "For the lady."

"Um . . . No thanks." She recoiled from his gift. "I prefer my flowers to be vegetarians."

"Suit yourself." Perch tossed the flower overboard. He stretched the stemmed portion out on the bench between Tad and Piper. "See, the bladderwort doesn't have roots. It just spreads across the bottom and lies there."

"I thought all plants have roots," said Piper. "That's how they get nutrients from the soil, right?"

"Not the bladderwort," said Perch. "The soil in the Oke isn't very fertile. It's especially poor in nitrogen, an important food for plants. The bladderwort had to come up with another way to get the nour-ishment it needs, so it evolved to trap insects and extract the nutrients from their little corpses, just like the Venus flytrap Tad mentioned. Only the bladderwort goes about it a little differently."

"I think I'm going to be sick." Piper gagged and pressed two fin-gers to her lips.

"Over the side, please," Perch insisted. "If you're gonna puke, you can at least feed the fish. Don't waste it."

Piper shot him a murderous look, but for once he wasn't paying any attention to her.

"Look here." Perch used his fingers to fan out the long, thin branching stem of the plant. The branch had hundreds of leaf shoots, and between the shoots were hundreds of tiny balloonlike structures, each the size of an apple seed. "These are called bladders. They're what give the plant its name." Perch tore off one of the biggest bladders and held it out to show them. "Each bladder is actually a tiny trap with a tiny trapdoor. There are trigger hairs around the door. When a little critter like a mosquito larva or a water flea brushes up against the hairs—snap!—the trapdoor opens and water rushes in and sucks the poor critter up like a vacuum cleaner into the bladder. There's no escape. Eventually it dies and turns to goo. That goo is what the plant draws its nutrients from."

Perch held the bladder up to the sun like a jeweler inspecting a diamond. "Whoa! There's a prize in this one!"

The kids huddled around him to have a look. Through the bladder's thin membrane they could see a tadpole squirming inside.

"Tadpoles are a little ambitious for a bladderwort," said Perch. "They're kinda like Thanksgiving dinner—too much of a good thing." Perch retrieved a Swiss Army knife from his pocket and carefully popped the bladder. He lowered it close to the water and squeezed it gently from one end, like a tube of toothpaste. The tadpole came out of the knife slit, but instead of making its escape, it turned and wriggled up Perch's finger. Its tiny mouth was opening and closing against the skin on his knuckle. Perch shook his hand over the water, and the tadpole fell off. It plopped into the water and swam away under the boat, no worse for wear.

"Well, that was weird!" Perch inspected his finger. "Felt almost like the dang critter was trying to bite me, which is odd because tadpoles are vegetarians! Well, that was a fine way to say thank you!"

"Maybe he's just a born hand kisser, like you." Tad snorted.

Perch laughed. He didn't seem to get that the joke was at his expense. "Maybe so."

"There's not a lot of meat on a tadpole," Creeper noted. "How come the bladderworts don't starve?"

"Don't forget," said Perch, "every plant has hundreds of bladders, so it can eat hundreds of critters at the same time. There are millions of bladderwort plants in the Oke. Scientists figure that together, the plants eat close to five hundred tons of meat every year. If I'm doin' the math right—and I'm great at math—that's the same as gobbling up fifteen thousand Creepers."

Creeper gulped.

Perch added, "After the gators, the bladderworts are the second most successful predator in the swamp. They're perfectly evolved killers."

"We should go," said Piper, feeling queasier by the second.

"Sorry if I ruined your breakfast," said Perch.

"You can make it up to me by getting us to Minnie with no more delays." She forced a fake smile, the kind she'd learned for pageants.

"I'll do my best," he promised. He returned the smile, only his was honest.

Around eleven thirty, the sun was on its stretch toward the top of the sky; it was already fiercely humid. The yellow flies began their strafing runs, but Tad's arsenal of insect repellents kept them from biting. There was no shade on the open water. Perch had a collection of soft, floppy bucket hats in the stowage compartment beneath his bench. Everyone took one except for Tad, who didn't want to owe Perch a favor. Piper's contribution to their comfort was a bottle of sunblock. They passed it around the boat until it was burping air.

Despite Perch's promise of a straight ferry to Minnie's Island, he kept stopping the *Mud Cat* to point out every plant or bug or crumbly bird nest he spied. He even brought the boat to a halt to fish litter out of the water. Fed up, Piper whispered in Tad's ear, "If you don't light a fire under this guy, we'll never get to Minnie's Island, which means we're never going to find Dr. Cole's last marker. Tell him to quit messing around."

"Fine," he hissed.

"Everything okay over there?" Perch asked.

"Not really," Tad said, trying to sound tough. "Listen, Perch, we paid you good money to get us to Minnie's Island, so if you don't mind, we'd like to take the express lane. No more stops."

Perch raised one eyebrow. "I see. I wasn't aware that this was a simple ferry job. I thought you wanted to see flowers."

"We do," said Tad. "The ones on Minnie's Island."

Perch was uncharacteristically quiet. He just sat on the bench across from Tad and Piper, glowering at them over the top of his sunglasses.

Macey, sensing the discord, throttled down the engine, and the boat slowed to a putter. "You want me to toss 'em overboard, Cap'n?" Piper couldn't tell if she was kidding.

Perch shook his head slowly. "That won't be necessary, Mace. They want to go to Minnie, then let's get 'em to Minnie. Take us to the Red Trail Spur through Floyd's Prairie," Perch instructed. "It's a shortcut."

"*Through* Floyd's Prairie?" Macey scratched her spiky head. "But that's—"

"The quickest way," he insisted.

"Aye, aye." Macey adjusted course, and the *Mud Cat* plied quickly in a new direction.

After a time, the open lakes and wide rivers turned into prairie. Swamp prairies looked a lot like the prairies of the Midwest, only here the grass was flooded. Macey nosed the boat's prow into the fringe. The grass and sedge parted, and the *Mud Cat* motored through it slowly.

"This is Floyd's Prairie." The excitement Perch had shown at the start of the tour was gone. His voice was terse and level now. "I want to show you folks something."

"Perch?" Macey seemed as confused as the passengers.

"Slide us over to a hammock," the captain ordered.

"What's a hammock?" Creeper asked. "You mean like the kind of net you sleep in?"

"No. You'll see," said Perch. "Be patient."

The boat broke through the far side of the "field" and slid out into a pond. At the center of the pond, floating on the surface, were three or four enormous mats of partially decayed vegetation. The largest was maybe thirty feet across. Macey swung the boat parallel and sidled up to it.

"Why are we here?" Piper was in no mood for jaunty side trips.

"Again with the detours!" Tad huffed.

Perch didn't reply. He sat on the gunwale and swung his legs over the side of the *Mud Cat*. Using the boat for leverage, he stood up on the mat. It held his weight. Then, after a dark glance back at Tad and Piper, Perch walked to the middle of the mat, turned, and addressed the group.

"This thing I'm currently standing on is called a peat hammock. It is one of the defining features of the swamp. Peat is made up of bits of decayed plants and other organic material. There are thousands of hammocks in the swamp, most of them here in the prairies. Hammocks are formed when peat collects at the bottom of the swamp. Over time, methane gas builds up inside the peat, eventually ripping big chunks of it free. Those chunks float to the surface, just like the one I'm standing on. They can get thick. Ten to fifteen feet thick. Thick enough for people to walk on. Thick enough to support trees."

"What's your point?" said Tad. "I thought we told you to head straight to Minnie's Island!"

"You're right, you did," said Perch. "But unfortunately that won't be possible today. This concludes your tour of the Okefenokee. Remember, tips are appreciated."

Piper was a mix of confused and furious. "What are you talking about?"

Perch spelled it out for her, this time without the droll antics. "Macey will take you back to the launch. Without me. I'm officially marooning myself here."

"Is this some kind of a joke?" Tad asked. "Because it's not funny."

Piper turned to Macey. "Why is he doing this?"

Macey just shrugged. "I don't know—ask him."

Perch gave them a fluttering wave that segued from a salute to a brush-off. "Don't come back now, ya hear?"

"Get in the boat." Tad didn't like Perch much, but he didn't want to strand him either. The Oke wasn't the kind of place where you leave someone behind and feel good about yourself.

"I'll make you a deal, Taddy," said Perch. "Why don't you come out on the hammock and escort me back to the *Mud Cat*? If you can reach me, I promise I'll come quietly. And then we can head straight to Minnie. My word."

"You heard him." Piper nudged Tad with her elbow. "Go get him."

"Go get him? Seriously?" Going and getting Perch seemed like the bonehead idea of the century. Worse, it felt like a trap. He didn't trust Perch as far as he could throw him. If Piper did, she was crazy. And if she didn't, then why was she sending him out on the hammock after the kid? It was something he needed to think about.

"Are you man enough, Taddy?" Perch taunted.

"Ugh. This is ridiculous." Tad slid across the bench to the starboard side of the *Mud Cat* and stood up. "Fine. Here I come, ready or not."

Perch smiled slyly and said, "Oh, I'm ready."

Tad climbed out of the boat and touched down in a crouch on the hammock. The peat beneath his feet sank several inches, and water rushed in around his ankles. It poured into the top of his sneakers, soaking his socks. "What the—?"

Piper scooted over to the gunwale to see if she could be helpful. "You okay?"

"I think so." Tad steadied and pushed himself into a standing position. He looked like a newborn deer finding its legs for the first time.

Perch goaded him forward. "Well, come on, then. Come get me."

Tad took a step, and the peat sank farther. The water rose to the bottom of his calves. He took a third step, then a fourth. The hammock shook beneath him. When he was halfway between the boat and Perch, Tad came to a halt. His legs were shivering as he struggled to stay upright. Beads of sweat bloomed on his forehead. Perch, on the other hand, looked comfortable. Like he was standing on a sidewalk.

"I can't go any farther," Tad said. "I think the peat is starting to weaken. I don't want to fall through it. Perch . . . help me. What do I do?"

"That's a real good question," said Perch. "I've got a question for you too. Tell me, Tad, do you know how the *Okefenokee* got its name?"

Tad furrowed his moist brow. "This isn't the time for a history lesson!"

"It's the perfect time," said Perch. "Hundreds of years ago, the Creek Indians named this swamp the Okefenokee. It means 'trembling earth.' I suppose you can guess why. These peat hammocks float on the water, unanchored to the swamp bed. They're unstable. They tremble when you walk on them. You can feel this one trembling right now, can't you, Tad? The Creeks were a nimble people. They could cross hammocks with ease. I haven't quite mastered it myself, but I've had practice, as you can see. There's a secret to it. I once watched a tourist fall through a hammock and plunge twenty feet to the bottom. Poor guy, ended up as alligator chow. I've been handing out liability wavers ever since."

"You're lying!" Tad snapped.

"Maybe I am, maybe I ain't. There's only one way to find out. Take another step."

Tad was frozen in an awkward position. It felt to him like a move in any direction would send him plummeting through the peat. "Why are you doing this? Are you a psychopath? Is that it? Are you trying to get me killed?"

Perch scratched his head. "That's up to you. I'll tell you what: I'll let you in on the secret to walking safely on a hammock—"

"Yes, tell me!"

"—but only if you share *your* little secret first."

"Secret? What are you—? Ack!" The peat sank another three inches toward the bottom, and Tad threw his arms out like airplane wings to steady himself.

"I should warn you," said Perch. "If you fall through, the peat will seal up above you. You'll drown. Or get eaten by an alligator. Or maybe you'll sink into the mud, and someone will find your body in two hundred years. Bog Man Tad. It has a nice ring to it."

"What do you want from him?" Piper yelled.

Perch yelled back. "I want to know what it is you folks are *really* doing here in the Oke! So far it's been nothing but a pack of lies."

"We told you," said Piper. "We're looking for flowers."

Perch's eyes narrowed. "Sticking to that story, huh? People who come to the Oke to look for flowers don't go to Minnie's Island. There's nothing special on Minnie." He gave them a sly look. "Or is there? You folks are after something—of that I have no doubt. I heard you whispering about a Dr. Cole. I'm familiar with all the legends in these parts, and I know all about that plant hunter. I know he came here looking for a unique flower. A silver flower. You've been lying to me from the get-go. Using me and my boat too. Listen up, Tad. If you want my help getting back to the *Mud Cat*, then you'll fess up. This time I want the truth. Otherwise you can sink, for all I care."

Tad would never betray Piper's trust. "My lips are sealed."

Perch growled. "Fine, have a nice swim." He started bouncing up and down on the hammock, causing it to quake and Tad to totter.

"All right!" Piper cried out. "I'll tell you, but you have to promise to save Tad."

"Go on," Perch said. "I'm all ears."

Keeping the story brief for Tad's sake, Piper opened up and told Perch about Grace, Tad's connection to Dr. Brisbane Cole, the botanist's incomplete journal, and the silver flower that had been the object of Cole's search now was hers. She cried as she confessed everything. When she finished, there was a long pause of silence intruded upon only by the distant clucking of alligator hatchlings calling for their mother.

Perch didn't say anything at first. He looked up at the sun and then down at his feet. Everywhere but at Piper. Finally, in a tone laced with unexpected tenderness, he said, "I can't help you. I'm sorry, but I just can't."

Piper lifted the collar of her T-shirt to her face and dabbed her eyes. "Why not?"

"Because I'd be giving you false hope, that's why. Look, I've been all over the Oke, even down to the part that spills into Florida. I've never seen anything like the flower Cole was searching for. Not once. It's just an old legend. Folks gave up looking for it long ago."

Macey, who hadn't said a word to this point, finally spoke. "Kids, even if this flower was around back when yer plant feller was alive, it's probably extinct now. Something that rare . . . you have to understand—the Oke draws lightning like an outhouse draws flies. It's a magnet for electrical storms. During months so dry that the catfish carry canteens, the lightning starts fires. This swamp burned to a crisp four times over since I was born, and, no, I'm not telling ya my age. There've been fires in the Oke every twenty years or so since folks started keeping record back in 1860. Had a big one in 2007 and one again in 2011. Each time, hundreds of thousands of acres burn. Maybe the reason no one's seen your silver flower is because it was burned up too."

"Macey is right," said Perch. "The trees on Minnie are relatively new timber."

Piper's heart sank. If the old trees were gone, Cole's marker was gone with them. There was nothing left to point the way. Without that marker they could wander aimlessly for years and still not find the silver flower. "I guess . . . I guess that's it, then."

"No! We can't give up!" Creeper declared. Piper had never seen such a look of bold resolve on his face, not even the time he tried to talk their parents into letting him climb the giant Christmas tree at the mall. "We owe it to Grace to at least try. Just one day, Perch. Let us look for one day. Please!"

Piper was proud of him. Maybe there was hope for her brother yet.

"I admire your conviction, Creeper. I really do," said Perch. "But I think it'd be best if—"

"Let's take a vote." Creeper threw his hand straight up in the air like he was snatching birds. "I vote we stay and look."

Perch knew Creeper wouldn't give up until he had his vote. "All righty, Almighty. We'll vote. Raise your hand if you want to stay out here and drag out this wild-goose chase."

Piper and Tad raised their hands and brought the count to three.

Victorious, Creeper dropped his hand into his lap. "Three to one. We keep looking."

"That's all fine and well," Perch said. "Unfortunately, maritime rules say the ship captain's vote counts as three and tie goes to the captain. At least that's the way it works on the *Mud Cat*. And I say we leave. I intend to spare you from a colossal waste of time when you *could* be home spending every minute you can with your sweet baby sister. That's what I'd be doing. That's what you should do too. Fire up the engine, Macey. We're going home."

But an unexpected thing happened. Macey raised one massive paw. "The tally is four to three," she said. "Sorry, son, but I'm siding with the kids."

"Mace?" Perch's mouth dropped open in disbelief. He wasn't used to being undermined by his first mate.

"Close yer jaw before a bird comes along and builds a nest in yer mouth." Her words were typical Macey, but her tone was much softer, almost maternal. "I think we should give them the day."

Perch didn't understand. "If this is about the money they paid, they can have it back."

Macey sighed. "It's not about the money, boy. It's about family. The Oke gets half a million tourists every year. Most people come here for this or that, birds or brags. Theirs is the best reason I've heard yet. They're here on account of family."

"But, Macey—"

She didn't let him finish. "Now, that's not to say yer wrong either, Perch. Finding that flower is as likely as finding an otter on the moon, but these kids deserve the chance to look, and we owe them our help. But it's your boat, Perch; democracy be hanged. You decide."

Perch looked from Macey, to Piper, to Creeper, then back to Piper again. "All right, if that's what y'all want. I spoke my piece on the subject, but I guess Macey makes a good point. There's nothing more important than family. But we still have a problem."

"You're right, I do!" Tad said. A frog swam between his ankles. "Piper told you the truth. Now you keep your word and tell me what to do."

"I wasn't talking about you," Perch said. "I'm talking about your plan. Macey told y'all: Cole's marker was probably lost in a forest fire. Without it we'll need a new course of action. Do you even have one?"

"Yes, I think so," Piper answered. "I mean, yes, I do."

"All righty, then," Perch said. "Let's get on out of here."

He strolled across the hammock, just beyond Tad's reach, and climbed aboard the *Mud Cat*.

"Hey! What about me?" Tad asked. "You can't just leave me!"

Perch lifted the lid of the bench closest to the bow and retrieved a spool of inch-thick rope from stowage.

"Great!" Tad reached out eagerly, wriggling his fingers at Perch. "Throw me an end."

But Perch didn't toss him the end of the line. He tossed the whole heavy spool instead. Tad yelped and caught it in his arms. The weight of the spool, added to his own, sent him plummeting straight down through the peat.

But he didn't disappear beneath the surface. Instead, he found himself standing in water that came up to his knees. His face turned an interesting shade of red.

"You tricked me!" he shouted.

"That's right," said Perch. "I'd never intentionally put anyone in danger. If you knew me, you'd know that. The prairies are shallow, barely two feet deep in most spots. I made up that part about the tourist falling through. I'm not fond of fibbing, but I needed answers, and I got them. But you lied to me first, so now we're even. And I hope I proved a point. You don't know squat about the Oke. Not the depth of her water or the depth of her danger. That's why I expect y'all to listen to me from now on. No ifs, ands, or buts. I'm in charge. Got it?"

They got it.

Perch waved Tad over. "Bring that rope with you. I'm sure I'm gonna need it today."

"What for?" Creeper asked.

Perch sighed deeply. "To strangle y'all for talking me into this mess."

August 9, 1823

Again Micanopy displays his sense of humor at my expense, only
this time I find his joke more frustrating than amusing. Neither
of the guides he assigned to my expedition speak English, and
perhaps more frustrating, the younger is barely thirteen, little
more than a boy! The man is named Nokosi (which, as I learned
at supper, is the Seminole word for "bear"). The boy, Bolek, is
the chief's nephew. It is clear from his constant mumbling and
glowering that he is no more amicable to the arrangement than
I. Would I could, I'd send him back to his mother, posthaste,
but to reject any part of Micanopy's generosity would be to
surrender the rest, and without the use of his canoes, I would be
figuratively and literally dead in the water.

At first light, my assistants carried our supplies to the shore
and loaded them into two dugout canoes, hollowed-out vessels
carved from cypress logs. Nokosi and I share one canoe while
Bolek transports our supplies in the other. The boy stares at me
with seething contempt, but he follows Nokosi's commands, and
Nokosi follows mine. This pecking order makes the arrangement
bearable.

The plan is simple. We'll spend our days on the water, in
search of the silver flower, and our nights camping on one of the
swamp's central islands. I have every confidence that we will
find the flower within the week.

We paddled toward the rising sun. A mantle of mist hovered
above the water, obscuring our way, turning twisted trees into
wizards, demons, and Plesiosaurs. The vocalizations of hidden
creatures rise and fall as we pass. The Okefenokee Swamp is as
mysterious and foreign as any land I've ever explored. China,
Borneo, India, my dreams . . . there is no greater diversity of
life or landscape on earth than here in this quixotic place. I

will return with my beloved someday so that she can see this place firsthand. My account will not do justice to this ever-shifting watery realm, where nature both placates death and conquers it.

7

Now that the jig was up, Piper felt no qualms about sharing Dr. Cole's journal with Perch and Macey. With Minnie's Island dismissed as a dead end, Piper's off-the-cuff plan B was put into action. They would travel to a different island, the one Cole returned to every night after spending his day looking for the silver flower.

Perch glanced at the map in the journal and recognized the spot immediately. "That's Billy's Island." He tapped a shape on the map, which, from above, looked a bit like an owl perched on the brush bow of a snow sled. "It's the most famous in the swamp, named after Billy Bowlegs, one of the last Seminole chiefs to live in the Oke. The man was a great fighter. During the Third Seminole War, Billy and his two hundred men conducted guerilla-style raids on white settlers, retreating to this island afterward. The army was powerless to stop him. Billy's Island is a regular highlight of my tours."

"Maybe Cole left some clues behind." Piper tried to sound optimistic. "I know it's a long shot, but at least it's something."

They all agreed, and Macey headed south toward the Red Trail, bound for Billy's Island.

As the day continued to warm, Perch warmed with it. Now that he knew the full truth and had agreed to help, he seemed to be his usual, happy-go-lucky self once again, animatedly pointing out the denizens of the swamp. Numerous basking cooters—the swamp's most extroverted turtle—scooted through the water, playing peek-aboo with the world above. An appearance by a pair of playfully twining otters prompted Perch to say, "I don't believe in reincarnation, but if I did, I'd want to come back as a swamp otter. Look at them. That's pure joy you're seeing there." The group saw egrets, ibises, herons, and more of the ruby-pated sandhill cranes. Smaller birds were plentiful, too. Piper thought of Grafton and wondered how he was faring in his search for the ivory-billed woodpecker. She hoped his quest was off to a better start than theirs was.

The dilating sun brought the swamp's most infamous inhabitants, the alligators, to life. Everywhere the kids looked they saw the large reptiles soaking up rays, basking on hammocks, logs, and sometimes even on top of one another. A clutch of newborn hatchlings formed a squirming crown on their mother's partially submerged head. The most daring of her brood slithered into the water, careful not to swim past the tip of Mom's toothy mouth, and clucked a challenge to the *Mud Cat* as it passed by.

"Junior's not a fan of the visiting team," said Perch.

Piper had to admit, the babies were sort of adorable. Still, in clusters, the big ones made her nervous. She thrummed her fingers on her bare knees and jerked her head toward every splash. Perch was astute enough to notice.

"You don't need to worry about the gators," he assured her. "They're afraid of people and just want to be left alone. In the last forty years, there've been only twenty or so fatal attacks in the U.S., and all but one of them happened in Florida."

"And the one?" Piper asked, of course.

"Well, that one did occur here in Georgia," he said, then quickly added, "but not in the Okefenokee. A woman was attacked while swimming in the waters off Skidaway Island. Twenty deaths total in forty years means attacks are super rare. You have a better chance of being stung by bees while getting hit by lightning as you're being run over by a bus. They're not man-eaters like the crocs of Australia and Africa. There's never been a single fatality by alligator in the history of the Oke refuge."

"So they aren't aggressive?" Tad asked.

"Oh, they're plenty aggressive during mating season," Perch said. "But mainly toward one other. They only attack humans when they feel threatened. We leave them alone, they leave us alone, and we get along just peachy. Still, it's best not to swim in the Oke for a whole lot of reasons, the gators being just one of them."

Shortly after noon, Piper's appetite returned. She declared it lunchtime and opened up her backpack, retrieving the two bologna sandwiches she'd made. She handed one to Creeper. Tad had brought a few slices of cold broccoli-and-mushroom pizza from last night's dinner. He opened the Tupperware container and offered a slice to Perch and Macey, but Perch declined and Macey preferred a smoke.

Piper hadn't realized how hungry she was, and before she knew it, she'd wolfed down her sandwich, the granola bars, and the apple. She peered into the bag, hoping she'd forgotten something, but it was empty.

"I've got some snacks inside my bench stowage," Macey told her.

"Thank you," said Piper. "Maybe later."

It was a little weird to see this side of Macey. Since Piper had opened up about Grace, the woman was treating her differently. Even Macey's physical appearance had seemed to soften a bit. There was motherliness there, despite what the crew cut and tattoos implied. *Tattoos*, plural. Earlier, when Macey was yanking on the motor's pull cord, her sleeve slid up to her elbow, and Piper noticed a second tattoo, this one on Macey's forearm. The word *Georgia* in simple black lettering. The woman seemed fond of one thing, at least: the almighty Peach State.

The dock at Billy's Island was long, narrow, and floating on the water next to two giant pond cypress trees. The water here was so reflective it looked as though the dock was hovering in the air. They moored the *Mud Cat* and headed onto the island.

They set their equipment down on the shore and put their heads together for another look at Dr. Cole's map. The plant hunter had marked his campsite with a triangle. His tent, maybe?

"Billy's Island is five square miles," said Macey. "That triangle ain't exactly a pinpoint, but I think I know where that is, maybe three klicks from here." Macey, former navy, still thought of distance in military terms.

"All right, Mace, we'll follow you," Perch said. "Lead the way."

They kept to the worn trail for about a mile, passing along the way the rusted shell of a discarded steam boiler, corroded metal containers, and the skeleton of a railway car. Creeper spotted a two-foot section of track that had become overrun by time and weeds. Nothing could seem more out of place than a train in a swamp.

"Used to be a logging camp on the island back in the nineteen-twenties," said Perch. "They built a railroad through the swamp to transport timber out of the Oke. This is all that's left of Billy's human occupants. This, and a little graveyard on the northern end."

Creeper, overcome by heebie-jeebies, rose on his tiptoes and squirmed. "Yuck! People are buried here?"

"Yes," said Perch. "Members of the Lee family, the first whites to settle and farm Billy's Island after the army chased off the Seminoles."

"How'd they die?" Piper asked.

"Pneumonia, cholera . . . sicknesses we've mostly got a handle on now. But the Lees ain't the only dead folks buried on Billy."

Before Perch could elaborate, Macey left the path, leading the procession into the tangled forest. For a huge woman, she had a quick stride. The kids had a hard time keeping up, and she wasn't waiting on them. Piper checked her phone for the time. It was 1:04 P.M. Even though the search had really just begun, she could feel the minutes slipping away, like the smallest fish wriggling free from a net, each one stealing off with a bit of hope, then disappearing into the murk of despair.

A twig snapped behind her. Piper spun in time to see something small and furry—a chipmunk, maybe—scamper up the back side of a tree. Her heart thrummed. A hawk screeched overhead. She almost stepped on something slithering beneath the leaf litter, but it was just passing through and was gone in a rustle. Up ahead, she saw a brume of black particles swirling close to the ground. It rose up and hovered between two oaks like a dark specter. When the cloud came into sharper focus, she realized there was nothing supernatural about it at all. The swarm of gnats swirled around a tree, and then the smoky black scarf of tiny insects abruptly disintegrated into thin air.

Piper found it hard to breathe. She feared the onset of a panic attack (having suffered a few since Washington). She felt like she was being smothered by nature, as though the whole forest was one giant eye, unblinking, watching her, judging her. It was a horrible, crushing feeling. A flutter. A hot, groping breeze. A scratching noise. Intense silence. The memory of a rabid wolverine stabbed into her brain, wresting the courage from her. She wanted out. *Out* of the forest, *out* of the swamp, *out* of the *out*doors before she went *out* of her mind. *OUT!*

Suddenly, mercifully, the woods released her from its shadowy clinch, as the group marched into a sunny clearing. A breeze caressed her sweaty face, and Piper felt calmer at once.

"We're here," Macey announced.

In the center of the clearing was a large grassy mound roughly twenty feet long by ten feet wide and three feet high.

"What is that?" Tad asked.

"Like I said, the Lees ain't the only ones buried on Billy," Perch said. "This here is an Indian burial mound. A mass grave."

"Is this some kind of themed tour you offer?" Tad asked sarcastically. "The Native American ghost tour? You don't charge extra for this, do you?"

"Don't be a wiseacre," Macey growled.

"Native Americans lived in the swamp first," Perch said. "Archaeological evidence—bits of clay pots and the like—says they were here as early as 3000 B.C. Over the centuries, the Weedens, the Timucuans, the Seminoles all made homes in the Oke until the whites drove them out. The Native Americans were the first to die here too. They buried their dead in mounds called tumuli. Once upon a time these graves dotted all the islands."

"The whites destroyed most of 'em," Macey added. "It's a dang shame. There's still a few around, but not many. This one here is special. Even the Lees knew better than to crack this one open."

"What's so special about it?" Creeper asked. "Looks like a big lump to me."

Perch said, "We think this particular tumulus—*tumulus* is singular—belonged to the Tasketcha tribe from South America. The story goes, they fled north to Georgia to—"

"Escape the invading Spanish," Tad finished Perch's thought. "The conquistador Pizarro destroyed the Incan army at the battle of Cajamarca in 1532, then he executed the Incan emperor Atahuallpa, kicking off the Spanish conquest of Peru."

The group stared at him.

"What?" Tad asked. "I pay attention in History class."

"That's exactly what happened," Perch said, impressed. "Which makes this here tumulus the oldest in the swamp, maybe as old as three thousand years. The tribes that came after the Tasketcha were afraid to go near it. They suspected the Tasketcha were practicing dark magic, and avoided them like the plague."

Creeper shuddered. "Spooky."

"Yayup," Macey said. "There's an Oke legend. Before the last Tasketchan died, he performed a ceremony over this mound. He used wicked magic to free all the spirits of the dead into the dark heart of the swamp. Their bodies remained here to rot. To avoid fading away like smoke, the spirits took possession of various critters, predators mostly. Gators, black bears, red wolves, and the like. When the animal hosts died, the spirits just jumped into other animals. Into people too. Some of those possessed folks may have wandered out of the swamp, spreading the Tasketcha evil into the world beyond. But some, the legend tells, are still here, waiting for their chance to leave the Oke too."

"That's a great story!" Creeper showed Macey his arms. "Look, I've got goose bumps!"

"The Tasketcha were gone way before Cole's arrival, right?" said Piper. "What does this tumulus have to do with him?"

Perch explained. "Around the time when Cole was looking for the silver flower, tensions between the Creek Indians and the invading whites were high. Some of the natives would have found pleasure in cutting his throat while he slept. Like Macey said, those tribes steered clear of the Tasketcha graves. Cole would have been perfectly safe camping beside this tumulus."

"Safest place in the swamp," Macey agreed.

Piper panned around the clearing. She hadn't expected to see Cole's abandoned tent, of course, not after all this time, but other than the mound, there was nothing there, not even the remnant rocks of a former fire pit.

"That's it, then," she said. "It's another dead end."

"We didn't expect to find a blinking neon arrow, now, did we?" Perch bumped her shoulder playfully. "If Cole left us any clues, nature probably gobbled them up a long time ago. We gotta look *deeper*."

"How do we do that?" Creeper asked.

"I'll show you." Perch fished into his pocket and took out an iPhone. He set his backpack on the ground and pulled a black cylinder-shaped object from a long pocket on the side. He tugged at both ends of the cylinder, and it telescoped into a three-foot-long wand, about the size of a walking stick.

"You said we had to dig deeper. That's a funny-looking shovel," said Tad.

Perch chuckled. "That's because it's not. It's a metal detector. But it's a little different from the ones you see folks using on the beach. This wand is a three-D ground scanner. It uses radar to penetrate the earth, and then it sends images to my phone's screen. Tourists drop all kinds of valuable stuff on the islands. This baby paid for itself in the first month. I've found rings, coins, even old mining tools. Found a kid's retainer once, but some things are best left buried."

The kids watched Perch in utter amazement as he assembled the pieces of the radar.

Perch noticed their reaction. "Well don't look so surprised, y'all. Just because I'm a swamper doesn't mean I'm a hick. Thought I'd proved that by now. Guess what, I've got a Mac laptop at home too. And Macey drives a hybrid. Now, c'mere and take a look."

They huddled in close to the screen. It was green, with little glowing blue and red spots. As Perch moved the wand, the spots moved with it. "Rocks," he said. "It'll be obvious if we scan something metal. Metal shows up on the screen as white."

"I'll sit this out." Macey retrieved a silver lighter from the pocket of her overalls. The navy insignia was etched in its metal casing. She lit up a cigarette with it, her fourth of the day.

"You smoke a lot," Creeper scolded her. "That's not healthy, you know."

"Well, bless your little pea-pickin' heart." Macey glared down at him. "Are you and me havin' what my daddy would call a teachable moment? Scram, boy. Let me smoke my 'backer in peace."

"She means *tobacco*, of course," Perch told Creeper as he ushered the group away from Macey. "It's best to leave her to her vices."

Perch began to walk the clearing in an orbit around the tumulus, followed closely by the others. He stepped slowly, deliberately, sweeping the scanner in front of him low and wide, like a blind man's cane. When he'd completed each lap, he moved a few feet farther away from the mound and started another.

The day slipped away. An hour passed. Then two. Then three. Piper knew that as their shadows grew longer, so did the odds of finding the flower. But this was their only plan, so they had to keep looking. Perch never complained, took a break, or even slowed down. He moved steadily around the mound like a planet circling the sun.

Roughly five hours had passed when he stopped dead in his tracks. "Whoa!" He raised the phone close to his eyes.

"What is it?" Piper asked. She jammed her nose next to his for a look. There was something new on the screen. It was about the width of a brick but twice as long. The radar displayed it as a luminous white rectangle.

"I don't know," Perch said. "But it's definitely nonferrous."

"Huh?" said Tad.

"Yeesh, you city kids need to pick up a book once in a while," Perch said. "Nonferrous metal. It means there's no iron in it. Could be aluminum, copper, lead . . ."

"Or silver?" Creeper asked. He was crouching down, staring intently at the spot on the ground directly below the tip of the wand.

"Unlikely," Perch said. "It's pretty big. A silver object that size would be worth thousands. I'm sure its owner would have returned for it. It's probably more trash from the mining camp."

"I bet it's buried pirate treasure!" Creeper started wringing his hands.

"Right," said Piper. "Because a pirate ship in a swamp makes total sense."

"I wouldn't be quick to scuttle the idea," Perch said. "Edward Teach, old Blackbeard himself, plundered the Georgia coast. Legend says he buried his treasure on an island and boasted that only he and the devil knew where. People assume he meant an island off the coast, but if I wanted something hidden, and hidden well, I'd sail the St. Marys River from the Atlantic Ocean to the Oke and bury it right here."

"I knew it!" said Creeper. "It's Blackbeard's treasure!"

"Probably not, but there's only one way to find out," said Perch. "Let's bring it up." He handed his backpack to Tad. "There's a folding spade inside. Start digging."

Tad found the tool, and they formed a circle around the object. Monitoring the screen, Perch told him where to thrust the shovel point. In short order, Tad had scooped out a rectangular moat around the hunk of metal.

"All righty, now try to get the spade under it," Perch instructed. "Then pry it up carefully. It could be very old. Go easy so it doesn't break apart."

Tad pressed down hard on the handle grip and got underneath the thing. He pushed down on the shovel, and the object rose up easily, in one piece.

"That was good luck," Perch said. He passed the metal detector to Piper to hold. He took the dirt-caked object in his hands and set it in the grass, brushing the dirt off. Yellow peeked through the crud. "Creeper, there's a bottle of water in my pack. Get it, quick."

Creeper did as told and handed him the bottle. Perch poured the water in a steady stream over the object, from end to end, revealing more yellow. In a fit of exuberance, Perch yanked off his T-shirt and used it to wipe away the remaining layer of soil, revealing luster.

Creeper's eyes bloomed wide. "That can't be for real."

Perch was grinning like a madman. "Oh, it's real, all right."

The thing in his hands was a cylindrical-shaped, slightly flattened box with a hinged door on it. The box was made of solid gold.

"This is unbelievable!" Tad exclaimed. "I know what it is!"

"You do?" asked Perch.

"Yes! It's a botanist's container for holding plant samples. A vasculum. Dr. Brisbane Cole's vasculum, to be exact. It's the same one he's holding in the painting at the Jesup Nature Center. And you're right; it's made of pure gold. That's why it's so well preserved. Unlike most other metals, gold doesn't deteriorate, because it's an element, not an alloy."

"This thing hasn't been opened in nearly two hundred years?" Piper could barely believe their good luck.

The kids looked up at each other and then back down at the vasculum.

"Wow . . ." said Creeper. "Buried treasure. We found buried treasure."

Perch gave the vasculum a little shake. Something fluttered inside. Dr. Cole had buried it for safekeeping. Only important things get buried for safekeeping.

"Gad night a living!" said Macey, arriving behind them. "Don't just squat there like dogs in high cotton. Open the dang thing up and let's take a gander."

8

Perch passed the vasculum to Piper. "Go ahead, Princess. This is your quest. You should open it."

Piper stared at the gold cylinder resting on her fingertips. It felt like the last unscratched box on a lottery ticket. She needed a sign to point them in the right direction. Without a new clue, the search would end there. The swamp was simply too vast to find the silver flower without the help of Dr. Cole. She breathed a quick prayer, then unlatched the little metal door on the vasculum's side. She opened it. There appeared to be a scrap of cloth inside. Piper pinched a corner, pulled it out gently, and handed it to Tad. He uncrumpled the cloth, then laid it out flat on the ground. It was dirty and blank.

Macey recognized the material. "That's vellum. Animal skin. You can tell by the little pits covering the surface. That's where the hair follicles used to be. Cotton or paper wouldn't have survived this long, not even inside a gold container. Vellum lasts for centuries."

Piper was devastated. "It's nothing, then? Just old animal skin?"

"The follicle pits are always on the back side," Macey said. "Flip it."

Tad turned it over.

"Well, how about that?" said Macey.

On the front side of the vellum, Dr. Cole had drawn a map of the swamp. They compared it to the more precise map provided by the welcome center. Perch was impressed by how accurately Tad's ancestor had visualized the Oke's layout. A few smaller islands were missing on the hand-drawn map, and the shapes and distances weren't perfect, but all of the swamp's major landmarks were there.

"Dr. Cole just earned my respect, big-time," Perch said. "Even today, with a GPS and other high-tech equipment, it'd take a surveyor half a year to come up with a map this spot-on. Cole did it in weeks, and with no real technology. He sure had a fantastic eye for detail. Color me impressed."

"And look!" said Tad. He pointed out several little Xs on the map. "They match up to the markers in his journal. There's the one we'd hoped to find on Minnie's Island. And these right here—"

"They're new ones!" Piper practically shouted. Her fingertip skated across the map. "Here, here . . . and here! Those aren't in the journal!"

She was right. Cole had gone to several locations after his stop on Minnie's Island, and he'd recorded them all on the map. More important, he'd drawn little arrows to show the progression of his journey.

"The last arrow leads to this spot right here." She tap-tapped inside a circle Cole had drawn then lapped over several times with his ink.

Piper's heart nearly stopped. "I don't believe it. . . ."

At the center of the circle was a faded, barely perceptible symbol that looked remarkably like a flower.

"He found it!" Piper jumped up and down excitedly. "Dr. Cole found the flower! It's there, inside that circle!"

"We can't know for sure," said Tad. "The facts suggest he was killed and never completed his quest, otherwise he would have put the flower in the vasculum, right? That's the whole purpose of the thing, keeping botanical samples fresh."

"He makes a good point," said Perch.

Piper shut the door on doubt. "Who cares? All I know is that this circle is where we'll find the flower. We have to go there!"

"Well, even if your silver flower *is* there, we may not be able to reach it," Perch told them. "First, the circle is west of the refuge's boundaries. There are insurance issues for my company."

Piper opened her mouth to argue, but Perch lifted his hand up and out like a crossing guard to cut her off.

"Relax, Princess, that won't stop me from taking y'all. My real concern is the swampscape. There was a huge fire in the western part of the Oke a few years back. We had a dry spell, and then a lightning storm set the trees ablaze. It torched a couple hundred thousand acres. The state paid to clean up the park, but dead trees outside the park's border were left to rot and fall. Could be treacherous to navigate through. In all honesty, I've never been that far west in my life. It's uncharted territory."

"Isn't that the best reason to assume the flower is there?" Piper reasoned.

"Piper's right," said Tad. "It's the most logical place to look."

"Fine. But there's another problem," Perch told them. "And this one there's no getting around."

"What is it?" Piper asked, positive she would.

Perch nodded up at the sun. It was on its descent, tilting to the west. "It's early evening. We still have to trek back to the boat. It'll take us a couple hours to get to the part of the swamp Cole circled on the map. Possibly more if trees felled by the fire are blocking the narrows. We'll only have a few hours of daylight left before dark."

"The western swamp won't be like Disney World, kids," Macey said. "No privies, no picnic areas, no docks. There'll be no creature comforts, just creatures. We'd be loons to head out now."

"But we're so close," Piper moaned.

Perch took a good hard look at the map and then a good hard

109

look at his passengers. "I'm double-minded on the problem. I told you I'd give you the day. But if I keep my word, that day would end with us motoring inside that red circle, and that'd be a mistake we'd all regret. So here's what I'm proposing: I'd be willing to give you an *extra* day, for no charge, provided you folks are willing to spend the night here on Billy's Island."

"You want us to sleep in the swamp?" Piper couldn't imagine a more repugnant scenario.

"It's perfectly safe as long as you don't wander off," Perch assured her. "No sleepwalkers in the group, right? We could start fresh in the morning."

"I can't," Tad objected. "My mom would kill me. She'd pound me, then ground me. And worse, she'd never trust me again. Piper, you can't be serious about this? You really want to sleep in a swamp?"

She didn't. Just the thought of it made her hands sweaty, but what she wanted was irrelevant. Piper was there for Grace, and fully committed to the search. However, there was her other sibling to think about. "Yes, I want to stay. But Creeper—"

"I'm staying!" Creeper avowed. "You guys can go home if you want, but me and Perch are gonna keep looking."

"It's gotta be all or none, buddy," Perch said. "We can't make the others swim home, right?"

"Piper, please . . ." Creeper begged. "We have to stay. For Grace."

"Okay," she agreed. "We'll stay."

"Not that anybody asked me"—Macey tamped her smoldering cigarette butt beneath her boot—"but I'm in. It won't be the first time I've slept in the Oke. Don't ask."

They all looked to Tad.

"Ugh!" he cried. "Piper, I promised you one day, and that's all."

"So did I," Perch reminded him. He was grinning at Tad like the Cheshire Cat, his naked torso rippling with muscles.

A camping trip with Piper wasn't the worst thing Tad could think to endure, but with shirtless Perch around, it felt like a train of regret he could see barreling down the track. He wanted to go home. Still, the way Piper was looking at him, imploring with those big, golden eyes . . .

"Fine," said Tad. "Let's stay."

Piper threw her arms around him. "Thank you! Thank you!"

"Oh . . . okay." Tad blushed darkly. Inside, his heart exploded into confetti.

Just as he lifted his arms to hug her back, she broke away and pulled Perch into an embrace. "And thank you too!" she said, pressing her cheek against his bare chest.

Perch chuckled "Well, ain't this a treat."

Tad didn't like "this." Not one bit.

"I have a question," said Creeper. "What does this word mean?" He pointed to the map. There was a word scrawled—or possibly smeared—in five large red letters, the largest on the map. Every letter was capitalized, as if to emphasize the word's importance. A line had been drawn from the word to the center of the circle, connecting it to the flower's location. The word was this:

MERGO

Tad scratched the letter G with his fingernail, and red powder flaked off under his nail. "Guys . . ." He grimaced. "I don't think this is ink." He licked his fingertip.

"Well? What is it then? Spit it out," Perch said.

Tad did just that. He spit on the ground and wiped his mouth. "Guys, I think the word *Mergo* was written in blood."

August 9, 1823

We have reached the end of the first day. My assistants and I
set up camp sixteen to twenty miles deep into the swamp, on
the south end of a large island. After covering our canoes with
palmetto fronds and reeds (there are other Creek tribes hunting
in the swamp, and it is best not to alert them to our presence),
we trekked inland through the forest until we came upon a
clearing. In the center of the clearing was a great, unnatural
mound. Nokosi instructed Bolek to help me pitch my tent while
he gathered rocks for a fire pit. Despite the language barrier,
the elder Indian takes direction well and absorbs language like a
sponge. We have developed a working system of communicating
through a smattering of English and Seminole words combined
with a dozen hand gestures. Nokosi seems to anticipate my
needs and is quick to fulfill them. Perhaps most useful of all
is his comprehensive knowledge of the swamp and his innate
sense of direction within it. He may yet prove to be an adequate
assistant. Time will tell.

Nokosi chose this spot for a reason, and although I'm sure
I missed the finer points due to our language barrier, I gather
that the clearing is a burial site, and the mound is filled with the
bodily remains of a tribe feared by all others. Nokosi assured me
this fear will keep us safe from attacks in the night and from
theft by day.

The youngest of our party has claimed ownership of this
place, thumping his chest, stomping the ground, and declaring
the land to be "Bolek's Island," although it sounded very much
like "Bowleg's Island," and I couldn't rein in a chuckle, earning
the lad's deeper contempt. Bolek is not bowlegged, of course,
being neither a horseman nor a sufferer of rickets, nor does it
matter to me if he plays at being boy-king, baron, or god of the
island, as long as he grants me refuge upon it and asks nothing

in remuneration. From the way he has fixated on my vasculum, I will be wise to use it as my pillow. Otherwise, this clearing seems as comfortable and safe as any place I've camped, and for that I am grateful. Safety is a luxury explorers such as myself must often forgo in pursuit of specimens, and many have died an untimely death: Forsskål from malaria, König from dysentery, Brunete from a fall from his burro, Dalton from freezing, Seetzen by poisoning. Of course the one that currently stands out in mind is John Lawson, a poor soul who was tortured and burned at the stake by hostile Indians. Why, then, do we choose a path so pockmarked with grisly fates? My friend William Bartram said it best when he wrote: "I might be instrumental in discovering, and introducing into my native country, some original productions of nature, which might become useful to society." It's true there are some vainglorious men who care for naught but fame and riches. But many of us hope to find some new specimen that can be used to enrich the lives of our fellow man. That alone is the reward of the risk. Let us see what tomorrow brings.

9

erch was hunched over the fire pit like a caveman. A caveman with a butane barbecue lighter. He'd put on a fresh Oke Dokey Boat Tours T-shirt. "I keep a dozen extra stored on the *Mud Cat* to sell to tourists at the end of their visit," he explained. Perch used his dirty old one as char cloth to start the fire. Tad was glad the show was over. He was sick of watching Perch parade around half-naked in front of Piper.

Creeper was busy unrolling one of the three sleeping bags Perch kept stored inside the *Mud Cat*'s benches. Say what you want about their flamboyant guide, but the kid was well prepared. They'd set up camp by the trail just a few hundred feet from the dock so they could keep an eye on the boat and stay within a short distance of any supplies they might need. The last bit of sunlight stained the water's ultrareflective surface ginger, and the stars began to poke through the darkening sky above.

"So what do you suppose *Mergo* means?" Creeper asked. "And why was it written in blood?"

"No clue, little buddy," Perch said. "Never heard the word before. Maybe it's from one of the Creek languages. Seminole, if I had to guess. *Mergo* probably just means, 'Ouch! I pricked my finger.'"

Creeper giggled.

"It's not Creek," Tad disagreed. "I think it's Latin. Definitely sounds Latin to me." He was sitting on a log, handing Perch sticks one at a time for kindling. He'd removed his sneakers and socks and placed them by the fire pit to dry. They were still wet from his dip in the prairie.

"You read Latin?" Piper asked from her seat on the log next to Tad. The vellum map was draped across her knees. She was straining her eyes in the fading light, studying it for clues. "I didn't know that."

"Not really," Tad admitted. "But botanists use Latin in taxonomy, the process of identifying and naming plants. I've seen enough Latin words in my science books to know the language when I come across it. I just can't tell you what it means."

Perch noticed Piper squinting. "It's getting dark out," he said. "There's a flashlight in my boat. Don't go ruining your eyes trying to read that map."

"I'll get it," Creeper said, and he ran off down the trail toward the water. Out here in the Oke, Creeper was a different kid. Eager to help. Piper could get used to this alternate-universe version of her brother.

Macey flicked a cigarette butt into the smoking weave of kindling. "Dang it, that was mah last smoke," she grumbled. "It's gonna be a long night."

Perch chuckled. "It ain't gonna kill ya to go without for a day. Probably the opposite." He looked to his elder. "Mace, you've been around the swamp longer than most; what do you reckon *Mergo* means?"

She sat down on a log across the fire pit from Tad and Piper and stretched her legs. "Who knows? Maybe Mergo is the name yer plant fellah came up with for the flower." In her thick Southern drawl, she pronounced the word as *Mergah*.

"I don't think that's right either," Tad said. "It's an ugly name for a flower Cole believed would save his wife's life."

"Tad, you said Cole's Seminole guide blamed his death on an evil spirit," said Piper. "What if Mergo is an evil spirit? A Tasketcha ghost?"

"Cole was a man of science," Tad reminded her. "He wouldn't buy into anything so hokey. The more likely theory is that he was killed by his guides, and his bones and buttons are rolling across the bottom of the swamp. He came to the swamp right between the two Seminole wars. There was a lot of bad blood."

"There's no point in busting our brains on speculation." Perch had coaxed up a flicker of fire. He fanned the flicker into a flame. Then he fed the flame a few sticks, waited for those to catch, and fed it a few more. "None of us here believe in evil spirits, right? The story of the Tasketcha is just that, a story. A folktale. Why should we care about some superstitious mumbo jumbo?"

"So you don't believe in the supernatural?" Tad asked. "Not that I do, of course. I'm a man of science, like my ancestor. I just figured . . . you know."

Perch bristled. "What? I'm just a swamp rat, so I'm sure to believe every tall tale I hear? Maybe I should change my company's name to Gullible's Travels—is that what you think?" Perch seemed genuinely hurt.

"Hey, man, I'm sorry." Tad didn't have a cruel bone in his body. He felt bad instantly. "I didn't mean—"

"I'm just messing with ya!" Perch guffawed, then slapped Tad on the back. "My feelings wear armor. But trust me, if I believed every legend I hear in the Oke, I'd be moving to the city tomorrow. Just last week a fisherman told me a story about a monster-size fish that got away. He claimed it was fourteen feet long. Of course, nothing makes a fish bigger than almost gettin' caught."

"Please don't talk about fish," Creeper groaned. He'd returned with the flashlight and handed it to his sister. "I'm so hungry. Is anybody else starving?"

"We're out of sandwiches," Piper reminded him. "You ate them all on the boat."

Perch stood and brushed off his knees. "Tell you what. Tad, you keep feeding the fire, and I'll go catch us some dinner."

"Forget it," said Piper. "I don't eat oak toad."

Macey smacked her lips. "You don't know what yer missing, girl." Piper couldn't tell if she was joking.

"I've got fishing tackle in the *Mud Cat*," Perch said. "The jackfish and warmouth get hungry at dusk. I'll be back in a jiff with dinner. Whaddaya say, Creeper ol' buddy? You want to help me catch some fish?"

"Sure!"

"Great. C'mon then. I'll get the fly rod while you scrounge around for some bait. Worms are good. Crickets'll do."

Creeper didn't wait for Perch. He bolted down the trail toward the water.

"This should be interesting," Macey said, pushing herself up from her log. She sauntered after the boys.

Piper realized she hadn't seen Creeper truly excited about much since they'd learned of Grace's illness. She was happy to see a spring in his step again. Even if they didn't find the flower, this trip had been good for him. And despite her hatred for the swamp, it had been good for her too. It had given her purpose, something she'd lacked for quite a while.

Tad strategically placed another stick on the fire. "Grafton is probably back at the car by now. He'll be worried when we don't show up. I know he said he'd leave without us, but I doubt he was serious. I wish we could call him."

Piper checked her phone for bars and frowned. "No signal."

"Yeah, same here. We could ask Perch to use his, but I'm sure he's in the same boat."

"Same boat . . ." Piper stared at the fire, deep in thought.

"That doesn't bother *you*, though, does it?" Tad asked.

"What doesn't bother me?"

"Being in the *Mud Cat* all day with Perch." As soon as he'd said it, he wished he could take it back. It was petty, the result of a stressful day. But Tad noticed the way her eyes lingered on Perch, and it hurt his feelings.

Piper glared at him. "Ugh, Tad. What is wrong with you?"

She really doesn't know, he thought, surprised. He tried a different tactic. "I'm just saying he's not so bad, that's all. Creeper seems to like him."

Her posture relaxed. "Oh. Yeah. I guess he's all right."

Tad smartly changed the subject. "Did you learn anything else from Cole's map?"

"No," she said, skimming the vellum with the flashlight. "But I keep thinking I've heard this word *Mergo* before. It rings a bell."

"Yeah?"

"It'll come to me, maybe."

As the sky darkened, the flashlight's halo grew brighter on the map. Piper trained it on the circle with the flower inside. "It's there," she said. "I know it. It's been there all along, just waiting for us."

"Let's hope so," said Tad.

Twilight was beautiful but brief. Darkness descended. In the Oke, night wasn't just a time of day. It was a transformation. The landscape shifted from swamp to ocean. An ocean of stars. Piper had never seen so many in her life. Or any so bright. She now understood how by simply adopting planets, stars could also be suns. And with the stars came music, the orchestral din of frogs. Each species added its own unique instrument: a trill, a bleat, a chuckle, a sound like the pluck of a banjo. The swell of throaty croaks was unsettling.

"I wish they'd hush up," Piper complained. "Stupid frogs are driving me nuts."

"The little ones got the biggest mouths," Perch said, emerging from the gloom. To demonstrate this point, Creeper skipped past him, singing loudly. "Fish for sale! We got fish for sale!" There was a chain of checkered-scaled sunfish dangling from his hand. It stretched all the way to his socks, enough meat for two meals, dinner and breakfast.

"Wow, great job!" Piper clapped.

"The warmouth sunnies were biting," Perch said. "Macey showed your brother how to tie a grinner knot. I've never seen her display such uncommon patience. I think they're best buds now."

A tiny, flitting orange light farther down the trail gave Macey away; she'd found an escaped cigarette at the bottom of one of her overall pockets and was taking her sweet time puffing the stick of 'backer down to a nub before returning to camp.

Creeper handed the fish off to Tad.

"Um, thanks." Tad had no clue what to do with them, so he just draped them over the end of the log and waited for something to happen to them.

"You hear those booming grunts?" Perch cupped his hand around his ear. "That's a pig frog. He's a little guy, a few inches long, but by sound alone, people mistake him for a bull gator."

"I wish he'd dunk his head," Piper growled.

"Don't worry," said Perch. "You'll get used to the music of the Oke. Y'all had a big day. You'll sleep fast tonight."

Piper knew better.

To Tad's relief, Macey took over the job of cleaning and gutting the fish. She was a flurry with a knife, handing chunks of meat off one by one to Perch, who ran them through with sticks and roasted them over the crackling fire. Tad passed out juice boxes. He'd brought plenty to go around.

"*Now* it's a party," Perch declared, stabbing the tiny straw into the top of his box.

They sat on their logs, awash in the orange glow of the fire, picking pieces of crispy flesh off their fish kebabs.

"This is delicious!" Creeper said, stuffing his mouth.

"Warmouth is my personal favorite," Perch said. "The meat's so flakey. Pickerel is good too."

Macey weighed in. "Nothin' beats a good catfish."

"I don't know," said Piper. "This may be the best fish I've ever had."

Perch waggled his eyebrows. "You could thank this swamp frog with a kiss, Princess."

Tad had had enough. "Let it go, dude. And quit calling her Princess. Her name is Piper."

Perch gave Tad a curious look. "Huh," he said. "I didn't pick up on it before, but I see it now. I'm usually quicker about this sort of thing."

"What are you talking about?" Tad grunted.

"Nothing," Perch said. "Nothing at all."

Macey stretched and yawned like a lion. "You kids can stay up jawin'. I'm hitting the hay. We get on the stick at dawn, so be up or I'll water yas."

Piper didn't know what "water yas" meant, and she didn't want to know.

There was one pup tent on the *Mud Cat*, and without being told, everyone knew who belonged to it. Macey unzipped the flap and disappeared inside. Two minutes later she was snoring like a buzz saw.

"I think I preferred the frogs." Piper snorted.

Perch grinned. "This *is* the Okefenokee, land of the trembling earth. Some days it trembles more than others."

Tad, reminded of his ordeal on the hammock, didn't think Perch's joke was funny.

The kids sat quietly for a while, listening to Macey snore. When Creeper finished his fish, he tossed his stick and fish bones into the fire and then bemoaned the absence of marshmallows. "What good is a campfire if we don't do campfire stuff?"

"What's campfire stuff?" Tad asked. He'd never been camping before. During his travels, he usually stayed in hotels, or at worst, hostels, which were a bit like the YMCA. Even the hostels had electricity and running water.

"You know!" Creeper said. "S'mores, sing-alongs, ghost stories."

Perch mulled it over. "Well, we don't have the ingredients to make s'mores, and if we sing, we might wake Macey—and trust me, you don't want to wake Macey. So I guess that leaves us with stories."

"Know any good ones?" Creeper asked. "The scarier, the better."

Tad had a request. "How about a tall tale from the Oke? As a swamp guide, you must know plenty. Tourists eat that stuff up, right?"

"I'm not in the mood for a ghost story," Piper said. "My nerves have been jangled enough for one day."

Perch thought for a moment, then said, "Actually, I have a story that might be right up your alley. It's about princesses."

"I don't want to hear some mushy story about a glass slipper and Prince Charming," Creeper groaned.

"It's not that kind of story. No kissing frogs either. This one takes place in the Okefenokee a long time ago."

Creeper perked up. "Okay, but if there's romance, tell me now so I can go to bed."

"Piper?" Perch asked permission.

She nodded. "Go ahead. But keep it light. Nothing too scary. I don't want Creeper having nightmares tonight."

Perch slid down to the grass and leaned back against the log, draping his arms over the top of it. He sat cross-legged to keep his feet away from the fire.

When he was settled comfortably, he told them the story of a magical island in the Okefenokee and the mystical people who lived on it. The story of the Daughters of the Sun.

10

"Thousands of years ago, the first humans arrived in the swamp and settled on an island somewhere deep within its dark heart. The legend says that the women of this tribe had black glistening eyes, like onyx, and skin the color of copper. They were so beautiful that any man who looked upon them would fall hopelessly in love forever. The women were, each and every one, princesses of the Oke, so beautiful that their island became known as the Land of the Daughters of the Sun.

"Naturally, the braves of the tribe wanted to keep these women for themselves and sought to safeguard them from invaders. When the first Seminoles arrived in the swamp and discovered the island, they became smitten with the Daughters of the Sun and begged the women to let them live on the island with them. The Daughters said no and warned the outsiders that their braves would be returning from a hunt soon and would surely kill the strangers on sight.

"The Seminole men left the island and returned to their people. But those lovesick puppies couldn't get the Daughters of the Sun out of their heads. So they gathered all their best warriors and set off in canoes. They figured they could use stealth and surprise to defeat the men of the island and take the squaws as their prize.

"As they neared the island, the Seminole warriors heard a horrible screeching noise above them, like from a giant bird. One they'd never heard before. An instant later, they were hit by a great wave that rolled in at them from across the swamp, seemingly out of nowhere. Most of their canoes were shattered and many men drowned, descending to their watery graves. The warriors who survived refused to give up, so bewitching was the beauty of the Daughters of the Sun. They continued on until they came to a wall of high sedge separating them from the island. They pushed through it, whooping and hollering their most fearsome war cries. But when they paddled out onto the lake where the island was supposed to be, they were met with shock and disappointment. The island was gone. Vanished without a trace. The Island of the Daughters of the Sun and its inhabitants had disappeared, never to be seen again."

Perch fell silent. He tore a few more strips of roasted warmouth off the bones with his teeth, then tossed the scraps into the fire. For a long while, he stared quietly, mesmerized by a fluttery moth that had come to court their flame. When Perch came out of his trance, he was surprised to find the others still staring at him with anticipation.

"Oh, um . . . The end," he concluded. "Forgot to add that part, sorry."

Creeper spread his hands to clap, but Perch raised a finger to his lips and glanced toward Macey's tent. "Bad idea."

Creeper whispered, "Do you suppose the sun people will ever come back?"

Perch lifted himself up onto his log and said, "It's just an old folktale, Creeper, my man. But to this day I still hear stories of some poor dummy who ventures into the Oke looking for the island and its women, and ends up lost."

"I bet the sun people are aliens," said Creeper. "And their island is a spaceship! I bet they come back every few years. Maybe Cole sneaked aboard their ship and was transported to some other dimension. I bet that's why he disappeared! Maybe he's trapped and needs our help!" Creeper was thinking like a true video-game addict.

"You're a fairly decent storyteller, Perch," Piper said. Stiff from sitting in the boat all day, she sat up tall on the log and twisted side to side until her back cracked twice. "But I think you got my brother worked up before bedtime."

"It's a work of fiction, buddy," Perch assured Creeper. "Trust me, if there was an island of beautiful women somewhere in the swamp, I would have found it by now." He knocked on the side of his head. "I've got built-in radar for that kind of thing. If you want my opinion, there's only one princess in this swamp, and we're sitting with her."

"Why do you keep calling me that?" Piper asked. "Who cares if I do pageants? It doesn't make me a bad person."

"Whoa there. I never said it did," Perch replied. "But for the life of me, I just can't figure you out. Tell me again. Why are you here?"

"What's that supposed to mean?" she asked. "I told you: I'm here to find the flower. I'm here to save Grace's life."

This answer didn't satisfy Perch. "This is a swamp. Pageant princesses don't come to swamps. For any reason. You're out of your element. It's painfully obvious how uncomfortable this all makes you: the alligators, the bugs, the heat . . . me."

Piper grew agitated. "So I'm not the best fit for a swamp. Big deal. What are you saying, that I should have stayed home and let my sister die?"

"Not at all," Perch said. "I'm saying most people would have just convinced themselves that the flower is a myth. But you did the opposite. You convinced yourself it's real. You believed, and it's because of you and you alone we're all here. That's what's got me stumped. There's some missing piece to the puzzle. Something you're not telling me. Something you're not telling any of us."

Piper picked with her fingernails at a bit of moss on her stump and sat quietly.

"I'm not wrong, am I?" Perch said. "Look, Piper, I'm going to help you find the flower if I can. You've made a believer out of me. Well, you and that vasculum. If I can trust you, then you can trust me."

Piper breathed a weary sigh. "I believe that the flower is a second chance. A chance to redeem myself for breaking a promise."

Somewhere off in the woods, a barred owl asked the strangest question: "Who cooks for you? Who cooks for you?" The call of this bird was unmistakable.

In Tad's mind, there was only one question that needed answering. "A promise to whom, Piper?"

The flames cast deep shadows across her face as she made a troubling confession. "A couple of years ago, I overheard our parents talking. They'd just come back from a visit to the doctor. My mother was crying. Dad was upset too. The doctor told them they couldn't have any more kids. Both of them came from big families. They wanted a big family too."

"I didn't know that," Creeper huffed. "Nobody tells me anything."

"You were the baby of the family," Piper told him. "And totally spoiled. You were so jealous when we got a cat that we had to give it away. Plus you were too young to know."

Her brother pouted. "Oh."

"Our parents weren't the only ones who took the news hard," she continued. "I was heartbroken. I desperately wanted a sister. More than anything. I'd always imagined what it would be like to have someone I could fuss over. Take care of. A little version of me I could teach things to, like how to catch fish or pitch a tent. A sister I could tell all my secrets to . . ."

"And the promise?" Perch asked.

"I remember the date, because it was just two days after Christmas, right after my parents got the bad news. It was nighttime. I was outside on the porch, staring up at the stars, freezing my butt off. One star drew my focus. It was pink, and at the time I hated pink.

But I sure didn't hate that star. It was beautiful, frozen in place, like God had pinned it to the sky just for me. I knew it had to be a sign."

"So you wished on a star?" Perch asked. "You wished for a baby sister?"

"Nope. I knew wishing wouldn't be enough," she said. "I felt I had to offer something in return. I promised that star . . . I promised the *whole* universe that if it would give me a baby sister, I'd take care of her like she was my very own. I would never be cross or mean or ignore her. I would keep her safe, no matter what. She could always have the last piece of cake, and I'd always let her watch her show on TV, even if *Supernatural* was on a different channel. I would do everything I could to make her life a happy one. That was my offer, and I knew that if I got my wish, I'd have to honor my promise no matter what."

"And then?" Perch prodded. "What happened then?"

Piper sniffed. "Ten months later, Grace was born."

A deep hush settled over their camp. The frogs were taking five, and the owl stopped interrogating them about the cook. The fire continued to pop and hiss, but even it seemed subdued, like someone had adjusted its volume control.

"That's an incredible story," said Perch.

"I don't put faith in astrology or omens or any of that stuff," said Tad. "But in your case, I think something special really did happen that night."

Feeling grateful, Piper put her head on Tad's shoulder. His support meant more than he knew.

"You made a promise, and the universe delivered," said Perch. "Seems like a bona fide miracle to me."

"That's how I felt," said Piper. "And I kept my part of the promise. For the first year, I acted like I was Grace's second mother. I couldn't have loved another human being more ferociously."

Perch thought he understood. "So you came to the Oke because you're living up to your end of the bargain. It all makes more sense now. I knew there was more to the—"

"No, that's not why I came." Piper could no longer hold back her tears. "Last year Grace was almost killed. I made a mistake, and I wasn't there to protect her. I blamed Tad unfairly, but it was my fault, not his. After that incident, I started to obsess over all the horrible things that might happen to Grace if I kept pretending I was her protector. I'd come so close to losing her once—I couldn't risk it again. I decided she was better off without me. I'd failed her, and rather than try harder, I pushed her away. I convinced myself it was for Grace's good, so I went back on my deal, and now the universe is punishing me. Grace is going to die, and I know it's because I broke my promise. I wished for a miracle and got one, and now she's fading away and there's nothing . . . there's nothing . . ."

Piper put her face in her hands and sobbed.

Tad slid across the log and wrapped his arm around her. "Grace did not get sick because of anything you did or didn't do. She got sick because people get sick. Even babies."

"I wish I could think that way." She sniffed. "But I can't. I believe in miracles."

"Well, like I said, you've made a believer out of me too," Perch said. "And that ain't an easy thing to do. You've earned your chance to make things right. If the flower is out here, we'll help you find it."

Tad gave Piper a squeeze on the shoulder. "Tomorrow we'll know."

Perch agreed. "I think that's our cue to get some rest. If we don't beat Macey to rise, she'll do as she threatened and water us. While that ain't as bad as you'd fear, it ain't as polite as you'd hope. Trust me, I know."

"Are you going to be okay, Creeper?" Piper received no reply. Not even good night. Her brother got up, dragged his sleeping bag a few feet farther from the fire, and wriggled his way inside. He rolled over, turning his back on her, and lay still.

"What's his problem?" Tad asked.

"Who knows?" Piper shrugged. "Past his bedtime, I guess."

The two older boys made sure the fire was well contained. Perch offered to stay up to watch for snakes. "The fire'll keep bears and gators away," he explained, "but rattlers are attracted to heat. I'm not worried, but since I don't sleep much anyway, I'll keep an eye out. Besides, Macey's got the tent, and I only brought three sleeping bags."

"If it's all the same, I'd like to take first watch," said Piper. "I already know I won't be able to sleep—I'm too anxious about tomorrow. And even though you said I'd get used to the frog jamboree, I'm pretty sure I won't."

"You want company?" Tad asked, hoping she'd say yes. "I can stay with you for a while."

"I'll be fine," she promised. "You guys get some rest."

"If you get chilly, there's a heavy blanket on the *Mud Cat*. Second bench. I can fetch it for you," Perch offered.

She smiled appreciatively. "I can get it. Thanks."

"Suit yourself."

"Good night, Piper." Tad didn't feel comfortable leaving her alone, but he could tell that's exactly what she wanted.

"Good night, Tad."

It wasn't long before everyone was fast asleep except for Piper. She hunkered down by the fire and tuned her ears to the rattlesnake channel. She thought of another rattle, the one in Grace's crib. Piper's heart ached at the mental image of her sister's perfect little face staring up at the lazily rotating teddy bear mobile above. Next she imagined the street in front of her house lined with police cars, their red and blue flashing lights shining through her neighbor's windows, drawing them out into their driveways in pursuit of gossip. She pictured police officers rifling through her house. The one in charge standing with a notepad, talking to her shell-shocked father. And another in the kitchen, pouring coffee for her sobbing mother. Several more were tearing her room apart, looking for clues that might explain why she and Creeper hadn't come home. It was all just horrible, and it was all her fault. She had to make sure the pain she was putting her parents through counted for something. She had to find the flower.

Piper drove the scenario from her mind and opened Cole's journal. Now that she'd spent time in the swamp, his insights made more sense. They weren't just the rambling of an excitable naturalist in his element, as she'd first thought. His account was a careful gathering of clues by a remarkably observant detective in pursuit of the swamp's number one most wanted—the silver flower.

When she reached the journal entry dated August 27, 1823, she reread a passage that brought her to a halt.

> *Because of my love of taxonomy, or perhaps out of sheer boredom, I have decided to assign this imaginary beast a fitting name. A good and proper Latin name. I have chosen one that translates literally as this: I drown, I bury, I overwhelm. I dub this laughable creature Mergo.*

Mergo.

There it was. She knew she'd seen it before. Cole hadn't just scrawled the word in blood on the map; he'd mentioned it in his journal too.

According to Cole's Seminole guides, Mergo was an evil spirit that existed solely to protect the flower from those who would seek to steal it from the swamp. Tad was right; Mergo *was* Latin. *I drown, I bury, I overwhelm.* She let that sink in. But Cole chose the name as a joke. Piper didn't think the joke was funny at all. She'd never really understood "nerd humor."

Piper decided not to share her findings with the others. The word meant nothing. Less than nothing. Slowly, quietly, she ripped the page free, wadded it up, and tossed it into the fire. She watched the paper blacken and shrivel until it fell between a gap in the charred kindling and vanished.

Mergo. I drown, I bury, I overwhelm.

Piper shivered.

She decided she wanted the blanket and set off down the trail toward the *Mud Cat*, using the flashlight as both a lamp and a snake detector. As Piper made her way to the dock, she had the unnerving sensation she was being watched from the shadows. And she knew it was likely that she *was* being watched. Not by evil spirits, but by the many nocturnal creatures that lived on Billy's Island. She played with one of the buttons on Perch's flashlight and discovered that by clicking the button, she could change the color from white to red to blue to green. She didn't know what the other colors were for, but white was brightest, so she clicked back to it. Bright was good.

When she reached the water, Piper crossed the dock and boarded the *Mud Cat* with great care. (Her brain couldn't fathom the horror of falling into the water at night. She would have a heart attack, for sure!) She retrieved the thick wool blanket inside the second bench. As she shut the lid, she heard a splash in the water behind her. Startled, she spun quickly and cast her light across the surface. At first there was nothing to see—just thousands of stars reflected on the swamp's mirrorlike surface. She breathed a sigh of relief.

But then she noticed that the stars had a strange greenish tint. They began to blink out, one by one. And then back on. And out again.

"Oh . . ." She understood now. They weren't stars at all.

She ran the beam up and out across the swamp, and everywhere the flashlight shone, it reflected back as tiny gleams in thousands of little eyes. All eyes were on her. They started moving toward the boat. Piper had never been so creeped out in her life. With the blanket in hand, she leaped onto the dock. Right into someone's arms.

"Gah!" she screamed.

"Don't be afraid," Perch said. "I've got you."

"What are you doing here?" she hissed, pushing him away. "You scared the poop out of me."

"Sorry about that. I didn't mean to. I woke up and noticed you were gone. I was worried, so I went looking for you."

"Well, you found me. I just came for the blanket you mentioned. I don't feel like standing out here all night." She moved to go around him.

Perch blocked her way. "You saw something upsetting. I can tell. What was it?"

"What did I see? Hmm, nothing much. Just this!" She shined the light on the water and waited for his appalled reaction, but he just raised one eyebrow and frowned. The green glints were gone. "I don't get it. . . . There were a gazillion blinking eyes in the water. Where'd they all go?"

"Probably just frogs. I'm not surprised they took off," Perch said. "You scream like a banshee when you're scared."

"Oh," she said, feeling stupid. "I suppose I did startle them."

"Yep."

"There were so many." she said. "Is that normal?"

"Frogs are amphibians and need both land and water to survive. I suspect they're displaying good sense by staying close to the islands."

"They're creepy. Why do their eyes glow like that?"

"It's not a glow," he corrected her. "It's a shine. Some animals have what's called a tapetum lucidum. It's a layer of tissue right behind the retina that reflects light. Humans don't have it. Most nocturnal animals do. Now, what's really interesting is that the color of the shine varies from animal to animal. Horses have blue eyeshine. Dogs and cats, green. Coyotes and rats have red eyeshine. Alligators have red eyeshine, too, which is why some folks think they look evil when you put a light to 'em at night. But the red is a reflection of the light, not of their nature."

"The eyes I saw were green," said Piper. "Maybe they were catfish."

He chuckled. "Nope, I was right. Frogs. Funny thing about them is how sensitive they are to their ecosystems. More so than any other species in the swamp. They're usually the first to know when something's off kilter in the water. Like if there's too much pollution or a surge in a predator species. I've noticed the frogs in the Oke have been acting a little screwy lately, but I'm sure it's nothing to worry about."

"Screwy? In what way?"

"For one, they're not as shy as they used to be. Well, you saw. They weren't afraid of you until you screamed at 'em. There were thousands, you say? That's an unusually big army."

"They were hardly an army," Piper scoffed.

"I didn't mean it to be cute," Perch said. "An army is the term for a group of frogs. Although come to think of it, they should probably be called a navy, since they spend most of their lives in the water. Dang it. I wish I'd brought my gigger."

"What's a gigger?"

"A frog gigger is a four-pointed spear especially designed for sticking Kermit. There's nothing more delicious than roasted frog's legs for breakfast."

"Ugh. You're like one of those pendulum clocks that swings back and forth between almost bearable and downright annoying. Please see a clockmaker to have that fixed at your earliest convenience."

"*Ha!* Well, Miss Piper, *you're* like a watch that's stuck on mean thirty."

"Mr. Gentner," she said in her best Southern belle voice, "I don't have to stand here and let you wind me up further." She shined the flashlight in his face. "You can come back with me to camp, basking in my spotlight, or you can stay here in the dark with more like-minded companions."

"Princess, you are a hoot." He took the blanket from her and tucked it up under his arm. "Lead the way."

Behind them, in the black water, a thousand eyes rose like bubbles to the surface.

August 27, 1823

Today is the nineteenth day of the expedition. While the swamp offers an embarrassment of botanical riches, the silver flower continues to elude us. Inclement weather has grounded our party on "Billy's" island for the day. The evening's downpour carried on into the morning and now into the afternoon. Nokosi believes it is safer to wait for the storm to pass, and I am left with no option but to defer to his timidity. As I write this entry, I sit just inside the flap of my tent, in the shadow of the great tumulus, watching purple veins of electricity pierce the dark skies in the distance. I understand the pivotal role that lightning plays in the swamp. It is the Lord's deputized arsonist. The fires sparked in its fury clear back the woody plants that would otherwise choke the waterways and make the swamp impenetrable. While I am grateful for this as a man of science, I am still just a man, and in that regard it unnerves me to be so flimsily protected inside the reach of nature's awesome tantrum.

But then there are a great many things that have tarnished my mettle over the last few days. It hasn't escaped my notice that Nokosi is deliberately keeping us on the cusp of some invisible border, confining our search to the east. I have heard one word repeated time and again during his heated conversations with Bolek, and always in fearful tones: *Isti-Papa.* I have yet to let on that I know this word. Isti-Papa is the name of the Creek culture's boogeyman, a name invoked to scare children into proper behavior. *Isti-Papa* translated literally means "Big Cannibal." I have yet to understand if and why this creature of bedtime stories is impeding my quest. It seems as though Nokosi believes Isti-Papa is real and that this creature, whatever it is, has laid claim to the west, establishing its monarchy there. I have traveled to the farthest reaches of the globe, immersing myself in many cultures, all of which told tales of wild beasts and malevolent spirits, and all turned out to be nonsense. I can no longer tolerate this fanciful impediment with good humor. I will speak to Nokosi when the rain breaks and insist that we forge west in the morning.

I admit I find the rather vague names the Creeks bestow on their natural surroundings to be a bit perplexing. Isti-Papa, for instance. A name should say more about a thing than just its dinner preference. A name lasts forever; therefore, it's important to put thought into the naming. Because of my love of taxonomy, or perhaps out of sheer boredom, I have decided to assign this imaginary beast a fitting name. A good and proper Latin name. I have chosen one which translates literally as this: *I drown, I bury, I overwhelm.* I dub this laughable creature *Mergo.*

Tomorrow, my guides *must* acquiesce. We will venture forth boldly into Mergo's sovereign domain together, or I will be forced to go alone. Tonight I will finish my work on the map. Even in this abysmal humidity, the vellum takes my ink well. Thank heavens for small blessings.

This lightning makes me silly.

11

At first light, Piper awoke to a soft hissing. She bolted upright in her sleeping bag and scanned the ground for snakes but saw none. The hissing, she realized, was the sound of their dying campfire being pelted by a drizzle of rain. Despite the fact that Macey was still fast asleep and dry in her tent, the group was being watered.

Piper and Tad scrambled to make sure Cole's map and journal were safely protected inside Tad's waterproof backpack. Perch and Creeper crammed the sleeping bags back into their compression stuff sacks before they could soak up moisture.

"Looks like we won't be cooking this morning," Perch said, pouring rainwater that had collected in Tad's sneakers into the sputtering fire to finish it off. A billow of smelly smoke rose like an evil genie, and Perch dispersed it with a wave of his hand. "I guess we'll have to make do with the snacks Macey keeps under her bench."

Tad snatched his shoes from Perch. "Great! Cigarettes for breakfast. Yum-yum."

"I heard that," Macey growled. The mama bear emerged from her nylon cave. She straightened slowly, one hand pressed flat against her lower spine for support. "Keep it up, boy, and you can starve."

Tad whispered to Piper, "Remind me to stop saying stupid things around that woman before she kills me."

"She's out of her 'backer," Piper reminded him. "Tread carefully."

Creeper was still in a dismal mood. He worked fine, carrying more than his share to the dock, but he didn't say one word during breakfast (crackers, peanut butter, Fruit Roll-Ups, and some of Macey's homemade deer jerky, which Piper couldn't eat because of the movie *Bambi*). His attitude remained sour even after they were back on the water and the drizzling had stopped.

"Sleep okay?" Piper asked him.

"I s'pose." He grunted, feigning an overly keen interest in a blue heron strutting in the shallows. The bird was looking for something edible to spear with its harpoon of a beak.

Piper figured her brother was just tired and didn't press him to talk. She, on the other hand, was wide awake, bursting with excitement. Macey had them plying the water at top speed (which was still slower than Piper would have liked, but Oke law stated that all boat motors had to be ten horsepower or less). They were heading west toward the spot Cole had circled on the map two hundred years earlier. No longer aimlessly wafting like a leaf, they were traveling straight and purposefully, like a torpedo.

A low fleece of mist hovered above the water in all directions. Piper drank in a deep breath. The Okefenokee was a swamp, so it would always have the musk of decaying plants and primordial earth, but after the rain, the air was fresher and the tannin-stained water gave off a pleasing scent like the iced tea at Cracker Barrel she loved so much.

"How long until we get there?" Tad asked Perch.

"Couple of hours. We got a good jump this morning, so with luck we'll be there before it gets hot."

For the first time, Piper noticed the red spiral cord running between a hook on Macey's overalls and a plug on the outboard motor. Piper plucked the cord. "What's this for, Macey?"

"Some people call it a dead man's switch, but that's a little morbid for my taste. Its proper name is a kill switch."

Piper didn't see much of a difference. "What's it do?"

"It's a safety precaution," said Macey. "If I fall out of the boat, the red lanyard"—she held up the coiled cord—"will tug on the kill switch and pull it free of the motor, shutting it down. Keeps the boat from leaving me behind, or worse, running me over."

"Couldn't Perch stop the boat and fetch you?"

"I used to cruise alone, so I needed it. Now it's just a habit." Macey patted her chest pocket again, but no cigarettes had magically appeared. "Sometimes good habits are as hard to break as the bad ones. Having a kill switch in place is never a bad idea."

An hour into the voyage, the Oke's ecosystem changed dramatically. The western half was much different from the eastern half. They left the prairies and hammocks behind as the waterways shrank and flooded forests dominated the swampscape. Pond cypress trees, some a hundred and fifty feet tall, compressed the passages, shaping the natural architecture of the west. Piper saw that the needles on the pond cypresses did not droop like the ones in Washington. Instead, they stood straight up on their branches, as if they'd seen a ghost. Maybe they had—the Oke felt full of them.

She noticed something else unusual about the cypress trees. A few feet from their submerged trunks, several small knobby stumps jutted up from the water. The stumps looked a bit like melted candles, but they were wood, not wax.

"What are those, Creeper? You're the tree expert."

He shrugged. "Dunno."

"Them're called knees," Macey said. "We don't know much about them. We think they're support systems, absorbing nutrients from the air and passing them along underwater to the tree."

"Cool!" Piper said. "Isn't that cool, Creeper?"

He shrugged again.

"Maybe after we find the flower, we'll stop and you can climb one of the big ones. What do you think?"

This time he didn't even give her the courtesy of a shrug.

Perch was unusually quiet too. He looked focused. Anxious, maybe. Piper hadn't known him long enough to read his serious face. She decided it would be best if she kept her enthusiasm to herself.

After another half hour passed, they came upon a gloomy, gray part of the swamp. It was as if all the color had been leached out of the world.

Perch said, "Stop the boat, Macey," and she did. "We've reached the part of the Oke that got burned up in last year's big fire. The Rowell's Island Fire."

Since they'd departed Billy's Island, the morning mist had dissipated everywhere else, but here it was corralled by the barren trees, a massive cloud caged by grotesque black spindles covered in scaly, charred bark. There was no green here. The intermittent strips of land looked crispy and fallow. Everything smelled of soot.

"This is horrible," Piper murmured.

"The trees look like burned pencils," said Creeper. "They're scary."

That's a first, thought Piper. Creeper had never met a tree he didn't like.

"Reminds me of the river Styx," said Tad. "The underworld, in Greek mythology. It's the river that separates the land of the living from the realm of the dead."

Piper agreed. It did feel as though they'd entered a murky netherworld, one completely devoid of life.

"It's the same thing that happens time and again in the Oke," Macey said. "Lightning."

"Like Macey mentioned before," said Perch. "This swamp is notorious for wicked lightning storms. We get them every year, May through September. It's especially dangerous after a long drought. Swamp fires can rage for weeks, if not months, sometimes smoldering underground for days, undetected, waiting to erupt."

Somewhere from deep in the mist came a hoarse, screeching wail. *Kee-eeeeee-arrr.* Piper stiffened. In the story of the Daughters of the Sun, the Seminole warriors heard a horrific cry right before they were hit with the wave that decimated their armada. Piper braced for a tsunami, but it never came.

"Red-tailed hawk," Perch said. "Nothing to fear. Some animals died in the fire, but most of the birds flew away and the burrowers burrowed. Turtles, snakes, gators, gophers—they're all fine. Looks like the critters are coming back."

"The forest itself seems pretty dead," Tad said.

"It's not," said Perch. "The ground plants will bounce back soon, but it may take several years for the canopy to fill in again. Fires are a necessary evil in the Oke. They clear back the invading brush and woody plants that'd otherwise clog the waterways and eventually turn the swamp into a regular forest. Heck, if it weren't for the fires, this swamp would be mostly woodlands now, and I'd have to hock my boat and start offering walking tours of the Oke. It'll be slow going, but this burned section is all that stands between us and the circle on Cole's map. In another mile we'll be outside the park's boundaries. Mace and I have never gone this far west before. Y'all ready for this?"

"We've come this far," said Piper, speaking for the group.

"Okay, then," said Perch. "Take us in, Mace. Go slow."

"Aye, aye." Macey adjusted the throttle, and the boat motored into the charred and flooded forest. Perch scouted ahead with keen eyes as he guided them through the maze of mist, crumbling trees, and shadows.

To Piper, it felt as though they were passing through an uneasy dream. In the mist it was impossible to see more than ten feet in any direction. It seemed to roll in behind them, erasing the *Mud Cat's* wake. Erasing the world. One by one, black trees emerged from the mist, then faded again as the boat passed. There were untrustworthy sounds everywhere. Some of them Perch could identify—the call of a screech owl, the splash of a turtle slipping off a log, splashing into the water; other sounds he could not, and was sometimes startled by them. Silhouettes were moving everywhere. In a branch hanging low over the water, they spied a large dark shape, like a snake wearing a Dracula cape. As the *Mud Cat* passed underneath the limb, the shape was exposed as an S-necked anhinga bird fanning its wings.

Underwater, things bumped against the submerged part of the hull. Piper feared there were creatures down there testing the boat's integrity for nefarious reasons. At least there were no fallen trees to trammel their way. Rather, the dead cypresses loomed tall above them, creaking eerily against the nudge of the hot summer breeze.

"Does this go on forever?" Creeper asked. It seemed that way. He was anxious to be out. They all were.

Perch pointed. "I see something up ahead."

"Well, I'll be jiggered," said Macey. "Jewelwing damselflies."

The *Mud Cat* was suddenly surrounded by hundreds of beautiful insects. They looked like dragonflies, only with leaner, teal-blue bodies that glinted like metal in the light. They flew on jet-black wings, jouncing like papery marionettes on wires. Full of curiosity, the damselflies flitted through the gawping group. Some of them landed, clinging to their clothes and hair and even to Perch's extended index finger, turning him into his namesake. The damselflies hovered around them for a short while, then regrouped into a loose, gleaming cloud in front of the bow. The insects moved ahead of the boat but didn't abandon it. The *Mud Cat* followed as they fluttered low above the water trail.

"Looks like we've got ourselves escorts," Perch said.

The damselflies ushered the crew and passengers of the *Mud Cat* out of the mist, and they emerged into a vista of jarringly vibrant greens.

The canopy returned, burgeoned with foliage thick and lush. Lichens and vines patinated the trees. The grasses growing on patches of land were garishly bright, almost neon—mint, lime, mantis, olive, chartreuse, pine green, and more. Even the water was green, carpeted in algae, lily pads, sphagnum moss, and all manner of aquatic plants, most of them exploding with flowers.

"Whoa." Creeper's eyes widened to take it all in. "Everything's so green! It's like we're in *The Matrix*!"

"We must have passed beyond the border of the fire," Tad said.

"I don't think so," said Perch. "Look at the tree trunks. They're charred and scaly, just like the ones in the mist. This part of the Oke was burned too."

"How is that possible?" Piper asked. "Everything looks so . . . alive."

"I don't know," Perch admitted. "I've never seen the swamp have such a quick and aggressive resurrection after a fire. This kind of recovery should take decades. Look at that tree—" He pointed at one of the tallest and most grossly blistered cypress trunks. It was veiny with bright green creepers. "Those vines are fresh. They sprouted *after* the fire. You can tell by the healthy coloring and the buds. But that makes no sense. See how they grew all the way up into the canopy? Normally, it would take ten years for a vine to grow that high."

Suddenly, as if they'd hit a wall of glass, the damselflies made an abrupt U-turn, orbited the boat one more time, and then fluttered away, back toward the mist.

Creeper craned his whole torso to see them off. "Bye!"

"Well, that was different," Macey grunted.

Piper sensed that if Macey hadn't encountered something in the Oke before, it must be truly rare.

The *Mud Cat*'s motor spit and sputtered, shoving them on down the narrow. For the first time since they arrived at the Oke, Piper saw the swamp through the eyes of Dr. Brisbane Cole and Perch Gentner. Especially here, in this greenest of places, the Okefenokee was a living, breathing paradise. A drowned but thriving Eden. She noticed everything: the cluster of little blue herons stepping high though a field of water lilies; a lovely purple gallinule preening its feathers in the muck, casting a watchful eye at the boat as it passed; a feather-light dragonfly lying in the film of the water's surface, resting before takeoff; glossy turtles and jewel-eyed alligators sunning. The life here, in all its forms, was beautiful.

"I wish I'd brought a camera," said Piper.

"I did, remember?" Tad said. "The disposable kind. I forgot about it. It's in my backpack, if you want to use it."

Tad's backpack was resting on the floor next to Creeper's feet. "Find the camera for me, will you?" Piper asked him.

He tossed her the backpack. "You find it. I'm not your servant." His attitude was still downright rancid.

"Ugh!" Piper found the camera and snapped off a few shots.

Tad saw something that excited him. He went to stand up for a better look, felt the boat rock, and sat back down. "Up there, look!" He pointed into the trees. "See those things that look like little tumbleweeds stuck to the branches? Those plants are called Bartram's bromeliads. They're named after one of the Oke's first explorers.

They extract nutrients right out of the air. So cool! I wish I had some of those in my greenhouse."

"That's sad," Perch snorted.

"What's sad?" Tad asked, bristling.

"It's sad that you have a greenhouse," said Perch.

"What's wrong with owning a greenhouse?" asked Piper.

"Greenhouses are nothing but glass cages. Zoos for plants. Look around, kids! This here"—Perch spread his arms wide—"is *my* greenhouse. All these plants are exactly where they're supposed to be, out in the wild green yonder, not stuck in clay urns."

"You mean flowerpots?" Tad was angry now. "My plants do just fine, thanks!"

"You're a jailer," said Perch. "A plant warden."

"You know—" This time Tad did stand up. "I've had just about enough of—"

The boat slammed to a halt, sending Tad sprawling across Perch's bench. Perch caught him and helped him up. "You okay?"

"Yeah, I think so," Tad said, checking himself over. "What the heck was that?"

The *Mud Cat*'s motor was still blubbering away, but the boat wasn't moving.

"Macey?" Perch asked. "Did you—?"

"Wasn't my doing," she said.

They peered over the side. There was nothing there, just black water green-topped with sprigs of algae.

"We're probably hung up on a sunken tree. Throw 'er in reverse," Perch suggested. "Let's give that a whirl."

Macey tried to take the boat backward. It lurched a foot or two, but then it stopped dead. She went forward, then backward again. After a few tries to shimmy the boat loose, the slack tightened and the *Mud Cat* was stuck fast. Macey declared the boat "dug in like a tic on a dog's behind."

"Now what?" Piper asked.

Perch stood up and took off his shirt.

"Here we go again," Tad muttered.

"I have to find out what we're hung up on," Perch told them. "That means getting in the water and going under the boat."

"Is that even safe?" asked Piper.

"Safe enough. Cut the motor, Macey," Perch ordered. "I'd prefer if the blades weren't spinning while I'm down there. I like my haircuts just a little off the top, and I don't mean the top of my neck."

His first mate threw the choke. The motor fell silent. "Be careful, son."

"Be back in a jiff." With a nimble leap, Perch was over the gunwale and in the water.

Piper knelt on the bench and leaned over the side. She found Perch bobbing there.

"It's deep," he said. "I'm treading. Not touching the bottom."

"How deep?" asked Creeper.

"The Oke is relatively shallow. Eight feet is considered deep," Perch said. "It's deeper than that, I think. Gonna see what's holding up the *Mud Cat*."

Perch took a gulp of air, then dropped down into the murk. All they could do was wait. And wait. And wait.

A minute passed.

"How long can a person hold their breath underwater?" Tad wondered aloud. "Isn't this pushing it?"

Fretful creases formed on Macey's brow. "In the navy, I was stationed in Japan for a spell. I met a pearl diver there who could stay under for seven minutes. But for most people, a minute is tricky. Perch was rightly named after a fish—he can stay under for two, but that's pushing it."

The second minute passed.

"That's it. Something's wrong. I'm going after him." Tad started to untie his sneakers. The sun had them half-dried, and he wasn't about to undo that progress.

"No, I'll go." Piper stripped off her shirt, revealing a polka-dotted swim top underneath. "I'm a better swimmer than you, Tad. I've got the Camp Get-Along Summer Games trophy to prove it."

"That was six years ago!" he reminded her.

Piper sat on the gunwale and tossed one leg over the side. The last thing she wanted to do was jump into a swamp full of alligators, but if something happened to Perch, the game would be stopped short of the goal line. Her fear of losing Grace was greater than her fear of losing a limb. Plus, if she had to be honest, Perch was starting to grow on her. "I got him into this mess. I'll get him out."

"Piper, wait—" Tad reached out to stop her, but she was gone.

For the first several seconds, Piper slowly flapped her arms underwater and refused to open her eyes. She was terrified of letting any invading microscopic monsters get past her lids. Plus she was certain that if she opened them, she would see something big and toothy coming for her, and then nothing ever again. But she couldn't help Perch if she couldn't see him, so she pried her eyes open and had a look around.

The water was a little clearer than it had seemed from above. Piper could see the motor's still propeller. Like the object of her hunt, it had silver petals.

The *Mud Cat* was completely free of obstruction. Perch had done his job. Piper turned a full three hundred and sixty degrees, but there was no sign of him anywhere. She looked down through her feet and spotted him. He was at the gloomy bottom, ten feet down, struggling inside of a growing cloud of silt. Struggling *against* something. Perch was snared in a web of thick vines. He must have removed them from the *Mud Cat* but got himself hog-tied in the process. Piper torpedoed down into the cloud to rescue him.

146

She grabbed hold of the thickest vine, the one looped around his thigh, and tugged. It was tight, and Perch's flailing made it even tighter, but she was persistent and managed to unbind his leg. The vine sank to the bottom. Next, they worked together to leverage him loose of the one that had cinched around his midriff. With the first two vines no longer weighing him down, he was able to snap the one around his wrist with a jerky uppercut, and just like that he was free. Completely out of air, Perch couldn't afford to wait on Piper. He bolted toward the boat like a water-to-surface missile. Piper tried to follow but realized that her ankle was snared in a swaying tuft of vines, and she couldn't get free. She'd come to save Perch but had merely taken his place.

She reached down and tugged with all her might. With her arms busy pulling instead of treading, she began to sink down into the tangle. There were so many vines, a jungle of them! If she didn't break away quickly, she'd find herself wrapped up like a mummy. Piper kicked and yanked and twisted, but the vine was like an animal snare, tightening as she struggled.

Something moved inside the tangle. Something big. Piper peered into the vines. Two round yellow eyes snapped open in scaly sockets and peered back.

An alligator burst through the vines, its mouth gaped wide, its pointed teeth exposed and lethal. The beast chomped down hard and missed her face by inches. She could hear the dulled clacking of the two halves of the gator's jaw slamming together like leather paddles over and over. Perch said alligators weren't man-eaters. He was so wrong! Piper swished backward to get away, but she knew the beast was in its element, easily the faster swimmer. She braced herself for the coming death roll, hoping she'd drown quickly so she wouldn't have to watch her limbs being wrenched away from her body then gulped down a monster's throat. No one should have to witness that.

But the gator was tangled up, too, and so much worse. It could barely move, other than to thrash its head and chomp empty water. Vines had coiled around its legs, tail, and neck. As desperate as it was, the alligator was unable to cross the distance between them. Why then, Piper wondered, was it so intent on killing her instead of saving itself? Alligators didn't have gills. They needed air or they'd drown. It didn't make sense.

Piper kicked at the beast, hoping it would break off the attack. The gator snapped at her foot but missed. Instead it snagged the vine knotted around her ankle and started swinging Piper through the water, before its sharp teeth shredded the vine, setting her free.

Without looking back to thank her savior, Piper swam toward the surface.

"There she is!" Creeper shouted when Piper's head bobbed up above the surface. Tad and Macey reached down to pull her aboard.

Creeper, near tears, helped her onto a middle bench. He sat close to her and kept patting her hand, asking over and over if she was okay. She answered with nods of her body.

Perch, she saw, was on the floor, unmoving. Tad hovered over his face. "I don't think he's breathing! I'm gonna try CPR." He leaned in to attempt mouth-to-mouth resuscitation.

Perch palmed Tad's face and moved it away. "Let's just stay friends," he croaked, staring blankly at the sky.

"Suits me," Tad said. "What happened down there?"

When Perch had regained enough strength to sit up, he squeaked out his story. They realized how lucky he was to be alive.

"When I dove in, I found a fat vine wound around a metal plate on the transom. I managed to yank it over the top of the plate, but then the vine looped around my leg and dragged me to the bottom, where there were more vines. I got all tangled up. Next thing I knew, I was fighting for my life. Honestly, Piper, if it weren't for you, I'd be a goner. I'm obliged."

"You'd have done the same for me," Piper assured him, and left it at that. She didn't see the point in telling them about the gator. It would only upset Creeper more, and he was already a mess.

Tad handed Perch his T-shirt. "Yeah, yeah, she's a hero and you're grateful. Now put this on."

"Thanks, buddy. I will." Perch wrapped the shirt around his head like an Arab kaffiyeh.

"I give up," Tad muttered, then plunked down on the bench.

Macey put her hand on Perch's shoulder. "You okay, son?"

"I'm good, Mace. Sorry if I scared you."

"That you did."

"Let's get out of here," Perch said.

They took their positions in the boat, and Macey fired up the motor. The *Mud Cat* was on the move again.

After just two minutes of travel, Tad jumped up and crawled to the back. He leaned over Macey, tracking something with his eyes. "Stop the boat!" he ordered.

Macey thumped him in the gut with her elbow. "Go sit, dummy."

"No! Stop the boat!" Tad was insistent.

"Mace, stop the boat," Perch ordered. "Let's see what his problem is now."

She throttled down. "Whadja see, boy?"

"Right over there," Tad pointed. "Look at those two big cypress trees."

"What about them?" asked Piper.

"See how they're fused together at the middle of their trunks? Like a squished letter *H*."

"So?"

"So? Look at Cole's map!" Tad said. "He drew those exact two trees."

Piper unrolled the vellum and held it up to compare. Tad was

149

right; they were a match. Cole had been right here, in this very spot, sitting in a canoe, some two hundred years before. Examining the map, Piper realized something else. "Guys . . ." She could feel her heart thrumming in her chest. The boys saw it too.

"How dumb could we be?" Tad said, shaking his head.

The *H* trees, they saw, were *inside* the circle Cole had drawn on the map.

"*We're* inside the circle." Piper was breathless. "We've *been* inside it for a while."

With the aid of a dead botanist, a long shot had just become a real chance. Almost there, Grace, thought Piper. Almost there. She took a photograph of the trees for posterity.

Click!

On the bottom of the swamp, directly below the boat, something massive and ancient was prodded aware. A faint current had poked at its mouth, and the thing opened wide. The current meandered across its fleshy pink tongue, carrying with it an unusual taste. One that pleased it very much. The ancient thing had lived in the swamp for more than two hundred years, and in that time it had devoured thousands of living creatures. But this flavor was unique. The ancient thing liked this taste very much. It shivered, sending plumes of silt rolling across the swamp floor. Frightened fish scattered in all directions; they'd been feeding in the ridges of its back and sensed that the buffet was closed.

The ancient thing craned its broad head toward the surface and saw the black silhouette of the *Mud Cat*'s belly.

The creature began to rise.

August 28, 1823

After much cajoling, Nokosi agreed to expand our search to
the western part of the swamp. It is clear that this decision
does not sit well with either of my companions, and for a few
tense moments, I feared they contemplated mutiny. Yesterday
I came to the final page of my journal while chronicling the
kidnapping of a baby alligator that was carried aloft in the
clutch of osprey talons and devoured by the bird's newly hatched
offspring. Fortunately, I thought to bring a new journal, and
this is the opening entry in what I suspect will be a fascinating
story when read as a whole. I left the completed journal with
my belongings at camp, and we set out in a westward line.
Several hours later, we crossed an invisible marker—I cannot
tell you exactly when—and found ourselves in a section of the
Okefenokee quite different from any we'd seen thus far: a self-
contained oasis of such monochromatic green that at times it
feels as though we are plying through chlorophyll instead of
water. Even the low-hanging clouds appear the color of mint, due
to the light reflected from the lush vegetation. These primordial
wetlands teem with life. The breezes come and go with such tidal
consistency that it feels as though the swamp itself is breathing.

My companions seem agitated. Nokosi fears this place. It is
evident in his eyes and his murmuring. Prayers stream from
his lips, but to which gods I cannot tell. The Creeks have many.
Bolek doesn't pray to anyone or anything. At times I catch him
staring at me. Sneering. At others I see his eyes lingering on
the satchel nestled between my feet in the canoe. His obsession
with my vasculum is evident. The great bard Shakespeare wrote
in *Othello*: "Beware, my lord, of jealousy; it is the green-eyed
monster which doth mock the meat it feeds on."

Even here, it would seem that the green of envy is the most
vivid green of all.

12

"That's crazy, Perch," Tad argued. "Plants simply aren't capable of doing what you're claiming. It's physically impossible."

Perch sat on his bench, swamp water dripping from his pant legs and pooling at his feet in the bottom of the *Mud Cat*. The happy-go-lucky kid they'd first met was gone. "I'm telling y'all, what happened down there wasn't normal. The more I think about it . . . yes, I'm certain. Those vines were trying to kill me."

Tad turned to Piper for her eyewitness account. "You were down there too. What did *you* see?"

"I didn't see anything, but that doesn't mean he's wrong."

Creeper was still sitting next to her, but he'd scooched across the bench a few inches to give her breathing room. At least he wasn't being an insufferable grouch anymore. They'd stayed on a steady course bearing northwest, confident in their heading. While Perch composed himself, Macey was pulling double duty as sternman and navigator.

"Piper, you must have seen it too!" Perch insisted. "How could you not?"

"I saw you tangled up in the vines," she told him, "but I never got the impression that they were deliberately trying to drown you.

If they were tightening, it was probably because you were flailing around in them."

Tad leaned back, confident that Piper's input had proven his take on events to be the more rational of the two. "Perch, it was dark down there. One minute you were freeing the boat and the next you were drowning. You panicked. No one could blame you for assuming you were under attack."

"Maybe." Perch flicked a piece of clingy algae off his forearm. "I can't deny it was confusing."

"Vines aren't boa constrictors," Tad said. "They don't deliberately strangle people."

Piper remembered the mimosa plant in Tad's greenhouse. "Are you sure? You said some plants can move quickly, right? What did you call it? Rapid plant movement?"

"Some plants can move quickly, yes," Tad admitted. "But not vines. And they definitely don't go after prey like Perch is suggesting."

"None?" she asked.

"No." But then Tad remembered an exception to the rule. "Well . . . unless you count *Cuscuta pentagona.* The dodder vine."

"The daughter vine?" Creeper misunderstood.

"No, *dodder.* Rhymes with *odder.* The dodder vine isn't capable of moving quickly, but it does hunt."

"It hunts?" Perch said. "What do you mean?"

"Plants get their energy from the sun," said Tad. "They absorb sunlight through the pigment chlorophyll contained in their cells, the same pigment that gives plants their green coloring. The dodder vine lacks chlorophyll. Without it, the dodder can't absorb sunlight and convert it into energy through the process of photosynthesis. This means that unlike most plants, the dodder can't make its own food. So it adapted the ability to 'smell' prey and literally hunt it down."

"What kind of prey, Big Brain?" asked Perch. "You mean animals? People?"

Great, Tad thought. A nickname. He shook his head. "No, the dodder vine is too small for that. It only grows to about three feet long. It preys on other plants. Its favorite is the tomato. When a dodder sprouts up from the ground, it has to find a host to feed on quickly, or it'll die. The vine starts moving its tip in little circles, like a blind snake sniffing for rats." Tad held up his index finger to mimic the dodder sprout. He whirled it in the sign for *whoop-de-do*. "It's searching for something yummy with its unique smell receptors. If the vine smells a scent it likes, it grows through the air toward it. When it reaches the other plant, it wraps itself around its victim's stalk, burrows its tip inside, and starts sucking down the plant's nutrients, like a vampire. The dodder feasts until the other plant dies, and then it has to start the hunt all over again."

"So you don't think the vines that trapped the *Mud Cat* and almost killed me could be related to the dodder?" Perch asked. He was having real trouble accepting that the whole thing had been an accident, and probably his fault.

Tad set him straight. "The dodder doesn't *lunge* at prey. It *grows* at it. Through the air. It can take days for the vine to reach a plant that's only a few feet away. Since the tomato can't uproot and run away, the dodder can take its sweet time. It doesn't strike quickly, like snakes."

Perch sagged. "I suppose you're right, then. I guess I was just careless. I feel as dumb as a box of rocks."

Piper rubbed his knee. "Don't be hard on yourself. You got us moving again. You were great."

"Thanks," he said, brightening a bit.

Macey brought them back to the present. "Y'all need to start payin' attention to the view. If Cole's map is accurate, we'll be on top of that flower of yours soon. I only got two eyes, so y'all better start looking."

The kids spread out in the boat. Creeper and Piper took lookout on the starboard side of the swamp, Tad the port side. Perch searched ahead, and Macey sat with her legs straddled over the back bench, making sure to catch the flower if it slipped past the others. For the next half hour, there was little chatter.

Although nature in this unexplored region of the swamp was wildly robust, the water looked putrid and stagnant. It wasn't brown like the tannin-rich waters of the Oke's lakes and canoe trails. Here, it was a vile shade of yellow-green, the color of cartoon acid. Of course it wasn't corrosive; the menagerie of animals darting around in it was proof that it was livable, but those very same animals made it no less dangerous than acid. This wasn't the Oke that Cole had been so enamored of. This place was something else, a primeval soup teeming with skulking life-forms. Some of them, like the alligator, had outlived the dinosaurs.

Macey unexpectedly powered down the *Mud Cat*, and it came to a stop.

"Gad night a living," she muttered. She was sitting up as straight as a post, staring back in the direction they'd come from.

"Macey, what are you—?"

She flapped her hand, and Perch shushed instantly. "Just *look*," she said.

Piper didn't see anything at first, save for a solitary sandhill crane gliding low above the water thirty yards off. But then, suddenly and in a powerful fit of violence, an enormous adult alligator burst upward from the lily pads, leaped ten feet out of the water, and snatched the bird in its powerful jaws. In that instant when gravity latched hold to pull the beast back down, it hung in the air, allowing Piper a good look at the rubbery white tile of its underbelly. Then the beast dropped like a stone below the surface, taking the doomed crane with it.

"Cool!" Creeper cheered.

"Why, Macey?" Piper wailed. "Why would you want us to see *that*?"

"Hush up, girl," Macey snapped. *"Keep looking."*

"I see them too," said Perch. "My God."

It took longer for the others to see it. They weren't used to spotting animals so expertly designed to blend in with their environment. But eventually they saw. A dozen or more alligators—big ones, judging by the width of the space between their raised eyes—were hanging back, lined up in a row, staring in their direction.

Piper gasped. "What are they doing over there? Are they following us?"

"No," Tad said. "They're *stalking* us."

"That's ridiculous," said Macey. "Gators ain't like that. They don't stalk boats, and they don't hunt in packs."

"Macey's right," said Perch.

"Sure looks like a pack to me," Tad agreed.

The alligator that had caught the crane surfaced in the center of the line. Soggy feathers stuck out sideways through the gaps between its yellow teeth. It almost seemed to be smiling.

"At least they're staying put," said Perch. "Keeping a reasonable distance. I don't think we have to worry about them."

"Can we go?" Piper asked, trembling. "Please? Can we just go?"

"I think that'd be smart," Macey agreed. She got them moving again.

But as the *Mud Cat* puttered northwest, the alligators followed. They didn't rush forward to close the gap. Instead, they hung back, leaving a thirty-yard span of water between their toothy line and the boat.

"They *are* stalking us!" said Tad. "Why are they stalking us?"

"I honestly don't know" was all Perch could say. "This is a first. I have to admit, they're giving me heebie-jeebies. This place . . . it's not natural."

Where the *Mud Cat* went, the alligators went with it. When it slowed, they slowed. When the boat sped up, they used their powerful tails as rudders, propelling themselves faster through the water to keep up. Perch asked Macey to throttle down so they could discuss a new plan.

"What do you think, Mace?" he asked.

"We're not gonna be able to shake them, that's for sure," she replied. "If I push the motor, the boat will reach twenty miles per hour, but we might plane out. Gators can swim faster than the *Mud Cat*'s top speed, especially those big bruisers. Some of them're at least fifteen feet long, judging by the width of their skulls."

"This doesn't feel right," said Perch. "I think . . . I think it's time to leave. Maybe we can find a detour. Or a strip of land, lead them around it, and—"

"No!" Piper couldn't believe her ears. "We can't go home now! We're so close. We have to be. We'll go back when we find the flower. Macey, tell him!"

This time, however, Macey sided with her partner. "I know what this means to y'all," she said. "Believe me, I do. But these gators, they're just not right in the head. Perch and I . . . we're responsible for you kids. I understand how you feel, but—"

"No you don't!" Piper shot to her feet and yelled in Macey's face. "How could you possibly know how I feel?"

Piper waited, fists clenched at her sides, chest heaving, for Macey to answer. The others were too stunned to speak.

There was a long, heavy pause as Macey sat on the bench, silent, a wounded look on her face. The deep folds in the weathered skin of her forehead squinched tight. She started to roll up her right sleeve. For a moment, Piper was afraid Macey might hit her, but the *Mud Cat*'s sternman was just uncovering the tattoo on her forearm. The one that read *Georgia*.

"Mace." Perch sighed. "It's none of her business."

"Yes, it is," Macey said. "I'm making it so."

"So what?" said Piper. "You have a tattoo that says 'Georgia.' What does that have to do with diddly?"

"It has everything to do with everything," said Macey. "Georgia was my daughter's name."

"Your daughter?" It never occurred to Piper that Macey might have a family—unless you counted Perch, which the woman obviously did.

Macey rubbed her arm, smoothing out the wrinkled and slightly sagging canvas of the tattoo. She eyed it sadly. "My Georgia . . . she liked to play with dolls. She was real good at it. Took them everywhere she went. Gave them their babas three times a day. You could set a clock by their feeding schedule. Georgia would have turned thirty-eight last month. Probably would've had two or three kids of her own by now. She would have been a terrific mother, that's for sure."

"What happened to her, Macey?" Tad asked respectfully.

"Georgia was only six. Her Jack Russell terrier Whipper got free from the yard. It was my fault. I'd forgotten to latch the gate. Georgia chased that pooch down the sidewalk. Whipper darted out between two parked cars into traffic. The dog made it across fine, but Georgia . . ." Macey faltered. She patted the top pocket of her overalls flat. "Lord, my kingdom for a cigarette. That'll teach me to pack light."

"I'm really sorry, Macey." Piper's eyes brimmed with tears. She'd been wrong. Nobody understood what she was going through better than Macey. "I'm so sorry for what I said." She felt a desperate need to hug the woman, but Macey seemed to shake off her melancholy, and the opportunity passed.

"It's okay, darlin'. It was a long time ago. A hitch in the navy seemed like a good way to get out of my head about it. One thing you'll learn in the service is that people have it rough all over. It helps to know we're not alone in our suffering. And I'll tell you one more thing I learned in my travels: hanging on to regret won't help anyone. Not me, not you, and not that baby sister of yours back home. What's happening to her is no more your fault than it is hers. You spend enough time in the Oke and you'll learn that lightning strikes wherever it dang well pleases, and there's nothin' we can do about it but fight the fires as best we can. And sometimes we lose. No matter what happens, you will go on, and you'll find a way to be happy."

Macey's words made Piper feel a little better and a little sadder at the same time. She wondered how different the woman would look if her daughter hadn't been killed all those years ago. Still big and burly, but instead of overalls she might have on a pretty blouse or a WORLD'S BEST GRANDMA T-shirt. And instead of a tattoo of a battleship, maybe there'd be a stylish scarf wrapped around her neck. Or possibly adoring grandchildren.

"I understand what you're saying." Piper reached out and took Macey's hand. "But, Macey, what if you could go back in time and latch the gate to your yard? Wouldn't you do anything for that chance? I believe the silver flower is my last chance to lock the gate on Grace's illness while I still can. I have to try. Please help me."

Macey gave Piper's hand a gentle squeeze. "You're a persuasive girl—I'll give you that. Not many people can get this old mule to change her mind. I'll leave it up to our captain."

"Piper, I don't want to give up either," Perch said, "but if someone gets hurt, I couldn't live with myself."

"You can have the vasculum," said Piper. "If you'll let us keep going, it's yours."

"What? No, it is *not* his!" Tad's objection was forceful. "Cole's vasculum is an important piece of science history. It belongs in a museum. It has value because of what it represents, not just because it's made out of gold. Perch would probably melt it down or pawn it off for a quick buck!"

"Now, hold on a minute, Tad—" Perch rushed to his own defense.

"No, you hold on!" Tad snarled. "That vasculum is going to the Smithsonian or, better yet, the Fernbank Museum so people in Georgia can enjoy it."

"On whose say?" Perch asked.

"On my say! Cole was my ancestor. By right, that makes the vasculum mine!"

Perch snorted. "Obviously, you haven't heard of a well-known legal precedent known as Finders Versus Keepers!"

Piper circumvented their argument. "Perch, think of it," she implored. "My dad was reading the financial section of the paper the other day, and I overheard him tell my mom that gold is worth more than a thousand dollars an ounce now. The vasculum has to weigh, what, two pounds? That's over thirty thousand dollars! It's probably worth even more to an antique collector or history buff. You could buy a whole *fleet* of *Mud Cats* with that kind of money. Think of what it would mean for your business."

Perch glanced past Macey, back at the gathering of alligators. They were buoyed in the water, as still as logs. There were so many, clustered tightly together, all in a row, findable by their raised eyes and nostrils. "It's funny; when I was a kid, I saw this one cartoon where Tarzan crossed a river by jumping around on the backs of crocodiles. Things sure seem more plausible in cartoons, don't they?" Perch sighed.

"Please," Piper begged.

"To be honest"—Perch stared at his toes—"business hasn't been that great lately. I wish I could afford to say no. Okay, Piper. We'll keep going for now."

"Thank you, thank you!" she said, then added "Thank you" for good measure.

"But if those gators get any weirder—"

"Then we'll go," Piper agreed quickly, giving him no time to change his mind. "Tad, give the vasculum to Perch."

Tad was seething. "I don't believe this! No! I won't!"

"Tad! Give it to him!" Piper made a grab for it.

Tad yanked the vasculum from her reach and held it over his shoulder. "Piper, this is important! It's a piece of history!"

"You're gonna be a piece of history if you don't give it to her!" Creeper threatened. He jumped up from his seat, ready to scrap. "This is about Grace! She's worth a lot more than some stupid gold box!"

Creeper was right, Tad realized. Of course Grace was more important than his ancestor's vasculum. He felt like a fool for forgetting what they were there for.

He was about to hand over the vasculum when Creeper and Piper lunged for it simultaneously. Startled, Tad dropped it behind him. The vasculum fell, clanged against the gunwale, and splashed into the water.

"No!" Piper yelped.

"You idiot!" Creeper cocked his arm back to swing at Tad, but Macey caught his wrist in her huge paw.

"No hitting," she said.

Tad turned pale. "I'm—I'm sorry! I'd decided to give it to you, I swear! You didn't have to attack me!"

Piper leaned over the side of the boat, hoping against hope that she could still rescue the vasculum. But all she saw was the reflection of her desperate face staring back at her. "It's gone. . . ."

"No it's not," Perch said, spanning his legs over the gunwale. "I'm going after it."

"The hell you are!" Like a linebacker, Macey brushed Tad and Creeper aside, grabbed Perch, and threw him onto his butt on the bottom of the boat. The look on his face was one of shock and betrayal. She pinned him down easily with one hand. "There's an armada of gators not thirty yards yonder, ya dang idjit!"

She let him think on this, and when she let him up, Perch scrambled onto the aft bench, out of her reach.

"That's thirty thousand dollars, Mace!" he cried. "We can't just let it sit on the bottom of the Oke! We need that money!"

"More than ya need your arms and legs?" Macey asked. "Boy, you haven't got the sense that God gave a goose."

"Well, you're not my mother or my boss. I'll get it," Tad said. "It's an important artifact. It would be a crime to leave it behind."

Macey literally growled. "You try it, boy—and this goes for you too, Perch—I'll bang you two dummies like cymbals." No one doubted she could make good on her threat.

Perch tried to reason with her. "Mace, you know how fast I can swim. I'll shoot to the bottom and be back up with the box before those gators cross half the distance."

"I said I'll do it!" Tad repeated himself.

"Shut yer traps," Macey ordered. Just like that, she commandeered the boat. "Perch, get me the portable depth finder."

Perch fished inside the bow bench and retrieved something that looked like a thin yellow wand with a button and a tiny digital screen on the opposite side of the handle. "Here you go." He handed it to the new captain.

Macey turned the depth finder on. "If the water is deeper than ten feet, the gold thingamajig stays on the bottom. Ten or less and you can dive for it, Perch. That's the deal—take it or leave it."

Tad didn't agree with her choice of diver. "I said I'll be the one—!"

"And I said Perch!" Macey thundered an inch from his face. Tad's mouth snapped shut and he plopped down next to Perch.

"I've givin' you a five Mississippi count, Perch. You do not linger. You go to the bottom, get the box and come straight back up. If you don't see it, you don't waste time lookin' for it. You come back up. You understand me, boy?"

Perch nodded rapidly, like a bobblehead doll.

"All right, let's see how deep this bathtub is." Macey set the depth finder against the hull, took a reading, and announced the result. "Twenty-one feet."

"That can't be right," Perch challenged. "The Oke rarely gets that deep, only in the big lakes. The finder must be busted."

"Let's go again." Macey took a second reading against the hull. "Twenty-one feet," she confirmed. "That's that. Good-bye, box."

"Maybe you're doing it wrong," Perch said. "It can be sensitive. You know how you are with electronics. Let me try."

She handed it over. "See for yerself, then, doubting Thomas."

Perch leaned over the side and dunked the depth finder right into the water. "Sometimes it works better when you do it this way." He clicked the button, waited a couple of seconds, and then took a look at the screen. He smirked. "See! This thing is busted. Now its reads *seventeen feet.*"

Tad leaned in to verify the result. "He's right. Seventeen."

"I'll try it again." Perch repeated the test, then laughed. "Eleven feet! What a piece of junk. One more time."

Dunk, click, check. "See? Now it says five feet! I think I proved my—"

Macey was the first to witness the ancient thing breaking through the algae. She yanked Creeper away from the gunwale. *"Brace yerselves!"* she warned just as the creature's massive shell made impact with the bottom of the boat.

The depth finder had been accurate at every reading, but the sonar wave had been bouncing off the hard shell of something following the boat below, hunting them in secret. They couldn't know that the readings had also been alerts, announcing the ancient thing rising, foot by foot toward the surface. Now it was too late. The creature rammed into the hull of the *Mud Cat*, lifting the starboard side of the johnboat high out of the water.

"*Gah!*" Tad cried, as he fell backward over the portside gunwale and into the water. Piper and Perch pitched forward and tumbled together over the starboard side. Piper twisted and back-flopped into the swamp, but Perch landed headfirst on the beast's jagged shell. Dazed, cut, and bleeding, he rolled off the shell and followed Piper through the thin film of algae.

Once again Piper was underwater, facing the surface but falling down toward the bottom. She could see the sun, distant, a pinhole of light. It was brashly bright compared to the dark tarp of algae sealing off above her head like a pool cover. She could still make out the solid underbelly of the boat, rocking side to side, settling after the crash.

No, not the crash. The attack.

Something had attacked them. And now she was in the water with it.

The last thing she saw before the algae blocked out the crepuscular rays of sunlight was the terrified expression on Creeper's wavy face as he yelled her name. If she died now, at least he was safe in the *Mud Cat*. He could go home and tell their parents what had happened. There was that, at least.

Piper was a sinker. She had to stop her free fall to the bottom, so she forced her limbs into motion. Falling became treading. Treading became swimming.

She tried to remember: had Perch fallen overboard too? And what about Macey and Tad? The creature, whatever it was, had nearly flipped the boat. It had been like one of those amusement-park simulator rides, bucking on tilting hydraulics. She looked around for the others.

The water was dim, scummy, and haunted by fluttery shadows.

Piper could see a bit, even with the algae overhead, but it was all so confusing. She thrashed and kicked hard, pirouetting to take in her surroundings. It was difficult to tell what was up, what was down, and where she was within it. The swamp seemed infinite in all directions—endless, like space. The green water was speckled with dark motes, creatures too small to identify and too light to sink. The water was polluted with hungry life.

Piper glimpsed a twinkle of gold far below on the bottom. She couldn't risk diving for the vasculum. There wasn't enough oxygen left in her lungs. And while the alligators seemed to be holding their position for now, that could quickly change.

Piper saw the ancient beast as a shadow first, like a zeppelin sailing dreamily through a cloud. She fought against the impulse to open her mouth and scream underwater—if she did, she'd drown.

The beast swam directly toward her, paddling with powerful scaly legs, its feet tipped with long, rakish claws more bearlike than reptilian. Its mouth was raptorial, hook-beaked for clasping and crunching prey. Its body looked like an enormous slab of jagged black rock.

Their attacker was unmistakably an alligator snapping turtle, easily the biggest Piper had ever seen. So big that she could feel a surging wave pushing ahead of it as it closed the gap between them. The alligator snapper, the largest of the turtle species, was common in southern waters, but never in her life had Piper seen one so massive. It looked about four hundred pounds, with a tail like a cudgel and an armor-plated shell several inches thick and six feet across. Something dancing inside its beak drew her focus. Piper stared with horror at the fleshy bubble gum–pink tongue that was darting about inside the turtle's open mouth. It looked like an earthworm in the throes of a seizure. The alligator snapper's tongue was the ultimate fishing lure. The turtle, she realized, was trying to entice her into willingly entering its bone-crushing jaws.

Piper flapped hard, desperate to get out of range of the beast's head. It was like trying to crawl from the path of an oncoming truck. The reptile was too big. She couldn't escape it.

Something grabbed her by the ankle and yanked her down hard. The turtle glided over top of her head. Its cross-shaped plastron—the yellow undershell—scraped her scalp. It was that close.

Whatever pulled her from the turtle's trajectory didn't let go. She thought of the vines that had snared Perch and instinctively kicked hard to free her leg, giving Tad a fractured nose in the process. Her friend had saved her, and she'd kicked him in the face for his troubles.

Covering his red-clouded nose with one hand, Tad pointed up with the other. Together they swam toward the surface.

With Creeper's help, Macey dragged Piper and Tad up over the gunwale and into the boat. "I thought you were goners for sure!" the woman said, her voice brimming with relief.

Creeper used a fresh Oke Dokey Boat Tours T-shirt to blot swamp water off his sister's face. Piper saw that he was trembling.

"I'm okay," she assured him. She took the T-shirt from his hand and ran it up and down her algae-specked arms.

"Did y'all see Perch?" Macey was in a panic. "Please tell me ya saw him down there!"

Piper shook her head. "No. I looked, but no."

"Me neither," Tad said in a nasally voice. He was sitting on the floor of the *Mud Cat*, pinching his nose closed with his fingers to stanch the flow of blood. Exhausted, he struggled to pull himself up onto the middle bench. Droplets of blood dripped from his face and spattered on the plastic seat cushion. "I'll go back for him."

Tad leaned over the gunwale just as the vasculum flew up from the water, cracking him in his leaky nose. He caught the gold container before it could fall back in, slipped on a puddle, and landed on his back.

Perch pulled himself up into the boat and plunked down next to

Tad on the floor. He ran his hands through his wet and bloody hair, clearing it from his eyes. There was a gash on his forehead where he'd landed on the turtle's jagged shell, but it was nothing a Band-Aid from the boat's first-aid kit couldn't patch. "Anyone get the license plate on that monster?" he joked, then he slapped Tad on the bare bottom of his foot. "Hey, man, did you know your nose is bleeding?"

Not bothering to get up, Tad reached out and presented Perch with the vasculum. "Take it, guy," he muttered. "You earned it."

The Field Notes of Botanist Dr. Brisbane Cole

August 28, 1823

Mother Nature saw fit to grant me a front-row ticket to the
second act of a wondrous and secret show. In the first act,
no doubt a spring performance, a mother alligator snapping
turtle swam up from the bottom of the swamp and crawled
onto the shore of a narrow strip of land. There she dug a hole,
laid her clutch of eggs inside it, and carefully buried them all.
Sadly, I was not in attendance. The second act, which was post-
intermission as I was passing, was by far the more interesting
half of the production. To my delight, the ensemble cast was
in the midst of a breakout performance. As many as twenty
hatchling turtles, each no bigger than a thumb's length, clawed
their way to freedom and began the epic four-yard trek to the
water. To see so many intrepid survivors made my heart leap
with joy. Turtle eggs are a delicacy for many forms of wildlife.
The usual cast of scoundrels—skunks, raccoons, and their
ilk—often dig up nests to abscond with the eggs and devour
them. Nokosi and I waited breathlessly until the very last turtle
emerged, but just as he crawled from the sand, the story took a
dark twist. A mink crept low and silent toward the hatchling,
licking its lips in anticipation of an easy meal. I'm not sure what
possessed me, for a gentleman knows that it's never proper for
the audience to interfere with the outcome of the story. But ever
since I was a young boy, I have always preferred a happy ending,
and so I smacked the surface of the water with my paddle,
soaked the mink, and chased it out of the plot. The turtle did
not stop to thank me, nor would it have been wise to do so. It
reached the water and swam downward to join its siblings in the
murk. The star of the show had triumphed in its quest. This was
an ending I could drink to. I raised my flask of water, sipped,
and wished him a long and prosperous run.

13

"**L**ook at it," Tad said. "That thing has to be a world-record holder, for sure."

The five of them sat in the boat watching the giant alligator turtle tread water fifteen yards away. Its craggy shell poked up through the algae like a barren island, midway between the *Mud Cat* and the alligators.

"People ask me all the time how big turtles get in the Oke," Perch said. "I had to do a little research so I could look them in the eye when I answered. The biggest snapper in the world weighed over two hundred and thirty pounds. There were rumors of one caught in Kansas that people claimed was four hundred pounds, but that was never verified. Donatello over there has to be at least four hundred. I'd be willing to go out on a limb and say he's a quarter-tonner."

"It would take forever for a turtle to grow to that size," Tad said. "A hundred years, at least."

"Try two hundred," said Macey. "I wouldn't be surprised if Thomas Jefferson was president when that beastie was a hatchling."

"It's just floating there." Perch slapped his palm against the outside of the hull, and hollered, "Here, turtle turtle," but the turtle ignored him. "Why isn't it leaving? Snappers are usually shy and only surface when they need air or lay eggs."

"They don't usually attack boats either," Macey reminded him. "What's normal doesn't apply to this part of the swamp. All the reptiles are acting crazy as an outhouse rat."

"I know what's wrong with them," Creeper announced. "It's that evil tribe you told us about. The Taska . . . Teska . . ."

"The Tasketcha?" said Perch.

"Yeah! Them!" Creeper nodded. "They must have possessed the turtle, and the alligators too. They're trying to get at us so they can jump into our bodies and take us over. They need to possess us so they can leave the swamp, just like Macey said."

"It's just an old folktale," Tad scoffed. "There's no such thing as magical tribes or evil spirits or possessed alligators. The animals are probably just really hungry."

"Is that supposed to make us feel better?" Piper asked. "And why would they be hungry? It looks to me like the water is loaded with their favorite foods."

Tad shrugged. "I'm just saying there has to be a scientific explanation for this. Something less crazy than ghosts."

"Well, one thing's for sure," said Perch. "We can't go back the way we came. Not with a five-hundred-pound alligator snapping turtle playing goalie in the narrow. We'll keep moving west."

Piper was relieved. She'd thought Perch might revive the idea of going home.

Creeper was pouting again, probably mad at Tad for shooting down his ghost theory. His arms were crossed and his chin was tucked close to his slight chest. He had such a big personality that Piper never thought of him as fragile, but seeing him now, tiny and dejected, it was hard not to fear for him. This wild place was dangerous. She wished she hadn't allowed him to come. Her goal was to save

Grace, not put her brother's life in jeopardy too. But he was here, and there was little she could do, other than try her best to get Creeper back to Jesup in one uneaten piece.

They motored west for a distance, a couple of klicks by Macey's count. (Piper was beginning to sense that a klick was the same as a kilometer.) Like the alligators, the turtle was following the boat. At times the massive terrapin disappeared under the water, but only for short intervals. It always came back up. It too was keeping a set distance.

"Look! Eels!" Creeper pointed to several long and thickly muscled creatures with black rubbery skin, writhing around in the algae soup. They looked like fat snakes to Piper, and she thought they might be cottonmouths.

"I hate to correct you, but them are sirens," Perch said. "Big salamanders with tiny forelegs and no back legs at all. Evolutionary throwbacks to when fish grew lungs so they could attack prey loitering on the shore. Mostly they stay in the water, but at night, during a rain, they can wriggle their way across land for short distances."

"They're gross," said Piper. "Why is everything in this swamp so gross?"

"Oh, it gets grosser," said Perch. "During times of extreme drought, a siren will stay moist by surrounding itself in a cocoon of mucus."

"Are they poisonous?" Creeper asked. "They look poisonous."

"No, but even if they were, their teeth are located in their throats, not their mouths," Perch said. "They can gum us, but they can't bite us."

Piper gave the final verdict on the sirens: "Disgusting."

Shortly after that, they spied another alligator snapping turtle. Not quite as big as the first, but still a giant. They passed tiny islands and drew more alligators too. They came sledding down the banks on their bellies, splashed into the water, and swam out to join the bizarre flotilla.

"Take a gander at that one," said Macey. An enormous bull alligator lay asleep in the mud. From tip to tail, it had to be eighteen feet long. "I thought only saltwater crocs get that large." The monster's eyelids slid open, and with yellow dragon eyes it observed the boat. The giant reptile crawled forward, slipped below the waterline, and vanished for a very tense minute. No one had to tell Piper that a beast that size could capsize their boat. They breathed a collective sigh of relief when they spotted it again, swimming away to join the other gators. This didn't mean it wasn't a threat—just that it wasn't a threat *right now*.

"Did you see that?" Tad asked, jumping up from his seat. He scrambled toward the starboard side for a better look. He gripped one of the tie-off cleats so tightly that his knuckles turned white.

"See what?" Piper asked.

"It's gone. It moved so fast," said Tad. "It came up out of the water—just a head."

"Ahead of what?" Perch asked.

"Not *ahead*. A *head*. It was a snake. A *huge* snake."

"Cottonmouth, probably," said Macey. "They're the biggest in the Oke."

"No, I've seen a cottonmouth in person," said Tad. "This snake was a lot bigger than a cottonmouth."

"I doubt that," said Perch. "Can you give us a little more description? 'Huge' isn't much to go on."

Tad kept his eyes on the fading ripples, hoping the snake would resurface. "I only caught a glimpse. It had two dark marks on its face, like it was crying black tears. Seen anything like that before?"

"Yes, but not in the Oke," said Perch. "Sounds like you're describing an anaconda. You probably saw another snapping turtle. Snappers have pretty big heads. You know that from experience."

"Maybe," Tad said. But he didn't believe it for a second. He knew what he saw.

"Let's unpack the facts and spread 'em out on the table," said Macey. "We're the grand-marshal float in a very strange parade. This isn't some random behavior. Those critters are following us like cans behind a wedding limo. They're definitely stalking us."

Piper thought of another possibility. "What if they're actually *prodding* us toward something?"

Perch furrowed his brow. "Prodding us toward something? You mean herding? You think they're behaving like sheepdogs?"

"Yes," said Piper. "Exactly like sheepdogs."

"And what do you suppose these scaly, aquatic sheepdogs are herding us toward?" Perch asked.

"I know!" Creeper said. "The Island of the Daughters of the Sun, that's what."

Piper shot Perch a dirty look. "See what you've done?"

"Don't blame him!" Creeper snapped. "Perch didn't make up that story; he just repeated it. And I think it's true!"

"Creeper, stop talking nonsense," Piper scolded. "You can't take Perch seriously. It's just an old campfire tale. There's nothing behind it. There are no boogeymen in the Okefenokee!"

"What about Mergo?" Creeper asked. "You believe everything on that map, so explain Mergo! I think Mergo is an evil spirit and Cole was trying to warn us!"

"Cole wasn't trying to warn anyone!" Piper was exasperated. "Look, the truth is, Cole made Mergo up. As a joke."

"What are you talking about?" asked Tad. "How could you know that?"

"I read it in the journal last night while you were all asleep. Tad, I told you I recognized the word. That's because I'd seen it before in one of Cole's entries. We both did, but you forgot. There is no Mergo. His guides were superstitious. They got scared and claimed there was an evil spirit in the swamp, so Cole made up a name for it. He didn't believe his guides; he was just poking fun."

"Did he explain what Mergo means?" Tad asked.

"You were right," she said. "Mergo *is* Latin. It means 'I drown, I bury, I overwhelm.' But again, it was just a joke. So let's just drop this whole mystical body-snatchers thing, okay? Mergo means nothing. Mergo *is* nothing."

Creeper wouldn't let it go. "If the word doesn't mean anything, then why did he write it in on the map? In blood!"

After two dips in the swamp and all the weirdness with the animals, Piper's nerves were fried. She'd had enough of her brother's ridiculous ideas. "Yeesh, Creeper, will you shut up about this?" she snapped. "I can't listen to your nonsense anymore! Read my lips: there are no ghosts, demons, aliens, vampires, or any other monsters in the Okefenokee. *So shut up!*"

Creeper pounded on his bench with his fist and exploded. *"No, you shut up, Piper! You shut up!* All you ever do is put me down and laugh at me! I get it. I'm stupid and my ideas are silly and I should just leave you alone forever, because you hate me anyway. *You hate me!* Admit it, you hate me and you wish I'd never been born!"

"What on earth are you talking, about?" Piper asked. "I don't hate you! You're my brother!"

"Exactly!" he roared. "I'm just your stupid little, pesky *brother*! The one you never wished for! Not on a star or a comet or even a lump of dog poop in the backyard. Well, I'm sorry I was such a huge disappointment! I'll do you a big favor—once we find the silver flower, you don't ever have to talk to me again, okay? I'll stay out of your way and you can pretend like it's just you and Grace and it can be like I don't exist, which is exactly the way you want it!"

Creeper's words were a slap in Piper's face. A wake-up slap. Her brother's sour mood since the campfire had been *her* fault. She hadn't considered his feelings at all when she'd gone on and on about wanting a sister.

"Creeper . . . Monty . . ." she started.

"Just leave me alone." Creeper leaped up and went to sit next to Macey at the back of the boat. Macey put her arm around his head and drew him in close, like a mother hen. Creeper buried his face in her overalls, hiding his tears from the group.

"We can't keep going like this," Perch said. "I don't care about that stupid vasculum anymore. With every new mile, things have gone from bad to worse. I've been used, lied to, and nearly drowned by killer vines—I don't care what you say, Big Brain, I *know* they were tryin' to kill me. On top of everything, my boat was just attacked by the King of the Turtles! And now we're turning on each other. Ghosts or no ghosts, there's something foul about this place, and I can't see no good coming from overstaying our welcome."

"Please don't turn us back now," Piper pleaded. "I know things are bad, and I admit it, I've been a horrible passenger. And a horrible sister to Creeper. And a horrible sister to Grace, and a horrible friend to Tad . . . I probably don't deserve anyone's help. To be honest, I feel like diving out of the *Mud Cat* and letting the gators do their worst. That'd be a fitting end to Pageant Princess Piper Canfield, and I'd be okay with that. But please . . . *please* keep going. I'm begging you, Perch. Get us to the flower, and then you can leave me behind, for all I care."

Perch stuck out his lower lip and blew a puff of air up his face to clear a sopping flap of hair from his eyes. He reached into his pocket and fished out a dime. "I'll tell you what I'm going to do. No more bargaining. Instead, we'll leave it to chance. We'll flip for it. I can't be any fairer than that."

Grace's life hinged on the flip of a coin. It seemed vulgar and wrong, but Piper understood that Perch had already gone further for her than most people would be willing to for strangers. After the turtle attack, she couldn't blame him for wanting to give up. She might too, if the *Mud Cat* were her boat and Grace weren't her sister. She would accept the result of the toss, no matter how it landed.

"Heads," she called. "Heads we keep going."

"All right, then," said Perch. "Tails we concentrate on finding a way out of here. Not sure how we'll get past Turtlesaurus and the Gator Gang, but we'll come up with a plan. Ready?"

She gave a sharp nod and dug her nails into the plastic of her bench seat.

All eyes were on Perch as he made a fist and balanced the coin on the back of his thumbnail. His eyes met Piper's and lingered there for a moment. Then he flicked his thumb, catapulting the coin high into the air.

Piper whispered a one-word prayer. "Please."

The dime tumbled over and over, sparking in the afternoon sun. Perch held his palm out to capture it.

Without warning, something big bumped against the port side of the boat, launching the *Mud Cat* sideways across the water. Perch grabbed the gunwale with one hand to keep from falling overboard and grabbed at the coin, but the boat had been pushed too far and the coin was beyond his reach. Just before it hit the water, the biggest fish Piper had ever seen raised its head through the thin pellicle of algae and opened its mouth wide, exposing a lining of alligatorlike teeth.

"*Whoa!*" Perch jumped back in surprise.

The dime disappeared inside the saggy pouch of the fish's lower jaw, then its mouth snapped shut. The fish rolled on its side, giving the group a good look at its torpedolike body. It was covered in thick, diamond-shaped scales that interlocked like chain mail. The fish was at least as long as the *Mud Cat* and looked positively prehistoric. With a swish of its tail and a burst of frothy spray, it was gone.

"What was that . . . *thing?*" Tad asked the captain, but Perch was busy counting his fingers to make sure he still had them all.

"*That* was an alligator gar," Macey answered. "I've never see one here. We have lots of the smaller Florida gars in the Oke, but the gator gar is native to the Gulf States. All the monster-size gator gars were fished off years ago."

"Apparently not," said Tad.

"Did you get a look at those scales, Mace?" Perch asked.

"I got eyes, don't I? Native Americans used the gator gar's thick scales as arrowheads. Makes a lot of sense now, having seen them up close."

"I bet you couldn't get a knife through them if you tried," said Perch.

"I hate to be the one to point this out," Tad said, "but the fish swallowed the coin. Anyone see how it landed?"

"No," said Perch. "I was busy tryin' not to follow the coin into the gar's mouth. Anyone else?"

"I did," said Creeper, still red skinned and pink-eyed from his blowup with Piper. "It landed on heads."

Perch eyed him suspiciously. "How could you have seen that from the back of the boat? You're not just saying that, are you?"

"We all saw it," Creeper said. "It landed in a head. A fish head. And that counts."

Macey smiled and patted Creeper's back. "He's got ya there, Perch. It's hard to argue with that kind of logic."

Perch huffed. "Fine. We'll keep going. But there's something we need to consider."

"What's that?" Piper asked. She was afraid he was going to suggest another sleepover or tell them they were low on gas.

"Piper, you had the theory that all these critters are behaving like sheepdogs, right? You think they're herding us somewhere?"

"Yes, it feels that way," she replied.

"That's exactly what I was afraid of." Perch's brow puckered above his nose. "Sheepdogs have masters, right? Did it occur to anyone that maybe these critters have a master too?"

The group looked back at the horde of animals churning the water with frenzied impatience as they let Perch's point sink in.

The afternoon stretched as the waterways narrowed. Stands of giant pond cypress rose from the water and closed in on them. The canopy of trees arched over the boat, forming a sheer tunnel, casting deep shade that bordered on gloom.

"Those are the biggest trees I have ever seen in this swamp." Perch craned his neck toward the sky to take them in. "All of the giants were cut down by the nineteen thirties. Before the lumber companies came, some of the cypress trees in the Oke were a thousand years old, although it's hard to determine their age because they grow hollow—no rings to count. We figured they were all gone. This part of the swamp looks completely untouched by humans."

As the corridors became more claustrophobic, the animals following the *Mud Cat* bottlenecked behind the boat. Their line stretched back fifty yards or more, with new animals joining as they passed. Piper was worried. What if they suddenly found themselves at a dead end, cornered like rats? But then they saw a brightly lit vista at the end of the tree tunnel, which could mean only one thing—open water.

The *Mud Cat* left the confines of the narrow and glided out into a crescent-shaped lagoon. On the far side, the lagoon was surrounded by forested land. Real land. This was either the western edge of the Oke or a very large island that extended as far as they could see in both directions.

Floating in the middle of the lagoon was a lone hammock of peat. It was maybe thirty feet across from all sides.

The hammock wasn't the most interesting thing in the lagoon.

That distinction went to the massive, leafless plant stalk rising up from the water through the hammock's center. The lime-green stalk was at least forty feet tall, and as thick around as a telephone pole. Tad had never seen a stalk that size, not ever, not even in books. None of them had.

Macey throttled down the motor until the boat came to a stop. The *Mud Cat* continued to drift toward the hammock under the power of its momentum. "Lord Almighty, is that what I think it is?"

Tad and Piper glanced at each other. Their internal reactions were uneven. In Tad's case, this was the sudden death of his disbelief. For Piper, it was belief rewarded.

"Have you ever seen anything so beautiful?" Piper breathed.

High atop the stalk, as silver as a newly minted quarter, was the largest, most dazzling flower Piper had ever beheld. It did exist. Dr. Cole had been right all along.

Tad snapped a photo with his disposable camera. Then a second. And a third.

"We found it," Creeper said, transfixed by wonderment. "Cole's flower is really real."

"Not Cole's flower," said Piper. "Grace's flower. It belongs to Grace."

"What are we waiting for?" Creeper raised his arms in victory. "Let's go get it for her."

In their exuberance they forgot something.

Behind them, the creatures of the swamp funneled into the lagoon and spread out inside it like a disease. Gliding silently underwater, they began to close the gap that had until now separated them from the *Mud Cat*.

August 28, 1823

We are being followed. It has been more than three hours since we entered the mysterious emerald corridors and the first alligator began shadowing our canoes like a stray mutt keeping cautious distance behind a baker's cart. Soon several others joined the first, and now they swim in a convoy of a hundred strong behind us. Nokosi believes they are prodding us toward our doom, but I am certain there is a commonsense explanation for this unusual animal behavior. Simple curiosity, perhaps. Regardless, we have no choice but to continue, for to double back would send us straight into their toothy midst.

The trees, laden with drapery of gray moss, conceal much of this realm from view, but what is visible is both mesmerizing and cause for deep concern. This is an unnatural realm, full of secret life.

A large insect of the pond skimmer family skittered up Nokosi's paddle and speared his finger with a sharp beak the length of a sewing needle. Nokosi flicked the bug away, but the damage was done. Blood streamed out of the wound, and the finger turned an angry red to the knuckle. He tried to stanch the flow of blood, but for a good while it continued unabated. Perhaps my friend suffers from hemophilia, a rare condition in which the blood is unable to clot properly, but it's entirely possible that the insect secretes some form of anticoagulant in the bite wound so that it may drink its victim's blood at leisure.

Nokosi unrolled the vellum map. Using his finger as a writing quill, he drew a circle around our location and then scrawled the word *Mergo*, the name I'd coined in jest. My friend mocks the mocker. While I still can't claim to share his superstitious belief in spirits and demons, I can no longer dismiss them so cavalierly. There is something here, bewitching this place. I sense it too. Something unnatural and yet also born of nature. We must remain vigilant.

14

"It's a straightforward plan." Perch attached the belt hook of his sheathed bowie knife to his belt with a carabiner. "Macey, you sidle the *Mud Cat* up to the hammock and drop me off. Then take the boat out away from the hammock—forty feet should do it. I'll tiptoe over to the plant stalk and saw a wedge out of it with my knife, bending the stalk in the direction of the boat. If I do the math right—and I'm good at math—the tip of the stalk should land right across the *Mud Cat*. Then y'all can cut off the flower with this." He handed Tad the fish scaler Macey had used on the warmouth. "Once the flower is safely aboard, come pick me up."

"Then we go home?" Creeper asked.

Perch winked. "Then we go home, buddy."

Tad had his doubts. "That stalk is huge. Are you positive it won't flip the boat? Or smash through the hull?"

"Nah, the plant isn't woody like a tree," Perch said. "Without branches, it'll be too slick to climb. Cutting it down is our best course of action. Not to worry, Big Brain. As long as the stalk hits the gunwales on both sides, the pressure will be distributed evenly. It'll bounce the boat a bit, but the *Mud Cat* was made to take a beating.

That's why I picked her. Just make sure none of you are directly under the stalk when it lands."

"Be careful, Perch," said Piper. "If the flower falls into the water—"

Perch chuckled. "Have a little faith in me."

Piper did. He'd earned it. "Okay. Let's do it."

Macey puttered over to the hammock and swiveled the tiller handle to swing the boat alongside it. Perch lowered himself overboard and tested the integrity of the hammock with the weight of one leg. They knew from experience that the water in this part of the swamp was much deeper than the water in Floyd's Prairie. Perch couldn't afford to be cocky.

"Wait—" Piper squeaked. She reached out and clutched Perch's pant leg.

"I got this," he assured her. "Relax."

She let go.

Perch kept a tight two-hand grip on the gunwale as he gradually lowered his full weight onto the peat. The hammock trembled. It was quaggy, but it held.

"It feels solid enough," he told them, standing slowly. "I think it's safe."

Macey wiped a dew of sweat off her forehead. "Good. Be careful, son. Go it slow."

"I will," he promised. "Take the *Mud Cat* out, Mace."

Perch began the twenty-foot walk between the edge of the hammock and the center, where the stalk had at one time burst upward through the peat then kept growing toward the sky.

Macey undocked from the hammock, took the *Mud Cat* forty feet out, and swung parallel to the hammock so that the stalk would fall across the middle of the boat, as planned.

Creeper glanced back toward the opening of the narrow, then did a double take. "Hey! Where'd all the animals go?"

"I plum forgot about them," Macey said. "Looks like they skedaddled."

"Why would they leave?" asked Piper. For the last few hours, the presence of the animals behind the boat had made her incredibly nervous, but their sudden absence worried her more. It didn't seem likely that after all this time, they'd collectively lost interest in the boat and its passengers.

"Let's just count our blessings and be grateful they're gone," said Macey. "This is going to be tricky enough without them milling around, waiting for table scraps."

Piper understood that by "table scraps" she was referring to Perch. If he fell though the hammock, he'd be at the animals' mercy.

When the *Mud Cat* was in position and Perch had reached the stalk, he unbuttoned the sheath and drew his knife. He eyeballed the boat, then glanced up to the tip of the plant. "Looks like you're in the right place, Macey! Here I go!"

He picked a spot on the stalk about three feet up from the peat, set the blade of the bowie knife against the rubbery green cellulose of the plant, and started to saw.

At the very moment the saw teeth of the blade ripped into the stalk, the peat beneath Perch's feet tore open, and the snout of an enormous bull alligator burst upward through it.

"Holy hell!" Perch yelped in surprise.

The gator opened its mouth wide and thrashed its head side to side as it tried to grab hold of Perch's leg. Perch lifted his foot high, avoiding the beast, but it was a narrow escape. When the gator made a second lunge for him, Perch let go of the blade handle and jumped back, leaving the knife embedded in the plant.

There came a chorus of warnings.

"Perch!"

"Look out!"

"Get out of there!"

The group was helpless to do anything but watch the attack unfold.

Perch needed a weapon. Luckily, he had one. He jerked the knife free of the stalk and cocked his arm back to put some weight behind his thrust. The gator didn't wait around to be stabbed. It dropped down through the tear in the peat and vanished.

"You okay, Perch?" Macey hollered. Her deep voice echoed around the lagoon.

"Yeah! I'm alive! I guess the gators weren't done with us after all!"

"Stay put!" Macey ordered. "I'm coming to get you!"

"No! Stay there! I'm gonna try again!"

Perch slipped the knife back into the groove he'd already cut— there was no sense in starting over. He checked the gaping hole in the hammock, but there was nothing inside it. He resumed cutting the plant. The juice just beneath the tender cellulose skin began to ooze out.

The weave of peat directly below Perch's shoes lifted several inches in the exact shape of an alligator snapping turtle's shell. Perch surfed down the side of the moving mound and it instantly fell flat. The turtle had dropped away from the underside of the hammock.

"Son of a gun!" Perch cursed. "Crazy animals! They won't let me finish!"

He took a step back from the deflated thatch and nearly tripped over the snout of another gator that had erupted through the hammock behind him. A third gator—or possibly the first one returning—started gnashing at the peat, but the dead vegetation snagged between its teeth and it couldn't break through, though not for lack of trying.

"Incoming!" Macey hollered.

Two huge sirens squirmed up out of the hole that the first alligator had made. They dragged their fat, slimy bodies across the peat, using their front, and only, legs. The stout amphibians wriggled toward Perch, their mouths agape and hissing like cats.

The first siren to reach Perch got the toe of his sneaker in its soft underbelly. The siren yelped as it flew through the air, then it landed on the fringe of the hammock and rolled off into the water. The second siren latched on to Perch's ankle. "Get off!" Perch yelped, shaking free. He punted it back into the hole. Without teeth, the sirens weren't a major threat. The gators were a different story. There were several of them now, tearing through the peat all around him. The hammock was bubbling. To escape their snapping jaws, Perch leaped high onto the stalk, wrapping his arms and legs around it tightly, dropping the knife onto the hammock in the process. The thick stem was too slick to climb, so he just hung on for dear life. The stalk was slippery, like a fireman's pole. As hard as he tried, Perch couldn't prevent himself from sliding slowly down toward the gnashing jaws.

But once again the attacks stopped, and the gator heads slipped back into the water. Perch waited until the hammock went completely flat. Then he dropped into a crouched position on the peat. He picked up his knife. He looked at it. He looked at the stalk. He looked at the knife. He looked at the gaping hole in the hammock. He put it all together.

"They're protecting the flower!" Perch yelled to the others.

"What are you talking about?" Tad hollered back.

"Every time I cut into the stalk, the animals go nuts! When I stop cutting, they fall back! I'll show you!"

Keeping a watchful eye on the peat, Perch set the edge of the bowie knife against the stalk, and with one swift stroke he sliced off a piece of cellulose no thicker than an apple peel, just a sliver. Instantaneously, bulges appeared in the hammock, like mice trapped under a carpet. Perch stepped away from the stalk and waited. As he'd expected, the bulges disappeared.

"The deeper I cut into this thing, the crazier they become, and the harder they try to get at me!"

"I think I finally understand what's been happening with the alligators and the other animals," Tad said.

"You do?" Piper asked, surprised.

"Yes," said Tad. "I think the plant is controlling the animals' minds."

Piper thought Tad's theory sounded like bull-pucky. "You mean it's using telepathy or something?"

"No, I'm talking about chemical manipulation."

Macey scratched her bristly head. "Speak English, son. You're not making sense."

Tad tried to put it into simple terms. "Every time Perch wounds the plant, the animals go on the offense. When he stops, they stop, right? The plant and the animals are connected. The plant is telling the animals it's under attack and commanding them to protect it."

"So you're saying . . . *the plant* is the sheepdogs' master?"

"Yes, Piper." Tad nodded. "There's a precedent."

"A president?" Creeper struggled more than the others to keep up.

"No, a *precedent*, Creeper," said Tad. "What I mean is, there are other examples of this phenomenon in nature. The acacia tree, for example. When its leaves are under attack by beetles, worms, or even hungry mammals, the tree releases a chemical distress signal called a volatile into the air. The volatile affects the brains of the ants that live on its branches. It whips them into a frenzy. The ants charge the invaders, biting them over and over in an attempt to drive them away from the plant. They've been known to chase off full-grown giraffes."

He continued. "Some species of plants can even summon specific insects based on the nature of the threat. Butterflies land on the leaves of the black mustard plant and lay their eggs. The plant sends a volatile into the air that is only attractive to wasps. The wasps fly in like the cavalry and attack the butterflies and their eggs, keeping them from hatching into caterpillars, which would feast on the plant's leaves."

"So you think the plant is sending out—what did you call it—volatiles into the air?" Piper asked.

"No," Tad said. "I think it's sending them into the water, which is something unheard of in science. And it's not summoning insects; it's—"

"Calling all alligators!" Piper blurted.

"Exactly," Tad said. "And every other slimy predator that lives in the water. The alligator snapping turtles, the gars, the sirens . . . the plant is mind-controlling all of them, and I think it has been ever since we entered this part of the swamp."

"I guess we finally know what happened to your ancestor," Piper said.

Tad frowned. "Yeah, I think we do."

Perch brought their attention back to his precarious situation. "There's no way these gators will let me hack through the plant's stem! Anybody got a plan B?"

"Are you sure you can't climb it, Perch?" Piper asked. "You won't hurt the plant if you climb it, right? The animals won't come after you, and even if they do, they won't be able to reach you."

"Unless he falls," said Macey. "A fall from even ten feet up might send him straight through the hammock. That'd be the end of him, for sure."

Perch glanced up the stalk to the flower. From the hammock, it looked like a tiny silver speck. "It's too tall, and the stem is too slippery! I'd try if I thought I had even the slightest chance, but I know better."

Macey had an idea. "What if we tie a rope around the stalk and use the *Mud Cat* to bend it down to the water?"

"Won't work!" Perch said. "I won't be able to get up high enough to rope off the upper part of the stalk. If I tie it too low, it'll just crimp the stem at the middle, and the whole thing will bend the opposite way, dropping the flower into the water."

Piper was beyond frustrated. She hadn't come all this way and endured a night on Billy's Island and two baths in the swamp only to be thwarted by the flower itself.

"Ugh! This is ridiculous!" she said. "There has to be something we—"

"I'll climb it."

All heads turned to the smallest member of their party.

Creeper stood up, his expression was one of stone-faced resolve. "I'll climb it," he repeated. "I can climb the flagpole at my school. I'm the only one who can reach the flag. I'm light and I know how to grip with my feet. Climbing is what I'm good at. I know I can do this. Grace is counting on me."

Piper loathed this idea, but they were out of options. They had to let him try.

Macey ferried Creeper to the hammock. Piper looked over the port side of the boat as the starboard side nudged against the edge of the hammock. She could make out the wraithlike animals swimming beneath the hull, orbiting the base of the plant below. Piper knew they were waiting for the plant to tell them what to do. She changed her mind.

"No. I'm not letting you do this, Creeper," she declared with finality. "We'll think of something else."

"It's not up to you," her brother said, untying his shoes. He slipped them off and set them to the side on the floor of the *Mud Cat*.

"Of course it is!" she shot back. "I'm the closest thing you have to a parent out here!"

Creeper responded with a derisive snort. "You don't have to

protect me. I'm not your perfect, wonderful sister. I'm the brother you didn't wish for, remember?"

He was about to climb out of the boat when Piper grabbed him and pulled him into a deep, crushing hug.

"I'm going and you can't stop me!" Creeper tried to wriggle free. He didn't understand that she wasn't trying to restrain him.

"I'm hugging you, dummy," she told him.

"Oh." He stopped fighting, but he remained stiff and suspicious. "What for?"

"Because I love you. That's why." She clutched his shoulders and moved him to arm's length. "I'm sorry if I ever said or did anything to make you think you're less important to me than Grace. I don't know if you'll believe me now, but I swear, you mean just as much to me as she does. You can be crazy and weird and impulsive sometimes, but those aren't always bad traits. I promise if it was you that got sick, I'd be right here looking for the silver flower. And if something happens to you . . ." A tear spilled out of her eye and rolled back toward her ear. "I just couldn't live with myself. I just . . . I couldn't."

Creeper smiled. He'd been waiting to hear those words. Not just this trip, but his whole life. "Stop blubbering. I'll be okay." He hugged her back.

Click. Tad took a picture. "Well, this is the strangest thing I've seen all day."

"Shut up," Creeper said, laughing.

"You don't have to do this," Piper said. "I can try to climb it."

"Sure, that's a great idea. Not! Unless Perch has a very long chain saw in one of the benches, I think it's all up to me." With that, Creeper scooted out of the boat and onto the hammock. It barely jiggled, he was so light.

"Take Perch's vasculum," Tad said, handing him the gold box, showing that he'd made peace with the treasure's ownership. "You don't mind if we use this to keep the flower fresh, do you, Perch? The moment Creeper cuts the flower off the stalk, it'll start to die. We stand our best chance of getting it to Grace alive if he puts it into the vasculum immediately, as soon as he lops it off. That's what they're designed for."

Perch gave Tad a thumbs-up. "Happy to help the cause. Bring it on over here."

At half Perch's weight, Creeper walked across the peat easily.

"Welcome to the party," Perch said. They high-fived.

"Here, you can hang on to this." Creeper gave the vasculum to Perch. "I can't climb with it. Think you can toss it to me once I get to the top?"

"You bet," said Perch. "Can you carry my knife with you, or do you want me to throw that at you too?"

"Uh . . . I'd better carry it. I'd like to keep my body free of holes. Er . . . except for the ones I was born with."

Perch grinned and handed him the bowie knife. Creeper put the handle in his teeth, leaving his hands free to climb. Perch helped Creeper up onto his shoulders, then gave him a boost up the stalk.

"Let me know when you're ready," Perch said. "I'll throw you the vasculum, and then I'm gonna walk out a ways. I won't leave you, but I don't want to be right near the stalk when you start cutting off the flower. The gators ain't gonna like it, and I don't want to be in the middle when the Whac-A-Mole fun begins."

Creeper took hold of the stem and started to climb. He scampered up the length of it like a lemur. His unbelievable dexterity reminded Piper of a documentary she'd seen about Hawaiians flying up coconut trees to gather nuts. In less than half a minute, he was eye-to-petal with the flower. The creatures below the hammock didn't seem to notice his accomplishment.

"What's it like?" Piper hollered.

Creeper took the knife out of his mouth. "It's pretty!" He took a good whiff of the flower. "Smells like Apple Jacks!"

"I'm going to throw the vasculum up to you," said Perch. "Ready?"

"Ready!" Creeper put the knife between his teeth again and leaned back, holding one arm out.

Perch held it with two hands between his legs, then tossed it straight up granny-style. It was a perfect throw; the golden box landed in Creeper's hand.

Piper clapped excitedly from the boat. "You're doing great! I'm so proud of you!"

Creeper tucked the vasculum between his stomach and the stalk and took the knife out of his mouth. "Where should I cut it, Tad?"

"The flower is attached to a smaller stem shooting off the stalk, right? That's called the peduncle. Leave some of that attached to the flower. So cut four or five inches below the petals."

"Okay. Here I go," said Creeper. "Ready down there?"

Perch repositioned himself halfway between the boat and the stem. They all agreed it was far enough. "Go for it," Perch said.

Taking hold of the base of the flower, Creeper started to carve away at the peduncle.

On cue, the animals went crazy. They thrashed beneath the water and clawed and chomped at the hammock's underbelly. A determined alligator got its nose through the peat, and then another one jammed its snout in next to the first to help widen the opening. As if that weren't terrifying enough, an alligator gar squeezed between the two huge reptiles and attempted to writhe through the hole they'd created, not seeming to care that as a fish, it couldn't survive out of water.

As Creeper sawed, their desperation to stop him grew. The hammock was quaking with movement. Sharp teeth ripped through it in a half dozen spots, and Perch had no choice but to step farther back toward the boat or risk being bitten. Piper wondered if they'd stop their frenzy once Creeper had freed the flower or if the plant would keep pumping out chemicals, demanding retribution for the theft. It was a horribly violent event, several species working together to destroy a single parasite. Her little brother.

"Hurry up, Creeper!" she cried. "You have to hurry!"

"I'm going as fast as I can!" he yelled. "It's like sawing through bone!"

An alligator managed to get its whole head through the hammock, and its two front legs quickly followed. It lurched forward, dragging its back half out of the hole and onto the hammock. The monster was at least fourteen feet long, big enough to eat a child whole. The gator lifted its head to get a look at the thing it had been ordered to kill, a little boy with a knife and a golden box.

"Hey, ugly!" Perch hollered at the alligator.

The beast swung its massive head in Perch's direction and let out a bellowing roar by blowing air from its lungs.

"I didn't think this through too well," Perch admitted to the gator. He stepped backward slowly. "I just figured we could have a nice little chat, man to man. Assuming you're a male. There's only one way to check, and I don't think we're quite that friendly yet."

"Get in the *Mud Cat*!" Macey ordered. "Dang it, Perch! Get in the boat right now!"

The alligator charged, pushing itself across the peat on powerful, stubby legs, swinging its tail behind it. Perch shuffled backward quickly, but he'd underestimated the speed of a gator on peat. When the reptile was almost upon him, the hammock beneath the beast's body gave way and it plunged down into the water. Perch was lucky. The peat was thick enough to support his weight, but not that of a six-hundred-pound monster.

Perch touched a finger to his forehead and snapped off a salute. "See you later, alligator."

"You almost done, buddy?" he called up to Creeper. "They're going nuts down here!"

"Got it!" Creeper held up the flower, beaming with self-satisfaction.

Carefully, he placed it in the vasculum and closed the lid. The five of them watched the hammock with bated breath to see what the animals would do.

To see what the plant would do.

The furor died down. The animals stopped attacking the peat. Some were still pushing up against it, but before long they ceased their attack entirely. Just like that, it was over. Creeper had the prize in hand. It was time to go home.

"Come on down from there!" Perch summoned. "Coast is clear!"

Creeper tossed the knife so the blade dropped flat. Perch snatched it out of the air by the handle.

"Good catch!" said Creeper. He tucked the vasculum under his armpit and positioned his feet to act as brakes on the slide down. "Here I come."

Unbeknownst to them all, the stem had been struggling to support Creeper's added weight at the top, and couldn't do so a moment longer. The plant buckled and crimped at a spot just a foot above the hammock, and the whole stalk bent and fell at an angle away from the *Mud Cat*. Creeper had no time to scream. For the others, the screams came after they watched him ride the top of the plant all the way down into the murky water.

August 28, 1823

At long last, our search is over. We paddled into a sunlit lagoon and found, at the center, sticking up through a floating mat of peat, a gigantic plant stalk, unlike any I'd ever seen. At the tip of the stalk was a solitary silver flower. Acquiring it seemed no simple task. My promise to Micanopy meant that I could not simply cut the stalk down. I would have to climb and pluck it from the tip. I couldn't trust Nokosi or young Bolek with the task. Severing the flower required the skill of a botanist, so the job fell to me. The stalk was slippery. I untied my boots and climbed with my toes, and in this fashion I nearly reached the top. I grazed one silver petal with the tips of my fingers. And then I slipped and fell straight down. Through the air, through the peat and into the gloomy water. Below, I beheld horrors beyond my imagination! I darted toward the surface at once. I climbed back up through the hole I'd created in the peat, but not before an alligator bit into my calf, taking a sizable chunk of flesh for its effort. The damage to my tendons rendered my right foot useless, making a second attempt to climb the stalk impossible. I crawled to the base of the plant and sat back against it to rest. I packed peat into my wound to keep it from bleeding further. The sphagnum moss in the peat has been used as a dressing for centuries, and as I'd hoped, I felt relief immediately.

I summoned Nokosi to come to my aid, but as he attempted to step onto the peat, a second gator, large enough to swallow the first, rammed into the canoe, launching it away and throwing Nokosi into the water. Moving at blinding speed, my friend drove his knife into the eye of the reptile, killing it instantly. Despite my warnings, Nokosi swam toward the drifting canoe instead of the peat. Like the plague of Exodus, thousands of frogs appeared. They darted to the surface and hopped on top

of Nokosi one by one until they covered him completely. He
shook them off, but more appeared immediately to replace them.
The fleshy pile grew, the weight of it driving Nokosi below the
surface. Soon there were too many frogs to count, hundreds of
pounds' worth, at least. The frogs formed a thick blanket on the
top of the water, directly above Nokosi, trapping him beneath the
surface. His knife flashed up in defiance. He stabbed and stabbed
until dead frogs covered every inch of the blade from tip to hilt,
but it was hopeless—there were too many, and soon the knife
stopped plunging and it sank into the pile and I knew my noble
companion was drowned. Their job complete, the frogs darted off
in every direction, their bowed legs flexing on sinewy hinges.
Bowlegs . . .

When I could find the wherewithal to turn away, I looked to
the second canoe. Bolek was sitting quietly, stone-faced, unmoved
by the unnatural death of his tribesman. I assumed he was in
shock, as was I. With Nokosi dead, I would have to abandon my
canoe and join the boy in his. I beckoned him over. Bolek lifted
his paddle, cut the water, and plied toward the peat. But when he
reached the other canoe, he backstroked, slowed, and sidled up
next to it. Bolek snatched my bag and set it at his feet. He rifled
through it, retrieved the vasculum, and placed it in his lap. Next
he found my field journal, *this* field journal, and tossed it across
the water to me. Bolek smiled a cruel, heartless smile. There was
no "boy" in that smile. It was the smile of a devious man finding
delight in the suffering of his enemy. Bolek canoed around the
peat mat, then paddled away, out of the lagoon, out of sight,
taking all hope with him.

15

While the others were too stunned to move, Perch didn't hesitate. He sprinted across the spongy hammock, not the least bit concerned that he might fall through. He leaped off the edge, diving into the water after Creeper.

Piper just stared at the spreading ripples on the surface where her brother had belly flopped through, and screamed inside her head.

Macey yanked hard on the motor's cord, firing it up. She steered the boat over the area where Creeper and Perch had disappeared, and cut the motor.

Piper used the short trip to gather her wits. She couldn't see any movement below the surface. It was too murky. She propped herself on the gunwale.

She heard Tad say, "You'd better not be doing what I think you're—" But Piper was underwater before he could finish. For the third time in one day, she was under the boat.

With the sunlight streaming down from above, she could see through the water a little more clearly. The hammock cast a deep shadow below, but Piper could still make out the thick base of the plant stalk running from the swamp floor up through the peat. The trunk of it widened toward the bottom. If she wrapped her arms around the base, she doubted her fingers would touch. The shaft of the plant must have been sixty or sixty-five feet from the base to the tip where the flower had grown. Now the flower was somewhere underwater, too. Even if she could find the vasculum, it wasn't waterproof. Exposed to the swamp's bacteria, the flower was already starting to rot. And if she couldn't save Creeper, he'd rot below too. Their quest was over. Now she had to find her brother, and fast. Before anything could eat him.

There were fifty or more large animals circling the base of the stalk, just under the hammock. They were ignoring her. She watched them swim in a counterclockwise path, waiting like soldiers for the plant's chemical orders.

The bulk of the menagerie was made up by alligators. Big ones. Any of them could swallow her brother whole, if that's how alligators fed. It wasn't. Piper had seen a documentary and learned how they latched on to their prey, then launched into a move called a death roll. An alligator grabs the victim's arm or leg (or possibly the head), and uses the powerful muscles in its tail and torso to roll in the water, spinning faster and faster, like a figure skater, twisting the part clean off its victim's body. She couldn't remember if gators could eat while submerged. Probably not. Her fear was that while she wasted time underwater, one had already dragged her brother onto the land to feast on him in the mud.

There were other creatures too. The turtle that had attacked the *Mud Cat* was using its clawed, paddlelike legs to propel itself languidly through the swift-swimming gators, like a school bus in the fast lane. And there were sirens, at least six or seven, wriggling between the bigger animals. Piper saw snakes. Lots of snakes. Mostly big cottonmouths, but that wasn't all. A much larger serpent, maybe thirty-feet long and as thick as her leg, was winding through the gloom. Tad had been right; he had seen an anaconda. All she really knew about the snake was that it came from South America and could unhinge its jaws to eat large prey, including humans. The anaconda stopped swimming and curled around the stalk. Piper inspected its body for any Creeper-size lumps. Thankfully, there were none.

The massive plant and its animal minions resembled a nightmarish carousel that had overturned in the water and was still churning away haphazardly below. Piper feared that if she lingered a moment longer, she'd be hypnotized and then meld into its living layers, becoming part of it forever. She scissor-kicked her way toward the bottom to look for Creeper there.

The water warmed as she descended, and there was a bit of a current, but it was pulsing back and forth like a washing machine, instead of in one direction like a river. Closer to the bottom, the swamp was clouded with silt and rife with hovering pom-poms of pulled peat.

Piper didn't notice she'd reached the bottom until she plunged her right foot into the cool sludge that had caked there over thousands of years. It was thick and clumpy, like oatmeal. She didn't want to know what might be crawling around inside of it. Piper yanked her foot free and treaded water above the goop, groping around in the roiling plumes of silt for Creeper. Gradually, the silt and plant debris began to settle, and her eyes adjusted to the gloom. She could make out a dozen or more enormous vinelike branches as big as bridge cables resting on the bottom. These branches radiated from the base of the plant stalk in all directions. Attached to the branches were dozens of enormous fleshy pods. They looked like figs, but each was the size of a small car. In addition to the twelve pod-covered branches, she counted four unique branches. These branches were gigantic, three times the size of the others, and they ran north, south, east, and west, like the cardinal points of a compass. If viewed as a wheel, the plant was the axle rising up from the water and its branches were the spokes radiating outward across the swamp bed. The whole layout looked like a set from a movie about aliens.

Piper swam above the pods, searching for a hint of red, the color of Creeper's shirt. The clusters of pods reminded her of a pumpkin patch loaded with record-size pumpkins, only these were yellow-green, not orange. Some of the pods were deflated, flattened out like beanbag chairs. She passed over one branch and was about to swim to the next, but a voice in her head told her to look back. She saw a flutter of movement inside one of the pods. There was something trapped within, struggling to get free. She could see the walls of the pod pulsing outward. At one point it stretched into a very distinct shape, the hand of a small boy. Her brother, she realized, was inside the pod, struggling to break out.

Piper was desperate for air, but there was no time to ascend. She swam back to the pod, crawled on top of it, and tried to rip it open with her fingernails. She'd grown them long for the upcoming pageant, but they barely made a scratch. She hunted for an opening or a seam, but the pod was tight as a drum. Creeper had gotten inside, but Piper had no idea how. She'd have to force her way in, and for that she needed some kind of tool. She looked around and spied something metal shimmering in the water, just a few yards away. It was sticking out of the muck, handle end up. Perch's bowie knife.

Piper liberated the knife from the muck. She swam around the pod, searching for the weakest point, and found an area that looked slightly thinner, close to the stem. She couldn't just stab the pod willy-nilly and risk skewering Creeper. She had to be careful even though her lungs were burning.

Leaning into the handle, she managed to drive the tip of the knife slowly and steadily through the skin. She was almost through when the knife stuck fast. It was wedged in so tight that she couldn't pull it back out. Keeping a firm grip on the handle, she took a sizable step back and set one foot high on the pod, intending to use her weight to unstick the blade. But her back foot grazed something whiskery, and an instant later she felt herself being yanked away by a powerful current as though she were being sucked up by a giant vacuum cleaner.

In a blink of the eye, Piper's found herself imprisoned inside the pod next to Creeper's. She was spinning around, disoriented and helpless. When the water within the pod settled, she came to a rest curled up on her back at the bottom.

Piper was out of air. She had to get free and to the surface immediately. She stomped her feet into the fleshy wall of the pod. It stretched but didn't break. Without the knife, she was in serious trouble.

Piper saw a pocket of air trapped against the roof. She jammed her face into it and drew a deep breath. The air smelled terrible, a musky, reeking stench, like rotting fish. But it still provided oxygen, and she was grateful for it. It would keep her alive, for now. She stopped thrashing and just floated. She needed to calm down and think. She hoped Creeper had a pocket of air in his pod, too. His rescue was taking way too long, and if not he might already be dead.

She ran the tips of her fingers over the wall's spongy pulp and tried to make sense of it all: a plant stalk the size of a telephone pole . . . the single flower sprouted from the tip . . . the network of thick branches running along the floor of the swamp . . . the lack of roots . . . the pods . . .

The pods.

No, not pods. Bladders. They were *bladders.*

Piper remembered the bladderwort plant that Perch had draped across the bench, with its feathering stems, pea-shaped traps, and its single flower sticking up out of the water like a beautiful, petaled periscope. On the surface, the towering plant was beautiful and enticing. Beneath the surface, it was something else entirely. Something horrific and savage.

Its given name crawled into her mind like a germy insect.

Mergo.

This massive plant with its hundreds of hair-triggered, trap-door bladders was Mergo. It had to be. In his journal Dr. Cole had mocked it, called it a joke. The joke had been on him. And she, Piper Canfield, was at that moment struggling to stay alive inside Mergo's sloshing digestive juices. If she didn't escape soon, she would never escape. And then, day by day, her body would decompose. Bit by bit, her liquefying corpse would be filtrated through the branches to be consumed as nourishment.

She would become plant food.

For a while, her body would remain mostly unchanged, like one of those perfectly preserved animals floating in a bottle of formaldehyde at the Jesup Nature Center. But then, over time, she would be dissolved and converted to energy. Energy Mergo would use to help it grow. To help it trap and feed on others. It would be as if she'd never existed. Never been part of a family. Never had friends or hopes or dreams or fears. Even bones vanish in time.

She kicked and clawed and pummeled the pod. She even tried to bite her way through, but the little pulp she managed to rip off with her teeth burned her tongue and made her gag. She hadn't considered that the plant might also be poisonous. Of course it was! She spit out every last bit. Fatigue had settled into her muscles, but she had to keep going. To her last breath she had to keep—

A faint beam of light passed through the pod and cut into the darkness inside.

Is this the light? Piper wondered. The light people see right before they die? No, it couldn't be. This light was moving, flickering and crawling across the surface of the pod. It was the beam of a flashlight. She reached out to touch it but yanked her hand away just as the blade of Perch's knife penetrated the pod's skin. The blade slid vertically, then withdrew. Then it came back and sliced horizontally, creating a cross-shaped wound in the wall. The blade vanished and was replaced by an arm. Piper grasped it. She took one more drag of air from the pocket, then Tad pulled her free.

She wanted to throw her arms around her hero and give him the tightest bear hug ever, but she knew she'd probably wring the air out of him, so she refrained. Tad pointed up. She shook her head and swam toward Creeper's pod. Tad followed. There was no sign of movement inside the pod. Piper thumped against the top of it. Still nothing. Tad saw the desperation on her face and understood. He handed the flashlight to Piper and started to saw into the pod with Perch's knife while Piper provided him with light to work by. When the hole was Creeper-size, Piper jammed her arm through it. She felt air. Air that was quickly replaced by the water pouring inside.

Piper lay flat against the pod and thrust her arm in deep. She fished around in the digestive juices until her fingertips grazed cloth. Creeper's shirt. She tried to find it again, but it was gone. Gone like the air in her lungs. Tad sensed she was in trouble. He grabbed her other arm and tried to drag her to the surface, but she jerked free. She couldn't leave, even if it meant she would drown there along with—

Inside the pod, warm fingers wrapped around her wrist. Piper heaved, and Creeper came halfway out of the pod. Tad grabbed the boy around the torso and yanked him the rest of the way out. Together, the trio made a break for the surface.

On the swim to the *Mud Cat*, Piper thought of Perch. She hadn't seen him since he dove into the water. Was he still there? Trapped inside one of the pods? Once Creeper was safely aboard the boat, she would have to go back for him. Perch had risked his life to recover her brother, someone he'd only just met. If there was a chance she could save him, she had to try.

They broke the surface and devoured air. Immediately they heard shouts coming from two different directions: one voice from the *Mud*

Cat—Macey's—and the other from somewhere in the distance. Perch was alive and urging them to swim toward him as fast as they could.

"They're coming for you!" he warned. *"Hurry! The animals! They're coming for you!"*

Piper zeroed in on his voice. Perch was safe, somewhere on the landmass at the far western edge of the lagoon. He was running down the shore, waving his arms. She panned around, trying to get a bearing, and found the stalk, broken and slanting down into the water some twenty yards away. They'd swum up at an angle to avoid the plant's protectors. What was Perch yelling about? Piper dunked down to have a peek.

Perch was right; the animals were abandoning Mergo's stem and heading in their direction. The alligators, the snakes, the snapping turtles, all creatures great and deadly, were spearing through the water, an array of living torpedoes. Mergo had sicced the animals on them, turning the sheepdogs into attack dogs.

Piper rose and shoved the boys, setting them in motion toward the shore. If they made a break for the *Mud Cat*, they would be intercepted long before they reached it. They had no choice but to try to beat the creatures to land and then hope they could get up into the trees before the gators could overtake them. She didn't know how fast gators could run, but in the kids' exhausted and waterlogged condition, she was worried it would be a hair shy of a photo finish.

"Keep going! Hurry! Hurry!" Perch was acting as their swim coach and lookout. The panic in his voice told them everything they needed to know: the animals were gaining on them.

Something got its mouth around Piper's ankle. She kicked at it with her other foot and removed it. She looked back and saw a siren falling away, dazed. If an alligator had chomped on to her, she'd be dead or swimming with one leg. Instead, she made it the shore right behind the boys, alive and in one piece.

"Give him here!" Perch threw Creeper over his shoulder, and they bolted to the tree line. From there they watched the animals closely.

"They're not following us," Tad observed. "They're staying in the water."

Some of the alligators were thrashing about in the shallows, slapping the water with their tails. They didn't appreciate being deprived of their prey, and vocalized their frustration with rumbling bellows. But they stopped their pursuit shy of the shore grass, as commanded. Piper wondered if Mergo had sent out a new kind of volatile that heeled them or if they were just mentally programmed to stay in the water to protect the plant. It didn't matter. The threat was over for now.

"They're heading back to the stalk," said Perch. He lowered Creeper and set him against the trunk of a black gum tree. "We're in the clear. I honestly didn't think y'all were gonna make it! That was a close shave."

Piper fell to the soft ground next to Creeper and draped her arms around him. He put his head on her shoulder and rested.

"I'm sorry about the flower," Perch said. "After all we went through to get here . . ."

Piper was heartbroken, too, but she was also filled with gratitude toward Perch and Tad. "Thank you both so much. Thank you for saving my brother."

Perch took an uncharacteristic pass on credit. "Tad did all the work. He's the hero."

"You dove in first," Tad reminded him.

"What little good that did," Perch said. "I looked for Creeper but didn't see him anywhere. There was nothing but weird blobby things at the bottom. Where'd you find him?"

Tad glanced down at Piper. "You're not going to believe us when we tell you, Perch."

"At this point, nothing will surprise me. But save the story for the ride home. We need a pickup." Perch jogged back to the shoreline. "Hey!" he yelled to his first mate. "We're okay!"

"Y'all scared me half to death!" Macey hollered. "Give me a minute. I'll swing on over and get you!"

Creeper squished his ear with his palm in an attempt to relieve the pressure inside. "Do we have to go back into the water? Please say no. I've never been so scared in my life."

Piper rubbed his shoulder. She was scared too. Not because of the animals, but because of Mergo itself. Another trespass violation seemed like more than it would allow. "I don't know. We'll find out in a second."

Perch heard them from the shore. "Macey'll use the steering lever to raise the motor and run the boat right up onto the bank. Curbside service."

"I gotta show you something!" Macey hollered across the lagoon as she yanked on the starter cord. "Yer not gonna believe it!"

The motor roared to life on the first pull and drowned out her voice. Perch attempted to read her lips, but he was no expert at the trick, and what he thought he picked up had to be wrong. It just had to be. Whatever Macey was trying to tell him would have to wait. He turned back to the tree line and waved the others over.

Piper helped Creeper to his feet, and Tad carried him piggyback to the shore.

Macey aimed the *Mud Cat* at them and squatted to sit down on the stern.

Madness erupted with a splash.

An alligator gar the size of a surfboard leaped from the water. The fish thwacked her in the ribs with its wide spotted tail, knocking her overboard, into the swamp. Macey resurfaced, sputtering.

The kids cried out to her.

Macey reached up, grabbed the gunwale, and started to pull herself back into the boat. Mergo had other plans.

The anaconda erupted from the water and coiled around her torso, adding a portion of its immense weight to her own. Macey's biceps bulged, and in a Herculean effort, she chinned herself up to the gunwale. Piper had never seen anything so extraordinary; the old woman was a fighter.

With the anaconda's lower half wrapped around Macey's torso, crushing her ribs, the snake's upper half slithered up her back and piled onto the gunwale. Under the combined weight of woman and snake, the *Mud Cat* began to capsize. Macey looked to the kids. Piper saw the fear in her eyes.

If the boat overturned, they'd all be stranded. Macey knew that too. She wouldn't let it happen.

"Hang on, Mace!" Perch rushed toward the water.

The snake was squeezing Macey tight, compressing her ribs against her lungs. She was forced to use her last bit of air to squeak one final order: "Stay!"

Perch moaned and howled and tugged at his hair, but in the end he obeyed and stayed out of the water. Macey's eyes locked on his face. She smiled lovingly at her friend. Then she blinked her good-bye. Perch collapsed to his knees, helpless to save her. "No, Macey! Don't let go!"

"Look away, Creeper," Piper said, making sure he did. She wished she could look away, too, but she couldn't. She felt an obligation to the woman to stay with her until the end.

Macey let go of the gunwale and grabbed hold of the snake with both hands, yanking it off the boat. The *Mud Cat* rocked level and slid away, safe. Snake and woman went underwater, locked in a deadly embrace.

And just like that, Macey was gone.

Heartbroken, Perch rocked back on his feet and sobbed. Piper went to put her hands on his shoulders, to comfort him.

Without warning, Perch let out a ripping growl and sprang upward, accidentally elbowing Piper hard in the head. He was too lost to notice.

Piper saw spots exploding in her eyes.

Perch bawled. "I'm coming, Mace! Hang on!" Sludge and swamp juice spattered up his pant legs as he thudded into the water. Tad chased after him, commanding him to stop.

Piper fell to the ground.

Everything went dark.

16

"Anyone sitting here?" The tall girl with the sparkling green eyes and the fishtail braid didn't wait for Piper to answer. She set her tray down across from Piper and made herself at home.

Piper didn't want company. She thought she'd made that obvious by the way she'd spread her lunch items strategically to cover most of the table, but without appearing crazy. This girl couldn't take a hint.

"I'm Olivia," the intruder said. "I'm sure you knew that, though. Everyone knows who I am. And who my friends are."

Piper didn't bother to look up from her creamed corn. "Sure I do. You're part of the pageant crowd. You won Junior Miss Tybee Island at the fair last summer. I was there."

"I won the summer before that too. I was also a judge at the baking contest."

Apparently, humble pie wasn't a dessert Olivia was familiar with.

"Good for you," said Piper. "Why aren't you sitting with your friends?"

"I was hoping *you and I* could be friends. Actually, I'm acting as an emissary. The girls and I have been watching you for a while. We think you'd be a good fit with our group."

They'd been watching her. How wonderfully creepy. "Why

would you think that? None of you ever talk to me. You don't know anything about me."

"Don't be silly!" Olivia lightly batted Piper's hand and gave a fake, buttery laugh. "Obviously you're pretty enough to hang out with us—that's never been in question. In fact, you'd be the prettiest girl in school if you didn't always dress like the janitor." She cackled. "It's nothing that a trip to Macy's can't fix."

"So then what's the problem?" Piper asked, although she couldn't care less.

"Oh, there's no problem. Not anymore. See, until recently your choice of friends has been a little . . . problematic."

"Oh yeah? How so?"

"Well, for one example, there's that boy you were always with."

"Tad? What's wrong with him?"

"Is that his name? How funny. Well, he's a *tad* too skinny. And a *tad* too bookish. And a *tad* too peculiar. If you want my honest opinion—"

Piper didn't. Just because she'd stopped hanging out with Tad didn't mean she'd allow this witch to insult him. "He's okay. Leave him alone."

"Oh, I'm delighted to leave him alone." Olivia smirked. "It looks to me like you are too." She rose off her seat and scanned the cafeteria. "There he is. Sitting waaaay over there. Seems like you two aren't very chummy anymore."

In ten seconds, thought Piper, this chick is going to be wearing a tiara made of creamed corn. "It's none of your business, Olivia."

"You're right. And I don't care." Unfazed, Olivia batted her eyelash extensions at Piper. "But now that you've shaken some of the fleas out of your coat, I don't see any reason why you can't be friends with the girls and me. What do you say, Piper? Ready for an upgrade?"

"I don't need friends," said Piper. What she meant was that she didn't *deserve* any friends. And even if that weren't true, she couldn't see how she and Olivia had the slightest thing in common. "I'm fine on my own."

"We're all *fine* on our own," said Olivia, twisting Piper's meaning. "But we're even finer as a group. You'd be amazed how much easier your life would be if you were popular like us. Everything is handed to you on a silver platter."

"Where's the fun in that?" Piper growled. She had reached her limit of this dingbat's nonsense. She started packing her tray to leave. She'd lost her appetite, and her temper would be next.

"You must be kidding! The fun, Piper, is in getting our way all the time! Why carry books when boys will line up to do it for you? Why bother studying when it's a fact that teachers give good-looking people higher grades than ugly ones for the exact same work?"

Piper didn't know where Olivia got her facts, but she didn't think that was true at all. This girl was living in her own little castle in her own little mind. Piper was ready to ditch her. Or hit her. She hadn't decided.

"And the best part of all?" said Olivia. "Nobody expects anything of us! People assume we're always busy doing charity work, or mentoring dumb girls from the elementary school, or cutting ribbons, and they don't want to heap more on our plates. But in reality it's not like that at all. I mean, it could be, sure, if we signed on for those things, but most of the time we're just hanging out at Penelope's house, sipping iced tea by the pool. Imagine a day with no responsibilities, then multiply that by three hundred and sixty-five days a year. Sounds pretty sweet, doesn't it?"

Piper eased her grip on her tray and leaned forward, finally joining the conversation instead of just enduring it. "That *does* sound good," she said, but not for Olivia's reasons. Piper wasn't afraid of hard work. Sometimes she even enjoyed it. But the idea of not having anyone depend on her, for *anything*, was exactly what she wanted. When people depended on her, things went wrong. People could get hurt. Promises were broken. If joining Olivia's group meant she could fly under the radar, then that's what she would do.

"Okay, I'm in," said Piper. "Where do I sign?"

"Wonderful!" Olivia clapped like an excited circus seal. "You'll have to spend time with the girls and me, obviously. Maybe a sleepover at Penelope's. Wait until you see her house. You know, her dad is the CEO of a company that makes software for music. Or music for software. I can't remember which."

"Good for him."

"Good for us! They have a home theater that's as big as an actual theater! With a popcorn cart and everything!"

"When do you want to get together?" Piper asked, already dreading her decision.

"Saturday night. We'll have a skin-cleansing party."

"What's a skin-cleansing party?" To Piper, skin cleansing meant thirty seconds with soap and a washcloth.

Olivia lifted her dessert, a cup of chocolate pudding, from her tray and placed it on the table between them. "Mud facials, silly goose! You'll love it!"

Now it was getting weird. "Uh . . . that's not mud," Piper told her. "It's pudding."

"Is it? Are you certain?" Olivia grinned, revealing the longest, pointiest, yellowest teeth. An orthodontist's nightmare. And worst of all, there was a bloody bird feather caught between two canine teeth, although now they all sort of looked like canine teeth. Or alligator teeth. "Look again, Piper."

The dessert cup was growing, expanding until it was the size of a punch bowl. Piper saw worms and pill bugs bubbling up through the jiggling pudding skin. Only it wasn't pudding anymore. It was indeed mud. "Olivia? What's happening?"

Olivia's head morphed. Her mouth elongated, pushing her eyes out to the side of her skull. Her skin turned green and scaly, her forehead flattened out, and her nostrils turned upward until the girl looked exactly like an American alligator. An alligator in a pink Ralph Lauren blouse.

Alligator-Olivia reached across the table, grabbed Piper by the cheeks, and with a booming grunt slammed her headfirst into the bowl. Piper felt the mud, cold and wet on her skin. She wanted to scream, but she knew that if she did, her lungs would fill with dank, buggy muck.

—Piper snapped awake and realized she was lying facedown on the muddy bank of Mergo's lagoon. She jumped to her feet and groomed her face frenetically like an otter. The intertwined memory and nightmare faded, replaced by the horrible realization that Macey was dead.

Creeper helped her to her feet and told her what she'd missed. When Macey was pulled under by the anaconda, Perch had bolted back into the water to attempt a rescue. There was no chance he would have reached her in time. Mergo had suffered damage and was now on the offense, no longer keeping its protectors close. Instead, it was sending them out into the water, like antibodies into the bloodstream, to deal with the foreign invaders. Somehow, while Piper lay unconscious, Tad had managed to drag Perch out of the water all by himself. He'd pinned Perch on the shore until the grief-racked boy stopped struggling. If Tad hadn't restrained Perch, he'd be dead now, just like Macey. Perch had to accept the truth: his friend was dead, and there was nothing any of them could do about it.

"You okay, sis?" Creeper asked.

She rubbed her forehead and felt a tender egg where Perch had clipped her with his elbow. She had a wicked headache too. "I just watched a twisted rerun of a bad lunch date in my head, but otherwise I think I'm fine."

Perch, on the other hand, wasn't fine at all. He was having a meltdown on the shore, and Tad was having a devil of a time trying to restrain him. The siblings scrambled to help.

"He won't listen to me," Tad said. "I'm afraid if I let him up, he'll dart back into the water."

"Get off me!" Perch roared. "She's drowning! I have to save her!"

"She's gone, man!" Tad pounded him with the awful truth. "Macey's gone. The last thing she'd want is for you to throw your life away by getting into that water again."

Tad was pressing down on Perch's back with both hands and had one of his arms pinned beneath his shin. It was an awkward, unbalanced position; he wasn't sure he could hold Perch for long. He'd wrested the knife free from Perch's hand and tossed it into the mud. If the kid had been in his right mind, there'd be no way Tad could have accomplished any of this. Tad needed reinforcements. "Creeper! Piper! Get over here and help!"

Piper jumped in and caught hold of Perch's free arm (at the time, he was using it to reach around and punch Tad in the leg). She grasped his hand tightly, squeezing it every few seconds. Piper could only imagine the depth of his anguish. Macey had been more than just his first mate. She was his family.

"I'm so sorry, Perch," Piper cooed. "Please don't fight us anymore. We want to let you up. We want to help you. . . ."

Perch flapped around on the ground for several more seconds, then abruptly gave up the struggle, falling completely limp. He dropped his chin into the muck. "Just leave me here," he sobbed. "I don't care anymore. Leave me here to suck mud."

"Macey wouldn't want that either," said Piper, choosing her words carefully. "She'd want you to survive this and get home alive. She'd want that for all of us."

Perch let out a grief-stricken moan, like the mooing of a sickly cow.

"Listen to me," said Piper. "Macey could have given up when her daughter died all those years ago, but she didn't. She had a good life and helped a lot of people in the process. And maybe in a way you were like her second chance, Perch. You were like a son to her; I could see that right away. She'd want you to keep going, grow up and grow old. Something Georgia never had the chance to do. Macey was a brave woman. She didn't let tragedy beat her, and now she's in a better place. She's with Georgia now. Let her be your example here."

Tad looked at Piper in amazement. Where had those words come from? It had been a long time, but there she was. The girl he'd fallen in love with.

"All right. I know you're right. Okay." Perch sniffled. "I'm good now. Can you please let me up?"

They did, but they formed a blockade between him and the water, just in case. When they were certain he wouldn't try anything stupid, they gave him some space.

For the next ten minutes, Perch didn't utter a single word. Like a shorebird, he just paced across the beach, staring at the mud. Finally he calmed down and began the task of cleaning himself up. He'd lost his T-shirt head wrap when he dove off the battery, so he had nothing to swab the mud off his body. He used his hands to squeegee as much of it off as he could. Then he combed his filthy hair back with his fingertips.

"I look like the Creature from the Black Lagoon, don't I?" he said in a fragile voice.

What he looked like to Piper was a strong young man made weak by a great loss.

"Nah. You're ready for the paparazzi." Piper rubbed the back of his arm. "Or at least a hike."

"A hike?" Perch balked at the idea. "We can't hike our way out of here. The last guy who tried was lost in the Oke for forty-two days. When I've rested a bit, I'll swim for the *Mud Cat*. It's our only way out of this place."

"I thought we agreed; nobody's going back into the water?" said Tad. "We'll hike west. Hopefully reach a road by tomorrow."

"No way," said Perch. "If we leave here and you're wrong, we may not be able to find our way back to our only mode of transportation."

Creeper stomped hard in the mud. "You can't go back into the water with that . . . that monster!"

"The anaconda"—Perch's jaw flexed involuntarily—"is busy."

"My brother isn't talking about the snake," said Piper. "There's something you should know about the plant."

"You mean other than the fact that it leaks out some kind weird Jedi-mind-trick chemical to control a legion of animals? And that it's holding a grudge against us for stealing its pretty corsage? What else is there to know?"

Piper believed that preposterous ideas needed to be stated in the most straightforward way possible. "I think the plant is Mergo."

"I do too," Creeper said quickly, in lockstep with his big sister now that she'd made amends.

Perch cackled. "You two must be drunk on the stink water. That thing is no monster or demon. It's just a stupid plant with a couple of nasty tricks up its leaves. Right, Big Brain? Tell them how crazy they sound."

Tad gazed off at the bent stalk in the middle of the lagoon. "Honestly? I think that plant is what my ancestor's guides feared. And I think it's what probably killed them all."

Perch rolled his pretty eyes. "Are you trying to tell me that this plant is some kind of deranged serial killer? Plants can't think! They don't even have brains!"

"Some of what you've said is true," said Tad. "Plants aren't, as a rule, murderous and evil. Their reactions are instinctual, not deliberate. They don't scheme like we do. But they *can* sense when they're being threatened."

Perch let this sink in. "So you agree, right? It's just a dumb plant."

"I think Mergo is a killer. I'd bet the vasculum on that. While the volatiles are a neat trick, the plant doesn't need the animals to kill for it. It's capable of doing its own dirty work. And it seems to be coordinating its attacks on us. That means something."

Perch threw his hands up in frustration. "Well, now you've lost me!"

Piper explained about how the pods had trapped and nearly drowned her and Creeper, and would have if Tad hadn't saved them. "It happened so fast. Sucked us right up and there was nothing we could do to stop it."

"So it acts exactly like a bladderwort," Perch said, satisfied with his assessment.

"No," said Tad. "The bladderwort reacts automatically when something brushes against its trigger hairs. Like how you can't help but kick when a doctor tests your reflexes by hitting you below the knee with a rubber mallet. But I think that even without a brain, or at least a brain in the traditional sense, Mergo has evolved some unique mechanism that gives it predator intelligence. It sensed our presence in its water, it tried to kill you when you cut into the stalk. And now it's reacting to the damage we caused it. A bladderwort can't do that. There are other differences too. I'm talking about Mergo's network of branches. If you think of the ones with the pods as veins, then the four giant podless branches would be the plant's arteries. I'm not sure where the arteries lead to or what their purpose is. To be honest, I think Mergo is a true miracle. It may be the forerunner of some evolutionary shift in the plant kingdom. Maybe someday plants will be at the top of the food chain, like how mammals took over for the dinosaurs. Think about it. We discovered Mergo! This could be the most important new species since—"

"Whoa, there," Perch cut him off. "It almost sounds like you want to join the misfit protection program with the snakes and gators. This monster you're in love with killed my friend. If I could, I'd rip it up from the swamp floor and jam it in a giant wood chipper."

Tad blushed. "That's not what I'm saying."

"Good," Perch said. "Don't get too attached to that . . . *thing*, Big Brain, because once I get you three to safety, I'm comin' back here to kill it."

"You mean *if* Mergo lets you," Tad said.

This challenge was the last thing Perch needed to hear. "You think that plant's gonna kill my Macey and get away with it? I promise you this, I'm gonna stick my green thumb right up its—"

"Stop it!" Piper was sick of the pointless posturing. At that moment, Mergo was holding all the cards. They were trespassing in its domain, and they needed to get far away from the lagoon. "Let's decide. I vote we try to hike out. I think getting back into the water would be suicide. Even if one of us did make it to the *Mud Cat*, that didn't stop Mergo from killing Macey. She was in the boat. The gar knocked her out, remember?"

"Stop calling it Mergo!" Perch flared. "It's just a plant!"

"I'm siding with Piper," said Tad.

Perch threw his arms up and danced a mocking jig. "Well, there's the surprise of the century! Tad votes with Piper!"

"What on earth is that supposed to mean?" Piper asked.

"Shut up, Perch." Tad warned him with a look.

"Wake up, Princess!" Perch said, then jerked his thumb at Tad. "This dope is in love with you! Are you really that naive?"

"What? No, he's not!" Piper protested. In a day full of outrageous ideas, this took the cake. If Tad, her friend of forever and a day, was in love with her, she'd be able to tell.

"You don't think?" said Perch. "I guess I know Big Brain better than you do."

"Shut *up*!" Tad snapped.

"Tad and I are just friends," Piper insisted. "We have been for years. Well . . . not this past year, but that was my fault."

Perch pointed out the flaw in her thinking. "So after a year of being a bad friend, you came to him with your problem, and Big Brain didn't tell you to go suck a lemon? He just said, 'Why sure, Piper! I'd be happy to go poking around the biggest swamp in the country to help you find a flower that nobody has ever seen in like . . . *ever!*' Yeah, like *that* makes sense, Princess."

Piper knew that Perch was in a dark place, so she tried to be patient with him. Only one person knew how Tad felt, and that was Tad. "Tell Perch he's wrong so we can drop this."

Tad stayed quiet.

"Tad? Tell him," she prodded.

Tad sighed. "I can't, Piper. I can't tell him that."

Piper was stunned. "So . . . it's true?"

Perch snatched his knife from Tad's hand and slammed it into the sheath on his belt. "Now that we've cleared the air, I guess we'd better get a move on. No need to finish the vote. I don't want any more dirty secrets stinking up my boat. We'll walk." He took one last long at the *Mud Cat*. "I'll be back for you, darling," he promised. Then he whirled off toward the forest with Creeper dogging his heels, leaving Piper and Tad to stare awkwardly at each other.

Piper's cheeks flushed pink, making her freckles disappear. "I . . . I didn't know."

"You weren't supposed to," Tad muttered. His tone was flat and frosty. "Don't worry about it. We won't talk about it again. And I'm sorry about the flower. I'm sorry about Grace."

Before she could reply, he turned and strode after the other boys.

Piper looked out across the lagoon and surveyed the damage she'd caused. The *Mud Cat* was abandoned and unreachable. Macey was gone. The flower was gone. Her one chance to save Grace was gone with them. It was all over. Well, not entirely over. They still had to trek their way to safety, and while they were leaving Mergo behind, the danger was still considerable. There were rattlesnakes and biting insects and the biggest threat of all: being totally lost with only five or six hours of daylight left before dark.

Her eyes lingered on the johnboat resting vacant in the water. It was full of camping equipment, but they'd have none of it tonight. Well, except for the flashlight. She patted the cylindrical bulge of it through the fabric of her shorts pocket. At least they'd have light. Until the batteries died.

Piper looked to the sky and peered hard in the direction where she hoped her star was. She imagined it looking down at her and grinning wickedly, as if to say, *This is what you get for going back on a promise.*

Cut me a break! she begged. *I'm trying so hard to make this right. Just let me get my brother home safely.*

At first there was no reply. There was just the expansive blue sky masking the stars. But then something skimmed across it. A hint of red, just a flutter. Piper couldn't believe it. She followed it until it vanished beyond the cypress canopy. Maybe it was a sign sent from above. She chose to believe that. The extinguished coals of hope began to glow again. Piper trotted after it with a fresh spring in her step. It had streaked overhead, traveling in the same direction as the boys. West. This was fortunate. She didn't think they'd listen to her if she asked them to change course. They were tired of Piper dragging them into trouble.

"Wait up!" she called, knowing full well they wouldn't.

17

"**W**e'll keep marching west until we stumble upon civilization," said Perch, taking point on the plan he had nixed just minutes earlier. His workload was light. This wasn't rain forest that had to be hacked through with a machete. The forest here wasn't much different from the one on Billy's Island, except the trees were crusted with black, fire-curled bark and laden with foliage so vividly green that looking up for too long intensified Piper's headache.

"This won't be like marching out of a desert," Perch warned. "We're not going to die of thirst or exposure to the elements. We just have to be careful to avoid stepping on rattlers, cottonmouths, and coral snakes. Or brushing bare skin up against poison sumac or ivy. Don't eat any berries you find until I've signed off on them. You might give yourselves the green-apple quickstep, and there are no toilets 'round here, I assure you. Oh, and if anyone asks 'Are we there yet?' I'm likely to blow my lid. Are we clear?"

"Got it," said Tad. "Besides, I'm pretty sure we'll know when we're there. We're not stupid."

"That's debatable," Perch growled. "This isn't a sightseein' trip. It's survival. Do what I say and we'll live."

Perch kept a good distance from Tad and Piper, but he found it impossible to shake Creeper, who had to run in periodic bursts to keep up because of his short legs. Tad and Piper were able to talk privately as long as they whispered, although Tad could barely look at her now.

"I messed up," Piper said. "This is all my fault."

"Not entirely," said Tad. "I could have said no. I could have, and you wouldn't have come here without me."

"You said yes because you never gave up on me, Tad, even though I was mean to you. If I hadn't pushed you away a year ago, it would have been easier for you to tell me how crazy this plan was. Instead, you went along with it because you . . ." She had trouble speaking the words.

"Go ahead and say it," Tad prodded. "The cat is out of the bag. I went along with it because I like you. A lot."

"See? It's all my fault."

"Let's just agree to disagree," he said. "Besides, I'm the descendant of Dr. Brisbane Cole. I suppose that made his quest mine too."

"Maybe," said Piper, but she knew he was just trying to make her feel less guilty. "Tad, I honestly had no idea that you felt so—"

"Drop it, okay? I don't want to talk about it."

"Sorry."

They passed through a tight corridor of saw palmettos and were forced to pay attention or get pricked. When they exited, Tad had a new topic ready.

"There's something I don't understand about Mergo," he said.

"Just one thing?"

"It's a freak of evolution, no doubt about that. But what I don't get is how it reproduces."

"Yuck. Who cares? As long as it doesn't spread to Jesup."

"Piper, this could be important. It's a flowering plant—we know that. The silver flower was the reason we came."

She slapped a yellow fly off her cheek before it could bite. "So?"

"Sometimes flowers can be self-pollinating, and maybe that's the answer, but most flowering plants need animal pollinators, like bees or bats. In Mergo's case, it would have to be something a lot bigger than a bee. Possibly a bat, but probably something bigger than that."

Piper's mind drifted to the story of the Daughters of the Sun. Right before the Seminole warriors were hit by a wave, some kind of creature had screeched. Something the Seminoles didn't recognize. But she'd scolded Creeper for believing that myth, and she felt stupid for considering it now. "Bats," she said. "Probably just bats."

"Fine, let's assume the pollinators are bats. That would mean there was more than one flower in the swamp, and the pollinators were traveling between them."

Piper stopped in her tracks and grabbed Tad's arm. "Wait! There may be two flowers in the swamp? Or more?"

"It's possible, I suppose."

"That's amazing news! Why didn't you say so earlier? Don't you get it? If there's more than one flower, that means we get another shot at saving Grace!"

"Piper, more than one flower means more than one Mergo."

"Oh," she said. "I hadn't thought of that." They started walking again.

"But to be honest, I think Mergo's flower is just for show," Tad said. "Maybe the plant doesn't reproduce through pollination at all. There is another way. Bladderworts reproduce through pollination, but also through fragmentation."

"I'm sure whatever that is, it's spectacularly gross, but Mergo *does* flower, so you can spare me the nasty details. Besides, if Mergo reproduces through some other method, then why would it need a flower at all?"

"Bait, Piper," said Tad. "The flower could be bait."

"Bait? Bait for what?"

"Who do you think? Bait for us. We came looking for it, didn't we?"

"Are you saying it knew we were coming? That it sensed us conspiring over Dr. Cole's journal all the way over in Jesup?"

"Don't make fun. I'm not saying it flowered just for us. Humans have been in the swamp for thousands of years. I'm sure the Creek Indians were tempted by it too. And the soldiers who drove them out, as well. And the lumbermen. All the early swampers. What value would the flower have to any creature but humans? If it's really a disease cure-all—and at this point I believe it is—then it's an enticing prize for the one animal that would know how to use it: people. I'm sure Cole wasn't the first or last person to make a grab for the flower."

"No, *we* were the last," she reminded him. "And now it's underwater and Grace is going to die."

"Sorry," said Tad. "I shouldn't have brought this up."

"You're overthinking things. Mergo is nothing more than the plant version of the board game Hungry Hungry Hippos, gobbling up any creature unlucky enough to swim too close to its bladders." Piper was tired of talking about it. Even if Mergo did grow the silver flower to bait humans, so what? It was waterlogged and rotting inside the vasculum at the bottom of the swamp, and every step they took away from Mergo was a blessing. Good riddance to bad roughage.

A few minutes later, without realizing it, they trudged into a graveyard. They mistook the first tumulus for a bump in their path. They walked around the burial mound, paying it little mind. But then they came upon another and another, and then they were surrounded by them on all sides. These tumuli were different than the one on Billy's Island. That one was the length and width of a mobile home and was likely packed tight with dead bodies, like a gruesome burrito.

The mounds in this forest were small, just roomy enough to fit one body each. They'd been there a very long time. Trees had grown up through some of them, splitting them open like baked potatoes. Thankfully, there were no skeletons dangling from the branches. To make matters creepier, there were fresh vines everywhere, growing over the tumuli, spreading across the forest floor. The vines were all thicknesses, from shoelace to gymnasium climbing rope. Several wound up around the trees and threaded through the canopy. Their tips split off into curled pinwheels that reminded Piper of fiddlehead ferns.

The kids stopped to rest and take it all in.

"I've never seen so many tumuli before," Perch said. "Most of the ones on the other islands were demolished and razed flat by the earliest white settlers."

"Looks like they missed these," Tad said. "There must be hundreds of them."

"Who do you think is buried here?" asked Creeper.

"Could be more Tasketcha," said Perch. "Maybe these are the ones who died of natural causes."

"These vines are weird," Tad remarked, leaning in close to examine one draped over a low-hanging branch. "They're everywhere."

"Reminds me of last Halloween when some teenagers TPed our yard," said Creeper.

"They remind me of the invasive kudzu vine back home," said Tad. "They're smothering the other plants."

Creeper reached out to touch one.

"Don't!" Piper warned. "It might be poisonous. The last thing we need now is for you to get some weird rash. You know how sensitive your skin is."

Creeper withdrew his hand.

"They're probably harmless," Tad said. "But to be safe, let's just avoid them."

They exited the far side of the tumuli graveyard and continued through the forest. The vines continued with them, covering the ground like a haphazardly cast fishing net, the threads crisscrossed atop the leaf litter. The group stepped high to avoid them, but Creeper was still exhausted from his ordeal in the pod, and his legs were shorter than the others'. He started dragging the tips of his sneakers, and inevitably he tripped over a vine, jerking it hard. Creeper landed in a clumsy heap.

"Are you okay?" Piper jogged ahead to help him.

"I think so," he replied. Creeper rocked back and sat on his calves. "I'm just really tired."

The sound of rustling drew their eyes to the forest canopy.

"You guys hear that?" asked Perch. The leaves were shaking. The timber was creaking. "Something's up there."

The curled leaves at the tips of the vines—Tad called them fronds—looked strange to Piper. Like something from the age of the dinosaurs. They resembled rolled-up octopus tentacles, but they were green and lined with fine hairs instead of suckers. "Huh." She squinted. "Those fronds . . . are they unrolling?"

She was correct—the fronds were rapidly unfurling.

"That can't be good," Tad said. "I think we ought to keep moving. Now."

They hustled through the woods, keeping a close watch on the canopy.

"Look!" Creeper yelled. "They're falling!"

When the tip of each vine had finished unfurling—most were as long as jump ropes—they snapped off, one by one, and dropped to the ground. It was raining vines.

When the vines landed, the most horrific thing happened. They slithered through the leaf litter silently, like faceless snakes, propelling themselves forward with a side-winding locomotion. Each and every one of them headed straight for the kids.

"Run!" Perch ordered. He didn't have to tell anyone twice.

The snaky-vines were fast. The group had to run at full speed to keep ahead of them; Perch led the way, followed by Creeper, then Tad. Piper brought up the rear. She didn't know what would happen if the snaky-vines caught up to them. She didn't want to know.

She found out anyway.

A vine dropped right on top of Piper's shoulder. Before she could shake it off, it coiled around her neck twice, crushing her windpipe. Piper stopped running and dropped to one knee. "Help," she wheezed, hoping the boys could hear her.

They hadn't, but Tad looked back to check on her anyway and saw that she was in trouble. He doubled back, dodging the vines raining down around him. The ground became a deadly obstacle course as the vines hit the earth with soft thuds and then sprang to the chase.

"Hey! Piper needs help!" Tad yelled, alerting the others. Creeper and Perch made a U-turn.

It was like being in a snake pit, only instead of hissing and biting, the snaky-vines were stalking their prey silently, twirling their heads (or bottoms—it was impossible to tell which end was which), sniffing the air for something good. Piper thought of the dodder vine Tad had told them about after Perch got tangled under the boat. She remembered Tad's exact words: *Plants don't hunt.* He was wrong. If these vines were hunting by scent, then the group was in serious trouble. They reeked of sweat and fear and probably smelled delicious.

Tad reached Piper. He jammed his fingers between the coils and tried to pull them loose. The vine wouldn't budge. In fact, it tightened.

Piper was turning a deep shade of plum. Her eyes were bulging in their sockets. She'd choked once before, on a Goldfish cracker. Her mom had saved her then with the Heimlich maneuver. The Heimlich wouldn't work this time.

Tad snapped his fingers at Perch. "Give me your knife!"

Perch unsheathed it and slapped it handle-first into Tad's palm. "What *are* these things, man?"

"Plantlets, I think." With extreme care, Tad severed the vine into three pieces. It fell away dead and Piper guzzled air.

Creeper saw the angry purple ligature mark around his sister's neck and started to cry again.

"Don't," she wheezed. "I'm okay."

He saw this was true, but he cried anyway because he loved her. She understood that now.

A snaky-vine wrapped itself around Perch's ankle and started to climb in a spiral route up his leg. Tad tossed him the knife and with a precise downward swipe Perch sliced it off before it could reach his thigh. "Plantlets? What are plantlets?" One half of the bisected snaky-vine made another charge at him, so he hacked off both ends to be safe. He minced the body for good measure.

Snaky-fronds were slithering toward them from all directions.

"Can't explain now!" Tad said.

Perch swung the knife over Tad's head and slashed a falling vine in midair, saving them both a lot of trouble.

"Thanks," said Tad.

"Don't mention it."

The boys checked on Piper. "Are you ready?"

"Ready."

They fled and the vines followed.

Perch took the lead again, ushering them through a thicket of twisted black scrub oaks. They had to slow down a bit to navigate around the curved trunks and duck under crunchy beards of Spanish moss that had been growing for so long they had nearly reached the ground. Rip van Winkle beards.

Something dartlike whizzed past Perch's face.

"Did you guys see that?"

"I did!" said Tad. "I saw it!"

Another dart zinged through the air, passing right through the fingers of Piper's outstretched hand. It hit the side of one of the oaks with a *thwok*, lodged in the bark, and vibrated there. *Thwok! Thwok!* More darts struck the trees.

"Someone's shooting at us!" Creeper yelled. "Stop shooting at us! We're just kids!"

Piper scanned the forest for their assailant, but there was nobody there. Maybe the shooter was hiding.

Pank! Perch deflected a dart with the blade of his knife. He seemed more surprised by this than anyone. It was a lucky accident that kept the dart from piercing his hip.

They kept going, running, clambering over fallen trees, dodging darts, staying just ahead of the slithering snaky-fronds. Suddenly, they burst from the forest into a sunny clearing. It was an empty field except for three or four big oaks clustered in the center. The shooter ceased fire immediately. The snaky-fronds, however, followed them out of the forest. They slithered into the clearing, unwilling to give up the hunt.

But then the oddest thing happened.

Piper saw it first. "They're dying!"

She was right; the vines were withering away. The moment they went beyond the tree line, the snaky-fronds began to spasm, roll into knots, dehydrate, and deflate, like a worm roasting on a hot sidewalk for days.

"Well, *that* makes zero sense." Perch stepped on the snaky-frond closest to him, and they heard it crunch. He ground it to dust with his heel.

"It makes a little sense to me," Tad told them. "Let's go rest against those oaks and we'll talk. I need to catch my breath. We all do."

They walked and limped across the clearing. Behind them, just past the edge of the woods, a dune of dying vines piled up.

18

In a fit of frustration, Perch used his knife to decapitate a bunch of flowering pickerelweeds, whacking the purplish heads off as they tramped by. "Stupid plants," he said.

"That'll show Mergo who's boss," Tad said, unimpressed.

"You know what?" Perch rounded on him and held the knife point out toward Tad's chest. "Stop calling it Mergo! Plants don't have names like people do!"

Tad froze on the spot. He hadn't known Perch long enough to assume the boy was bluffing. "Calm down. I'm not the one who named it," he reminded Perch. "Put the knife away."

"It doesn't deserve a name!" Perch flared. "It's just a freakin' weed. A weed that killed my friend! Killed Macey! I'll come back for it soon. I'll load a boat with bags of herbicide and dump them in the water. That'll do the trick."

"I doubt that," said Tad.

"Perch, put the knife away." Piper tried to calm him. "You're not mad at Tad; you're mad at Mer—" She caught herself. "I mean, you're mad at the plant."

"Yah, yer right," Perch said. "I am." He slid the knife into its sheath. They gave him space as they finished the walk to the center of the clearing.

They rested in the shade of a gnarled oak. As plants go, the tree seemed safe enough. Creeper scampered up to the highest bough that was still within hearing range of the conversation.

"Tad, if you know what that crazy obstacle course was all about, please clue us in," said Piper. "You said those strangler vines were plantlets. What were you talking about?"

"Remember I said there's another method of plant reproduction besides pollination?"

She nodded.

"Some plants reproduce through plantlets. I have several kinds in my greenhouse. A parent grows tiny baby plants in the margins of its leaves. Eventually, these plantlets break off and take root in the soil, where they grow into adult plants, like their parent. I think those vines that tried to choke us to death might be Mergo's plantlets. Or, technically speaking, Mergo's babies."

"Merglets!" Creeper coined a horrible new word.

"How is that possible?" asked Piper. "We left Mergo back in the lagoon, didn't we?"

"Did we?" Tad asked. It was an odd question.

Perch said, "What I want to know is who was the jerk firing darts at us, and why."

"Nobody was firing at us," said Tad. "No human, I mean."

"Then what?" asked Piper.

"First off, they weren't darts. They were nettles. Hollow stinging hairs that cover the leaves of some plants." Tad held out his fist and opened it. There was a nasty-looking woody thorn resting on his palm. "This is a nettle. They're usually a lot smaller than this one, like the hairs on a peach. If you brush up against a normal nettle plant, the nettles will break off and stick in your skin. Some act like hypodermic needles, injecting toxic chemicals produced by the plant into the bloodstream. Depending on the plant species, some of the chemicals can do serious harm to a person. They can blister the skin, cause excruciating pain, hallucinations . . . blindness. I've never heard of a plant that can shoot nettles like darts. Maybe the wind shook them down on us."

"There's no breeze here," Creeper said, wiping sweat from his face. It was always hot in the Oke during August, but today the air was especially still and muggy.

Perch took the nettle from Tad and examined it. It was long enough and sharp enough to sew buttons with. "So you think the whole swamp is out to kill us? Is that it?"

"You should know better than that," said Tad. "You work here."

"Then what?" Perch asked.

"If I tell you what I think, you have to promise you won't call me crazy," said Tad.

"Can I at least *think* it?" Perch asked.

Tad shrugged. "I think Mergo's reach extends beyond the lagoon. I don't know how, but I believe the plant is hunting us on land too."

Perch broke his promise. "That's the most insane thing I've ever heard!"

"Perch . . . let's just listen." Piper didn't want arguments. That's not what they needed. They needed ideas, and so far Tad was the only one who seemed able to offer any.

"Fine." Perch huffed. "We're all ears."

Tad thought Perch was ninety-nine percent mouth, but he kept that thought private. "When the Spanish conquistador Pizarro reached Incan territory in 1526, under royal order, his army conquered the forest people, turning many into slaves. One of those tribes, the Tasketcha, fled to the Okefenokee, and probably brought along things they'd need to survive, right? They'd want to bring seeds, of course.

Maybe one of those seeds came from a unique species of plant. A plant found only in the dark heart of the South American rain forest. From those seeds would grow their protector, a monstrous killing machine to fend off any intruders who might want to harm them—or possibly steal their women. Picture it? Now what if this *protector* grew too large and too hungry and started preying on the Tasketcha too?"

"I'm not sure I'm following you," said Piper. "Are you saying that Mergo was the Tasketchas' . . . pet?"

"Not pet. Protector. And I think the campfire story Perch told us may have some truth to it. I have a hunch that the Daughters of the Sun and the Tasketcha tribe were one and the same. There are similarities. Many South Americans have bronze-colored skin and jet-black hair. . . ."

"And they *are* often beautiful," Piper chimed in. "Contestants from Venezuela won Miss Universe in 2008, 2009, and 2013."

Creeper snorted. "You *would* know that."

"Hush up," she scolded.

"I don't think the Tasketcha were mystical or evil at all. I think they were innocent people who tried to escape Pizarro's army, sought refuge in the Oke, and accidentally released an invading plant species that thrived here and eventually got too big and too hungry to handle. It responded to the poor quality of the soil by evolving quickly into a carnivore, and as time passed, it developed a ton of biological weapons, weapons it's using against us."

He carried on with his point. "There's a botanical garden just outside a castle in England called the Alnwick Garden. I've been there. It's walled off behind big black gates, for good reason. This garden is home to hundreds of the most deadly poisonous plants found anywhere on the planet. Now imagine if a single, extraordinary plant species—a super-adapter—evolved to take on the deadly properties of all of those plants: rapid movement, trap bladders, venomous nettles, plantlets that break free and hunt large game, animal-controlling chemicals, and a flower so tempting that it lures humans right into its clutches. When you think about it, Mergo is the perfect predator."

"Get creepy much?" said Perch.

"Sorry." Tad realized he was coming off as a little too enamored with the plant. "It's just that there's never been a discovery of this significance. Not since Pando."

"Who's Pando?" asked Creeper. "Mergo's cousin?"

"No," said Tad. "Pando is the largest living thing on the planet. A single male quaking aspen in Utah that produced an entire forest colony of clonal trees—trees that have the same genetic code. The trees share a single underground root system, technically making it one living organism. Collectively, Pando weighs over six thousand tons. It's also one of the world's oldest living things, having probably sprouted from a single seed more than eighty thousand years ago."

"Wow," said Creeper. "I didn't know trees could live that long. I definitely want to climb Pando someday."

"What does the name mean?" Piper asked. Tired of standing, she hopped up on one of the oak tree's branches and almost ran her head through a spiderweb, but she noticed it in time and ducked. Piper scooted down the branch, away from it. She hated bugs more than anything, but after being imprisoned inside one of Mergo's bladders, she had a little more empathy for them.

"*Pando* is Latin for 'I spread'," said Tad. "And boy, did it. The root system and its trees spread out across a hundred acres."

"Do you really think Mergo is as big as Pando?" Piper asked. "I mean, as far as I could tell, it's just one stalk and some underwater bladders."

Tad saved his most disturbing theory for last. "Remember I said that Mergo might be hunting us on land? I think I know how. I believe its four main branches run along the bottom of the swamp for quite a ways. All the way back to where the vines tried to drown Perch. Maybe farther. They run beneath this forest too, feathering out into thousands of smaller branches, creating a network that could run for a mile in all directions. So yeah, I think Mergo is as big as Pando. Maybe bigger. The one thing I haven't figured out yet is how the plant seems to know where we are at all times. The attacks just keep on coming, even though we've put some distance between us and the stalk."

Out of the corner of her eye, Piper caught sight of the web's owner returning home from work. The ferocious-looking spider, a golden orb weaver, was two inches long and had a fat black abdomen covered in yellow markings. It skittered to the web's bull's-eye and parked. An orange ladybug hovered down onto one of the web's sticky strands. It struggled to free itself, sending a pulse of vibrations along the thread and into the heart of the web, where it was noticed. The spider went to dinner.

"I think I know how Mergo is tracking us," said Piper excitedly. "Look!" She pointed out the web. The spider was busy wrapping the ladybug up in a silk straitjacket to keep it from escaping.

"Well, that's gross," said Perch. "Thanks for that. Anything else you want to contribute to the conversation?"

"What does a spider have to do with Mergo?" said Tad.

"The plant may be working the same way a spider does," she explained. "The vines covering the forest floor must act like a web. Every time we brush against one of the vines hanging from the trees or step on the ones on the ground, we're letting Mergo know exactly where we are. But Mergo doesn't build a web—"

Tad smacked his forehead. "Duh! Mergo *is* the web!"

"Exactly," she said. "Remember those plantlet things didn't start falling until Creeper tripped over a vine. Maybe all those vines are actually branches shooting off the four large underwater branches.

They poke up through the ground and send signals to Mergo, alerting it to potential snacks. You called it tropism in the greenhouse, Tad. A plant reacting to touch."

"That's right. Actually," Tad said, remembering, "the alligator snapping turtle attacked shortly after the *Mud Cat*—shortly after Perch got tangled up in those vines. Maybe they weren't vines. Maybe they were Mergo's branches, and that was probably the exact moment that Mergo was made aware of our presence in its territory."

"Wait, the animals started following us before that," Creeper reminded him from above. His legs were hooked over a branch and he was hanging upside down like a bat.

Tad said, "True, maybe the boat brushed against other vines along the way. Honestly, though, we just don't have enough information yet to understand the effect Mergo has throughout the swamp."

"Well, now that we have this far-fetched intelligence, what are we supposed to do with it?" Perch asked.

Piper knew that "intelligence," when used in this context, was a military word. He must have picked it up from Macey. People do that, she thought. They pick up ideas and pass them along like gifts to people they care about. Gifts that can be helpful long after the giver is gone.

"We keep moving west, right?" Piper suggested. "Maybe we've gone beyond Mergo's reach. Its plantlets died at the edge of the forest. That's a good sign."

"Maybe," said Tad. "Or maybe it just means that Mergo's babies are only meant to serve its parent for a short time and then die. Maybe a limited life is part of a plantlet's genetic code. That way they can't grow big and become competition for their mother."

"Oh, so now Mergo is a she?" Piper was mildly offended.

"Sorry," Tad said. "The bottom line is that while Mergo may be a wonder of nature, *he's* also firmly in charge of everything around *him*, including *his* offspring."

"Better." Piper smiled weakly.

"Enough with the chitchat," Perch said. "We'll start walking again when we're rested and just hope this place isn't an island, or we're trapped like that ladybug."

Perch tossed the nettle back to Tad. Tad was looking right at him, but the nettle hit his shirt and rolled off to the ground.

Piper touched Tad's arm. He flinched. "Tad? Are you okay?"

Tad furrowed his brow. He poked at the back of his neck, and his sweaty face contorted in pain. "I didn't want to say anything. I was hoping it was a temporary problem. . . ."

"What's wrong?" Piper jumped down from her branch.

Perch stepped close to Tad, leaned in, and inspected the boy's darting eyes. "Where did you get that nettle, buddy?"

"That's the thing." Tad sighed. He turned around and showed them the back of his neck. There was a huge, angry red lump on it, like a poisonous bug bite or a boil. The welt was inflamed. The redness was spreading down his nape and through the valley of his shoulder blades.

"Oh, Tad," Piper gasped. "You were hit in the neck?"

Tad faced them. "I can feel Mergo's venom in my system."

Piper took his hand in hers. "Tell us what's happening."

"Guys, I think . . ." Tad's eyelids fluttered rapidly. "I think I'm going blind."

It was a shocking admission, which led to another.

Perch had been hiding something too.

19

"**W**hat *do you mean the vasculum is on the* Mud Cat?"

Piper had never felt so stunned or betrayed in her life. She wanted to punch Perch right in his handsome face until pieces fell off like Mr. Potato Head. "How is that even possible? And how could you have hidden that from us? Answer me!"

"I didn't say it's *definitely* on the *Mud Cat!*" Perch backed away from Piper when she came stomping across the dried grass toward him. "I said it *might* be on the *Mud Cat!* Big difference! Besides, you three were the ones who wanted to leave my boat behind!"

"*Because we didn't know the flower was onboard, you jerk!*" She lifted a fist, ready to launch it at him if he said just one more stupid thing. "Tell us again, Perch," Piper demanded. "Why do you think the vasculum is on the boat? The last time we saw it—"

"I had it in my hands when I fell," said Creeper. "I dropped it when I hit the water."

"Are you sure about that?" Tad asked. "Or did you drop it when the stem broke? Think hard, Creeper. This detail is important."

Creeper made his scrunched concentration face, which was simi-lar to his "I ate too much Halloween candy and now I'm constipated" face. "I can't remember, honest. It happened so fast. I guess I could have dropped it as soon as I felt the stalk start to fall. I didn't have it in my hands when I went under the water. That's all I know."

"So Creeper might have dropped it onto the hammock," Tad said. "That still doesn't explain how it got into the boat."

"Macey," Perch said. "Macey must have grabbed it while we were all underwater."

Tad wasn't sold. "Perch, are you sure you heard her right?"

"I already told you, I didn't *hear* her at all. The motor was loud, and I was on the shore, too far away. She pointed to something in the boat. I couldn't see what it was. I tried to read her lips. It sure looked like she said 'I've got the vasculum,' but I can't be certain."

"That's not good enough," Tad said, staring slightly to Perch's right. "We can't go back through the woods . . . back into the lagoon, on such flimsy evidence. We'd be risking our lives, probably for nothing."

Piper didn't mince words. "I guess I just have to come out and say it. Your life is *already* at risk, Tad. Mergo is something unknown to science, right? That means the same can be said for its venom. Even if we're able to walk out of the Oke and get you to a hospital, there's no guarantee there's an antivenom. I mean, do they even make antivenoms for plants? I'm betting Mergo's flower can fix you, though." It became apparent to all that Piper had already decided on a course of action.

Creeper started creeping down the oak's trunk. "So we're going back for the vasculum?"

"No, *we* are not going back," Piper replied. She paused, then said, "I am."

"Not without me, you're not!" Tad protested.

"You can barely see! We can't afford the time it would take to guide you through Mergo's web," she told him. "It will be far easier if I just go back myself. I'm nimble-footed. Now that I know to avoid the branches, I think I can get back to the lagoon without drawing any attention."

"I'll go with you," Perch offered. "Two heads are better than one, Princess. If you get caught up in those . . . Merglets, you'll be grateful to have me and my knife along to cut you free."

"And if we're both killed trying to get to the vasculum? Then what?" Piper shook her head. "No, Perch, you have to stay. If I don't make it back, I need you to get Creeper and Tad out of the swamp. You'll have to lead Tad by the hand. And you'll have to look out for my brother. Promise me you won't let him out of your sight."

"Fine," Perch grumbled. "You hear that, buddy? I'm your new babysitter."

There was no complaining. No reply at all. Perch and Piper looked up to the branches, but Creeper was gone. They panned around the clearing and caught sight of him just as he leaped over the pile of dead Merglets. Creeper stopped at the forest's tree line and looked back. He cupped his hands to his mouth and hollered to them.

"I'm going to get the flower! I'm the brother! It's my job! I'll get it for Grace! You guys, um . . . sit! Stay!" When he was done addressing them like puppies, Creeper gave a sad little wave and disappeared into the gloomy woods.

Perch was a fast runner. Maybe faster than Donny Foster, Jesup Middle School's all-time track-and-field ribbon winner. He left Piper in the dust, although that wasn't a major accomplishment, since she was dragging nearsighted Tad by the hand across the clearing.

"Get him, Perch!" Piper screamed. "Don't let Creeper get away!"

Why? Why did I let Creeper come along? she thought with thundering regret. She could have said no back at the Citgo gas station on Temple Street. Then she came to her own defense: *How was I supposed to know we'd be attacked by a giant salad?*

Perch was in the forest long before she and Tad arrived at the threshold. "Tad, just wait here, okay?" Piper insisted. "I'll have a better chance of finding Creeper if I go in alone."

Tad acquiesced but added, "If you don't come back in ten minutes, I'm coming in after you. I'll feel my way through the forest if I have to."

"Don't do that." She waved her hand in front of his face to gauge how much his vision had worsened. He caught her by the wrist.

"I can see well enough, at least two or three feet ahead," he said. "Everything past that is a haze, like I'm surrounded by fog. If you don't want me to follow, then you'd better come back soon."

"Fine!" she said. There was no time to argue. She left Tad and the sunlight behind in the clearing.

In the woods she was alone. There was no sign of Creeper or Perch. At first she moved stealthily, afraid any noise would trigger a response from Mergo. Then she remembered what Tad told her in the greenhouse: *Plants are as deaf as a doornail.* She hoped that was true.

She cupped her hands to her mouth and called out for her brother. "Creeeeeeeper!"

"Creeeeeeeeeeeeeeeeper," the forest echoed dimly.

She hollered for Perch, too, but there was no answer, save for the swishing wake of leaves kicked up by a marsh hare that had been eyeing her from behind a mossy cypress stump. Piper froze in her tracks, waiting to see if the hare's flight would trigger an attack from above—nettles, Merglets, or God knows what. Nothing happened. Maybe the hare is too light, she wondered. Maybe it's beneath Mergo's notice (assuming anything was beneath the notice of such a gluttonous life-form). Either that or the hare was just smart enough to avoid Mergo's sensitive branches. Some animals have a sixth sense when it comes to evading predators.

Piper heard noises up ahead: cracking twigs, the rustle of leaves being raked across the ground. The scream of a boy. She raced toward Creeper, hopscotching through Mergo's web. She wouldn't be much use to Creeper if she was dead, so that meant paying attention to the ground and going more slowly than she wanted to.

When Creeper came into her line of vision, he was on his butt, scuttling away from something blocked from her view by overlapping trees.

"Creeper!"

He heard her. "Piper! Help me!"

She closed in and saw the threat, a black bear swiping the ground with its shaggy forepaws in a bullying gesture.

"I'm coming! I see you! I'm coming!" Her careful trot turned into a thudding sprint. Maybe Merglets fell—she didn't know. Maybe nettles launched. It didn't matter. All she cared about was reaching her brother.

During their RV summer, she'd watched from the opposite side of a river in Montana as an adult grizzly smacked trout out of the water. Although black bears were half the size of grizzlies, the one that was intimidating Creeper was still impressive and clearly powerful. What did she know about black bears? The noisier they are, the less likely they are to attack. This one was stomping its paws, popping its jaw, and huffing in loud snorts. It couldn't make more noise if it tried. She also knew that the best way to scare off a bear was by standing tall, puffing out, and being noisier than the animal. Black bears weren't like grizzly bears. They didn't like to fight.

She waved her arms as she approached. "Hey! Over here! Look at me! I'm in your face! I'm big and bad! You'd better run away!"

"What are you doing?" Creeper asked. "Are you crazy?"

"I'm saving your life!" she snapped.

She stomped her feet and clapped her hands. "Hey, Yogi! Over here! Look at me!"

The bear did as she'd asked—it turned its attention to her. But instead of running away like the wilderness books promised, the bear charged toward her.

Piper saw why her tactic hadn't worked. Several of Mergo's nettles were lodged in its nose and face, and like Tad, the bear was nearly blind. It was acting out of fear and confusion, using its acute smell and hearing to lash out at an unseen assailant.

Piper tried to escape, but her foot caught on one of Mergo's branches. She tripped and fell onto her backside. In a flash, the bear was on top of her. It opened its mouth wide and roared like a train in her face. A blast of hot, stinking breath flooded Piper's nostrils. A rain of spittle spattered across her cheeks and lips. She was going to die. She knew it.

But not yet.

Two thick green tentacles sprang up from the ground and wrapped around the bear, one across its shaggy neck and the other around its broad chest. The end of each tentacle tapered out into a broad, flat tip, a bit like a pizza paddle. One side of each tip—the side stuck to the bear's fur—was lined with fat, clear hairs. Each hair was tipped with a gland like a red dewdrop, dripping with glistening mucus. The hairs wriggled into the bear's fur, finding purchase on its hide. They made a sickening squishing sound, like sticking your hand in soggy macaroni. Seeing the tentacles digging into the bear made Piper want to vomit.

The tentacles yanked the bear off Piper. They lifted the four-hundred-pound animal into the air, and then slammed it hard into the ground by her feet. The bear clawed at the dirt, desperate to escape, but it was no use. The tentacles were too strong. Like the anchor chain of a freighter retracting into its hawse, the tentacles dragged the bear backward through the forest, down into a hole, sucking it into the earth.

Piper heard the animal's muffled cry of anguish traveling beneath the ground, until it went silent abruptly, definitively, and Piper knew the bear was dead.

Creeper flew to her side. "Did it bite you?"

Her heart was drumming in her ears; his question barely registered. "No, it never got the chance," she said, panting, as Creeper helped her to her feet.

"What the heck were those thingies?" he asked, referring to the tentacles. "Giant Merglets?"

"I don't think so; they looked different. Have you seen Perch?"

"No."

Piper yelled for Perch, but there was no response. She grabbed Creeper by the hand. "Let's get you back to the clearing before more of those things show up," she said. "Watch your step, okay?"

They moved as one, marching in high steps over Mergo's tropistic trip wires. This plant was no shrinking violet. Mergo *wanted* to be touched, and not in a warm, fuzzy way. It wanted to be touched so it could touch back.

Piper and Creeper made it a quarter of the way back to the clearing when she saw movement through gaps in a large thicket. It was a wave of small dark-brown creatures plodding across the ground, negotiating a path through the leaf litter. Hundreds of them. Piper hooked a hand over Creeper's shoulder and brought him to a stop.

"Shh. Look." She pointed.

"What are they?" Creeper bent low to find a better viewing hole through the thicket.

"Turtles?" Piper said. It was a fair guess. They had smooth brown shells, like the swamp's numerous basking cooters; they were six or seven inches long; and they were traveling in a herd. She'd seen enough nature documentaries to know that turtle hatchlings often came out of the ground in great numbers and then made a dash together to the water. But then again, these creatures weren't heading to water. They were heading away from it, deeper into the forest. It was bizarre behavior for turtles, if that's what they were.

"What are they pushing?" Creeper asked.

Every creature was rolling a clear ball in front of it, nudging it across the ground, butting it with its shell. The balls were the size of softballs and jiggled a bit with each shove forward.

"I don't know," said Piper. "They look like water balloons."

Despite their size and their shells, Piper decided the ball rollers couldn't be turtles. Turtles didn't have the dexterity to roll balls through a forest. The only time she'd seen this kind of behavior was in a documentary about beetles. The dung beetle got its name for being the most disgusting creature on Earth. When an animal like a cow or a horse poops, the beetle collects chunks, then rolls them into a ball three times its size. Then, like King Sisyphus of Greek myth, the beetle rolls the ball to its burrow for safekeeping. For when it's hungry. Because all true dung beetles eat just one thing—poop. Vile insects. But the creatures marching through the forest weren't rolling balls of poop. Poop isn't clear. And the rollers were way too big to be dung beetles.

To the Canfields' right, a second wave of rollers flushed a pair of mourning doves from the grass.

"I know what they are!" said Creeper.

"Which one? The balls or the things rolling the balls?"

"The things rolling the balls. They're beetles."

"No, they're too big to be dung beetles. I already thought of that."

"Not dung beetles. Titan beetles."

"Huh?"

"Titan beetles. They're super-huge beetles from South America. They're as big as a man's foot, and they have jaws like wire cutters. They can snap a pencil in half. I saw it on Discovery Kids."

South America. That made a weird kind of sense, thought Piper. Another nasty life-form imported to the Oke by the Tasketcha. Just like the anaconda. Just like Mergo. But what were the insects doing? Gearing up for a game of dodgeball?

A new stream of beetles swarmed out of a hole not five feet in front of them. The hole had been covered over by a rug of sphagnum moss. If the kids hadn't halted when they did, they would have fallen down into it.

Piper stiffened, ready to defend Creeper if she had to. If the beetles could snap a pencil with their jaws, an army of them working together like piranhas could probably make short work of a human. At this close distance, Piper got a good gander at the balls they were pushing around. They were thin-skinned, semitransparent. She could see liquid sloshing around inside them. She could smell it too: a faint chemical odor, like kerosene.

The beetles ignored the kids. They'd crawled from the ground with a singular purpose. As each beetle came to the base of a tree, it clutched its ball with a pair of spiny front legs and used its four other legs to carry the ball up the trunk. The beetles deposited the balls in the crotches of branches, in hollows, in nets of moss, and even in an empty hawk nest.

"They're loading the trees," Piper said.

"Yeah, but why?"

When they'd finished the job, the beetles didn't return to the ground. Their shells split down the middle, and the two halves lifted to expose a set of veiny, papery wings. The insects beat their wings furiously, making a loud thrumming sound like thousands of little helicopters. They lifted off the branches and flew into the air. If she hadn't seen it with her own eyes, Piper would have never believed that an insect so bulky could fly.

The beetles regrouped in the sky. The swarm dove and came at them, like a hail of bullets, through the forest.

Piper's eyes grew owlishly wide. "They bite, you said?"

"Yeah," said Creeper. "Hard."

"Then duck!"

Piper pulled her brother to the ground. They covered their heads with their arms for protection. The bugs buzzed over them. There were so many, Piper could feel the wind generated by their furious wings.

One landed with a *thud* on her back. It had a potato's weight. She could feel the spikes on its legs pricking her skin. It was a horrible sensation, but she didn't dare move. Piper prayed that the beetle wouldn't bite into her flesh with those wire-cutter jaws. She hazarded a glance over at her brother. He had three big beetles on him, two on his back and one on top of his head, flogging his hair with its segmented antennae. Thankfully, Creeper had the good sense to stay still.

After what seemed like an eternity, the swarm passed over and vanished into the forest. The beetles on the siblings took flight and departed with them.

"I think they're gone, Creeper," Piper said, relieved.

There was no response, because he was gone too.

Piper whipped around and saw her brother being dragged, feet-first, by a tentacle through some holly bushes. The tentacle had sneaked up behind them, latched on to Creeper's ankle, and stolen away with him. Piper leaped to her feet and chased after him.

"Fight back!" she screamed. "Don't let it take you underground!"

"Piper!" he cried out. "Help me!"

"Dig in!" she ordered. If he put up a fight, used his limbs to turn himself into a grapnel, it might slow the tentacle down long enough for her to reach him. "Grab on to something! Anything!"

Creeper threw his arms around a tupelo sapling, but the tentacle was too insistent, too strong, and it yanked him off the tree with ease. The boy was as helpless as a fly in a gale.

Piper was swift and made up ground. She was only a few feet from Creeper's outstretched fingers when the tentacle and her brother disappeared down a hole in the ground.

Without thinking, Piper dove in after him.

The tunnel was narrow, not much wider than the septic pipe in her family's backyard that had to be dug up last spring when the dumb roofers backed their truck over top of it and cracked the concrete casing. It was a tight squeeze, but the walls were soft, so there was leeway where she needed it. But they were also caked with wet dirt itchy with little bits of life: worms, beetles, and pill bugs. She was entrenched in a nightmare. In a moment of quirky thinking, she wondered how Olivia would like this mud treatment.

Piper wriggled headfirst down the shaft until the last vestige of light faded behind her. She paused for a moment to catch her breath and listen for her brother's voice. She lay on her belly and thought about Tad. Is this what her friend would be forced to cope with for the rest of his life? Total darkness? All because of her? No, not if she saved the silver flower. That would fix him, she was certain. But first things first—saving the troops. Somewhere farther down the tunnel she'd find her brother. Alive, if she was quick enough. Until she saw his dead body, this was still a rescue mission.

She remembered the flashlight in her pocket and hoped she hadn't broken it when the bear attacked and she fell to the ground. She squeezed her right arm back until she was able to slip her hand into her pocket. The flashlight was still there, in one piece. She brought it up to her face, and pressed the ON button with her chin. A beam of white light flew down the tunnel.

It looked like a dead end up ahead, but then Piper realized she was heading toward a bend in the tunnel. She wormed her way to the elbow and peered around the corner. The tunnel continued. So did Piper.

The air smelled bad. It had that same acrid chemical stench as the jelly balls. It burned her nostrils and made her tongue tingle.

"Creeper?" she whispered. No answer. Clearly, Mergo was capable of things beyond any plant she was familiar with. Maybe Tad was wrong. Maybe it could hear too. Not in the conventional way, but perhaps even the slightest vibrations would tip it off to her presence. Sound was nothing but vibrations after all, and vibrations were waves of pressure. Mergo was sensitive to pressure, she knew, and the mechanisms the plant used to detect pressure could be numerous.

The tunnel roof rose. Piper was able to get to her hands and knees and crawl. The walls in this part of the tunnel were lined with holes, entrances to other passages. She heard something moving in one of the tunnels to the right and froze. She placed her hand over the light, dimming it until she could barely see.

A tentacle slithered out of the tunnel on the right, stopped, and lifted its paddle-shaped tip until it bumped against the roof. It swayed there like a trapped kite. The tentacle's red, gland-tipped hairs were moving in waves, scrubbing the air.

Its hairs are probes, she thought. But what were they searching for? A foreign smell? A source of light? The vibrations of a pounding heart? Because at that moment she was all of those things.

The tentacle swiveled in her direction and slowly advanced down the tunnel, heading straight for her. Piper stayed perfectly still and prayed it couldn't detect her.

A dulled tapping sound echoed through a tunnel on the left. The tentacle retracted partway into the right tunnel then rocketed tip-long into the tunnel on the left in the direction of the sound. Piper watched the tentacle flow between the two openings. It just kept going and going. She wondered if it had a tail end like the Merglets or if it was part of Mergo itself. Eventually the tentacle stretched taut and she had her answer. It was an offshoot of one of Mergo's main branches. Being so close to any part of Mergo made her skin crawl.

Piper waited until she was sure the tentacle wouldn't bungee back, and then she crawled over it with extreme care.

Piper wasn't sure if she was headed the right way, but getting far away from Mergo seemed like the smartest plan.

Minutes passed. She hoped Creeper was okay. Bad things happened quickly in this godforsaken place. In Vietnam, her grandfather had been a tunnel rat, a member of a group of specially trained infantrymen whose job was to enter enemy tunnels, flush the enemy out, and destroy the tunnels with explosives. Now she knew how he must have felt: claustrophobic, numb with fear, but also determined to complete the mission.

"Creeper . . ." she hissed. She knew it was risky to make noise, now that she'd seen the tentacle lured away by tapping. It may have been a coincidence, but she couldn't take that chance. There were so many side tunnels, though. It was like being lost in a giant ant farm. She couldn't just keep crawling aimlessly underground. Even if Creeper couldn't reply, she needed him to know she was coming for him. She would never abandon him. Not ever.

"Creeper . . . can you hear me?" she called out.

A voice wafted to her. It was faint and oddly singsong and chipper, ridiculously out of place. Piper turned her head and cupped her ear in an effort to determine if it was coming from ahead or from one of the side tunnels. Ahead, she was sure of it now. She waggled toward the voice.

Piper reached the end of this tunnel. Beyond it was a round cell with cylindrical earthen walls. The tunnel's exit was at the crest of a downward-sloping bank. At the bottom of the bank was a sheer drop-off, maybe six or seven feet, ending in a pool of clear liquid. The walls of the pool were slick and green, with faint white spots. The music, she realized, was coming from the little boy bobbing in the liquid. Why Creeper was singing and wearing the goofiest smile was beyond her.

"Creeper! What's wrong with you? Are you hurt?"

He didn't reply. He floated on his back and started singing their dad's favorite song, "Copacabana," by Barry Manilow. His caterwauling echoed through the chamber.

"Shh," she scolded. "Stop singing, dummy! Mergo will hear you!"

Creeper launched into a revision of the song. "Her name was Mergo! She was a show-plant! With silver petals in her hair and her branches everywhere!"

There was something seriously messed up with Creeper's brain. If she was going to get him out, she would have to go down and fetch him.

Carefully, she inched her way down the bank to the lip of the pool. The ground was crumbly, so she took her time.

"I'm coming, Creeper."

"Oh! You must be the pool waitress!" he said. "I'd like a Mello Yello, hold the yellow." Then he brayed like a donkey.

"I think what you need is a Dr Pepper, hold the pepper," she replied.

"You can't hold a pepper! Peppers are born to be free!"

Piper slipped and surfed dirt down the bank. Her heart leaped into her throat. She managed to use the side of her foot as a brake to stop her momentum, keeping her from falling over the lip of the pool. She caught her breath and scooted her butt back up the bank a bit. It was a miracle she'd hung on to the flashlight.

"Swim over here and give me your hand," she ordered.

"I can give you a hand from right here!" he said, then started clapping.

"Stop that, stupid! You're going to draw attention."

"I'm pretty good at Pictionary, but that'd be a tough one." Creeper seemed to have no sense of the danger they were in. He was doggie-paddling in tight circles, occasionally lifting one arm or leg out of the water, like a drunken synchronized swimmer. Perch was missing, Tad was blind, Creeper was loopy. . . . Piper had her work cut out for her.

"What is that stuff?" she asked, taking a whiff. The liquid filled the cell with a crisp, minty scent. It made her a little woozy and reminded her of Olivia's mother, who called herself a socialite, which was apparently another way of saying someone who drinks alcohol during the day. Whenever Piper visited, she'd usually find the woman gliding around her house with a mint julep in one hand. Maybe that explained why Creeper seemed drunk. If he'd swallowed some, he probably was.

"Pay attention. I need you to swim over to me so I can pull you out," Piper said. "You can't stay in there. This stuff is making you goofy, like how you get on cough syrup right before it puts you to sleep. If you fall asleep in there—"

"You're pretty bossy for a pool waitress." Creeper giggled. Then he pinched his nose shut and submerged. He didn't stay under long.

Creeper burst from the minty liquid, screaming at the top of his lungs. "Ah! Ah! It burns! My feet! It burned my feet!" Tears streamed from his eyes, and his face twisted up like a baby in the throes of a tantrum. Creeper had a high threshold for pain, handling his yearly flu shot like a trooper. Whatever he'd touched below had hurt him terribly.

"Grab my hand!" Piper leaned out over the liquid as far as she dared. There was nothing secure to hold on to, so she could only extend herself as far as her body weight allowed. "Hurry, grab my hand!"

Creeper thrashed around in the liquid, screaming bloody murder. Piper had hoped the intense pain would at least sober him up, but instead he seemed more disoriented than ever. His head kept slipping under the surface. She had to do something, quickly, before he swallowed more of the heady liquid, but she couldn't just go in after him. The walls of the pool were too smooth and too steep. There was no ladder bolted to the side, like the pool at Olivia's house. And then there was the intoxicating effect of the liquid to worry about. Once she got in, she might succumb to it as Creeper had, and then neither of them would ever get out. She needed a rope of some kind. She thought of the spool on the *Mud Cat*, the one Perch had tossed to Tad that sent him plunging through the hammock back at Floyd's Prairie. It would do her no good now, but it gave her an idea. There was something she could use; indeed, there was. A possible lifeline of sorts. She hated her brain for even thinking of it, but what other choice did she have? Desperate times . . .

"I'll be back," she promised, and scampered up to the tunnel. She crawled inside it and searched ahead with her flashlight. Way down, she could see Mergo's tentacle still stretched between the two side tunnels. She would need both hands free for the insane thing she was about to attempt, so she jammed the handle of the flashlight into the soil of the wall and screwed it there tight. The beam illuminated the first few feet of the tunnel and cast a dim halo of light into the chamber. She was ready.

"*Hey, Bear Breath!*" Piper called out. She thumped on the walls of the tunnel with her fists. "*I don't know if you can hear me, but I bet you can sense me somehow! I'm right here. A sitting duck! Come and get me, Mergo!*"

She fell quiet and listened. When the echo of her taunt died away, the tunnel went silent. She was about to try again, when she heard something slithering in the darkness. Slithering toward her.

Here it comes.

She braced for impact and counted down: three . . . two . . .

The tentacle flew out at her from the darkness, its red-tipped hairs wriggling like the bloody fingers of a murderer. Piper dodged to the right and grabbed the tentacle in a choke hold directly below the paddle-shaped tip. The tentacle whipped side to side in the tunnel entrance, attempting to break free, while the thick gluey hairs did the opposite; they tried to latch on to Piper's chest. Piper was counting on this and let them. The moment the hairs stuck fast, Piper leaped backward, out of the tunnel and into the chamber, using the tentacle as a rope, like a rock climber rappelling down a cliff. If she hadn't caught the tentacle by surprise, she'd be no match for its strength, but by using her weight and momentum, she was able to yank the tentacle down the bank, over the lip of the pool, and into the sweet-smelling liquid. With her torso stuck to the tentacle tip, her arms were free to make a grab for Creeper. She lunged but fell short.

"Creeper, give me your hand! Reach for me!"

She could already feel the powerful tentacle towing her through the water, back toward the wall of the pool. She kicked hard and tugged against it, but it was no use; she kept moving backward, away from her brother.

"Piper . . ." Creeper murmured. "I don't feel so good."

"Creeper, please! Take my hand! I can't lose you!"

She lunged for him again, missed, sunk half a foot, and felt a searing pain on her feet and ankles, as though she'd dipped them into scalding lava. There was another kind of liquid directly below the surface layer, one that was corrosive to the touch. She jerked her knees up to her chest, and the pain subsided. She reached for Creeper again, but it was no use; the tentacle had dragged her too far. She would never reach him now.

"You're my brother!" she pleaded, hoping her words would jar him to his senses. *"It's your job to save me! I need you!"*

Creeper blinked and woke up. He swam toward his sister and grabbed on to her ankle. The skin there was still tender from the liquid burn. His grip hurt, but Piper was too happy to care. She cried out, "Yes, Monty, yes! Hang on! Don't let go!"

A hole opened at the bottom of the pool, and the liquid started to spin and drain, forming an eddy. It sucked them down, playing tug-of-war with the tentacle, and for a moment Piper wasn't sure which would win.

The tentacle was stronger. It dragged the siblings out of the pool, up the bank, and into the mouth of the tunnel.

"Let go of me now, Creeper!" Piper ordered. "You can't help me! Find Perch and Tad and get out of here. Do you understand me?"

Creeper let go. But he wouldn't give her up. He jumped on top of the tentacle and pounded at it with his fists. Clawed at it with his nails. Dug his feet into the dirt and pulled against it. Creeper grimaced and gritted his teeth. His little muscles strained to their limit, but Piper knew it was no use. The tentacle was a powerhouse, way stronger than her little brother. They'd watched a tentacle drag a four-hundred-pound black bear to its doom. What chance did a seventy-pound boy have against one?

"Creeper, let go." Piper didn't yell this time. She talked to him calmly, patiently, fighting back tears. "It's okay. You're safe. That's all I care about. Just let go. I won't be mad. Go home to Mom and Dad. Go home to Grace."

"No!" he roared. "I won't! Not without you!"

Piper tickled Creeper under his arm. He yowled and fell away. For her brother's sake, she didn't resist the tentacle. She folded her arms, relaxed, and let it drag her away from Creeper, away from the flashlight, down the tunnel, toward pitch-black darkness. She accepted her fate.

Perch, however, did not. He came out of the darkness beside her and hacked away at the tip of the tentacle with his bowie knife. He carved it up like a Thanksgiving turkey, spattering bits of juicy pulp everywhere. With one final chop, he severed the tip. Separated from its feeler hairs, the decapitated tentacle thrashed about blind. It slipped away down the tunnel, presumably back into the black hole it had crawled out of.

Perch wiped plant gunk off his face. "Miss me, Princess?"

Piper embraced him. "You found us. How did you find us?"

"The flashlight. I was crawling around in the dark looking for you when I saw it." He grinned. "It's the light at the end of the tunnel, literally."

Piper called out for her brother. The light came bobbing up the tunnel toward them. When Creeper reached his sister, he fell on her, and they hugged each other tightly. Piper stroked her brother's filthy hair.

"Don't ever tickle me!" he said between racking sobs. "Don't ever tickle me! I've told you a zillion times! Don't ever tickle me!" He tried to sound furious, but he couldn't hide the relief in his shimmering eyes. "Now I have to pee."

"Can you hold it?" she asked.

He wiped the tears away and nodded. "I think so."

She gave his hair another tousle. "Good."

Perch helped Piper peel the amputated tentacle tip from her body. It took real effort, but they got most of it off. She'd scrub the rest clean when they got home, with a Brillo pad, if she had to.

"Have you seen Tad?" she asked Perch. "I left him at the edge of the clearing, but I'm worried that—"

"I did," Perch said. "I was in the forest looking for Creeper. I saw Tad wandering between the trees with his arms outstretched like a zombie, stumbling around, lost. I called out to him, but then one of those grabby arms—"

"Tentacles," Piper corrected him.

"Yeah, one of those tentacles came out of the ground behind him. I blinked and he was gone."

"Then he's down here." Piper sighed. "I told him not to come into the woods, but he never listens. And now Mergo has him."

"What are we gonna do?" asked Perch.

"*We?* Nothing. *You* are taking Creeper topside, then you're getting him to the *Mud Cat*. I'm staying down here to rescue Tad."

Or die trying.

20

With the flashlight aimed ahead, Perch led the Canfields on a crawl through the tunnels. Piper was behind him. Creeper brought up the rear, keeping a safe distance from his sister's butt, in a position he referred to as the "cootie caboose." The liquid he'd nearly drowned in was still messing with his brain. He was "higher than a Georgia pine," as Perch described him, fluctuating between moments of zany highs and nauseated lows, like he was riding a sugar-rush roller coaster. They took a side tunnel here, a side tunnel there, straight tunnel, side tunnel, straight.

"How do you remember where you're going?" Piper asked, awed by Perch's sense of direction.

"Years of paying attention in the swamp," he answered. "It's ridiculously easy to get lost in the Oke. All of us guides go astray every now and then. The best swampers learn to develop an eye for details. Bird nests, for example. Each one is different from the next, and if you can remember them all, then you can use them as markers to find your way home. That's how they did it in the old days."

"But you traveled these tunnels in the dark," Piper said. "You wouldn't have seen any markers at all."

"True. I had to get creative. Smells can be markers too. Lots of distinct stinks down here, most of 'em foul enough to gag a maggot. Still, I'm glad I spent the extra money and got a waterproof flashlight. Makes the trip back a lot easier."

"I've been meaning to ask you," said Piper. "Why does it shine in four different colors?"

"It's helpful in the swamp. The white light is best for all-around use. Red helps preserve our night vision, since the rods in our eyes are less sensitive to it. Plus, during night tours, I can shine it right in an alligator's eyes and it won't flinch. They can tolerate it longer than white, which burns their retinas." Perch clicked the button, and the beam ahead turned red.

He was right, thought Piper as her eyes adjusted; it did help her see more easily, although it made the tunnel appear ten times creepier than it already was.

"The green light is the best one for reading maps at night," Perch said.

"And the blue?" she asked. "What does the blue light do?"

"It's good for pretending you're a mermaid, I guess. I've never found much use for it," Perch said. He voiced his objection again. "For the record, I think this is a horrible plan. I don't see why you can't take Creeper to the *Mud Cat* while I stay down here and look for Tad. I mean, I'm a guy and you're—"

"Easily angered by chauvinists?" Piper's tone warned Perch to choose his next words wisely.

"I was going to say you're Creeper's sister, so you should stick with him."

"Sure you were," she said. "Think about it, Perch. If something happens and I don't make it back, you're the best chance I have of getting Creeper and the flower home. Like you said, you know the swamp. I don't. Plus I have no idea how to work the *Mud Cat*."

"It's easy," he assured her.

"Most important, Tad is my friend, not yours. I'm the one who got him into this mess. I need to be the one to get him out."

"Well, I don't exactly hate the guy," said Perch. "If he hadn't stopped me from rushing into the swamp after Macey, I'd probably be dead too. So I kinda feel like I owe him. Maybe we shouldn't split up at all. I can stay down here and help you look for Tad. Then we can make a run for the surface together."

Piper scuttled the idea. "Absolutely not. Creeper is still messed up from his pool party. He has to get to the boat now. I need you to do this for me. Please."

"You trust me with your brother's life, huh?"

"I do," she said, meaning it.

"We've come a long way in a day, you and me."

"That we have, Mr. Gentner," said Piper, returning his smile.

They crawled through the last few turns of the labyrinth and came to a stop in front of a curtain of thin hanging roots.

"Any tunnel past this point will lead you topside," Perch told Piper. "'All roads lead to Rome,' as the saying goes. Can you remember the way out?"

"I think so," she said. "What's your plan?"

"I'll get Creeper to the shore, and we'll see what awaits us in the lagoon. Hopefully the animals have left by now. Why would Mergo keep pumping its mind-control chemical into the water after the threat was gone?"

Piper hoped he was right. She leaned back against the wall to let Creeper pass. He looked sickly, like he might hurl any minute, but at least he seemed a little more clearheaded. The wacky juice was wearing off.

"You okay?" she asked him.

"Not really," he said. "I have a headache. And I want to barf."

"Sounds a bit like a hangover," said Perch. "An affliction Macey suffered from time to time."

"Perch is going to get you back to the boat," Piper explained to her brother. "You have to go with him. Do as he says. I'll join you soon."

"Okay," Creeper said.

Piper knew that if he wasn't so befuddled, he'd probably put up a fight. She pulled him in for a hug and kissed the top of his dirt-crusted head.

"I'll get him to safety," Perch promised. "We'll wait for you in the boat."

"Okay, but not for long," she told him.

Perch nodded his understanding.

"I love you, Creeper," Piper said. "You know that now, right?"

He squeezed her in return with his scrawny arms.

"Good." She kissed his head again.

Perch handed the flashlight to Piper, the red beam swinging between them. "We're not far from the surface now. I can get us the rest of the way in the dark. You'll need this more than we will. Take this too." He gave her his knife. "Just in case you need to make a salad."

"Thanks," she said. "For everything."

He gave her a worried look, then said, "See you soon, Princess."

Perch and Creeper crawled through the curtain of roots, leaving Piper all alone. A whisper in the back of her mind tortured her. It told her she'd never see her brother again. As the soles of Creeper's stinky swamp shoes—the last thing she saw of him—disappeared, her heart throbbed with a dull ache. With the flashlight aimed ahead and the knife in her other hand, Piper turned and crawled in the opposite direction, down, down, down the shaft, back into Mergo's damnable kingdom.

Piper had no idea where she was going or where Tad had been taken. She just kept her eyes peeled and her ears open and followed the red beam and her gut. She moved in constant fear that a tentacle would come slithering down the tunnel toward her. In such confined space, there'd be no place to hide. She'd be forced to fight.

The minutes dragged on, but there was no sign of Tad *or* Mergo. She couldn't help but be amazed by the complex network of tunnels the plant had bored for itself through the ground. But with so many side passages and turns, she soon found herself hopelessly lost, with no sense of her bearing to the surface. She considered turning around, going back the way she'd come, but her instinct told her to keep crawling forward. She was rewarded with a sign.

One of Mergo's tentacles slithered between two side passages and crossed her path thirty feet ahead. It was dragging a small alligator by its tail. The gator, barking its objection, tried to roll, flip, and bite the tentacle, but there was no escape for the outmatched reptile. The alligator death roll works only when the alligator is the predator, not when it's the prey. The tentacle and its prisoner disappeared into the opposite side passage.

Piper climbed into the tunnel behind them and followed. Her hope was that the tentacle was forwarding the gator to the same place the other one had taken Tad. She kept a safe distance, afraid the tentacle might see her as a more enticing prize. She tracked it by the claw marks the gator was digging in the soil and by the echo of the animal's grunts. Something else reached her senses too. The same kerosene smell she'd gotten a whiff of earlier in the forest. The farther she went, the more intense the odor became.

This tunnel was long, but it did have an exit, and beyond that was inky blackness. She caught a glimpse of the tentacle hauling the alligator through the darkness, and then plant and beast dropped down out of sight. Piper crawled to the lip of the exit and peered out into a black void. She leaned forward into it and felt a surprising chill on her face and arms. It was a very big chamber, airy and dark.

This can't be good. This can't be good at all.

Piper shined the flashlight into the chamber, but the beam couldn't illuminate more than a fraction of its space. She raised her light to the ceiling. It was high. She was deeper underground than the gradually sloping tunnels had led her to believe. The roof was supported by a tight lath of branches. It sagged a bit at the middle, but the meshing was a sufficient bulwark against the relentless pull of gravity. She aimed the flashlight outward. It was powerful, but not powerful enough to reach the far wall. The beam dissolved in the dark. Piper couldn't tell if the chamber was empty or if there was something waiting for her inside.

She turned around and wriggled backward through the tunnel exit. She lowered herself carefully over the lip. She wasn't tall enough to reach the chamber floor—it could be two or twenty feet below her, she didn't know—so she was forced to drop into it blind. Piper didn't fall far. When she landed, she felt something crunch beneath her feet. She swept the light over the floor and squealed. It was covered with bones. Not just covered—*piled* with bones. Her right foot was lodged inside the rib cage of a small mammal, a raccoon or possum, maybe; she was wearing it like a shoe. Piper kicked it away in disgust, and it clacked apart in the shadows.

The chamber was filled, wall to wall, with skeletons, some whole, some disassembled, some ground into splinters and powder over the course of centuries. Even the dirt walls were packed with skeletons, like a relief sculpture of embedded bones and deep shadows. Nearly every vertebrate in the swamp was represented, from fish to birds to mammals. Not even Mergo's reptile defenders were safe from its voracious appetite. The flat, broad clothespin-like skulls of the American alligator were present in great numbers, and empty turtle shells were strewn everywhere, like shields on a battlefield. There was clearly no clemency for loyal service.

Piper waded through the dunes of bones. The red filter of the flashlight made them look awash in blood, so she clicked the button on the handle until the beam was back to white and she saw that, for the most part, the bones were perfectly cleaned, almost as though the flesh had been boiled away.

She clamped her hand to her mouth to suppress a scream. There was a human skeleton in the mix. It was clad in the scrap remnants of a soldier's uniform. Piper could tell by the style—gray wool, with a belt that held a cartridge box and an empty scabbard—that this man once fought for the Confederate army in the Civil War. Maybe he'd been pursued by Union soldiers, attempted to hide out in the swamp, and encountered Mergo. Of course, bayonets and bullets would have been useless against a giant carnivorous plant.

The soldier was the first of many human skeletons Piper found in the chamber. Whatever Mergo couldn't digest remained on the bodies and spoke to who these people had been when they were alive. These clues offered a history lesson in human occupation of the swamp. There were skulls capped with miner helmets, a collapsed rib cage wrapped in the mackinaw jacket of an early nineteenth-century lumberjack, Creek Indians draped in shreds of buckskin, and even a hunter clothed in the latest L.L.Bean gear. Piper noticed that the great majority of the dead were wearing jade jewelry. Jade, she knew, was a South American mineral. There must have been at least a hundred Tasketcha entombed here, all bedecked in finery that could only be funeral attire. They'd died first and *then* Mergo ate them. Were the Tasketcha feeding their dead to the plant? Then why had they bothered to build tumuli in the woods? She worked out the ghoulish answers in her head. The Tasketcha *had* buried their dead. And then Mergo tunneled its way underneath the tumuli and snatched the bodies from *below*, stealing them without ever being noticed. That's why some of the tumuli had collapsed inward. The plant was a clever grave robber. This also explained how Mergo developed a taste for human meat. If the Tasketcha had brought Mergo as a plantlet with them from South America with the expectation that it would grow to become their subservient protector, they'd misunderstood two key things: fully grown, the plant would accept no master, and to Mergo, *all* meat was *good* meat.

An anguished roar echoed from somewhere beyond the chamber. The alligator had just died horribly. Piper had to know how Mergo killed it. She had to know if Mergo had killed Tad too. She moved swiftly in the direction of the gator's death cry. The carpet of bones grew deeper the farther she went, until she was forced to use her arms to help her scamper up and over the ever-shifting piles. "Forgive me, y'all." She felt a pang of guilt—she'd been raised to respect the dead, not step on their skulls and use their bones as ladder rungs.

Piper came to a gap in the far wall of the chamber. The kerosene stench she'd smelled on the beetle balls and in the tunnels was wafting in through the hole, pricking her eyes and polluting her taste buds with a chemical flavor. She crawled through the gap and found herself inside the second half of a double chamber, not unlike the shell of a peanut. This half was somewhat larger than the one with all the bones, but it contained something far more disgusting.

Piper's first impression: the chamber reminded her of a factory. Her aunt Cindy worked at the BMW factory in South Carolina and had once given Piper and Creeper a tour of the assembly floor. As she observed the vast network of Mergo's tentacles whipping about the chamber, busy in their tasks, she thought of the giant mechanical arms that moved car parts around and welded them into place.

The tentacles were everywhere, snaking in through holes riddling the walls like Swiss cheese, engaging in a range of duties. Most, like the one she'd followed, were hauling captive animals of all kinds into the chamber and bashing them senseless against the walls.

The room was filled with dead and dying creatures. Even with the intense stench of kerosene hanging in the air, she could distinguish the metallic odor of blood.

Above, descending from the center of the ceiling like a living chandelier, was an immense, closely knit cluster of orange tentacles, each one covered in wicked thorny barbs. One of the tentacles stretched down, harpooned the carcass of a deer with its barbs, and hauled it up quickly. The dead animal disappeared into the wriggling bouquet, and Piper threw up on her feet.

This wasn't a factory at all. It was a slaughterhouse.

The ground below the chandelier of tentacles was covered in a web of vines, just like in the forest, except these were bigger, as thick as the anaconda, and occasionally they would shiver like a snake about to shed its skin. It seemed that the deeper Mergo penetrated the earth, the more vile and ugly it grew.

"The light . . ." A faint voice drifted to her from the shadows.

Piper swung the beam toward the voice and found Tad slumped on the ground between a gap in the web. He was facing her direction, but his eyes were darting about, struggling to zero in on her.

"Tad!" she cried out.

"Turn off the light. . . ." he moaned, his voice weak and raspy. "They . . . they can see it."

Her friend's warning came too late. A tentacle flew at her from nowhere, coiled around her leg, and dragged her through the gap between the two chambers, dumping her onto the floor. Its hairs hadn't managed to adhere to her yet, so she was able to pull free.

"Get away from me!" She thumped the tentacle on the side of its paddle head with the sturdy flashlight, knocking it away. Three more tentacles zipped through the air in her direction.

Tad mustered the strength to holler. "Turn off the light! Now!"

Piper clicked the flashlight off and plunged the chamber into pitch darkness.

She didn't move. She held her breath, afraid that by sending the slightest signal of her existence she would give herself away. She could hear the tentacles swooshing through the air around her. One brushed against her leg. Its smooth, rubbery skin dragged across her own. It didn't attack. None of the tentacles did. With the flashlight put out, Piper had become invisible to their senses. Tad was right.

"They can't see you in the dark. It's okay to talk," Tad told her. "They can't hear us. Just don't make any sudden moves until you're sure they've given up looking for the flashlight. That's what got their attention. The beam."

Even though Tad had assured her it was fine to make noise, Piper remained silent. She didn't know if opening her mouth to reply counted as a sudden move. After an extremely tense minute, she heard the tentacles slither away. They'd lost interest in her.

"How did you get here?" she hissed in Tad's direction. "I told you to stay in the clearing."

"When you didn't come back, I headed into the woods. I didn't get far. A tentacle came out of a hole in the ground and dragged me into the tunnels. I ended up down here. Is that what happened to you?"

"One grabbed Creeper. I followed him into the ground," Piper said. "I thought only animals had tentacles. Is Mergo part animal?"

"No, it's part *Drosera*," Tad said. "It's the Latin name of the sundew plant, another type of carnivore."

In the dark, surrounded by the killer plant, Piper was a big ball of jittery nerves. Talking made her feel better. "So the sundew is like an octopus or a squid?"

"Not at all. The sundew's tentacles are actually modified leaves designed to attract, trap, and eat insects. The leaves put out a sweet odor, attracting bugs. The bugs get stuck on mucus-coated hairs covering the tentacle. The tentacle then curls around the bug and holds it fast until its digestive glands can suck out all the nutrients in its body."

"So disgusting!" She shuddered.

"The only method of trapping Mergo hasn't adopted is the one used by pitcher plants like the hooded cobra lilies we saw in the swamp earlier."

"How do pitcher plants trap?"

"They have leaves shaped like water pitchers filled with sweet-smelling digestive juice. The leaves are super slippery, so insects that come to have a sip of the juice fall in it and can't get out. Some pitcher plants are large enough to catch rats and birds."

Piper thought of Creeper swimming in the minty liquid. "Mergo has at least one pitcher trap too. A big one. The size of a swimming pool. I pulled Creeper out of it. It had a sweet, minty smell."

"Like *Sarracenia leucophylla*," said Tad. "The white pitcher plant of the Gulf Coast. It has a minty smell too. The plant's digestive juices contain a chemical sedative that relaxes prey. Keeps their victims from struggling. Helps them accept their fate."

"That explains why my brother was acting so dopey," she said. "Creeper and I were lucky to escape it alive."

"You were," Tad agreed. "How'd you get out?"

For the sake of brevity, she skipped the part where she'd tricked the tentacle into dragging them free. "Perch saved us. Then he took Creeper to the surface. I insisted."

"And you stayed down here to look for me. It figures. Perch saves the day, and I end up the damsel in distress." He sighed audibly. "You shouldn't have come back for me, Piper. You should have gone with them. You should have gone home."

"As if! Is that what you would have done?" she asked.

"No . . ." Tad admitted. "I would have done the same thing you did. It's selfish, but I'm glad you're here."

A horrible squeal filled the chamber. It went on and on until it faded to a gurgle and then ended with a pitiful moan. Another animal was dead.

When the chamber fell quiet again, Piper was raring to depart. First she had to get Tad. "I'm going to try to make my way over to you."

"Don't!" Tad shouted. "You'll step on one of Mergo's branches! The only reason I've gone undetected since I was dumped here is because I've stayed in one spot. The animals aren't smart enough to do the same. They scramble around the chamber, step on a trigger branch, and—"

"And then those tentacles on the ceiling shoot out like harpoons."

"Is that what's happening? I just knew that something in here was killing them. Mergo's venom really wrecked my eyes."

"So what are we supposed to do?" she asked. "Stay in here until this creepy plant evolves legs and walks away?"

"Be patient. I'm working on a plan. I just wish I could see what I'm doing. If I had use of the flashlight, even for a minute . . . but the tentacles would be on me in seconds, not nearly enough time."

Piper thought back to her first visit to Tad's greenhouse. "You said plants can see different colors of light, right?"

"That's right. Red, white, and blue. So?"

"What about green light?"

"As much as I'd love for the Green Lantern to come swooping in here to save the day, Piper, that's not going to happen."

She could hear him fidgeting with something. It sounded like he was ripping cardboard. "I'm being serious, Tad."

"The chlorophyll in plants absorbs most colored light, but it reflects green. It's the reason why plants look green to us."

"So the answer is . . . ?"

"No, Piper, plants can't see green light."

Green . . .

Piper turned the flashlight back on. White light landed everywhere.

"Hey!" Tad yelled. "What are you doing? Turn it off! Turn it off!"

Three more tentacles whirled in the air and faced Piper. One had

269

a struggling raccoon stuck to its tip, but it released the animal. The raccoon fell to the ground and scampered away.

Piper had given away her position. The tentacles knew exactly where she was. They came for her.

21

Piper clicked the flashlight's smaller button, trying to remember the order of the colored lights. If she dithered between the wrong ones for too long—red, white, or blue—she'd be dead.

Click, red.

Click, blue.

A tentacle swiped at her leg. She played skip rope with it.

On the third click, the beam and the chamber turned green. The tentacles froze in midair. The largest parked directly in front of her face and hovered there. If Piper leaned forward just a few inches, her nose would stick to its writhing hairs. Close up, those hairs looked like glistening lime lollipops dripping with spit. They were its "eyes," she knew. Primitive eyes that had just been tricked by the green light. Piper had pulled a Houdini. She'd vanished.

"What's happening?" Tad asked, hysterical with worry. "I see the green light! Did it work? Are you okay? Answer me!"

Piper didn't dare. She was so close to the tentacle's hairs that even the draft from a whisper could undo the magic trick. She let Tad worry until, just like before, the tentacles withdrew and returned to their business of murder. Except for one. It slithered to the gap between the two chambers and coiled up inside it, blocking the only way out.

Piper exhaled. "I'm okay. They're blind to green light, just like you said they'd be. But I think Mergo knows I'm here now. One of its tentacles is guarding the exit. If we're ever getting out of here, we'll have to deal with it first."

Tad was furious with her. "Piper, when I said plants can't see green, I thought you were talking about *normal* plants! I have no clue what Mergo can or can't see. It's totally unique! You took a huge gamble!"

"Says the guy who was certain Mergo is deaf. It worked, so hush. I'm coming to you."

Somehow, the factory chamber bathed in the sickly, green glow seemed even more chilling than the bone chamber lit with red. To Piper, an outdoorsy girl, green had always represented vibrant life. But now she saw that it could also be the color of death. She stepped carefully between the hair-trigger vines covering the ground and was halfway to Tad when a huge rat came scampering toward her, making a break for the exit. Piper tried to get out of its way, but the rat landed on a branch at her feet, and in a flash one of the tentacles on the ceiling zipped down like a chameleon's tongue, barely missing Piper's leg with its barbed tip. With the accuracy of a sniper, the tentacle harpooned the squealing rat and bungeed it up to the ceiling. Piper hopped the rest of the way to Tad and fell to her knees at his side. She threw her arms around his neck and mashed her cheek against his.

"I missed you too," he said.

"How are your eyes?" She held three fingers up close to his face. "How many?"

"Three," he answered.

"Can you see my face?"

Tad sighed happily. "I sure can."

Piper lingered on his smile. Until that moment, she'd never realized how handsome it was. "Now what?" she asked.

"I have a plan," he said. "Give me some light."

She trained the spotlight on his hands. He was holding the disposable Kodak camera. The sound of ripping cardboard she'd heard in the dark was Tad removing the box it came packaged in.

"You still have the camera?" she asked. "Does it work? Wasn't it underwater?"

"It was one of the things I thought important enough to store inside a ziplock bag," Tad said. "Then I put it in my utility belt. It's as dry as a—"

"Don't say bone," Piper implored. "I'm sick of bones."

"—a cracker." Tad slid the latch on the side, and the back half of the casing popped open, exposing the film to the flashlight.

"Why did you do that?" she asked. "Won't the light ruin the film?"

"I don't care about that," Tad said. "We need this camera for something more important than taking pictures." He noticed Perch's knife in her hand. "Can I borrow that, please?"

Piper handed it to him.

Tad fingers moved nimbly over the camera. He popped out the battery. "I did this once before. Forgot to take the battery out and gave myself a nasty shock." Using the dull edge of the knife, he pried off the faceplate, exposing the circuit board. He cut all the wires attached to the flash. He made a few more adjustments, reinstalled the battery, and reassembled the camera.

"Voilà," he said proudly.

"Um . . . voilà what?" Piper asked. It didn't look like he'd accomplished anything besides destroying his property.

"I converted the camera into a Taser. Like the ones the police use to zap criminals. It'll transmit a pretty painful jolt of electricity now. We can shock the tentacle guarding the entrance."

"What good will that do?" she asked. "Won't it just alert the other ones to what we're up to?"

"I don't think so," he said. "I remembered a story about the Venus flytrap. A while back, some scientists conducted an experiment. They wanted to see exactly what caused the flytrap's lobed leaves to snap shut. They discovered that they could force the traps to spring without touching the trigger hairs at all. By sending an electrical charge through the stem, they tricked the plant into closing *all* its traps at once. See, it's not the touch itself that causes a plant to react. It's the electrical signal that results from that touch. The mild current fooled the Venus flytrap into thinking it had already trapped its prey, and therefore there was no reason to open the traps again for a while. I'm hoping I can do the same to Mergo with the Taser. If I'm right, an electrical shock will convince Mergo that all its traps have already been sprung, and that'll give us a chance to get to escape."

"Are you sure about this, Tad?" Piper asked.

Tad pressed the camera's charger button. The exposed wires sticking out from the casing crackled with electricity, spraying sparks into the air. "No, I'm not sure. But honestly? At this point I'd rather have a weapon than a camera."

"Speaking of weapons . . ." she said. "When Creeper and I were on the surface, we saw an army of giant beetles crawling out of the ground. They were all carrying clear balls filled with some kind of fluid. They smelled like this place. Like kerosene. The bugs left them all over the forest. What do you suppose Mergo's up to? Should we be worried?"

"I'm not sure. Although . . . it might have something to do with a process called guttation, where a plant excretes droplets of sap. Mostly the drops are just water and sugar, but sometimes they contain pesticides and other chemicals. You say they smelled like kerosene? I wouldn't be surprised to find that Mergo's droplets contain an explosive liquid. Everything about the plant is dialed up to eleven."

"But why would Mergo leave them in the woods?" Piper asked.

"The most likely reason is to start fires in the forest. To burn back encroaching trees and other plants that threaten it."

"Mergo lives underwater. And underground. What could threaten it on land?"

"But its traps are in the lagoon. Remember, Perch told us that if swamp fires didn't burn up the woody plants, over time the waterways would close off and become land. If that happened to the lagoon, Mergo's bladder traps would become landlocked and useless. I guess it adapted to take advantage of lightning, and if that isn't a sign of intelligence then I don't know what is. One bolt is all it would take to set off a chain reaction, cleaning out the forest like Drano cleans pipes. All while Mergo waits comfortably below for the fire to burn itself out, just like all of the swamp's other burrowers . . . the turtles, the moles, the gators."

"But why is it moving the guttation droplets to the surface now?"

"Because of us. We damaged the stalk. Cut off the flower. My guess is that Mergo is pulling out all the stops. Setting all its traps, above and below. Because it knows we're here and it feels threatened. It wants to make sure we're dead, because we hurt it."

"God, I hate this plant." Piper groaned.

"I don't hate it," Tad said, "but I'm ready to get the heck out of here."

Piper was sitting across from Tad in the dirt, staying close enough so that he could see her. Again, she thought back to the day when she'd sneaked into his greenhouse. He'd sat across from her in the pea gravel and listened so patiently. But that was Tad. He had *always* been patient with her. *Always* cared about her. He'd always been right there waiting for her.

"I'm sorry," she whispered.

"For my vision? It's nothing that a pair of Coke-bottle glasses won't fix. Or maybe a Seeing Eye dog."

"I'm sorry for your vision, yes, but that's not all. I know I've already apologized for putting our friendship on hold, but until the last couple of days, I never realized how much I'd truly lost by pushing you away. You're like . . . the best guy ever. You'd have to be, to follow me into this mess."

"I'm glad we're friends again," he said. "I just wish Perch hadn't told you . . . you know . . . how I feel about you. It wasn't his business. I was okay with just having my best friend back. I don't want you to feel weird around me anymore."

"I don't mind that you have feelings for me," Piper said.

Tad chuckled. "Great. That's just what I was longing to hear."

"I didn't mean it that way," she said. "I guess I'm just a little shocked that you *like me* like me. I'm nothing special. Perch was right—I'm just a stupid girl who collects stupid tiaras."

"Perch and I see you very differently," Tad said.

"And how do you see me?" she asked, searching his failing eyes.

"Right now? You're a little blurry."

"Stop. I'm being serious. I need to know."

"Piper . . . I don't think this is the right time—"

"We may not get another chance to talk about this," she pointed out. "This is important. Please."

"Okay. This whole shallow-girl facade you've been wearing? It's not you."

Piper cringed. "I can only imagine what you thought of me when I started doing pageants."

"Well . . . I'm not a fan of your girlfriends—they're truly horrible people." He chuckled. "But there's nothing wrong with pageants. They can open up doors . . . opportunities for you to do great things, right? A lot of winners have gone on to make the world a better place through charity work. I figured you would too. And who says you can't be Miss America *and* a soldier like you always wanted, right?"

"I kinda gave up on the whole soldier thing after Washington," Piper admitted. "People depend on soldiers. They're trustworthy. After what I did . . . who could ever trust me again?"

"I would," Tad answered. "With my life. You came back for me, didn't you? Piper, you have to stop beating yourself up over what happened in Washington. You've gone through a lot of pains to put things right. Grace is lucky to have you as a big sister. So is Creeper. You're the most amazing person I know. There's so much more to you than meets the eye. More than just what people see on the surface. You're . . . beautiful."

"Your eyesight must be worse than I thought." Piper snorted awkwardly, feeling instantly self-conscious. She was caked in grime, and her hair dangled in clumpy strands in front of her face. She assumed he was making a joke.

"Piper . . ." His tone was soft, tender. "I've never needed eyes to see what makes you beautiful."

Piper felt something she'd never expected: the sudden overwhelming urge to kiss her best friend. But then she remembered they were in a dank cave filled with dead animals, and decided that a first kiss, even a spontaneous one, should wait for a less disgusting setting. But then she also remembered they were probably going to be eaten by a giant plant, so what the heck. She leaned in and pressed her lips to his.

Piper had never kissed a boy before. She had no clue if she was even doing it right, but she was happy because if this was her first kiss—and probably her last—at least she'd picked the right guy to share it with.

After a while, Tad mumbled something, and Piper let him have his mouth back.

"Did I do something wrong?" she asked.

"Not at all! It's just . . . I'm having a hard time breathing . . .

because of Mergo's venom. It took my breath away." Flustered, he jumped to add, "The venom, I mean. Not the kiss. Uh . . . not that the kiss didn't steal my breath! I mean . . . I don't know what I mean."

"Oh," she said, not entirely sure if the kiss was successful. "I'm sorry."

"Don't be." He grinned. "I'm not."

Embarrassed, Piper stood up quickly. "We should get a move on."

"Sure. Right." Tad patted the ground next to his leg, looking for the repurposed camera. It wasn't there. "Where's the Taser?"

The sizzling crackle of blue electricity lit up Piper's face, and a smell like a thunderstorm filled the air. She was pressing the charge button, testing the Taser.

"It's not a toy, Piper," Tad said, struggling to rise to his feet. "And it has a limited charge on the battery. Hand it over."

Piper could feel her body tingling. At first she assumed it was a light feedback of electricity from the Taser coursing through her arms, or maybe the rush of adrenaline flooding her system. But no, it was more than that. It was the exhilarating feeling of renewed confidence after doubting herself for far too long. She'd never felt so alive, so eager to test her mettle against their tormentor. She was ready to fight, for Tad, for Creeper, for Grace . . . for herself.

"You're nearly blind," she said. "I should be the one to shock Mergo. If it doesn't work, I'll have a better chance of dodging those tentacles on the ceiling. You said there's more to me than meets the eye. Did you mean that?"

"Yes, but—"

"Then let me do this. Trust me."

Tad gave in. He had to, because Piper was right. "I trust you."

"Good," she said. "I'll guide you across the floor of the chamber. We'll use the Taser on the tentacle guarding the exit. If your theory pans out, Mergo will seize up, and then we can slip past it."

It was slow going. Tad's arm was draped over Piper's shoulders. Hers was hooked around his waist. She used the flashlight to illuminate their route through the net of trigger vines crisscrossing the floor of the chamber. A few times Tad came dangerously close to stepping on one, and it didn't help that Piper's concentration was frequently broken by the random shrieks of dying animals.

"That's it—we made it," Piper said as they cleared the last trigger vine successfully.

"One hurdle down," said Tad.

"One more to go," said Piper.

They were standing in front of the gap. The neck that joined the two chambers. The doorman tentacle was still there, coiled inside. As they moved toward it, the dewy hairs on its tip started wagging in every direction.

"It's sniffing the air," said Piper. "Do you think it knows we're here?"

"I doubt it. The stink here is overpowering. But then again, a shark can smell a drop of blood in the water from three thousand yards away. Who knows? Maybe Mergo's sense of smell is just as keen. Be quick, okay?"

"Like a mongoose," Piper promised.

Tad got the reference. Mongooses picked fights with cobras and were so fast that they usually killed the snake. "Be faster," he advised. "Sometimes the snake wins."

"Get behind me and grab on to my waist." Piper stepped in front of him. Tad tucked Perch's knife through his belt loop and did as he was told.

With Tad in tow, Piper inched toward the doorman tentacle, both her arms stretched out in front of her. In one hand she held the repurposed camera; in the other, the flashlight with the green beam shining ahead. The tentacle seemed agitated. Its hairs were waving in unison, and its lithe body was shivering like the tail of a rattlesnake. Even if it couldn't see her cloaked by the green light, it seemed to sense she was near.

This is it, she thought. God, grant me speed.

"*Now!*" she yelled, pressing the button on the makeshift Taser. Current flowed through the plastic case. Blue sparks shot out the wire ends. The tentacle rose up menacingly; its paddle-shaped head bumped against the arch of the gap.

"You can see blue light, can't you?" Piper taunted. "Oh, yes you can. You want it? Come and get it, then."

The cobra struck fast. The mongoose was faster.

She jammed the Taser into the tentacle's hairs and sent five hundred volts of electricity coursing through the plant's rubbery flesh. The tentacle convulsed violently, and smelled like fried zucchini. She kept her finger mashed on the camera's button until the plant stopped moving. Piper pulled the Taser back, ready to shock the tentacle again if she had to.

She didn't. The tentacle was frozen and harmless. Tad's theory had paid off. Piper looked around the chamber and saw that *all of the tentacles* had been immobilized by the electricity. "It worked!" she said. "Tad, your plan actually worked! I shut Mergo down!"

"There's no telling how long the effect will last," he said. "Let's go."

Piper let Tad into the gap first. He was bigger than she was, so he had to shimmy through it sideways. When he was on the other side, Piper went to follow, but she heard a rustling sound above her head and stopped in her tracks. She shined the flashlight at the ceiling. The chandelier of tentacles had already shaken off the effect of the Taser. The cluster, which in that moment reminded her of a giant squid, was awake and seemed keenly aware that it had been attacked. And worse, it knew *where* it had been attacked.

Several of the orange tentacles rocketed down toward her. Piper managed to dodge the first few, but they were too fast and too many.

One of them lashed across her backside, hooking into her flesh with barbs the size of an eagle's talon. She shrieked in pain.

"Piper!" Tad called to her from the bone chamber. "What's happening?"

She wanted to warn him. To tell him to run. To get away while he could. But before she could get a single word out, she felt the barbed tentacle jerking her upward, lifting her off her feet and into the air. The ground fell away below her. Through a fog of excruciating pain, she remembered she still had the camera Taser. She touched the prong of wires to the tentacle and pressed the shutter button, bracing herself for a shock (the electricity, she knew, would pass through the water-filled tentacle and into her own body). The wires smoked, but no sparks came off them. She'd used up the entire battery on the doorman tentacle. The Taser was useless.

When she reached the ceiling, dozens more barbed tentacles closed in around her like wicked fingers curling into a fist. Mergo gripped her tightly.

August 28, 1823

The nature of Mergo has become clear. It is no ghost or devil
or great beast. Instead, it is a marvel of botanical inventiveness,
unique in both its organization and its appetite. A carnivorous
plant so voracious and successful that it upends my understanding
of the food chain.

       During an expedition in Malaysian Borneo, I came upon
a species of pitcher plant so large that it was able to hold and
consume frogs and rats in its leaf traps, and frequently did so.
The *Nepenthes rajah*, as it is called in the scientific community,
is known to the locals by another name—monkey cups. Upon
dissecting a specimen of the plant, I was surprised to find the
skeleton of a juvenile goblin-eyed tarsier at the bottom of the
pitcher. This discovery sent my mind reeling like no other. For
you see, the Creator had seen fit to design a plant capable of
eating primates, an order of mammal that includes among its
ranks the chimpanzee, the great mountain gorilla, and of course,
humans. At the time I shuddered to think that the *Nepenthes
rajah*'s ability to predate on larger primates was restricted
only by the size of its pitchers and that perhaps somewhere in
the wild there might exist a species of carnivorous plant large
enough to consider people as prey. Never did I dare to dream
that such a life-form existed right here in the Americas. Perhaps
this creature is the vanguard in an evolutionary shift in power.
Perhaps the dawn of plants as the dominant predator is upon us.
I can only wonder.

       Mergo is a marvel of nature; I cannot discount that. But as
I learned while staring down a man-eating tiger in Sumatra, at
times nature harbors monsters.

22

Piper was inside Mergo.

Her body was compressed inside a fleshy sac hidden within the cluster of orange tentacles. The one that had carried her there was gone, leaving behind three nasty gashes on her back and shoulder. How she'd managed to hang on to the flashlight she didn't know, but if she was going to find a way free, she needed to have it. The sac was lined with something that felt like fur but looked like the fluffy floss found inside a milkweed seed. Her forearms were pinned against the sides of her legs. She could hear a rhythmic whistling of air above her head that sounded a lot like labored breathing. She couldn't cut herself loose; Tad had the knife. Piper had no weapons at all. No way to free herself. She thought of the screams of the dying animals and knew that unless she came up with a plan of escape, and soon, she'd share their fate.

Something wet splattered on her bare shoulder. She squeezed her arm upward until the flashlight illuminated the liquid. In the green light the liquid appeared black, but she knew it was really red. It's hard to mistake blood for anything but blood. It was dripping on her from above. Piper looked up.

The sac, she saw, tapered outward, opening into a bell-shaped cell above. The cell was the size of her bedroom and crisscrossed with a cat's cradle of taut branches. The branches held dozens of animals, most of them dead, and the live ones were on their final breaths. All of the animals were in some phase of being digested.

The walls were lined with several openings, small tunnels that only a rat could pass through. Or a beetle. The Titan beetles were there, traversing the branches, treating them as a network of bridges to get to and from the cell's centerpiece, an enormous cluster of guttation drops bunched together like oversize grapes. This was where they originated. One by one the beetles would pluck a guttation drop from the bunch and then skitter off into the little tunnels. New drops were constantly forming to replace the stolen. Combined with the chemical stink, the pain, the bugs, and the dead animals, it was more than Piper could stomach. She threw up, hoped it was over, then threw up again. When she had thoroughly emptied her stomach, she felt a little better.

"Tad! Can you hear me?" she hollered. There was no answer. The flossy lining was acting as soundproof insulation. She tried again. *"Tad!"* It was no use.

She searched overhead for the raspy breathing sound and spotted the source. The fattest branches at the very top of the cell were covered with fleshy nozzles. The nozzles bulged, then widened at their mouths. They sprayed a blast of mist into the air of the cell. It had the same odor as the guttation droplets and probably came from the same source. The mist descended in fine droplets over everything. As the droplets fell through the branches, she saw the flesh of the animals caught up in them start to bubble and melt. A heron squawked once, shuddered, and died. The mist was corrosive. More of Mergo's acidic digestive juice, like the liquid that had burned her feet in the pitcher pool.

Some of the droplets reached Piper and spattered on her face. She felt an intense burning sensation on her cheek, as though rusty razor blades were raking across her skin. It was the most intense pain she'd felt in her life.

Dozens of ropelike tendrils appeared from out of the walls and carried Piper aloft, closer to the nozzles. She wouldn't survive a concentrated blast of spray. Piper kicked and thrashed, trying her best to break loose, but the instant she pulled free of one tendril, another whipped out and took its place. She looked around for anything she could use as a weapon. Maybe a bone from one of the animal carcasses. Many had been dissolved down to their skeletons. Close to the bunch of guttation droplets she spied an enormous turtle shell. It had been flushed clean of its former occupant and then split into two halves, the top and the underbelly plastron. Squirrel skeletons hung from the branches like furry pennants. The awl-shaped skull of a crane scratched her arm as she passed by it.

Piper reached up, wrenched the leg bone off a deer skeleton, and proceeded to club the tendrils with it. The tendrils wrapped around the bone and confiscated it with ease, like candy from a baby.

The tendrils carried her up into the midst of the dead and dying animals. There was the massive carcass of a bear. Piper suspected it might be the one that had attacked her in the forest. The beast was dangling from a branch, belly up. Piper reached out to it. If she could swing underneath it, it might act as an umbrella from the next round of spraying. She set the end of the flashlight between her teeth and pumped her arms back and forth until she started to swing toward the bear. She raked the animal's fur with her fingertips. The flesh beneath it was still warm. It was definitely the bear from the forest.

One more swing should do it, she thought.

Back and then forward. She swung under the bear and kicked her legs up, wrapping them around the carcass. The bear's muscles shuddered beneath its shag. She felt its rib cage expand between her thighs as it took a deep breath of air.

Oh, God . . . it's . . . alive!

The animal regained consciousness. It was still clinging to life, and Piper, unfortunately, was clinging to its body. She was riding a panicked bear. Upside down! It started to thrash about, swiping at the tendrils, shredding them easily like party streamers with its razor-sharp claws. Several snapped. Piper reached out and grabbed the closest hanging tendril. At the last moment, she swung away and watched the bear fall several feet before a dozen new tendrils whipped out and coiled around its neck. Piper heard a *snap*, and the bear fell motionless. When she looked up, back to where the bear had been, she saw the horrific thing its bulky mass had been blocking from her view. Piper tore her gaze away, but only for moment. It was just like when her uncle Jake's body was shipped back from the Middle East and she'd attended his wake. She didn't want to look in the open casket, but she needed to see him. And now, just like then, she wished she hadn't.

Macey's corpse was caught up in the branches, hanging like a ghastly scarecrow. Piper wasn't sure exactly how it had gotten there, but it was evident that Mergo's army of swamp creatures wasn't allowed to keep what it killed. The woman's body was partially digested already. Her spiky white hair was streaked with black slime. The skin on her face was torn and peeled like paper in spots. Piper could see Macey's skull peeking through. Her overalls were sopping wet and covered in muck, but the digestive juices hadn't burned through them yet. The boat's kill switch was dangling from the belt loop.

Oh, Macey . . . Piper was beset by deep sorrow. *You deserve so much better than this. . . .*

The sight of Macey's body extinguished Piper's last flicker of hope. Even if Perch got Creeper to the boat, without the kill switch they weren't going anywhere. They were all fated to die in this god-forsaken place.

Pfssssssss.

The nozzles above swelled and opened again. Another blanket of mist spread through the air. Piper used her forearms to protect her face. The mist landed, burning her neck, her arms, her shoulders. She knew in that moment what it felt like to catch fire. Pain beyond her wildest nightmares. She chomped down hard on the plastic shell of the flashlight handle. It helped a bit.

Through the fog of agony, she had a moment of clarity. An image flickered in her mind. An object. A weapon, maybe. Just a flicker.

She fought back hard against the tendrils, swimming through them in the air toward Macey's body. A couple of thin ones snapped under her momentum, and she moved even more quickly. From above, a fresh tendril lashed around her ankle just as she reached Macey's body. It tried to pull her away—almost as if it sensed she was up to something—but Piper was able to grab on to the straps of Macey's overalls. The tendril lifted her up, and Piper dangled vertically, upside down. The buttons that fastened Macey's overall straps to the bib popped off. The straps began to tear at the joint seams on the back. Piper let one strap go and used her free hand to unbutton the left bib pocket. She jammed her hand into the pocket and found something cold and metal at the bottom.

Macey's lighter.

It had been underwater, though. Piper prayed it would still work. She flicked the hinged lid open then rolled her thumb across the flint wheel, sparking the wick. A beautiful yellow flame sprung up from inside.

The strap tore off the overalls. The tendrils jerked her away from Macey and hauled her up quickly through the branches.

Her plan, she knew, bordered on suicide. She intended to set fire to the guttation droplets. It would be like tossing a lit match into a full can of gas. The explosion would likely kill her, but if there was even a one percent chance she would survive, then she had to go through with it. For Tad's sake. If she died, he'd be lost in the dark, unable to find his way out.

Up, up, up she went. As she neared the cluster of guttation droplets, something hard clunked her on the back of her head. It was the top half of the giant turtle shell. The shell was spiky, thick, and formidable. It looked like an ancient shield.

A shield!

She grabbed hold of the shell's rim and tugged, freeing it easily from the thin tendrils holding it aloft. The shell was heavy. It took all the strength in her left arm to heft it into place in front of her torso. She needed the right arm free to start the fire.

The tendrils carried her and the shell to the height of the guttation droplets. She heard the raspy breathing sound again and knew without looking that the nozzles were swelling and spitting digestive juices. Piper maneuvered her body, slipped under the shell, and tucked her knees up close to her chest. The spray of mist spattered against the shell's spiked scutes, but not a single fleck landed on Piper. When the valves closed and the spray dissipated, she twisted around to face the guttation droplets. She held the lighter out past the shell and laid her thumb on the flint wheel.

This is it.

Piper flicked the lighter and conjured the flame. In her head, she said a blanket prayer that covered everything. She signed off with: *You know, just in case I'm incinerated. Amen.*

She hesitated, surprised by a fleeting pang of remorse. Mergo had existed in the swamp for thousands of years and was, as Tad said, a marvel of evolution. A one-of-a-kind life-form, unique in every way. But it had also blinded Tad. Killed Macey. It had tried to eat Creeper. For those reasons, Mergo had to die.

But even here the plant had defenders.

Piper yelped. One of the Titan beetles landed on her hand and bit into her skin with mandibles like scissors. Another flitted down onto the upper rim of the turtle shell, peered down at her, clacked its formidable jaws, and hissed.

It didn't matter. They were too late. Piper lifted the lighter to the nearest guttation drop. It sizzled as the thin casing melted away, and then it exploded. They *all* exploded.

Piper was pummeled by teeth-rattling shock waves and scalded by searing heat. The turtle shell took the brunt of the blast, but the explosion still tossed her about the cell like a sock in a dryer. The flossy walls shredded, and in a literal flash, the tendrils, the dead animals, and the beetles were cremated.

Piper plummeted to the floor of the chamber and thudded hard in the dirt. The turtle shell landed on its rim and rolled way. Above, an orange tentacle, severed and on fire, was falling down on top of her. She flung herself out of the way, and it crashed down beside her, flopping about, curling and uncurling like a beckoning finger.

A massive fireball churned inside the shaft where the tentacle chandelier had nestled. The flame was spreading down and out across the ceiling. A web of hairline cracks spread across the ceiling too. The chamber was crumbling.

Flashlight in hand, Piper raced for the gap between the two chambers. It didn't matter if she stepped on the trip-wire branches now. All the ceiling tentacles were destroyed, and the paddle-headed ones were roasting or retreating out the holes in the wall, carrying the fire with them.

Just as Piper reached the gap, she heard a loud groan and then a roaring *crunch* behind her. The ceiling collapsed. A waterfall of swamp water dumped in from above, dousing the blaze. This part of Mergo's domain was directly under the swamp! A billowing cloud of steam filled the chamber. The factory had been destroyed.

Piper darted through the gap and ran smack into Tad as he was rushing in.

"You're alive! I heard—"

"No time!" She grabbed him by the arm and dragged him toward the exit on the far side of the bone chamber.

Water came rushing in behind them, spreading quickly across the ground. The surge mopped up skeletons and turned the chamber into a disgusting, frothy soup of swamp sludge, water and bones. The wave reached Piper and Tad, swept them off their feet, and sent them crashing into a large heap of skeletons. They clambered up and over the pile, then jumped back into the water and waded toward the exit tunnel on the far side of the chamber. The shock waves from the explosion must have weakened the chamber's support structure, because the tunnel collapsed in front of their eyes. They were trapped.

"Where do we go?" Tad asked. "I can't see! Piper, where do we go?"

"I don't know!" She clicked the button on the flashlight, and the beam turned white. She scoured the chamber walls with it. "There! Another tunnel!"

They waded toward it. The water level reached Piper's midriff, rising fast. In a minute it would be up to her neck.

At the tunnel entrance, Tad froze.

"What's wrong?" she asked.

"We don't know where this tunnel leads. What if it collapsed inside? Or what if we get deep into it and find it's a dead end? We'll be stuck! The rising water will fill it up and we'll drown!"

"We'll drown if we stay," she said. "What choice do we have? Come on!" Piper climbed into the tunnel and pulled Tad in after her.

At first the tunnel's shaft sloped up at an incline, which was a positive sign. They were definitely heading toward the surface. But then it started to run downhill again and the kids entered shallow water.

"We're heading back into the chamber, Piper!" Tad panicked. "It's a loop!"

"No, we didn't make any turns. This has to be a way out."

"But the water—"

"The water is going to get deeper," she warned. "But it's still the way out. Stay at my heels. Trust me."

Piper was right; the water in the tunnel did get steadily deeper. It lapped at their chins, and the tops of their heads scraped the roof.

"It's no good," Tad said. "We should go back and look for another way out."

Piper was positive that the tunnel was an exit. "It's just a little farther. We can swim for it."

"A little farther? It's a dead end, Piper! There's no way we're—"

They heard a splash somewhere back down the tunnel, in the direction they'd come from. Piper aimed the flashlight at the source. There wasn't any movement except for squiggles of light on top of the water.

"What do you see?" he asked.

"Nothing yet. Shh."

Two red pinpoints of light bobbed to the surface twenty feet away. *Red eyeshine.* The eyes were too far apart to belong to a rat, and it surely wasn't a coyote. The alligator glided in silence toward them.

"Get behind me," she ordered, squishing Tad against the wall. "I'll try to fend it off."

"Fend what off? Piper, what is it?"

She gripped the flashlight tightly, preparing to bash the gator on its snout the second it opened its jaws. It wasn't a very big alligator, maybe five or six feet long, but its size didn't fool Piper. It was still capable of tearing off her arm in a jiff.

The gator wasn't interested. It rolled one crimson eye at her as it swam past and continued on down the tunnel. Free of Mergo's mind control, the beast had a new priority. Escape.

"Was that . . . was that an alligator?" asked Tad.

"Would you believe me if I said it was an otter?"

"No."

"Okay, it was an alligator. But the good news is that this tunnel *must* be a way out. Gators sense these things. They're burrowers, so they know. We're gonna follow it."

"How? The water level is almost to the ceiling."

"We'll have to swim underwater the rest of the way. I'll go first. Try to hang on to my ankle. I won't kick. I can pull myself along the bottom with my arms. Count of three?"

"Why not?" said Tad. "I've followed you this far." He wasn't just referring to the tunnel.

"I know you have," she said. Then she kissed him again. This time there was no clunky awkwardness to it. She kissed Tad and he kissed her back, and if it was the last thing they did on this earth, then she would be okay with that. It was the kind of kiss she'd read about in English class. Epic. Shakespearean, even.

When they finally pulled away, Tad sighed. "To be continued."

On three they took deep breaths and submerged. Piper held the waterproof flashlight out with one hand and used the other to propel her body down the tunnel. She moved as fast as she could without pulling away from Tad. The water was murky, but the light was bright enough that she was able to see a few feet ahead. A small fish darted through the beam. The exit was close, Piper was sure of it. She knew exactly where the tunnel was leading them.

Tad squeezed her ankle to let Piper know he was almost out of air.

Just a little farther.

Her lungs burned. She was almost out of air too.

Just a little farther.

The water grew brighter. *The light at the end of the tunnel.* An exit appeared.

They swam out of the tunnel and into the lagoon. Piper spied the lower half of Mergo's giant stalk. The plant's animal servants were gone. The lagoon had been evacuated except for a dark shape float-ing on the surface above them. It was long and rectangular and could only be one thing: The *Mud Cat*. The kids swam for it.

Tad and Piper broke the surface on the port side of the boat, gasp-ing for air. Because of Mergo's venom, Tad was too weak to get into the vessel without help. Piper would have to pull him into the *Mud Cat*. She reached up to the gunwale and tried to heft herself up. She strug-gled and groaned and swore that if she made it home, she would buy a chin-up bar during her next trip to Target. Despite her best effort, it was hopeless. She hung there by her arms, emptied of strength.

Two shocked faces peered down over the gunwale. Perch and Creeper. Her boys were safely aboard.

They reached down and dragged her into the boat so fast that she almost lost her shorts. They hoisted Tad aboard next.

A great *whoosh* sound reached their ears. It was the rush of air being sucked down into the earth in great gulps as a section of the forest caved into the tunnels. The fire was spreading underground, and the trees would burn as kindling. Black smoke billowed up and came rolling out of the woods toward the lagoon.

"We may be out of the frying pan," Perch noted with urgency, "but the fire's just getting started." He yanked on the motor's cord, but nothing happened.

"What's wrong?" asked Creeper.

Perch looked the motor over for problems and found a big one. "The kill switch is gone! I can't start the boat without it! Macey must have pulled it free when the gar knocked her out of the boat!"

Piper fished into her pocket and yanked out the plastic lanyard. The kill switch was dangling on the end of it. "Please, don't ask how I got it. Just take it."

Perch plugged the kill switch into the motor. This time it fired right up. He took over the sternman position. The others sat to the sides, giving him a clear view ahead. Perch brought the engine to full throttle and they moved swiftly toward the opening of the narrow, zipping around a rapidly widening whirlpool created when the chamber collapsed.

Piper looked back and saw several new columns of smoke rising from the trees beyond the lagoon. Mergo's lair had become its subterranean funeral pyre. Piper didn't know if the plant could survive the fire or not. She'd done it great damage, but Mergo was a resilient life-form. Almost alien, in many ways. It probably came from South America, but it could have just as easily ridden to Earth on a meteor. Was it truly a glimpse into the future of plant evolution? Piper feared it could be.

"What happened down there?" Perch asked her.

"I blew it up."

"Yeah, I figured that part. With what, though? We heard the explosion, like a bomb went off."

That sounded accurate to Piper. "Mergo secretes these things called guttation drops—"

Before she could finish her story, the biggest tentacle they'd seen yet shot up out of the *Mud Cat*'s wake, arced high in the air, and landed with a sound like the slap of a wet towel on the right side of the boat's transom.

The *Mud Cat* came to a jarring halt, throwing everyone backward. Perch hit his head hard against the motor casing and was knocked senseless. Creeper fell onto the floor and slid against the bench. The motor was gargling swamp water, trying in vain to propel the boat forward. Piper and Tad scrambled to remove the tentacle before it tore off the back of the boat.

The tip of the tentacle forked into a dozen smaller tentacles, each one dripping with a vile yellow mucous which discharged a powerful odor like rubber glue, the kind used to assemble model cars or rockets. These smaller tips were stuck fast to the *Mud Cat*, holding it hostage in the lagoon.

"Quick! Give me Perch's knife!" Piper ordered.

"Can't! I lost it in the tunnel," Tad told her.

"What else can we use to cut ourselves free?" She shouted to be heard over the violent popping of bolts being torn out of place.

The tentacle started to tow the boat backward. Toward the expanding whirlpool. The bow rose a foot into the air.

"It's pulling us under!" Creeper yelled.

"I know! I know!" Piper snapped.

Tad fumbled for the motor and felt his way around until he located the steering tiller. He leaned his weight on it, and the bottom of the motor lifted out of the water. The three blades on the end were buzzing loudly in the air, sounding like a WeedWacker, which is exactly what Tad intended to use them for. He swiveled the motor to the right and lowered the blades on top of the tentacle. Bits of shredded plant pulp spattered everywhere. Tad kept raising and lowering the motor blades, chopping through the plant's flesh little by little until he'd cut completely through. The damaged tentacle dropped into the swamp with a slapping splash and sank out of view.

"Did I get it all?" Tad asked.

"It's gone! That was quick thinking," Piper said, patting him on the back.

"It does happen from time to time." Panting, Tad wiped plant gunk off his face with his forearm.

With Piper acting as sternman, the boat sped out of the lagoon and into the narrow. She got the hang of it fairly quickly. Perch was right, it wasn't hard at all, but as soon as he shook out the cobwebs, she gladly retired. Piper went and sat at the front, next to Creeper.

"Are you okay?" he asked, examining the horrible burns on her body. "Is that from the fire?"

"The burns on my hand are. The rest are from Mergo. It tried to digest me."

"They look really bad," her brother said.

She downplayed the pain for Creeper's sake. "It hurts, but it could have been worse." The truth was she was in agony. As the danger and her adrenaline subsided, the pain became more pronounced. She put on her brave face and draped her arm around Creeper's scrawny shoulders. "Don't worry about me. Let's just be glad we're going home."

"Home," Creeper muttered. Just the thought of it caused his whole body to relax. He put his head on Piper's shoulder and sighed deeply. "Home to Mom and Dad. To Grace."

Grace! The siblings bolted upright at the same time.

Piper clambered over the benches, frantically searching the boat.

Wild-eyed, she asked, "Did you guys see it when you came aboard?"

"See what?" asked Tad. "I can't see anything, remember?"

"The vasculum!" she said. "Creeper did you—?"

"No! I didn't even think to look!"

She whirled on Perch. "Macey said it was on board, right?"

"I didn't say that," Perch reminded her. "I said she *might* have said it was on board. I'm not a lip-reader, Piper!"

The vasculum wasn't there.

"The benches!" Creeper leaped up from the one he'd been sitting on. He threw back the cushioned lid. "Check inside the benches!"

Perch and Tad watched the Canfield siblings scrounge inside the bench stowage compartments, tossing out the bigger stuff, like the sleeping bags and Macey's pup tent.

"It's not in this one!" Creeper shouted.

Piper used both hands to rake the contents of her bench to the sides. Then she raked it all into a pile in the middle and sifted through it. "Nothing!"

There was only one bench left to search. If the vasculum wasn't inside it, then there was only one other place it could be—the bottom of the swamp.

Perch slowed the boat to a stop and stood up. He nodded at Piper. Piper nodded back. She held her breath.

Perch lifted the seat of his bench. He reached inside. When Perch straightened again, he had a grin on his face and the golden vasculum in his hands.

The mental dam that had held all of Piper's fears and emotions in check to this point shattered completely. She plunked herself down on the bench next to Tad and burst into racking sobs. Perch handed the vasculum to Tad, and he set it gingerly on Piper's lap. Smiling, but still crying too hard to speak, she gave him a grateful shoulder bump.

"Open it," Tad said. "Go ahead and open it, Piper."

With trembling fingers, she unhooked the latch on the side and lifted the vasculum's small plate door. Hidden inside the box of gold was silver. Wonderful, glorious silver. Creeper was right—it *did* smell like Apple Jacks.

August 28, 1823

It's interesting how, at the end, the mind will trek beyond
the body to far-off places, to avoid the here and now. I recall
the continent of Australia. My Edwina was born there, the
daughter of the governor of one of England's first crown colonies
established on the continent. It's where we met, where we fell
in love, and where I made her my wife before stealing her
away to our new life in America. First established as a prison
colony, Australia was, until now, the most diverse place I'd ever
explored, and one of the most inhospitable too. Everything seems
to have evolved to kill: venomous snakes, man-eating sharks,
poisonous jellyfish, and vicious crocodiles rank as just some of
the deadliest animals in the world. It was no surprise to find
that the arsenals of the indigenous plant life are also creatively
lethal. For example, the *Drosera glanduligara*, a type of sticky
trap plant. Not content with waiting patiently for insects to land
on its gluey hairs, the carnivorous plant uses rings of snapping
tentacles to catapult insects onto its digestive leaves, a two-punch
adaptation that has proven quite successful for the species.

The gympie-gympie tree is a type of stinging nettle plant
with neurotoxins so potent they can cause extreme pain that
can last for weeks or even months; or, in worst-case scenarios,
it can kill a man. And then there is a type of eucalyptus tree
that produces extremely flammable oil. The tree explodes
during forest fires and emits clouds of flammable gas into the
air that can turn into massive fireballs when sparked. A forest
fire, accelerated by the tree's oils, will burn up all other plants
encroaching on its territory and blocking its sunlight. Deep
inside each eucalyptus is a fresh shoot, protected by its outer
shell. When the smoke clears, all the surrounding trees are dead
and the eucalyptus stands as the lone survivor. The tree is the
ultimate example of the kill-or-be-killed nature there.

And yet Australia is where I found Edwina. To think! Such exquisite beauty living amidst the most abhorrent life-forms. But this is the mischievousness of nature, for some of the most inviting flowers bloom on the unwelcoming arms of the cactus, and the most ornately painted birds thrive in the emptiness of the sun-scorched desert. Beauty within the beast.

EPILOGUE

They left the lagoon, Mergo, and their nightmare behind. They were bushed. Physically and mentally spent. Tad's eyesight was worse; he could detect only light and shadow now. Piper could no longer pretend she was okay. The burns caused by Mergo's digestive juice were unbearable. She had ugly white-and-yellow blisters on her right hand, her neck, her face, and her shoulders. Added to this was the pain of the wounds the tentacle hooks had carved into her back. Piper lay on the bench and writhed in agony.

Seeing his sister this way was more than Creeper could bear. He went into the vasculum and tore off one of the flower's petals.

"Don't do that!" Piper scolded. "Grace needs that!"

He batted her good hand away. "So do you! Now be quiet and lie still."

Piper wasn't used to Creeper taking care of her. She was angry that he was wasting even a bit of the flower on her, but she was also proud of him for taking charge, and she was in no condition to resist. Plus she needed to know if the flower was really the miracle cure Cole believed it would be.

Creeper folded the petal into a thick pad and gently patted her ugliest burns with it. Piper screamed and pushed him away.

"You're torturing me!" she cried.

"I'm not! I'm helping you! You have to let me, okay?"

"It hurts so bad . . ." she whimpered.

"I'm sorry," he said with all sincerity. Then he began to treat her again.

Gradually the pain lessened. After a while the areas Creeper labored over the most started to feel numb. Eventually Piper felt well enough to take over the job herself. Creeper sat next to her, relieved. She dabbed at her blisters and cuts with the soft petal until they faded into discolored spots or disappeared entirely.

"I'll be danged," said Perch. "It works."

Piper decided her thigh could wait. "Your turn, Tad." She tilted his head back and wrung the petal until a little liquid dripped into Tad's open right eye. She saved some for the left. Piper pressed the petal to the right socket. He put his hand on top of hers, and they held it there together for several minutes. When they removed the petal, Tad found that much of his vision had been restored. He could see everything, although things far off in the distance were still a little blurry.

He sighed. "So much better." He switched the petal to the left eye and nursed it for a while.

Through it all, Perch didn't say much. He just sat on Macey's bench and stared ahead with his piercing green eyes.

Piper sat down next to him and kissed his cheek and offered quiet comfort. There was no miracle fix for the loss of a loved one. Piper thought back to when she'd hurt Creeper's feelings and Macey had sheltered him under her strong arm. Against her big heart. Piper hadn't known Macey long, but she would certainly remember the sacrifice the woman had made for them all. Especially for Grace, whom she'd never even met.

"I think she'd be okay with this," Perch said when he finally spoke. "I knew Macey better than anyone. Her only real regret in life was what happened to her daughter. She'd be glad to know that her sacrifice helped save your sister's life."

When they reached the part of the swamp that had been shrouded in mist and watched over by jewelwing damselflies, they found the mist and the dazzling blue insects gone. A unique *kent-kent-kent* call drew their eyes upward. There was something else flitting about, high in the charred, scaly trees.

"I don't believe it," Tad said. His vision, fully healed, was now the sharpest among them. "There must be hundreds of them. . . . How is that possible?"

The trees were teeming with birds. Many of them had a red peaked crown, but some did not, a distinction between male and female. The birds were primarily a blue-black color, but they also had white markings trailing on the undersides and upperparts of their wings, and a narrow white stripe running up their necks and ending at their bills. Their bills were white. Ivory white.

"I don't believe it either," Perch said. "Those are ivory-billed woodpeckers. Every one of them."

"I thought they were supposed to be extinct," said Tad.

"They were," said Perch. "But here they are."

"I saw one earlier," said Piper. "Right after Macey died. It flew over the lagoon. I took it as a sign."

Some of the birds were hammering their beaks into the bark in search of hidden insects. The distinct double-tap drum offered positive identification of a species that had reached near-mythical status almost a hundred years ago.

Tad chuckled. "Grafton would flip his lid if he were here to see this. I wish I still had my camera. Each bird sighted has a fifty-thousand-dollar reward attached, right?"

Perch did the math. "That's roughly fifteen million dollars' worth of woodpeckers in those trees. I don't get it, though. Why are they concentrated here? Why don't they spread out through the rest of the swamp?"

"I know why," said Piper. "It's because here they have a protector. A guardian from hunters, careless campers, and polluters."

"Mergo," said Creeper. "Mergo keeps them safe."

"Yeah. Or at least it *did*." Perch nodded at the ribbon-wisps of smoke behind them, now far off in the distance. "We may have just killed the woodpeckers' last best hope for survival."

"I honestly don't know how to feel right now," Piper admitted. "If Mergo does burn to ash underground, then it can no longer prey on unsuspecting people. But on the other hand, it's the protector of a fragile species. Without Mergo, those birds might be doomed."

"That's a somber thought," said Tad.

Piper watched the precious woodpeckers darting in and out of holes, oblivious to the probable death of their custodian. Sometimes the cosmos awards custody of fragile life to the most unlikely keepers. A few years ago she'd bargained for a baby sister, and then her beloved Grace was born. Here in this secret green cradle called the Okefenokee the cosmos had seen fit to appoint a giant killer plant as the ward of some of its most vulnerable creatures. Who was she to say that Mergo was a monster? Who was she to destroy something so utterly and wonderfully unique? After all, until they'd come along, Mergo was just following its survival instincts. Was it so different from any other living thing? Was it so different from her?

Tad read her mind. "Charles Darwin believed it wasn't necessarily the strongest or the most intelligent creatures that would survive but the ones that could best adapt to change. Until now, Mergo could adapt to anything. My guess is it'll survive this, too."

"I wonder what Darwin would think about us," said Piper. "About what *we* just survived."

"I don't really know," said Tad. "But after all we went through to keep each other alive, I'd say we're more than just survivors." He glanced around the boat. At Creeper and Piper. Even at Perch. "Darwin also believed that a species whose members could work together as a team has the best chance of success. I think we proved his theory today."

"Smart fella, that Darwin," Perch said. "I bet he would have loved the Oke. I still do."

"You know," Piper said, "when we get home we're going to have to tell people about Mergo. We can't let it kill again."

"I know," Tad said. "It's the responsible thing to do. Let's just hope that if it's still alive when they come to study it, they'll also come to protect it. And the woodpeckers too."

They traversed the swamp, eventually crossing back within the boundaries of the state park. It was dark, deep into the evening when they reached the demarcated canoe route known as the Red Trail. The refuge typically cleared out at dusk, but tonight it was a highway of brightly lit motor boats, puttering along at duck speed. Their people on the boats were using megaphones, calling out the kids' names.

"It's a search party," Perch said. "I didn't think. Of course people would be out looking for us."

It was by sheer coincidence that the first boat to meet them would be piloted by someone Perch knew. It was an overweight man with a bushy white mustache—Bill Kite, from the park office. Bill was traveling in an airboat, the kind with an enormous fan on the back. He was sitting in the elevated pilot's seat closest to the cage. There were three or four other people in the lower seats, all with flashlights aimed in the *Mud Cat*'s direction, making it hard to see their faces.

Perch steered the *Mud Cat* into their path, and Bill swiveled the boat's pole-mounted spotlight to better see who was on board.

When he recognized Perch's face, Bill pumped his fist in the air and whooped.

"We found them! They're all right!" Bill hollered over the hum of the boat's fan to his shipmates. "Let the others know!"

One of Bill's men raised a plastic gun into the air and shot a sizzling red flare into the sky. A single firework to celebrate the good news. Piper heard dozens of muted boat horns sounding off in the distance.

"You kids okay?" Bill asked.

"We'll be fine after a hot shower and a couple dozen pizzas," Perch replied. "Hold the veggies. We've had our fill for a lifetime."

As the two boats gently bumped prows and came to a stop, the kids were greeted by an unexpected voice.

"You losers were supposed to meet me at the car," Grafton scolded them from his seat below Bill's boots, but the look on his face was one of pure relief, not anger. He was wearing the same clothes from the day before, which meant he'd never left the swamp. Grafton lifted a megaphone to his mouth and blasted them point-blank with "You're a little late, don't you think?"

"Just by a day," said Tad over the ringing in his ears. "I thought you swore you wouldn't wait on us."

Grafton lowered the megaphone and grinned. "I honestly didn't think you'd be stupid enough to get lost out here. I guess that was my mistake. My dad is so angry, he wouldn't even ride in the same boat. He's somewhere behind us with your parents."

"Whose parents?" Creeper asked.

"*All* of your parents," said Grafton. "And half the town of Jesup too. You got us into quite a mess. Thanks to you, I had my driving privileges revoked for six months. I'll be ticked at you later. Right now, I'm just glad to see you alive. It almost makes up for not spotting my woodpecker."

"About that . . ." said Tad.

"All right, you've had your little reunion," Bill huffed. Piper could tell that the man was ravenous for answers. "I want to know what happened out there, and you'd better have one heck of a story or I'd advise you to make one up."

"We do, Bill," Perch promised.

The man stopped him. "Not from you, silver tongue. I need to hear from a passenger. How about you, girl?" Bill gestured to Piper. "Where the heck have you kids been for the last thirty-six hours?"

"Go ahead," Tad put his hand on her shoulder. "It's okay. Tell him everything."

Piper Canfield took a full breath and began.

August 28, 1823

The sunset paints the lagoon in lavish hues of coral and salmon
and molten silver. The orange sphere dips to meet its watery
twin while clouds that remind me of panicles of lilac float across
the dimming sky above it. But it's not the shimmering light
dancing on the surface of the water that I should concern myself
with, but the shivering life-form that awaits hapless victims in
the murk below.

Nokosi is dead. Bolek has betrayed us both. I am injured,
and my canoe was apprehended by a patch of reeds near the
shore. Despite the bleakness of my situation, I can't help but
feel a sense of wonder. I think of my unborn child, and I hope
he or she will have a chance to see such places of breathtaking
beauty someday. What traits of mine will be passed on to the
little one and perhaps to subsequent generations? My spirit of
adventure? My inclination to root out nature's hidden treasures?
Or maybe just an illimitable appreciation for the simple miracles
that surround us always. Why do humans choose this lonely
life fraught with hardship to seek out something so common as
plants? Since Queen Hatshepsut of ancient Egypt sent the first
plant hunters to retrieve frankincense trees from the land of
Punt, there has existed a burning passion to find new specimens,
many of which have changed the course of history. We venture
into the wild, I believe, to both lose and find ourselves within
it. The great adventurer Alexander von Humboldt once said,
"This view of a living nature where man is nothing is both odd
and sad. Here, in a fertile land, in an eternal greenness, you
search in vain for traces of man; you feel you are carried into a
different world from the one you were born into." And yet I now
understand that there is nothing so important as the bonds we
make in this life. Our friends. Our family. Those we hold dear.

To pass from this world alone . . . that is the true sin against nature.

With Edwina in my thoughts, I'll make one last attempt to reach the flower. I leave the story of my journey on these pages in the hope that should I die, someone will find this journal and learn from my effort. If I fall short, then let my words be a testament not to my failure but to the boundless love one person can have for another.

It is getting late. And so I climb.

ACKNOWLEDGMENTS

A tremendous amount of credit goes to my agent, Lauren MacLeod, for setting me on the grisly path of middle-grade horror and for not blocking my e-mail address even though I routinely send her links to gory science articles whenever I'm doing research for a new book.

A huge thank-you to my insightful editor, Ricardo Mejías, and the terrific team at Disney•Hyperion for a job well done. And to Mark Fredrickson for another fantastic cover. And to Maria Elias for her superb design. I'm fortunate to work with some truly talented people.

A special thanks to Chris Cannon, Rosemary Olairez, Zoraida Cordova, Funmi Oke, Anna Berger, my agency siblings, and the fine folks of Write-O-Rama for supporting my work in various important ways.

A posthumous bellow to Oscar the alligator (and his harem of girlfriends), who left behind thousands of toothy descendants in the Okefenokee. The swamp's thriving gator population is just one of the many, many reasons why the Oke is such a remarkable place to visit.

To learn more about America's largest blackwater swamp, visit the following websites:

U.S. Fish and Wildlife Service, Okefenokee National Wildlife Refuge (http://www.fws.gov/refuge/okefenokee)

http://www.facebook.com/okefenokeewildliferefuge

Or better yet, just visit the Oke.

And thank YOU for reading *The Murk*! Until next time—see you later, alligator!